MW01139110

NEVER
THE
ROSES

NEVER THE ROSES

ROSES

JENNIFER K. LAMBERT

BRAMBLE

TOR PUBLISHING GROUP
NEW YORK

NEVER THE ROSES

Copyright © 2025 by Jennifer M. Kennedy

Map by Jennifer Hanover

A Bramble Book
Published by Tom Doherty Associates / Tor Publishing Group
120 Broadway
New York, NY 10271

www.torpublishinggroup.com

Bramble™ is a trademark of Macmillan Publishing Group, LLC.

The Library of Congress Cataloging-in-Publication Data
is available upon request.

ISBN 978-1-250-36034-2 (hardcover)
ISBN 978-1-250-42098-5
(international, sold outside the U.S., subject to rights availability)
ISBN 978-1-250-36035-9 (ebook)

Our books may be purchased in bulk for promotional, educational, or
business use. Please contact your local bookseller or the Macmillan Corporate
and Premium Sales Department at 1-800-221-7945, extension 5442,
or by email at MacmillanSpecialMarkets@macmillan.com.

First Edition: 2025

Printed in the United States of America

0 9 8 7 6 5 4 3 2 1

King's City

Oneira's house

ONEIRA'S
HOUSE

SOUTHER

NORTHERN LANDS

STEARANOS'S
CASTLE

KING'S
CITY

Stearanos's Castle

Queen Zarja's Citadel

ANDS

QUEEN ZARJA'S
CITADEL

NEVER
THE
ROSES

The sorceress Oneira retired from the gilded courts of men after the last war. Her last war, that is, as she'd resolved to absent herself from such conflicts for the remainder of her life.

She built herself a house on a spit of land between the mountains and the sea, close enough to both that she could descend the long series of white steps to the pink-pebble beach below or follow the narrow trails left by forest animals through the hills rising behind. Large windows looked out in all directions, commanding views of the wave-tossed horizon, the snow-capped peaks, and the forest canopy between. She raised a tower with a single room at the summit and nothing in it, and topped it with a bubble of crystal she breathed into being like a dream that could never shatter.

Alone in that tower, she watched the sun rise and set, the stars spin into a diamond-splashed array of contained chaos. And she set her wards, meticulously guarding all approaches to her solitary fastness, especially the one road that led there from the world of men.

In this way, she lived at an intersection of the elements of nature. If she could remove that sole unnatural element, she would have. She loathed that pulsating scar through the forest left by the hungry axes of men, one last ugly link that rendered her forever tethered to their world of debts and allegiances and endless plotting. She didn't care if she never saw another human being. Even in their noisy, greedy midst, she'd been isolated in her power and her soul-ravaging sorrow.

At least now she would have silence.

Though wardmaking wasn't the strongest of her skills, she didn't concern herself overmuch. Her weakest ability—whether in drawing runes, mind-reading, divination, healing, and so forth—still exceeded the best most magic-workers could muster. Only someone like Stearanos Stormbreaker could outmatch her there, and only because he was a powerful chartomancer, able to channel his magic through runes of all kinds, particularly wards. And Stearanos, the nemesis she'd never met, had no reason to attack her and every reason not to. Especially now that she'd been freed of the blood geas that had bound her since childhood.

For the rest of the world, magically gifted and otherwise, her reputation was enough to terrify all who'd heard the tales, even the ones that hadn't been liberally embroidered. Also, she'd been coldly clear as to the consequences of anyone who dared disturb her retirement. No one could or would dare trespass on the privacy of her exile.

So, no one did, for a very long time.

She found a solace of sorts in the silence that wasn't silent at all, but simply devoid of idle chatter, angry debate, and the shouts and screams of the dying. Away from the crowded world of people, other sounds emerged. Oneira learned to appreciate the subtle harmonies of the crash of surf against the rocks far below, the sifting rustle of the leaves as the winds changed direction, wafting cold alpine air over the forest one moment, salt-drenched ocean warmth next.

Oneira had never been one to talk to herself. She'd learned the lesson early in her education to be very careful of what she put into words. For any sorcerer, but particularly a powerful oneiromancer like her, giving voice to thoughts gave them a tangible reality that could lead to disastrous results. When Oneira spoke, she scrupulously said nothing of import or she deliberately shattered entire realms. It was far easier to say nothing at all, to allow the small sounds of the world to fill her ravaged, empty spaces.

She spent her days doing little. Nothing that affected the fate of anyone, let alone realms and entire populations. At most, she changed the course of fate for the fruits and vegetables in the garden she planted, learning what to do from the books she'd brought with her, working with her hands, using a bit of magic here and there. She'd sworn to never again use her sorcery at the behest of another, no matter who asked it of her, regardless of the reward offered or the threat levied, but that didn't mean she'd forsaken magic altogether. She might as well attempt to stop breathing.

It might come to that, someday—stopping breathing, stopping *being* altogether. Although, within the healing silence of her white walls, that eventuality seemed far less likely than on the day she'd raised them, pulling what she needed from the Dream and meticulously shaping it all to fit more or less seamlessly into the waking world. Still, the imminent inevitability of death had weighed so heavily on her mind while she built her house that, when she finished, it occurred to her that she had created for herself a sort of massive tomb, a mausoleum for one occupant: her eventual corpse, no doubt perfectly preserved, given all the magic that had coursed through her mortal form.

The prospect of her death gave her no sense of sorrow, only a kind of warped delight at the image of herself lying on her back, hair streaming in a silver-threaded crimson river to the floor, no virginal princess, but a woman matured and molded by the cruelties of a lifetime, both dealt to her and dealt by her. Some prince might happen along, somehow evade her wards and traps—through the purity of his heart or some such; it was only a dream of a tale, after all—and attempt to awaken her with a kiss.

Whether her mythical would-be lover was motivated by true love or inconstant lust, it didn't matter. Oneira had long passed any interest in such things. Though she remained awake and alive, her sexuality had fallen into deep slumber, if not killed along with the last remnants of her humanity.

Besides which, no sorcerer capable of laying such a deep enchantment would enable a simple key to unlock it. The prince would flail and curse the fates and go away disappointed. So much for heroic glory. Better for him to learn such things were the stuff of dreams, illusions only.

The image of that fairy-tale scene tickled her enough, however, that she'd giggled aloud. The sound echoed through the forming walls, halls, and archways of polished white stone, absurdly melodious given the deep grating despair of her thoughts. (She'd chosen white for obvious reasons: purity, simplicity, restfulness, atonement, a longing for an innocence forever lost.)

Unable to resist making one aspect of it real, Oneira searched the Dream and found a bier. Enough people dreamed about their own funerals in vivid detail that the pedestal needed little modification to blend into reality. She centered the bier in a large room that formed the heart of the house and created skylights, focusing them to shine upon the pedestal, spotlighting it with a touch of theatrical drama that would have been embarrassing, had there been anyone else to see it.

In the ensuing days, she took to laying fresh flowers upon her bier daily, first wildflowers that she picked on her rambles, later blossoms harvested from her increasingly bountiful garden. She arranged the flowers so they'd frame her corpse, so she could simply lie down, exhale her last breath, and have done. When the snows on the peaks behind the house crept low enough to sprinkle the garden with hints of frost, she dried blossoms and petals, storing enough to decorate the bier for an entire winter.

The ritual of it pleased her. Someone would mourn her passing, even if it was only herself.

The laying of flowers on her bier also reminded her, in the haze of honeyed autumn, that she'd need food stores for the frozen months. Food from the Dream rarely tasted right and was never properly nutritious, being the stuff of dreams and not reality. She wouldn't starve—she couldn't die that easily, not from such a basic bodily need—but hunger distracted and annoyed her. It made her mind too muzzy to read, forcing her to descend from her tower to eat, or left her legs too weak to ascend the many stairs from the beach or the hills beyond where she roamed without purpose.

Knowing she'd feel more alert with a balanced diet, she searched the vast library she'd brought with her, some of the titles from her own lifelong collection, others she'd helped herself to when she left, figuring they owed her far more than that. She found a tome with instructions on agromancy, a field of magic she hadn't learned. The academy that had purchased her life contract didn't deal in such low-return employment as farming. Agromancers never earned enough to pay off the debt of their schooling, much less deliver a profit.

Oneira enjoyed learning the simple enchantments of growing food. Living things weren't like the inanimate; nothing in the Dream was truly alive, not even the monsters extracted from nightmares and set loose in reality. Thus, she couldn't bring plants from the Dream and expect them to be anything useful in the waking world. But basic agromancy, coaxing existing fruit trees, grains, and vegetables—and flowers for the bier, of course—to sprout and flourish fell easily within her abilities as a sorceress. Sometimes she smiled, thinking of the warlords who'd employed her world-scathing skills seeing her on hands and knees, planting seeds, soaking the soil with magic.

She also learned to take pleasure in working with her hands, making porridges from grains, brewing soups from vegetables, and baking bread from flour she ground with her own hands. In learning to feed herself, she discovered a kind of affection for her own body, a basic sensuality she'd lost along the way. She'd never again have a lover—that sort of thing did require another person—but she began to forgive her own failings in that realm, content to allow her libido to slumber on. She found a peace in puttering around in the kitchen she later added on to the house, the need for one never occurring to her when she built the original.

She, of course, could not bring herself to eat meat of any sort, not even the pearlescent oysters that perched amid the pink-rock tidepools along her narrow beach. All life had become precious to her here at the edge of the world, far too late for it to make any kind of difference. Regardless, she refused to kill ever again. She couldn't undo what she'd done, but she could do that much.

Those simple things formed the bones, breath, and flesh of her days and nights. She nourished the garden, tinkered with recipes in the kitchen, arranged flowers on the bier. As impulse led her, she prowled the pink-pebble beach, or wandered the high hills, depending on how far the snowline crept down. The wildlife who shared her small, private realm—or, perhaps, it was more accurate to say she'd inserted herself into theirs—came to know her and ignored her presence, a restful novelty for her, who had always stood at the center of attention, usually the dangerous kind.

Where once a forest of birdsong had fallen silent at her approach, the feathered creatures now sang away. The sorceress who'd once frightened horses so badly that she couldn't be near them, either to ride or be pulled in a carriage, now sat quietly with paper and ink, sketching the does and fawns in springtime as they grazed trustingly nearby. Her scintillating, sharp-edged magic had retracted its spines and settled around her into a soft cloak, harmful to none. She liked the feeling, though she didn't care to examine the implications for herself as the battle sorceress she'd been or whatever kind of creature she'd become. So she encouraged the magic to wrap itself about her, making another layer of stillness and silence.

After some time—she'd lost track of how long in the seamless slide and tumble from season to season, all circling around to the same, yet different points—a visitor arrived. Not the hapless, yet heroic prince looking to awake his sleeping princess. It was too soon for his doomed attempt, Oneira not quite ready to lay herself upon the bier amid her flowers.

It happened on one of her rambles through the mountains, the full summer allowing her to hike higher and deeper, the meadows purple with wildflowers and the sky so close that wisps of clouds formed just above before whisking away again. As the afternoon wore on, those playful strands would weave together with dizzying speed, becoming storms with thunderous rain and lethal lightning akin to the sort she'd once brought out of the Dream and wielded with such unthinking destruction.

Oneira lowered her gaze from silent contemplation of the frisky clouds condensing white against blue and scattering again to find the creature there, without warning of its approach, watching her with keen intent.

It came as a bit of a shock, not being ignored after all that time. She almost looked around, about, behind herself, casting for the true object of its attention. But no, it saw *her*, standing as if pointing her out to some companion, all lean, alert hunter, canny, deep-blue gaze fixed on her and unmoving. Dangerous. Capable of dealing death, even to one such as herself.

Oneira held still. Not as frozen prey. No amount of solitude and silence could ever make her anything but the apex predator she'd been born as and molded into. She could kill this creature, except that she was done with killing.

Even in self-defense? Part of her ruminated over the philosophical question, one she'd mulled more than once.

Perhaps, perhaps . . . came the eternal answer. She couldn't simultaneously exist as the woman who valued her own life so little that she decorated her own bier daily and as a sorceress willing to kill to save that life.

She'd also pondered whether she'd kill to save someone else, an innocent or someone she cared about. Or maybe to save many people, their numbers adding weight enough to offset their lack of innocence and her lack of caring about them. All academic, as she cared for no one, and innocents weren't exactly thick on the ground.

All she truly wanted was to be left alone to ensure that such predicaments didn't arise.

And now she faced one.

She knew what the creature was. Though she'd never seen its like in life, she'd learned of their ilk way back in the early days of her compulsory education. He—definitely male—stood out in her mind against the softer magic of the landscape, the magic breathed by natural living things. He'd been created, not born, radiating the enchantment that had crafted him and his kind, long before Oneira had been born.

In her mind, though not aloud, never aloud, she named him: *scáthcú.*

Dread wolf.

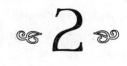

If anyone had asked Oneira what manner of creature she anticipated would be the first to break the solitude of her self-imposed and vigorously enforced isolation, she would not have picked a near-mythical wolf designed by an ancient mage to wage brutal war. Though, given the life she'd led, it really just figured.

The *scáthcú* sat on his haunches, eyeing her with riveted attention. Dirty ice matted his coat, turning him brown instead of his native white. Filth coated his belly, encased his great paws, and hung off the feathery underside of his long tail, which now curved around in front of him, the tip lifted in question. The unnatural magic that created his ilk shimmered about him, radiating a shade of purple not found in nature, an implicit warning to anyone with the wit to see it.

He must have come down from the forever-frozen peaks looming above. The ancient tales spoke of the packs of *scáthcú* who'd gone feral following the demise of their creator, roaming the cave-riddled wilderness of those altitudes too extreme for ordinary lungs to draw breath. Oneira had heard rumors from time to time of some ambitious young mage, burdened by oppressive debt and made brave by the desperation to rid themselves of it, attempting to ascend to the thin air and desolation of those peaks. They thought to obtain a *scáthcú* and make their fortune.

They died. Or disappeared. Or returned crushed in body and spirit, realizing their own insignificant skills could never allow them to survive the extremes a created being so thoroughly permeated with magic could.

If those mages had bothered to read the books Oneira had, those hubris-laden and impetuous fools would have known that even if they could manage to ascend to such heights, they would return unrewarded. *Scáthcú* chose their own sorcerers. The fabricated dread wolves had been embedded with a craving for magic. The more powerful the sorcerer, the more attractive to them. If they befriended a mage, their loyalty was unbreakable, and they formed a symbiotic relationship with their sorcerer of choice. As an enemy, however, the *scáthcú* fed their hunger another way, devouring the sorcerer they found wanting.

Oneira knew herself to be wanting in many ways—but were they the ones that mattered to a *scáthcú*? She waited with distant curiosity to discover the outcome of the test. Perhaps death had finally sought her out, impatient with her dithering. Truly, it would be a relief to have the decision taken out of her hands.

The *scáthcú*'s massive jaws opened, revealing ivory fangs. A black, forked tongue flicked out to taste the air between them. Jaws widening beyond what would be physically possible for a natural wolf, he revealed his pink maw and his native magic coiled out like that black tongue, visible only to her sorcerous senses. Braced, she held her magic in a still, folded cloak, allowing him to taste it . . . and he settled into a canine grin, giving her a yip of greeting.

Oneira sighed. There would be no getting rid of him now.

"There's no meat in my house," she told him, her voice an odd, rusty sound after such long disuse. "You feed yourself."

She turned and walked away. Whatever would she do with such a creature? Undaunted by her lack of welcome, the *scáthcú* followed at her side, establishing a pattern that would endure.

"Don't make me sorry," she added, and laid a hand in the ruff of coarser hair around his neck and shoulders. Such was his height that her hand rested there easily, her elbow at a relaxed and comfortable bend. As if they'd been sized for each other. "Perhaps you can address the rabbits savaging my garden," she suggested.

He emitted a growl of pure delight. It didn't count, Oneira decided, if her *scáthcú* committed bunny murder. After all, the rabbits were far from innocent, determinedly avoiding her nonlethal deterrents with arcane cleverness. She'd spent an undue amount of time—not to mention magic, though she had plenty to spare these days—on devising wards that wouldn't injure the fuzzy pests, but her humane solutions left loopholes for them to get in and savage her greens.

Many of her former cohort in the world of the ruthless employment of magic would construe a lesson from that, along the lines of kill or be killed. She willfully refused that premise. Or, rather, she'd done enough of the former that she'd resigned herself to the latter. Eventually, anyway. In the meanwhile, it could be frustrating that the immensely powerful magic she possessed all lay in the realm of the Dream. And that she excelled in destruction above all else.

Well, now she apparently had a pet *scáthcú* to kill for her. How scandalized her former handlers would be to know she planned to use such a lethal weapon for gardening.

❧

Oneira decided to call the *scáthcú* "Bunny," in honor of his labors on behalf of her greens. She'd gotten him to bathe himself in the deep, freshwater pond she'd added to the walled garden. It was easy enough to coax him into it as Bunny gleefully took to water. She then spent several nights by the fire—she lit a fire every evening, regardless of the weather, for its quiet comfort—meticulously combing the snarls from his matted coat. His fur turned out to be as soft as a rabbit's and as pristine white as their winter coats.

She ended up with a pile of extracted fur that she regarded with considerable bemusement, recalling excursions to various outlying fiefdoms where the women—it was almost always the women—would gather to spin piles of fluff like it into threads or yarns or some such. Oneira had always regarded their chattering circles, busy hands, and clacking instruments with a similar sense of befuddlement. Their lives had so little resemblance to her own that they seemed like a foreign tribe, a people who existed in spaces that weren't battlefields or council chambers crowded with greedy or frightened men. It didn't matter which emotion motivated the men, as they behaved in the exact same ways.

The women, though, they'd appeared content enough from a distance, as unmoved by the scheming of their men as the sheep in the meadows. It had seemed an enviable sort of peaceful ignorance and a kind of magic Oneira lacked, one made of nimble fingers and keen attention. As if by focusing on the simple tasks, they elevated the importance of small creations, putting the epic sweep of wars and kingdoms into the far distance, a tumult of landscape irrelevant to them.

So, remembering their ability to retire violence to the background of their lives, and confronted with a pile of white fur, Oneira attempted spinning.

She located a book in her library with instructions on the techniques, and which included several illustrations of the necessary tools. Selecting the spindle as something that looked as easy to use as a child's toy, she entered the Dream to find one.

Oneira was powerful and skilled enough to travel physically through the Dream that connected all living beings and emerge in a location where she could purchase—or steal, depending on the provenance of the item—anything she needed. But to create something as simple as a spindle, she needed only to reach mentally into the dream, which was much easier, though by no means easy. Stilling herself, allowing her folded cloak of magic to unfurl just a small amount, she walked her thoughts along the familiar pathway into the Dream.

A place as fantastic and unreal as the dreams that made up its fabric, the Dream was wildly confusing to magic-workers not experienced in that ever-changing, undulating landscape. Even naturally talented oneiromancers could become lost in bubbles of dreams that popped or spontaneously sealed themselves off. For Oneira, who'd traveled this mutable land intuitively since she was a small child, then with more skill as she learned from the best, skipping through dreaming minds to find a spindle took only moments.

She located one that looked like a simple version, similar to the book's illustration, from the dream of a woman surrounded by endless piles of wool and spindles that ever eluded her grasp. Extracting it from the Dream, Oneira pulled herself back to the waking world, the spindle in her hand. As always happened with items from the Dream, it wasn't exactly right. Though it looked like wood, the substance of the thing was flimsy, too soft for real-world work. There came in the true craft and skill of this sort of oneiromancy.

Using her magic with finely honed precision, Oneira recast the substance into something much more like the wood it was supposed to be. It would never be exactly like the real-world version, but it would more than suffice for her purposes. Especially with no one but herself to see and hold it. Other people tended to be unsettled by the vaguely foreign aspects of items built from the Dream, something of no concern in her exile. Another bonus.

Amused at herself that her self-imposed rules allowed her to obtain a spindle from the Dream, but not cheat any more than that, Oneira bent herself to the new task.

Within an hour, she wished she'd simply thrown the whole pile of fur on the fire. This was why she'd become a sorceress and not a weaver or spinner or maker of things.

Well, this and that she'd never had a choice. As a child of power, the recipient of magic that flew to her like birds to seed in winter, Oneira had begun to study sorcery so young that she had barely understood that people led any other kind of life. It had never once occurred to her to stop and chat with those women she'd observed, to ask to be shown how the tools they used worked to transform one thing into another.

Faced with a mountain of fluff, sore fingers that bumbled every movement, and a *scáthcú* who watched her as if he suspected she'd lost her mind, Oneira regretted that she hadn't ever taken the time to linger by those chattering groups, to observe, or possibly even ask. The book could only give her words; she lacked the translation that would make her hands *do* the thing.

Still, giving up had never been in her nature. She possessed an innate stubbornness that had frustrated her teachers and handlers alike, but her obdurate nature had also seen her through knottier problems than fur that flew up her nose and made her sneeze or fingers that reddened and ached in every tiny bone. Out of pride, and honestly a lack of much else to do, she persevered, working the strands of soft fur into, if not actual thread or yarn, then at least a lumpy tube with aspirations.

Hours later, the windows open to the warm summer evening and the languid chorus of crickets singing in counterpoint to the bass beats of the surf below, Oneira dubiously confronted the coil of dirty white ropelike stuff. Nothing remained of the prodigious pile of fur but for a few wisps tumbling idly over the stone floor, dancing with the night breezes. Beside her, Bunny gave her creation much the same look that she did. In retrospect, she should have spent time removing the various inclusions, all the thorns, bits of rubble, and other unidentifiable detritus Bunny had collected in his fur like an avaricious minor lord wearing his wealth on his costume.

At that point, she very nearly did pitch the ugly product of her work into the fire. Probably she should have—it served no useful purpose—but she couldn't quite bring herself to do so. She'd made it, however useless and unlovely, and that meant something. Probably not much, but something. Even if she didn't know what that was. For someone who'd never created anything without a purpose, that she'd made this useless, artless *thing* felt like a step toward an unknown destination.

So, she coiled it carefully, though the uneven lumps and occasional extrusions meant it would never look neat—*neatness counts*, her teacher Zoltan had endlessly exhorted—and she set it on the mantel, which had been otherwise bare. She couldn't have said why she had one to begin with, except that mantels went with fireplaces in the visions of most dreamers, and so it had emerged from the Dream that way. She hadn't cared enough either way to pare it off.

She paused, studying the soiled, brownish, and lopsided column precisely centered on the pristine white shelf, surrounded by equally pristine white walls, then went to bed. Bunny followed along, so he could lay himself in his accustomed spot across the threshold, where he'd remain until she awoke. As was her habit, she rested a hand between his shoulders as they walked, the newly combed fur soft as down. That was an accomplishment: not the making of the object she turned her back on, but the creation of the absence of filth.

As the sorceress and wolf walked away, the coiled rope re-mained on the mantel, a dubious occupant of the lone place of honor in an otherwise empty house.

The next creature to find Oneira arrived like a literal bolt from the blue. She was out in the garden picking the last of the to-matoes, the as-yet unripe green ones, as the cold wind blasting off the ocean shouted of a hard frost to come that night. She'd learned to listen for those sounds, too: the land, water, and sky speaking of their immediate plans, of the weather traveling from far beyond her fastness, bringing with it the imagined scents of exotic lands she'd once visited, occupied, or overthrown. The lash of the wind against her bare neck—for she'd braided her long, crimson hair and coiled it around the back of her head, so it wouldn't snarl—felt like a well-deserved punishment from those faraway places.

You abandoned me.

You laid waste to me.

You made me bow to your might and left me broken.

You made me into a nightmare landscape of nothing, nothing, nothing . . .

Pressing her lips together, she didn't reply, even in her mind. She didn't have anything to say back to them. The voices on the wind told her nothing she didn't already know, nothing she didn't already regret to the depths of her pitiless soul, nothing she hadn't already considered how to redress, except that nothing could.

Nothing, nothing, nothing.

So she accepted their castigation as her due, plucking each hard, round, brightly green fruit with care—*neatness counts*—as if each tomato saved from the frost might compensate for some small portion of the land she'd destroyed.

The sound hit her barely before her aerial wards blazed the warning through her mind, then shredded in the wake of the creature that plummeted from above, shrieking a bloodcurdling cry as it fell. Oneira leapt to her feet, dirt-encrusted hands stretched to the sky in a gesture that had nothing to do with defense, and everything to do with strike-first violence. Without thinking about it, she'd opened a portal to the Dream, iridescence tracing the outline of a doorway, the Dream seething beyond, the night terrors summoned by her instinctive fear throbbing with the need to be released. Struggling against her darker instincts, she caged the restless, potent magic, restraining the terrors, prepared to call something else from the Dream instead. Something less lethally nightmarish.

She would *not* kill rather than die.

At least, not until she knew what hurled itself toward her.

Acutely cognizant of that irony—that all her noble aspirations fell apart depending on context, and her emotions of the moment, marking her indelibly as a monster, forever and always— she sent a seeking eye upward. Aiming her far-vision at the rent in her wards, she was rather astonished to discover the culprit: a tiny kestrel, brilliantly colored in ruby rust and sapphire gray, diving straight for her. She turned her raised hands in time for the creature to land on her forearm, small, black-tipped talons easily piercing her sleeve to dig into her skin, drawing blood.

Oneira winced, but held steady, regarding the bird—no taller than her hand was long—with considerable bemusement. This small raptor had been able to slice through her wards as if they were nothing. Was that the fault of her less-than-sterling ward-making or its own ability? Would it be able to similarly shatter the wards of a powerful wardmaking sorcerer like Stearanos Stormbreaker? It would be interesting to try, though she'd never meet her nemesis in battle now that she'd retired. Not that they'd ever been likely to collide, always positioned against the other as a threat between the warring nations that held their leashes, a promise of mutually assured destruction.

Apparently uninterested in her musings, the kestrel stared her down, glistening obsidian eyes knowing, hooked beak sharp for killing prey. Another meat eater. She considered asking why it had sought her out, knowing there would be no more answer than to whether she could have defeated Stearanos in battle—she was certain she could have—or to the endlessly cycling, far more pertinent question of how to atone for her past.

She could, however, answer the question of the tiny raptor's identity. Stilling herself, she queried the Dream, seeking similar images. The vivid coloring, the metallic gold sparkle of the ring around its eyes, its ability to penetrate her wards. The answer bubbled up from countless numinous dreams.

This was Adsila, hunting companion to She Who Eats Bears, goddess of old.

Oneira had not asked for Adsila, nor did she want the attention of She Who Eats Bears. Attracting the notice of a deity always led to trouble, and Oneira's entire plan at the moment hinged on being so thoroughly forgotten that she'd be left alone. "You should go," she whispered to Adsila, who cocked her head, an obdurate glint in her bright eyes, a mirror to Oneira's own stubborn nature. The wind tugged at the knot of Oneira's hair, pulling it free of the coil and sending it whipping about them, stinging her face bloodless from the cold.

Bunny nipped a green tomato from the basket and ate it, grinning at her.

F**ull** winter enclosed the white halls of Oneira's fastness, layers of drifted snow washing against the high-walled garden like the foaming surf lashing the cliffs below, the blizzarding clouds swirling over the forever-frozen peaks above.

Winter days flowed quietly, with fewer sojourns into the world outside her walls. The heavy snows piled in waves against the gates, sealing them closed, and she didn't care to free them. Sometimes rows of days passed when she didn't venture outside, instead reading her books by the fire or in her dome surrounded by snowfall, getting up only to make soup, or turn the bread dough. Bunny and Adsila went in and out, but she'd quickly tired of playing servant to them. She might be embracing humility of circumstance, but she hated to be disturbed while reading. Or disturbed at all. Old habits die hard.

So, she spent a morning creating egress and ingress for her self-invited living companions. For Adsila, she added an aerie to the top of the house, not high enough to interfere with the view from her tower, but enough to satisfy the bird's desire for a lofty roost. She made it cozy enough for security, then added glass for viewing the landscape. It was simple enough to set a ward on the glass, as the goddess's bird could come and go freely, as if it didn't exist.

The solution to Bunny's independence took a bit more doing. In the summer, it had been simple enough to leave the glass doors open to the warm air, but the winter winds blew less kindly.

Though Oneira's fire burned without wood, and she could warm the house by pulling from dreams of hot summer lands, she discovered she disliked cold drafts nearly as much as being interrupted. And Bunny, accustomed to roaming the high peaks, liked to get out and frolic in the snow until he'd resemble a creature crafted from ice rather than pure magic. Then he'd roar in again, like an ice-ridden alpine wind, scattering snow—and snowmelt—on his hurtling path to the fire, where he'd roll belly-up until he reached roasting temperatures. Then he'd repeat the process.

The nth time Oneira stepped barefoot into a shockingly cold puddle of melt on her warm stone floors, she shrieked, pulled from deep thoughts, and seriously considered at least singeing an unrepentant Bunny. Instead she made a tunnel. It burrowed beneath the house wall and emerged some distance away in the garden. She would not make a ground-level access to her home from outside the walls, wards or no. That was a nonstarter. Bunny could stay in the garden for the winter before she'd risk that. Oneira trusted her skills in wardmaking only so far.

The tunnel functioned to cut the drafts and to absorb the water shed by Bunny as he raced through it. By the time he emerged into the house proper, he had dry fur again. Pleased with herself, Oneira considered the tasks well-accomplished and she turned back to her studies.

But magic liked to be used and her spell-working had tickled awake old habits and inclinations. Restlessness filled her, her agile mind no longer satisfied with making soup and baking bread. She sometimes walked with Bunny in the garden, donning her fur cloak she'd made from a dream of arctic climes, treading the weaving paths he'd tamped down in his circling. The snow rose on either side of her at hip height, the trees draping heavily laden branches nearly to the ground so it seemed at times that she moved through a tunnel of black, leafless skeletons fleshed in snow dropped again in sifts and clods, the landscape as bizarre and unreal as any she might tread within the Dream.

If she allowed her fancy to take her there, the soft plopping and the visual comparison to flesh melting from bone could remind her of the nightmare aftermath of battlefields. Or of lands destroyed without the opportunity to raise even a word of objection, like at Govirinda, the job that had tempted her with a startling revelation, the alluring possibility of ending the years of growing, restless dread. The one that had paid her enough to allow her to retire, to exile herself and leave it all behind. That guaranteed she'd never again open the Dream to bring in nightmare monsters to reduce a population of hundreds of thousands to sludge dripping from bones.

A quiet whuff from Bunny told her she'd stopped and was staring darkly at a pile of limbs half-buried in snow. They looked nothing like the mortal corpses of the dream that had invaded her mind, dredged up from memories that refused to be purged, and yet . . . She'd stood there long enough for her feet to grow cold and numb, and for the normally ebullient wolf to tug at the hem of her cloak with gentle teeth. Absently patting him on the head, she resumed walking, resting her hand on Bunny's shoulders as he paced beside her. He steered them back toward the house, showing a concern that she wasn't entirely sure how to wrestle.

As they approached the house, white on white against the gray sky, a *something* shifted. Oneira halted, not quite alarmed, Bunny mirroring her stillness, lifting his muzzle to sniff the snowflake-dense air. Adsila burst out of her aerie above, a streak of rust-and-blue smoke, cutting through the mist in skipping bursts. Oneira's mind did likewise, leaping along the smooth surface of her wards. No breaks, no intrusions or testing.

And yet, a *something* was somehow inside her wards and walls, arriving without a ripple of the many alerts that should've kept it out. "Who are you?" she asked on a whisper, threading it with a command to reveal itself truly. Under Oneira's hand, Bunny quivered, but didn't move.

A shape undulated out of the lacy curtain of falling snow, white going to gray and darkening to black as deep as shadowy corners on a moonless night. Graceful as smoke, liquid and dancing on great, soft paws, the cat flowed toward her, emerald eyes penetrating the mist with a sharpness at odds with all of its otherwise fluidity.

Ah. The knowledge came to Oneira on the wings of a dream. "Lady Moriah," she murmured. The cat's whiskers twitched up in a half smile, eyes glittering. The antimage, the witch's familiar, the feline in form but not function, repository of all the spells in the world. Before this moment, Oneira would have called Moriah a myth, a simple metaphor for the techniques ancient witches used to cast enchantments. But then, she'd also have called She Who Eats Bears a construct of human longing for a protective deity and the *scáthcú* nothing more than a tale told to ambitious young wizards hoping to shortcut indentured servitude.

Third time's a charm. Why these semimythical creatures had converged upon her aloneness, Oneira had no idea. She was no apantomancer, to work magic through chance encounters with animals. If these truly were chance encounters. She rather thought otherwise, but she also could no more refuse this guest than she had the others. She sighed and swept a hand at the house.

The three of them went in through the door to the kitchen, the side that faced the ocean and thus was regularly swept bare by the offshore winds. Adsila arrowed in over their heads, making one loop before exiting to her aerie. Moriah gave the bird a thoughtful, watchful glance. "Only if you care to anger a goddess," Oneira advised, figuring Adsila was on her own in this battle. Oneira had retired, after all, and was done with assisting anyone in their wars.

Moriah gave the feline equivalent of a shrug and ambled her way through the kitchen and into the rest of the house, looking it over thoroughly before finding Oneira's bier and leaping onto it. She swiped away a few of the dried garlands, then stretched herself out on the white stone, tail draping lavishly over one side nearly to the floor.

Oneira considered objecting, but she'd already said more words in a row than she had in weeks, possibly months, and found herself wearied. It had been an unusual day, what with Moriah's arrival and the uncanny visitation of that nightmare of her ultimate crime at Govirinda, and she apparently had lost all resilience for accommodating even the smallest variations in her days. She'd sought the numbing sameness of isolation and the gentle abyss of the blank slate. That had meant forgetting and thinking of nothing at all. Even the words of the books she read had slid into and out of her mind without leaving a trace.

With the advent of Moriah, Lady of Night and holder of all the spells of the world, things changed. Not to discount the disturbances created by Bunny and Adsila, but Moriah had tipped the balance, permanently disturbing the frozen sea of Oneira's mind. Thoughts trickled in through the cracks, small green shoots thrusting through the desolate frozen soil of her being.

She still submerged her waking hours in reading, sleeping, making soup, and baking bread, but the words she read ran around in her thoughts as they hadn't before. They marched in columns and reassembled themselves into new formations. When she slept, she dreamed of words. These dreams didn't come real, of course, as she'd long since mastered disconnecting her sorcery from her dreaming mind. Still, she dreamed vividly of lines of text, running backward and forward, upside down and sideways, the glyphs breaking up and rearranging.

For the first time since the moment she'd dumped out the chest of coin at Queen Zarja's feet, Oneira considered what she *was* doing. She'd rained a pile of bloodstained gold to drip down the stairs of the dais and told the queen and that roomful of astonished men to consider her debt paid and beyond, that she was done with them and their wars, to release her from the blood geas, that she was leaving and to disturb her at their peril.

"But what of Stearanos Stormbreaker?" Queen Zarja had demanded, barely suppressing the quaver in her voice. "Without you here, there's nothing to stop the Northern Lands from wielding him against us. We'll be conquered."

"Don't tell them I'm gone," Oneira replied. Stearanos and what he might or might not do was no longer her problem. "I'll go in secrecy and stay in secret, but I *am* going."

She went, and she'd gone on to find the place, build the house, ward against intruders, learn to sustain her life until she made the final decision to be done with it, to embrace the death she'd earned as surely as she'd earned those gold coins.

All of it had consumed her. But it had all occupied her as dreams devour a sleeper.

The time had passed in a mist of snowfall and summer leaves and ocean spray. Now, like a dreamer awakening, she wondered what she'd been looking for in all those books she'd read. At first she'd immersed herself in books because she finally had the long stretches of time to read everything she wanted to. All her life, she'd collected books, depositing them in the house she'd never truly lived in, in the suites of rooms in castles, palaces, and citadels that had been hers and not.

Her life had been an itinerant one, moving at the behest of the queen, or those requiring her services enough to pay her exorbitant prices. The time she'd spent in her ostensible home had been limited to visits to a place that felt more unfamiliar than the fortresses, forts, and castles she'd returned to again and again. One thing had become abundantly clear over the course of her career: the same places formed the nexus of the most trouble.

The abodes of those warlords had become more familiar to her than her own titular home. In some cases, they'd maintained a suite of rooms for her, kept solely for her use, furnished grandly and lavishly, always a reflection of what they thought she should like. Never had anyone asked her what she actually liked. To be fair, if they had, she wouldn't have had an answer for them. The house that had belonged to her hadn't held anything she particularly liked either. People gave her things. Gifts as payment, as tribute, as hints, to curry favor. Spoils of war that smelled eternally of the blood spilled to take them and echoed with silent screams of agony and injustice. She'd deposited them all in that house.

And when it came time to leave, she'd taken only the books. All those books she never read, all the more valuable because she couldn't pull them from the Dream. For some reason, people didn't dream in printed characters. Books from the Dream looked real enough on the surface, but the pages of the books they dreamed came glued together or were always out of focus, the words formed of nonsense shapes.

It had taken time with some of the books she'd collected to purge them of their violent pasts. When she could, during rare breaks in her schedule, she tended to her newest acquisitions, assuming responsibility for their rehabilitation.

With some tomes, the simplest and fastest way to cleanse them had been to pry the jewels from their covers. Usually with men, it was the jewels they wanted, not the books themselves. Or the information inside that would lead them to wealth or power, or both, as the two often went together, or one led to the other. She threw the jewels into the ocean, with apologies to the abyssal deities, and after cleansing the gems to the best of her ability. Sometimes she stripped off the binding, too, if the gold leaf had been too deeply embedded for her to remove it.

With the truly damaged books, she'd had to go to greater lengths, glad of the time in her exile to take on the extended process. To purify them, she returned to the ancient practices, the foundational magics, alternating bathing the books in the light of the full moon and burying them in trunks filled with the tiny, round, pink pebbles from the beach below. With some of the bloodiest books, the process took months or years. But she was patient, considering the labor one of love. It wasn't the books' fault that people had used them to commit horrors.

She put each one through the purifying and purging cycle, digging it out of the shining pink grave and carefully assessing the pages with her sorcery, continuing until nothing remained but the characters committed to substrate—and perhaps the intent of the long-ago author, though such things couldn't be relied upon. What the author intended and what the reader took away could be as distant from each other as the icy mountain peaks from the wave-lashed beach. She recommitted the contaminated pink pebbles to the sea, who was ever infinite in her forgiveness, replacing them with fresh sand deposited there by the everlasting surf, pinking with Oneira's magic. Why she'd made her beach pink, she couldn't say, except that it pleased her. She'd seen it once in a dream and never forgot.

One book she couldn't redeem. It had been written on human skin flayed from a victim of torture. The unfortunate person's identity had been forever lost, but not the pain they'd suffered, nor their even more acute longing for the loved ones who would miss them and never see them again. If Oneira's heart hadn't withered to dust long before, she would have wept over that tome. There were others similarly made, written on the skin of humans, or animals, or—in one salient case—a creature she couldn't identify, not even in the Dream. Those she was able to purge of their suffering, with patient attention and what passed for love. She'd learned early in her schooling that scrupulous, careful attention to a thing could be substituted for the love many spells of creation or redemption required. *Neatness counts.*

Of course, for the destructive sorcery almost universally requested of her, none of those kinder feelings had been required.

She began with meticulous care and eventually learned to love her books, even the ones written or published in pain. Except for the one. Concerned that fire would only concentrate its malevolence into indestructible ash, she debated for some time what to do with it. Even the sea, in her vastness and eternity, wouldn't forgive the introduction of such an evil thing.

Finally, Oneira carried the cursed book to the tops of the mountains. It took a long time, but one cannot travel via the Dream to a place where there are no dreamers, and she needed a place where nothing could live. Not even the *scáthcú*. She hiked three days and two nights to the remote glaciers that never melted in the thin air of the blue-black sky.

Pulling precise flame from the Dream, she carved a hole in the deepest glacier, displacing the upper layers of dirt and exposing the ice-blue heart, sending the benighted tome to rest deep inside. She didn't know what knowledge it had contained, as she hadn't dared touch it, much less crack its pages, and so she was at a loss as to how to memorialize the moment she sent it to its icy grave. Still, it felt wrong to say nothing. She stood there a while, idly smoothing over the wound she'd made in the glacier, swirling the lighter snow and soil together in small whirlwinds, like stirring honey into her tea in the mornings. In the distance, far below, the *scáthcú* howled, white ghosts racing the alpine winds.

In the end, she offered a song of benediction, a nonsense lullaby she was surprised to recall from her long-forgotten childhood. Nonsense words were always best, lest one manifest something into reality unintentionally.

She'd left it there, sealed in ice until time itself ended. Or until the mountains melted.

Whichever came first.

4

In time it became evident that Oneira had read every book she'd brought with her at least once. Many, possibly most of them, she'd read multiple times. And in this feeling of waking from a long sleep, all those words she'd consumed she'd also digested. Combined with the new sense of restlessness, the words spilled atop each other and recombined to form a nebulous inkling that prodded at her. Somewhere in mulling this odd sensation, she realized she'd been seeking an answer.

An answer to what, she didn't know, which presented a problem. How could she know the answer if she'd not yet identified the question? That must be why all those words hadn't yet formed a pattern. She had no architecture to offer them, no scaffolding upon which they could hang themselves and be assembled to form an image.

Or an idea.

She looked up from the slightly withered carrots she'd been chopping, meeting the inscrutable gaze of Moriah, who had draped herself over the counter beneath the windows, where she could keep an eye on the birds harvesting the remnants of the winter garden as the early morning sun melted the frost from the thawing soil.

"I need more books," Oneira said aloud.

Moriah flicked an ear, though the cat's feigned disinterest didn't fool Oneira in the least. The cat possessed the knowledge of all things and could send Oneira to the book that held the question she sought. Well, she could if Oneira could articulate the question that would lead to it—and how did one form a question to solicit a question? The mirror loop was endless. She could only hope she'd know it when she saw it.

"Any advice?" she asked Moriah. In the old tales, the cat could speak, though she'd never given any indication to Oneira that she possessed the ability. Like all cats, Moriah did exactly as she pleased and would no doubt speak only when it suited her purposes. Which it did not in this case. Moriah lowered her chin to her great, fluffy paws, giving Oneira a gleaming, knowing look, and flicked the tip of her tail. "I don't know why you even came here," Oneira grumbled. "You're not at all useful."

Bunny ambled into the kitchen, wagging tail high and ears perked. "You either," Oneira said, pointing her finger. "Uninvited guests who never leave are the bane of a peaceful mind."

Wagging his tail harder, Bunny grinned, tongue lolling to the side. Outside, Adsila called, a circling silhouette against a bluing sky. Shaking her head at herself and this menagerie that had foisted itself upon her, Oneira set the soup to simmer over a low flame and ascended to her tower.

Up in her crystal bubble, she felt like part of the sky. Did Adsila feel this way, soaring with spread and steady wings through the variations in blue and mist? It seemed so clean and restful, just the self and the air, nothing between. Oneira had never tried to fly in the waking world, only in the Dream, though it was theoretically possible for her to do so. The ability hadn't been anything useful to her clients in winning their wars and required extensive time and study—not something the magic academy that had acquired her had wanted to invest resources in.

She had the time now to learn, but still no need to fly, beyond the idle temptation to join Adsila, who zoomed past in a blur of russet and indigo, circling the dome playfully. Besides, she could travel more swiftly to anywhere she wished via the Dream.

She settled herself in the center of the floor. In this room alone, she'd layered carpets and color over the bare stone. Thick, hand-woven rugs, soft as Moriah's fur and brilliantly colored, depicted exotic flowers, birds, and insects from a distant arid and sunny land. She'd plucked them from the rooms maintained for her at one of the fortresses she'd used to frequent, after discovering that meditating for hours on a stone floor left her too stiff and creaky for comfort. The rugs were priceless in the world of men, but valuable in their own way to her. She supplemented them with pillows she extracted from the Dream, jewel toned and swirling with fantastical images from dreamers.

Crossing her legs, setting her hands palms up on her thighs, closing her eyes, Oneira cleared her mind and prepared to physically enter the Dream.

The Dream is different from dreaming and yet the same. Every oneiromancer first learns to differentiate their own dreams from the dreams of those around them. Later, they learn about the Dream itself, a conglomeration of millennia of dreams that has taken on a life and landscape of its own.

Oneira's sorcery first manifested when she walked through the dreams of her family, bending them according to her toddler whims. She'd quickly discovered she could pull what she found in those dreams into the waking world, doing so with the glee-ful abandon of a child discovering a new box of toys. She barely remembered a few snippets of people crying, shouting, and, as a result of their chaos, feeling afraid for the first time in her young life. Most of her "memory" was a construct of what others, mostly her teachers, had explained to her about it later. Nevertheless, the sequence of the ensuing events came easily to mind, though mostly through the lens of other eyes.

The maestro from the Hendricks Academy for Sorcerous Pursuits had arrived, a brilliant smear of fur-trimmed teal, green, and golden robes, standing out amid even her noble family like a peacock amongst drab sparrows. In the ruin of her family home, littered with twisted creatures never meant to escape the Dream, he'd kindly explained that their young daughter, still unsteady on her physical legs, was a powerful oneiromancer. That she had danced through their dreams without barrier and was capable of laying open their psyches and plucking what she wished from them. In that moment, she'd stopped being their beloved child and became a terrifying predator.

One image Oneira could clearly recall was the revulsion on her mother's face as she held her daughter out at the full length of her shaking arms, handing her weeping, begging child over to the maestro, scrubbing her hands against her skirts as soon as she let go. Her father hadn't looked, averting his eyes, his jaw tight and flexing, as he accepted the coin for Oneira's purchase.

The price that the Hendricks Academy for Sorcerous Pursuits paid for Oneira had been plenty to rebuild the castle with sufficient left over to add significant improvements. She remembered that, too, though her young mind shouldn't have been able to grasp that discussion, or perhaps she'd filled that in later, with her mature understanding of debt and finance. Somehow, though, she recalled one part of her standing aside and thinking, *so this is to be my life*, even as she sobbed, wailing without words and reaching for her mother from the prison of the stony arms of an academy nurse.

They'd taken her away to the private academy—the very best of all the academies of magic, public and private, though she wouldn't understand that either until much later—and surrounded her with trained oneiromancers with the skill to keep her out of their dreams. At least, until she outpaced them in ability. They renamed her Oneira, in honor of her nascent talent, so rare in its sheer potency, and in anticipation of the force of magic she'd become.

She didn't remember what name her parents had called her.

That massive initial price paid to her family was the first debt on Oneira's ledger and only the beginning of the eventual enormous amount of money she owed the academy by the time she graduated. That debt included over two decades of room, board, and—especially expensive—private tuition. All magic-workers were identified as children, bound by blood geas first to the academies who bought them, then to their eventual clients. They all spent the first few decades of their careers working off the price of their education, and Oneira had started out with more than most, thanks to paying for what she'd done to the ancestral family home.

In her favor, she was also the best of her generation and quickly developed a reputation as the most fearsome sorcerer in existence, except perhaps for Stearanos Stormbreaker. He possessed an enviable flexibility in his talents, but she exceeded him in power in her sole competency. The fees she was able to command helped to gnaw away at what she owed—then to Queen Zarja, who bought her contract to have her own anti-Stearanos to guard the Southern Lands—but the system was stacked against her. The world operated on the labor of everyone paying off the debts incurred by their education, magical and otherwise. Those who'd bought their way free in any profession were few and far between. It served no one in power to have the lower classes accumulate personal wealth.

Thus, even her wages from Zarja and other would-be tyrants who hired her to win their petty squabbles hadn't been enough to free Oneira anytime soon. And she'd been desperate to be free, so she took the job at Govirinda, not realizing she'd deal herself the worst and final blow by doing so.

Oneira set aside those old memories and concerns, uncertain why they'd bubbled up in that moment, except that they seemed to be part of the idea she was assembling, hanging each scrap of thought upon a scaffolding that as yet promised no answers.

As always, reaching into the Dream felt like slipping her hand into an old and familiar glove, like moving into a place more familiar than reality. She'd certainly spent enough time in that self-enclosed world that was independent of the dreaming of people, in the way that the ocean is independent of the shore. The ocean waves end up on a beach somewhere, touching before receding again. Thus, just as any shore may be reached by the water, anyone's dreaming mind can be accessed from the Dream.

Oneira floated through the Dream, at first only mentally, leaving her body behind. She engaged much more fully than when she simply reached into the Dream, searched for an object, and extracted it, but less than if she'd entered the Dream physically. She needed no portal for this, only a lowering of the barriers she normally held in place against the Dream's seductive call.

Enfolded in that embrace, one she knew from her earliest memories, preceded only by the loving arms of her parents and enduring long after, she felt whole and not at all alone. She knew the landscape there better than any in the living world. It felt like coming home to walk those undulating paths again, enough so that she wondered why she'd denied this to herself. But then, she was a different person within the Dream, one who possessed fewer qualms and sensibilities, which was part of the problem.

Within the Dream, nothing felt exactly real. It was only when she reentered the waking world and witnessed the impacts of what she'd wrought from inside the Dream that the consequences of her actions drove home with bone-melting reality.

But that wasn't what she was doing in the Dream now, she reminded herself before her heart could quail. Nothing from this place of infinite power would be extracted through her to create nightmares to plague humanity, no night terrors unleashed. She only walked the Dream, at one with the flow of it as her mental feet coasted the waves. Sometimes, standing on the cliff point just outside her walls, gazing over the endless sea, she imagined stepping out onto that water and walking the surface in exactly this way. In her darker moments, she'd nearly tried, even knowing that would lead to drowning. Only the thought of her bier stopped her. She'd gone to so much trouble to perfect that spot that she couldn't bear to lose the moment of finally laying herself upon it and letting go . . .

But not yet.

She had an answer to seek and a question to pose, so she surfed the tossing waves of the Dream. Beneath her feet, the vast depths of the entangled dreams of all living creatures surged and billowed. This was how most people experienced the Dream, as part of the contiguous sea created by themselves and everyone else in the world. Every time someone dreamed, they added to the pool, and the dream creations remained behind. Some settled to the bottom, forming the nutrient-rich floor that sprouted new stalks that swelled and burst, scattering seeds to inform and turn the direction of new dreams. Others lived on, sharking through the collective, invading nascent dreams or consuming them.

With her sorcery, Oneira detected the minds in the Dream, those people actively dreaming, mentally tiptoeing over their heads, touching just enough to ascertain their identity and physical location. It was a delicate art. Not enough contact and she'd glean too little information; too much and she'd affect their dreams. People tended to draw toward them the wandering elements of the

Dream that they most needed, but an oneiromancer interfered with that natural process.

Most oneiromancers—the kind who brought good to the world—operated as healers, helping dreamers attract those seeds and elements that helped purge old traumas and repair wounds. Usually people hired them to banish nightmares and night terrors, two very different phenomena.

Regardless, that sort of dream-healing oneiromancy worked best at lower levels of power. As Oneira's sorcery was the magical equivalent of a burning sun at high noon in the desert, she simply wasn't capable of that level of precision. She left scorched earth behind her sorcerous touch, as all the world knew, either by direct experience or the tales told and retold. As Govirinda would know, if anything had been left alive there. Oneira was a destroyer, not a healer. No one wanted her in their dreams. So, she trod carefully, touching just enough to glean a sense, never enough to affect the dreamer.

In this way, she moved through the world at large, leaping great distances with no more than a thought, as the Dream has no physical reality. This is why dreams shift so suddenly, moving from place to place seamlessly.

It took little time for her to find the mind she'd sought without consciously making the decision to find him. Perhaps because he'd just been in her thoughts. More likely because, according to rumor, he was the possessor of the most extensive library known to exist.

Stearanos Stormbreaker. Sorcerer of the Northern Lands. The nemesis she'd never met. The one sorcerer in all the world who could potentially defeat her.

The fact that Oneira and Stearanos had never met was, by itself, the stuff of legends. Much had been made of the possible conflict of giants, ballads composed speculating in the most florid terms what a duel between them would be like and which of them would win. They possessed different skills, their greatest powers lying in very different areas, so the stories spun about the potential war between them depended heavily on the arena of the conflict. Most of those tales culminated in mutual destruction, which Oneira had cynically decided expressed the wishful thinking of a world wiser than the nobles that held their leashes.

Oneira spent no more time touching the dreams of the sorcerer than she had with any others. Just enough to ascertain she'd found the right mind, which didn't take much, as even his dreaming self shimmered with magic, restless power, and the violence of countless wars. She recognized something of herself in the fragments of undying memories crowding his dreams, the remembered horrors attracting the scavengers of the Dream who lived to feed on pain and misery.

These things would exact their price, one way or another. She might've felt pity for Stearanos, but she knew how richly she deserved the punishing nightmares dealt by the Dream. He would be the same.

Instead of lingering out of the pleasure in his suffering one might expect her to have for her enemy, or even some misguided sense of camaraderie, she used the sorcerer's connection to his mortal body to ascertain that it was an hour or so before dawn where he slept, a powerful time for dreaming, which meant a powerful time for her.

With a gentle caress of her power, she ensured the sorcerer would remain asleep, along with all the denizens of his immense palace, from the housekeeper down to the mice in the walls. Connecting to her own physical body again, she rose to her feet and sketched a portal in the veil that separated waking from dreaming. The outline shimmered with iridescence, opening into the landscape few ever saw with mortal eyes. Wielding her skill with casual ease, she did what she would never have dared while the queen still held her leash: she cleared a pathway for herself, pulling her physical body through the Dream, and stepped into the library of her nemesis.

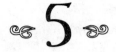

5

Few oneiromancers could physically step from the Dream and into a specific room. That was part of what made Oneira the best of her kind. Not only could she find a specific dreamer and go to their physical location, she could then survey the general area and move to a nearby place of her choosing.

The ability had made her a devastating secret weapon. None could ward against her arrival, as everyone dreamed. Some of those unfortunate enough to be her enemies had attempted countermeasures, usually enchantments to keep themselves and the people around them from dreaming, but that sort of thing backfires quickly.

The Dream doesn't like being suppressed, and it's a force more powerful than any human sorcery, even Oneira's. Such spells lasted only a short time before the Dream found a way through, like a rain-swollen reservoir eroding a leaky dike. If they tried to keep people from sleeping entirely—which some leaders did, thinking having everyone awake and working would bring additional value—the Dream eventually swept into waking minds, invading reality in disastrous ways. Oneira had taken advantage of situations like that more than once, riding dreams into the waking world. An exhilarating ride.

But using their own dreaming against innocents, time and time again, had led to her crisis of—if not conscience, as it could be argued she didn't have one, then—such deep moral misgivings that she'd done something even more terrible to escape it all. She was aware of the inherent contradiction, though it hadn't bothered her at the time.

Though her handlers had occasionally discussed—or, more aptly, fantasized—about sending Oneira to assassinate Stearanos, they'd always talked themselves out of it, to her vast relief. The odds were too great that he'd outmatch her and Oneira would end up dead instead. They never quite worked themselves up to run the risk.

These days, of course, she no longer cared if she lived or died. Nevertheless, it gave her a long-withheld sense of satisfaction to know that she *could* have succeeded. So much for the vaunted wardmaker.

Stearanos Stormbreaker's library lived up to its reputation, Oneira decided, surveying the large room. In those wee, small hours of the morning, when sleep was deepest and dreams dominated and lasted longest, no lamps were lit, only moonlight showing her the way. Tall windows glowed with light scattered from the moon shining on a sea far gentler than her own. She had no idea which of the seas abutting the Northern Lands it might be. That was one disorienting aspect of physically traveling like this. The Dream didn't come with labels or dotted lines showing borders. One ended up where the dreamer was, with no other information about the place.

Casting her senses over the castle to be certain of her safety— attention to detail had saved her skin more than once—she verified that her enchantment had put all living things within the walls into deep sleep. Suppressed by her magic, their dreams burbled quietly in the background, with occasional stabs of disturbance from Stearanos, like garish heat lighting in an otherwise calm sky. With a thought, Oneira found the lamps distributed around the room and lit them with a touch of flame, a relatively simple sorcery, common to most magic-workers. She winced at the sudden blaze of light. The man sure did like to have a lot of lamps.

But then, the library *was* cavernous, going on through several connected rooms, shadowed alcoves eating the light. Not knowing quite where to start—how did one search for a thing without knowing what it was to begin with?—Oneira browsed the shelves, running light fingers over the spines, enjoying the sheer variety and unfamiliarity of it all.

Titles and authors flowed into her mind from a myriad of languages. The Dream contained all the minds in the world and thus all living languages, plus quite a few dead ones that lingered still in the dreams of scholars and the ghostly remnants of civilizations long gone but immortalized in the Dream. Many of the books she'd read already, or was familiar with and had chosen not to read, but many more were new to her.

Stearanos had clearly read—or was familiar with and had chosen not to read—all of these books. Oneira supposed the sorcerer could have hired a librarian or archivist to do the work of shelving them, but she had a feeling it was all him.

Also, Stearanos had left a trail of himself on these books. Analyzing remanence wasn't the greatest of her skills, but Oneira could do so adequately, given time and quiet. A powerful psychometrist could delve through the layers of all who'd touched an object, peeling back to the origin of the item, potentially able to discern even the preceding influences on the constituent materials of the object. Oneira couldn't do that, but she could usually tell who'd last touched a thing, especially in this case, where book after book whispered of the powerfully magical touch of the same person. If she hadn't recognized Stearanos by his dreaming mind, she'd have built a picture of him from the years and decades he'd spent holding these books.

Without exception, he'd been the last person to touch each

and every one. Belatedly it occurred to her that he'd likely detect her own remanence left behind on the leather spines and gold-leaf lettering. He was not a highly skilled psychometrist, though—according to his dossier—and not an oneiromancer at all, so he wouldn't have any way to know who had appeared in the night to peruse his precious books that no one else touched, all while he slept oh-so-vulnerably. The thought of his ire made her smile for no good reason—and the stiffness of the skin around her mouth made her wonder just how long it had been since she'd last done so.

She set those musings aside. How Stearanos reacted to her nocturnal visit mattered nothing to her. Finding her question did matter, so she set herself to discern the organization system, in order to conduct a more organized survey of his collection. From what she'd been told of him over numerous, fairly detailed briefings intended to arm her with knowledge should the Northern Lands decide to throw all caution to the winds and pit Stearanos against her, he was meticulous to the point of being obsessive. Therefore, there must be a system. She need only bend her own intellect to the puzzle.

The problem was, the books were not categorized by language, author, subject matter, or title, but rather by an arcane system that seemed impenetrable initially. Gradually, however, as she made her way through shelf after shelf, climbing the ladders that slid on silent rails, she began to fathom something of the labyrinthine mind that had put these tomes into such a bizarre order.

He'd organized them according to meaning, possibly theme. Here were books on water of all types—oceanography, hydromancy, sailing, precipitation, even poetry on aquatic themes—and within that set of shelves, he'd arranged them grouped by salt water versus fresh, then application of the water. An excellent method to keep anyone but him from finding the book they wanted, she thought with irritation.

Well, she amended, anyone but him and Oneira, who had cracked his code. Had she known the theme of the question she wished to pose, she could have found it quickly. But, of course, she didn't know, instead letting intuition guide her. Soon it became apparent from the intensity of his lingering presence on those tomes what Stearanos's most recent area of concentration had been.

Oneira slowed, then lingered over those shelves, sensing the bright passage of recent days in the vivid remanence glittering against her fingertips. And ... *there.* Ah, there was the book that Stearanos had been reading that very evening—in truth, late into the night, as it had been replaced on the shelf only hours before. The sense of the sorcerer came to her vividly, his intense interest and eventual fatigue. The reluctance of relinquishing a quest. Intrigued, she pulled the book from its neat slot on the shelf—neither too compressed by its neighbors nor rattling in a too-big space— and perused the title.

It was written in ancient Veredian, which she could read, though with difficulty, and seemed to be about flower cultivation, which struck her as an oddly frivolous topic to keep an iron skull like Stearanos awake past midnight. He'd marked a page midway through with a scrap of paper with nothing on it, probably intending to continue the read.

Feeling that same mischievous spark as before, the one that had brought the unaccustomed smile to her mouth—and aware that she didn't have all the time in the world to settle on her choice—Oneira decided to take that book. It wasn't as if she had a clearer option and it pleased something in her that hadn't experienced pleasure in a long time to mess with her old enemy, even if he was an enemy only in an academic sense. Besides, she wanted to know what it could be about flower cultivation that consumed the dread Stearanos Stormbreaker.

Now, to leave the obvious gap, shuffle the books together to create temporary confusion, or replace the tome with something else? She decided upon creating symmetry of a sort and, reaching through the Dream, plucked a book from her own library, one she'd kept out of habit more than anything, as you never knew when you'd want some tidbit from the classic reference books. She could easily replace it from any bookseller, should she want to, which made the book innocuous and ubiquitous enough to puzzle Stearanos exceedingly. He was an overthinker, following every clue relentlessly down a rabbit warren of logic. In the past, when she'd planned strategies to counter the Stormbreaker, should they ever clash, she'd had to account for his remorseless attention to detail. In this instance, she would use that to confuse and annoy him.

Inevitably, the book would bear the imprint of her touch, but not much more so than any of her other books, and less than ones she'd read more recently. Not that it would do him any good to detect her presence without context.

She rather enjoyed the prospect of Stearanos trying to discover who she was. He wouldn't be able to, which also deeply satisfied her in the same way she'd once taken pride in her work. Deep down, she'd always nursed the certainty that, should she ever be pitted against Stearanos, she would've won. In her more pitiless days, she'd been almost sorry their kingdoms had shied from the prospect of the destruction they'd cause.

That would have been a battle for the ages.

Instead—in her old age, she thought mirthlessly to herself— she settled for a bit of harmless mischief. Perhaps a part of her missed strategizing against her nemesis, and this would give her a bit of that old stimulation, the thrill of outwitting her enemy.

She inserted her book on the shelf, aligning it perfectly, just as its predecessor had been. In an excess of caution, she ran a finger along the spine, removing as much imprint of her house or companions from the book as she could. Just in case. It would be insane to compromise their safety over a whim.

Casting a look about the library, she snuffed the flames in the lamps, allowing the filtering moonlight to return to the quiet, breathless room. Wandering over to a window, she observed the single deep armchair placed there with a small table and a reading lamp beside it, all of which fairly radiated the sorcerer's presence. She didn't dare actually sit in the chair, but angled herself to take in what view Stearanos would see.

Endless views of that ocean that was far more tranquil than hers. Some part of her approved. Another, wiser and more cautious part of her, observed that the horizon had lightened with approaching dawn. They were facing east then. And it was past time for her to go.

Reaching for the Dream, she drew the portal in the air, poised on the silvery threshold, one foot in each world, and cast her mind back over the sleeping castle. She withdrew the sleep enchantment with such gentle precision that they didn't awaken yet— and shouldn't until the rhythms of their own bodies prompted them.

Their minds billowed back into the Dream, from the smallest mice up to the vivid, ghastly tumult of heat and light that was Stearanos.

She stepped into the Dream, neatly avoiding all their minds, and was gone.

6

Stearanos awakened with an unaccustomed start and instinctively lay still as death.

He didn't know what had startled him awake, but he'd slept on too many battlefields, had caught snatches of sleep in too many war rooms to dismiss the internal alarm that alerted him to . . . something.

A *something* that had changed, a subtle wrongness he couldn't quite identify. Not yet, but he would. Casting his senses over the castle, he verified that most everyone was sleeping still. A few of the cooks had just begun to stir, unusually late for them. Bethany should be already in the kitchen, humming a tune as she punched down the dough she'd left to rise overnight for morning buns, but she had just left her bed. Nothing was as it should be for this time of the almost morning.

Including the *something.*

It smelled like magic—and not his own—but oh-so-faintly. In his younger days, he might've dismissed it as not important, the whiff was so barely there, but he'd learned over the years that sometimes the most elusive clues hinted of the worst dangers, especially in the fraught world of sorcerers. A light touch of magic could indicate an expert practitioner. Young sorcerers tended to paint the landscape with floods of magic, indiscriminate in both their resources and their wielding of it, drunk with the newfound power. As they aged, over the slow course of their extended lifespans, sorcerers good enough to survive their various battles— and the magical executions that were one of the few things that could bring an untimely end to their lives—learned to hoard their reserves and to wield power with skill. Having immense magical ability meant nothing if you exhausted it all in the midst of a battle. The precise attack, the one so honed and delicate that your enemy never saw it coming, that was what won wars. The showy stuff only sent up flags, painting a bright and shining target on the sorcerer.

So, this . . . this faint vibration of magic been and gone, inside his own castle, within his excellent and intact wards that evinced no sign of being tested, much less tampered with or crossed, this alarmed him greatly. So much so that he didn't move for some time, careful to ascertain that no magical trap had been set while he slept away, blissfully oblivious to the intrusion. The possibility infuriated him beyond reason, but addressing it would have to wait. He'd castigate himself and review his errors after the immediate danger had been quantified and dispensed with.

At least, he eventually determined, the invader hadn't been in this room. Not physically, though they'd left a faint dusting of enchantment behind. To accomplish what?

Moving slowly, just in case he was wrong, Stearanos crawled out from under the covers and stood naked in the center of his bedchamber, scratching his balls sleepily, in case this magicworker spied on him via remote viewing. Psychic magic of that variety could theoretically slip inside his wards. He didn't like to think so—he was by far the best wardmaker in existence—but he knew of other sorcerers who'd been taken in that way. Psychic or mentally derived phenomena didn't operate in the same way as other magic, and it was the careless sorcerer who failed to account for that possibility.

Nothing stirred, however, the sense of the *something* rapidly fading. Whoever they had been, whatever they had done, it was over, the trail cooling rapidly, evidence evaporating like dew as

the rays of the rising sun steamed it into nothing while he dith-
ered. Stearanos hated dithering, in himself or in others, and that
he'd become this person in his surprise at the invasion rankled.
It made him feel slow and old, and—while he'd been feeling his
years with a kind of grim weariness grittier than depression—he
had too much time ahead of him and too many enemies to allow
himself to deteriorate, even if he was on sabbatical.

He wasn't exactly sitting in a rocking chair on the porch of the
general store in the bleak steppe town he'd grown up in, jawing
with the other oldsters about all the terrible ways the world had
changed. There was a time he hadn't been so cynical, so poised
for disaster, but Stearanos had grown excessively cautious to the
point of outright paranoia. As if part of himself couldn't quite
relax, catastrophizing every minute change in his surroundings,
just in case envisioning the worst-case scenario could prevent it.

A paranoid and crazed recluse of a sorcerer. The rocking chair
might've been better.

Yanking on his pants in short jerks of disgust at himself and
at the world that had morphed him into this paranoid version of
his former self, he bundled back his long braids and tied them off,
then stalked barefoot and shirtless through the halls, sniffing out
his prey like the timber wolves that preyed along the outskirts
of that long-ago hometown. A few of the early-rising staff spotted his approach and vanished themselves, long familiar with his
moods and the roiling magic that preceded him like outstretched
claws and billowed in his wake, scouring the halls. He tried not
to be too difficult to live with, but he was also no gentle man.
That ship had long since sailed. He paid his staff well to tolerate
him and willingly released those with too little resilience to withstand his moods.

No trail presented itself to his sorcerous senses, which confirmed that the intruder hadn't traversed the corridors of his

castle. Their magic lingered throughout, however, a sheen of it left behind on virtually every surface. They'd been everywhere and nowhere, which made him want to growl under his breath, though long discipline kept him as silent as his footfalls. With no trail to follow, he looked for the newest and greatest concentrations of the magic they'd left behind like pollen shaken from a lily, bright, leaving an indelible stain.

He ended up in his library, the intruder's magic giving evidence of their actual, physical presence, and that they'd lingered there for some time. It gave him pause. Who went to the trouble of such a significant magic-working to evade his wards and invade his castle, only to visit the library? None of these books were objects of power. He didn't store such dangerous artifacts on these shelves. Anyone with the ability to do what this sorcerer had done would have easily ascertained that much. They'd have known in an instant that he'd locked away all of his arcane artifacts, especially the malevolent, quasi-sentient tomes. He could get to them should he encounter a grave enough emergency, but otherwise they were safely beyond reach behind immutable wards layered into indestructibility.

Apparently, this magic-worker had come for ordinary books. And, yes, he knew that in some circles the reputation of his library eclipsed even his own as the greatest sorcerer in the world, but still . . . it seemed like a lot of trouble just to visit his books. Especially when a quick census revealed that none of them had been taken. His posotomancy, the ability to quantify anything, lay at the core of his sorcery and he did it reflexively. Some might say compulsively, but much had been made over the years about his obsessiveness, as if striving for perfection was somehow a flaw.

A soothing habit, his counting didn't take much, if any, of his attention to assess the human denizens of the castle—seventy-nine, besides himself—or the plates in the cupboard—one-hundred and forty-three, which was one short because Ionos, the new washing lad, had broken one the day before and the replacement plate had not yet arrived—or the number of books in his library: ten-thousand, nine-hundred and fifty-three.

See? That sum demonstrated right there he wasn't *that* compulsive about numbers or he'd either have collected forty-seven more books to round up to ten thousand, ninety-one hundred, or—ideally—eliminated nine hundred and fifty-three to achieve an even ten thousand. He'd strongly considered the latter, but that was a lot of books to cull and he couldn't think of *one* he could do without, let alone nearly a thousand.

He prowled through the library, following the taste of foreign magic to its strongest point. Realization dawned as he neared the shelf that contained his current read. Surely not . . .

But yes, there—where *his* book was supposed to be, where he'd personally replaced it the night before—an imposter occupied the spot. A growl of utter rage welled up in him, almost immediately silenced. He yanked the offending tome from the shelf and glared at it. *Dragon Anatomy: From Tooth to Talon*, a treatise that had been copied countless times and could be found in any of the hundreds of magic academies, far from unique or interesting. Nothing to compare to the exceptionally rare book on the cultivation of Veredian roses that he had been studying, with an eye to adding those finicky bushes to his garden. That was, if any could still be found in all the world, since the last known specimens were lost on the island of Govirinda when it was destroyed. Worst of all, the new addition didn't even fit the theme of the surrounding books!

With effort, he mastered the surge of irritation at the mismatch, suspecting that his unknown visitor had done it on purpose, the person somehow divining that it would upset Stearanos's world in a meaningless and yet profound way. Was that the entire purpose of their visit, simply to aggravate him, to put him off-balance? Wars had been waged and won on the backs of such subtle tactics. In the arcane realm of sorcerers, confidence could make all the difference between victory and ignominious defeat. Undermining an opponent's belief in their skills, especially in the sanctity of their home—in his case, particularly in the impenetrability of their wards—could launch a gradual erosion of their ability to muster a solid defense, much less an aggressive offense.

Still, why taunt him in such an innocuous way? If this sorcerer had been hired by an enemy, then laying such subtle groundwork seemed excessive when a conflict had yet to be declared. Because if there had been even a whiff of a conflict, King Uhtric would have summoned him immediately, ignoring the sanctity of a sabbatical. If this sally stemmed from a smaller squabble, then everyone involved would already know that he'd taken a sabbatical. He wasn't available for hire at the moment, and this sorcerer should be off harassing some other magic-worker, not him.

Unless this was some sort of clever subterfuge on the part of one of his disappointed would-be clients. A number of them still sent messages, imploring him for a few days of his time, offering enticements should he agree to one more job. As if he wanted to spend his time and energy telling people what to do. A few cited their longstanding relationships, claiming friendship, even kinship, as if he meant something more to them than a tool in their wars of greed and pride. Maybe they thought to circumvent his determined refusals by drawing him into a personally fueled conflict. *You know that sorcerer who's been harassing you, infiltrating your home? Well, they've been hired by the Narphesiens. Here's your chance to destroy them on a fair field of battle. Wouldn't you like that?*

The final possibility was that this was personal.

That seemed to be the most likely scenario. He'd made many enemies over the years and no friends to speak of. Everyone he could count on as an ally either worked for him, owed him something, or held his leash. He suspected that this was true for all the world, and the concept of friendship a mass joke perpetuated on the gullible. He didn't care that some might call this a paranoid and cynical view.

Holding *Dragon Anatomy: From Tooth to Talon* in his hands, he plumbed it with his senses. Psychometry wasn't the strongest of his talents, but it extended naturally from his native ability, and he wielded enough to immediately discern that whoever had left this book in place of his had excised their own remanence with deliberate skill. They hadn't wanted him to know who left this substitution. But then why leave one at all? And why take his harmless book on growing roses so difficult and prickly in every sense of the word that they were almost certainly extinct? Stearanos cared about Veredian roses, but for his own reasons. No one else did. Wars were not won or lost because of rosebushes.

Forcibly calming himself, he paged through the book, searching for clues. There were none to be had. Stearanos had read the book back in his academy days, quite a long time ago, and it seemed exactly as he remembered it. In fact, he already possessed a copy. Fetching that one, he sat at his desk, laid the two copies side by side, and did a line-by-line analysis comparing the two.

They were nearly identical, with only the minor variations that came from hand-copying by the apprentices assigned the task. The two books had likely been sold to the magic academies and private tutors in the same batch. The comparison told him nothing he hadn't known before.

At last he closed both books. Leaving them side by side, he went to his reading chair to think, seating himself and looking out at the view, which calmed him under normal circumstances. Not this time. Unease crawled under his collar.

The intruder had stood here, he realized, and had remained stationary for quite some time. They hadn't been so reckless—or so deliberately provocative—as to sit in his chair. He ran his hands over the bloodred leather, verifying as much. No, they hadn't touched his chair, but they'd lingered, leaving behind a concentration of their passive magic, which tended to sift from the physical bodies of magic-workers like dandruff and stray hairs, hanging in the air like the heavy perfume from a social-climbing courtier.

Why? The mystery plagued him. He was not the sort of person who could be sanguine about unanswered questions and unsolved riddles. Which any enemy of his would know—which brought him around full circle to the conclusion that this . . . this *taunting* was personal. Whoever it was, they wanted to show him their power over him. None of the details mattered here, not the book they'd taken, nor the one they'd left behind. The entire point had been to get under his skin and send him into exactly this tailspin of doubt and obsessive wondering.

The question was: How to respond?

Surely this person would return. They'd left their book behind for a reason, as a message, perhaps. They'd rubbed his nose in their ability to evade his wards and frolic through his house as he slept. All of it had been too easy for them to be able to resist a second visit.

Well, Stearanos would be ready for them this time. Rising from his chair, he went to the twin books on his desk and took up the one the intruder had left behind, shelving it where it belonged, with the other books on scales combined with fire. Returning to his own copy, he considered, then put his plan into motion.

7

*R*oses. The book Oneira had borrowed from Stearanos's library had been, in truth, literally and entirely about cultivating Veredian roses. She'd never heard of them before, which put her in good company, as few people had, apparently. With dark foliage, wickedly long thorns, and small leaves, the Veredian rosebushes added nothing ornamental to anyone's landscaping. In addition to that the fact that they bloomed only once a year, for a few days at midwinter, when the nights were longest and most bitter, no one really pursued cultivating the things. Which in part had led to them dying out.

Gazing up at the cloudless blue sky—for she'd been lying on her back on a pile of pillows in the center of her dome to read—Oneira held the book in one hand, arms flung out like she was a starfish caught above tide. Thinking. Why would a sorcerer of Stearanos Stormbreaker's caliber and fearsome reputation spend his time reading about cultivating rare and undeniably ugly rosebushes?

She'd been so sure there would be some hidden meaning in the tome, a deeper significance, some sort of meticulously encoded information, perhaps, on the location of ancient Vered and their magics, rumored to have been greater than any known to humankind today. Not that humankind needed greater magics, especially as it seemed they only wanted them for more magnificently vile acts of destruction.

And not that the book hadn't been interesting, though it hadn't pointed toward the question she'd been seeking. Veredian roses turned out to be exceedingly difficult at every stage of the process. Virtually impossible to grow from seed, they needed to be either transplanted—which they hated—or grafted, which they hated apparently only slightly more. Then they perished at the least bit of variance from ideal conditions. They'd all but vanished from the world.

Eerily enough, the last place they'd been known to flourish was the island of Govirinda.

Discovering that startling bit of information had made her ill enough that she had to set the book aside and close her eyes for a while, willing the nightmare memories of what she'd done to subside. Could it be a coincidence? She didn't believe in coincidences. Still, she'd gone seeking a question, following intuition and guided by the Dream, and she'd found this. It might have meaning. Perhaps she was meant to restore Veredian roses to the world.

It would be within her power to do so. If anyone in the world could find a Veredian rosebush, she could, via the Dream. From there it would be relatively straightforward to transplant the thing to her walled garden, as straightforward as anything to do with the cultivation of the finicky things was. She'd have to plant the ugly shrub inside the walls, in order to stabilize the microclimate—the book was most insistent on the critical parameters of that—and she could use the various magical tools at her disposal to keep it alive. No one but her would know or care about this little bit of restoring of what she'd destroyed. Still, she was tempted, even intrigued by the challenge, which perhaps spoke to something she'd been unwilling to entertain until this moment.

It could be that she'd become bored.

"I think I'll grow a Veredian rose," she said to Moriah, who lay with her back pressed to the crystal curve of the dome, idly flicking the tip of her tail. "That will show Stearanos Stormbreaker," she added, though she had no idea what she meant by that. Except that she was now quite sure that he contemplated cultivating the rare blossoms for some arcane reason of his own. She might discover his plan by being first to locate and grow the roses. From what she'd learned, he lived in entirely the wrong climate for the persnickety roses to thrive. Not even his oh-so-impressive wards could create the much-vaunted microclimate under those conditions.

Taking the book with her, but not Moriah, who elected to stay in the sunbeam she'd found, Oneira descended to the main level, then went out into the walled garden. Bunny came galloping up in wolfish joy, delighted to see her emerge. With her hand resting on his shoulder, the book dangling loosely in the grip of her other hand, she strolled with him in the muddied track of their regular perambulations. Sunshine draped over her hair and shoulders, warming them, hinting of spring and languorous summer heat to follow. A good time to plant her roses.

She'd have to wait for nighttime, preferably those hours after midnight and waxing toward dawn, when dreams predominated, to enter the Dream and seek out the roses. She'd have to go physically, in order to bring one back, but the search could likely take a while. If they still lived anywhere, though, some dreaming mind would know about them.

For the time being, she planned her Veredian rose garden, consulting the book for specifics, using magic in exacting doses to prepare the soil, warding it against the burrowing rodents that the book warned liked to chew the tuberous roots. Through a stroke of serendipity, she'd hit upon exactly the right season to establish her new bushes, which she took as a promising omen. Perhaps this book, and the resulting inspiration to plant these roses, were part of her journey to discovering the question she sought.

Satisfied with her preparations, she turned to the problem of the book itself. She had planned to return it, but clearly could not do so, not if she wanted her roses to succeed. Oneira possessed an excellent memory, but she would need to regularly consult this book, itself exceedingly rare. Too bad she'd left Stearanos such a bland and worthless replacement. If she'd realized she'd have no choice but to keep his book, she'd have left something better, something of more equivalent rarity.

She hadn't checked to see if he already had a copy of *Dragon Anatomy: From Tooth to Talon* in his library. He almost certainly did, as it was required reading at most of the magic academies, including the one he'd attended, she was sure. One never knew when checking an arcane fact about dragon anatomy, especially verifying the precise location of their few vulnerable points, could win a battle.

There was nothing else to do but go back, retrieve her copy of the dragon book, and leave him something else. Something of equivalent scarcity and value. The risk of return didn't concern her; she'd be surprised if he'd noticed her visit, beyond possibly looking for his book and missing it. Surely an active sorcerer of his stature was much in demand and had little time for reading or sniffing out elusive nighttime visitors. He no doubt had storm-breaking to do, though she had no idea what that would entail. No one ever had been able to tell her the exact act that had led to his nickname. He should be Stearanos Wardmaker, if these things followed any logic.

What *did* concern her was the foreign—to her—sensation that she owed him something.

That was nonsense, of course, as they owed each other nothing, except perhaps a swift, merciful death should they face each other on the battlefield. Still, the imbalance of what she'd taken from him and what she'd left in its place plagued her. Only restoring that balance with an appropriate offering would settle this. But what could it be?

She spent several hours contemplating the choice. It had to be a book, to balance the other, but she loathed the prospect of parting with any of the valuable and rare ones she'd brought into exile. The ones she could spare weren't good enough, for exactly that reason. She could travel via the Dream to steal or buy one, but that felt wrong, too. It needed to be a book she already possessed, and one she cared about. Nothing less would resolve her debt—and never would she be in debt to anyone, ever again.

After far too much time sorting, she ended up with a pile of books scarce enough to fulfill that aspect of the requirement and beloved enough to give her physical pain to contemplate parting with them forever. One was a favorite novel from her teens, *The Folded Pages of Isabelle Blue*, a first edition she'd found in a second-hand bookshop in a city she'd since forgotten. Firmly, Oneira set that one aside. Sentimentality, yes—but also the Stormbreaker couldn't possibly appreciate what made that book special.

Another was an obscure text on mystical representation in dreams and pervasive symbology across cultures of various nightmare elements and themes in night terrors. It had taken her years to locate it, as it had been enchanted with a forgetfulness spell, one she'd paid dearly to have removed. Her attachment to that one derived less from nostalgia than from the sense of victory in finally acquiring it and from the edge it had given her in tormenting foreign armies. She wouldn't use it anymore, obviously, but she was loath to put it in the hands of someone like Stearanos. So far as anyone knew, he possessed zero talent in oneiromancy, but that didn't mean he couldn't hire an oneiromancer to assist him.

Ultimately, she settled on a children's book, one of the very few things she'd brought with her when she left her parents' home. *The Adventures of the Beastly Bunny* itself wasn't particularly rare, though it was old enough to have belonged to her grandmother when *she* was a child. The velveteen cover had worn down to the nubs, barely showing any of the deep green it had once been, plush only in the few patches where grubby fingers left it mostly alone.

Stearanos would likely be baffled by the thing, but what mattered in these sorts of exchanges was intent. The Veredian rose book had come to be precious to her—had given her a surprising amount of pleasure already and, more important, a renewed vitality, an opportunity for redemption, however small—and so she'd leave something in return that was similar in inherent quality. A reminder of family and love, little as she'd experienced it herself, to match the simple joy of gardening. If that's even why he cared.

Worn out by her nocturnal travels from the previous night and unusual flexing of her oneiromancy—she'd grown far rustier than she'd realized—she napped away the remainder of the day and evening. Rising at midnight, she tucked *The Adventures of the Beastly Bunny* into a pocket of the cloak she donned in case it was cold where she ended up, since she'd need to be outside to excavate her rosebush.

She'd sketched her doorway in the air and opened the portal into the Dream and was just about to step across the shimmering threshold of starlight and night when Adsila flew into the tower room and lit on her shoulder. Oneira raised her brows in surprise. Like most raptors, the tiny kestrel tended to sleep during the nocturnal hours. Adsila blinked back at her, winding her talons decisively into the padded shoulder of the cloak.

"The Dream can be disorienting," she told the bird, who emitted a whistle of contempt. True. Adsila belonged to a goddess, so likely the Dream paled in comparison to the silver paths trod by the deities. "Don't let go," Oneira added, just to be sure. People could be lost in the Dream, wandering there eternally if not anchored to a portal. She didn't know if a goddess's avatar could manipulate the Dream enough to create her own way out without being connected to one who could, but Oneira worried about the possibility. She did not want She Who Eats Bears to arrive on her doorstep asking after her gift that Oneira had carelessly lost.

She stepped into the Dream, Adsila a rust-and-sapphire light on her shoulder, less like a kestrel in that nonwaking world than ever. Gradually, Oneira accelerated her pattern of searching, moving in ever larger circles, seeking someone dreaming of Vered. She'd gleaned ancient Veredian from the Dream in order to read the book, but that didn't help her as much as she'd have liked with identifying the modern version of the language.

So she modified her search, seeking Veredian creations—some snatches of song, a few myths, an image embroidered into a tapestry she'd seen in a palace after her victory as the soldiers pillaged it. She'd nearly claimed that tapestry for herself. If she'd been in the habit of collecting things, she would have, liking the unusual lavender roses depicted in it. Roses she now knew to be the rare ones she sought. Her attraction to them had been an omen of things to come, no doubt.

The search took hours, something she kept high in her awareness, closely tracking the passage of time in the outer world via the mental anchor she kept to her portal in the tower. Inside the Dream, time moved differently, compressing and expanding in response to the dreamers forming it. Thus, with every dreaming mind she skipped across, lightly as a flat stone over still lake water, time folded into a different pattern. With this person, years passed in a flash, taking them back to childhood. With another, a moment played out with infinite slowness. Another mind circled endlessly through the same sequence, visiting and revisiting a memory that grew increasingly distorted.

Eventually, after spiraling in a search pattern through hundreds of thousands of minds, she found some Veredians. Fortunately, people tend to gather like to like, and she found more people linked to those. After that, however, it took nearly as long to find anyone who knew much about the elusive roses, much less anyone still growing them. A search of that specificity for something so rare required that she delve into minds far more deeply than she liked.

At one point, she glanced upon someone dreaming of the Veredian roses on Govirinda, the dream symbols full of grief and rage for what had happened to the place, redolent of the anguish of having lost a home forever. Oneira extracted herself immediately from that mind, thought it may have given her clues, unable to take the risk of losing her own control to the consuming memories. All the time, Adsila remained a still and steady presence on her shoulder.

Rattled by that encounter, Oneira began to tire. Also, the control required to search all those minds without affecting them and from being in the Dream for so long drained her magical and mental stamina. She might have to resume the search the following night. She hesitated to do that because it would take so much time to find her way back to these far-flung dreamers. Besides, she wanted to drop off the replacement book to Stearanos's library, to close that loop and be done with the debt. She disliked the irritating feeling of having unfinished business there, fully acknowledging it was her own cursed fault for starting it. She supposed she could do that without obtaining her rose first, but she wanted to be able to tweak the Stormbreaker's nose with her triumph where he had failed, even if only she knew about it.

She'd very nearly resolved to withdraw from the Dream, lest she tire too much and lose her anchor to the portal, relegating herself to becoming one of the lost wraiths forever trapped there, when she found it. An ancient woman dreamed vividly of gliding through a snow-covered garden blooming with lavender roses on black-emerald thornbushes. Veredian roses.

At last. Oneira stepped through into the woman's location, immediately closing the doorway behind her so nothing from the Dream would leak into the waking world, and keeping a mental thumb on it, much like marking her page with a finger in an otherwise closed book.

In the close darkness, she surveyed the small dwelling, which smelled of soil and green leaves. It wasn't the opulent palace she'd expected, some noble's castle with a collection of the rare and fabulous, along with an experienced gardener dedicated to preserving the roses, but rather the modest home of a humble person devoted to their passion.

Though she'd have liked to waken the sleeping woman and talk with her—and where did that impulse come from? Oneira hadn't wanted to converse with anyone at all in ages—she instead cast a light enchantment to ensure the gardener slept on undisturbed. Strolling outside, Oneira took in the elaborate nighttime garden with raised brows, Adsila giving a chirp that sounded delighted.

Here was the lavishness she'd expected. To this person, the interior didn't matter except as shelter for sleeping and storing necessities. This woman truly lived outside, in this extravagant garden that went on forever. Oneira could spend days exploring it and, much as she loved the gentle cloak of night, she briefly regretted that she couldn't see it in daylight.

She also worried about the time it would take to find the roses in such an expansive garden. It seemed she'd have to return the next night after all. At least she knew the pathway now, which would all allow her to travel more directly. She sighed. Ah well, however much time it took, she'd find her roses eventually.

"How did you come to be here, Dreamthief?" the old woman asked behind her in the language of Oneira's homelands.

Oneira turned in considerable surprise. The woman should not have been able to shake off the enchantment at all, much less without Oneira feeling the spell break. The woman stood with a straight spine, though her gnarled hand gripped a walking stick made of polished blackthorn, and she gazed at Oneira with penetrating, dark eyes, her long hair cascading around her in the moonlight shades of age.

"Why would the Dreamthief visit my humble garden?" the woman mused. "And with the avatar of She Who Eats Bears on her shoulder."

This woman presented quite the puzzle. She possessed no magic, but she'd shaken off Oneira's enchantment as if it were cobwebs and she knew things no common person should—including Oneira's identity. Though it should be no surprise that the person who managed to grow practically extinct roses that bloomed only at midwinter could navigate magic in unusual ways.

The woman laughed and waggled a finger at Oneira. "I will have answers from you, child. Cat got your tongue?"

Oneira finally found her tongue, not stolen by felines after all. "How do you know these things?" she asked in return, more in wonder than anything. "How did you escape the sleeping spell I laid upon you?"

The gardener smiled. "You are no doubt powerful, Dreamthief, but you are also young. Surely even one such as you realizes there is more in the world than you know."

It had been ages since Oneira thought of herself as young. And ages since she'd discovered something she didn't already know.

A flicker of a feeling akin to excitement fluttered through her blood. Following the roses had been the right path to travel to find her question.

The old woman nodded sagely, as if she divined Oneira's thoughts. "I'm supposing the likes of you has come for something rare in my garden. You are not the first to come, reeking of powerful magic, to raid my plants that I nurture with such care. Which are you after and did you plan to simply take them without a word?"

Oneira saw no reason to temporize. "The Veredian roses."

"Ah." The gardener nodded again. "I should have known you would want them, you with your eyes and skin luminous as the moon, and power blazing brighter than the noonday sun."

Oneira considered her. "Who are you?"

"A simple gardener. Let me show you where the roses are." She began walking, leaning slightly on the walking stick, seeming unbothered to be out in the cool night in only her sleeping gown.

Oneira fell into step beside her. "Why would you show me where they are if you fear that I'll steal them from you?"

The woman slid her a canny glance. "I fear nothing. I'm too old for that nonsense. And you can't steal them from me as they don't belong to me."

Aha, then the gardener did work for some collector. "Who do they belong to?"

"Themselves." The woman shrugged, chuckling softly. "I am simply their caretaker, providing what they need. Will you give them what they need?"

"Yes," Oneira answered with confidence. "I've been studying their cultivation in preparation."

"Hmm. You do have the scent of plants and soil about you, but you also smell of pain and suffering. Death and destruction. Oceans of blood," she added, not quite accusing, but close.

No longer surprised by what this woman knew, Oneira only nodded, oily shame coating her heart, an abyss of regret opening beneath her feet. "So much that it will never wash away."

"Perhaps washing is the wrong analogy."

Oneira thought about that. Washing did imply that something had been clean once and that the taint could be removed. She, herself, hadn't been innocent of destruction since her childish plundering of the Dream. Every action since, every decision, had cascaded from that moment. She could hardly return to a state of childhood innocence, even if she wanted to. "What is the correct analogy?" she asked.

"Ah, now that is the question, Dreamthief."

It was a question, but not *the* question. At least, so Oneira supposed.

❧ 8 ❧

The gardener descended steps cut into stone, bracing a hand against the high wall of a narrow stairwell open to the sky. Oneira followed behind, feeling as if she might still be in the Dream, but subsumed fully into the gardener's dream, one of nighttime gardens lit by silvery moonlight.

"There," the woman said with pride, waving a hand over what seemed to be a sea of rosebushes, long canes and curved thorns gleaming black-emerald in the faint light of the crescent moon. "They're not blooming yet. They won't until midwinter. Did you plan to uproot them or take cuttings to graft some?" She eyed Oneira keenly, and the sorceress knew this to be a test.

"From what I've read, they're more likely to survive uprooted."

"Nothing likes to be uprooted. The trick is to set new roots. Can you do that, Dreamthief?" She asked the question not unkindly and Oneira knew they no longer discussed roses.

"I don't know how," she admitted, realizing in that moment she'd been rootless since she'd been torn from her childhood home. Even in her final refuge, the white walls she'd pulled from the Dream with magic and refined to fit the waking world through her own will, she still felt adrift, wandering between the mountain peaks and the seashore, a living ghost. "I'm hoping to learn," she added, wondering if this was part of why she wanted the roses. Knowing at the same moment that she couldn't possibly tend them as they deserved, not if she planned to die.

"Veredian roses are not for amateurs," the woman noted

thoughtfully. "You have the power to take them, but no magic in all the world will enable you to keep them alive, to help them thrive. Dealing death, leveling destruction, stealing from dreams, those things are easy. Creating, sustaining, nurturing—those take true skill." She reached out and tapped a crooked finger over Oneira's heart. "They require something of your self that cannot be bought or stolen."

Oneira bowed her head, humbled, embarrassed. "You are wise. I shall go."

"Without the prize you chased through the Dream with such determination?"

"It seems the better part of valor," Oneira noted wryly. "I was following a whim, like a child wishing to take something because it caught her eye."

The gardener tilted her head, looking at Adsila. "And this one, did you take this pretty bird on a similar whim?"

"No," Oneira answered, a bit shocked by the implication. She might be prideful, arrogant, and a thief, but she would never steal from a deity. And not only because She Who Eats Bears could squash her like the tiny gnats that bounced soundlessly in the still shadows, but also because even Oneira respected some things as sacred. She ran a light finger over Adsila's feathers, the kestrel softly trilling in response. "Adsila came to me. I don't know why."

"Don't you?" The woman smiled gently, laying a hand on Oneira's cheek in a way that felt almost maternal. "You are a troubled child."

"I have not been a child for many decades."

"We are all children in our deepest hearts." She took her hand away and gazed at the crooked fingers. "Sometimes I see my hands and I'm startled, thinking my grandmother is here. In a way, I suppose she is. You may have three of these rosebushes, Dreamthief. My gift to you."

Oneira caught her breath, taken aback by the surge of relief, of . . . hope. "What if I can't tend them properly?"

"You must learn to do so."

"Perhaps I should learn first."

"Is that how you learned your sorcery—or did you learn by doing?" The gardener nodded, needing no answer. "Pick out your roses and I shall dig them up for you." She turned to a door set in the stone wall, opening it to reveal various gardening implements.

"I can dig them up," Oneira protested. It would be the work of a moment. Adsila left her shoulder, flying to a low branch hanging over the stone wall to observe.

"No magic." The woman handed Oneira a shovel, then dug around and extracted some rough-woven bags. "That is the primary condition and this you must promise me. With these roses, you must use only the work of your hands and heart."

So much for Oneira's plans to manage the microclimate. "I already created a bed for them using magic."

"Then you must dig a new one. You may keep that shovel."

And so it was that Oneira put her soft hands to the handle of the shovel, the gardener patiently showing her how to leverage her weight to push into the soil, how to know where the root boundary lay, how to work with both strength and gentle precision. Oneira bundled the roses into their rough cloth bags, their wicked thorns piercing her unscarred skin painfully.

"This, too, is important," the gardener said, drawing her own callused fingertip over the cuts and punctures. "This is good blood."

"Because it's my own?"

"Because of the reason you shed it. I'm surprised you don't know that, Dreamthief."

"There is much I don't know."

The gardener nodded, a smile bending the wrinkles of her face like the rays of the sun traveling through a crystal prism. Oneira realized dawn must be coming, the sky lighter. She would be almost out of time to visit Stearanos and leave the book, finish their transaction.

"At least you are learning to ask the right questions," the gardener replied.

❧

By the time Oneira walked out of the Dream and into the Stormbreaker's darkened library, the room resounded with a predawn chorus of birdsong. She paused midstep, so startled that she automatically double- and triple-checked that the sleep enchantment she'd cast over all the denizens of the castle remained effectively in place, before realizing the wild symphony sounded so loud because a window had been left open.

Still cautious, she surveyed the area for any tricks, just in case the Stormbreaker had detected her intrusion from the night before. She'd rather been counting on him not noticing, but in taking the book he'd been in the midst of studying, she'd invited discovery.

Sure enough, Stearanos had attempted to protect himself from her sleep spell this time, the reinforced wards shimmering along the walls of the castle. He'd gone about it the wrong way, however, in guarding himself against an external attack, rather than realizing it was his own sleeping self that sabotaged him. A common error. No one could ward against their own dreams. Oneira tsked at him mentally, savoring the delight at having put another over on him. It would be different if he'd figured out who she was, but as things stood, she had him at an enjoyable disadvantage.

Setting down the gift shovel and her roses, their root balls safely wrapped in their native soil and deftly swathed in the rough sacks the gardener had also given her, their tiny night-dark glossy green leaves wreathed in thorns protruding above, Oneira cautiously investigated the open window. The one left ajar was the one by the sorcerer's reading chair. Adsila whistled a question, then hopped off Oneira's shoulder to sit on the sill. Oneira hoped the kestrel wouldn't fly out, but she was her own bird.

Was the open window some sort of message? If so, Oneira had no idea what it was meant to communicate. Perhaps it indicated that Stearanos knew she'd looked out this window, but if so, the rebuke—if a rebuke was intended—was mild to the point of meaninglessness. She was likely overthinking, reading too much into it. Much more likely, the window had been left open through forgetfulness. It was warded, regardless. She, herself, would never leave any ingress or egress entirely unmonitored, and she didn't live and die by warding the way the Stormbreaker did. She doubted Stearanos would be any less paranoid than she was, and likely far more.

With interest, she used her sorcerous senses to probe the window frame in its entirety, and in more detail along the edges of the open section. An intricate webbing protruded from the frame, which seemed to be infused with concentrated magic, one that stirred in response to her own. Warily standing back, she studied the clean-painted wood in the faint light, noting a bit of a pattern, brown on dark brown. She didn't dare touch it or add magical illumination, but the substance looked like dried blood. Canting her head, she narrowed her eyes to focus, making out what looked like an equation. Mathematics had never been her strong suit, but she knew Stearanos used the method extensively, an appropriate one given his affinity for numbers and counting.

Fascinated, she had to restrain herself from poking at the ward just to see what it would do. She revised her initial supposition:

the window seemed to have been left open in invitation to her—as a trap. Without knowing who she was, Stearanos wouldn't be able to guess how she'd invaded his home, only that she had done so.

Despite the ancient gardener recognizing her so easily, oneiromancers were far from common or expected, especially those who could use the Dream to physically travel to other locations. In fact, she knew of no other oneiromancer alive who could do so, likely because the learning curve so easily resulted in amateurs getting lost in the Dream.

That aspect of her powers had always been kept quiet, a secret weapon against the enemies she'd been hired to defeat, so Stearanos would be unlikely to think of this possibility. Also, surely news of her retirement had traveled to the Northern Lands. That, on top of the fact that she'd never disturbed the Stormbreaker when they had been positioned against each other as enemies, made it unlikely that he'd suspect her. No, Stearanos had followed logic to the most likely possibility: that someone had penetrated his wards and somehow climbed the walls of the castle. Wily of him to offer an apparently easy route for ingress, and make it into a trap.

She left the window untouched and investigated what else the sorcerer had concocted to ensnare her. It amused Oneira to think of the angry Stormbreaker waking to discover his castle had been invaded again, his trap intact and unsprung. Having fun now, Oneira easily avoided the strands of alarm spells and immobilization enchantments Stearanos had scattered about the room and went to the book of dragon anatomy she'd left in place of his book on Veredian roses.

Dragon Anatomy: From Tooth to Talon was precisely where she'd left it, apparently undisturbed. Before touching it, however, she probed for another trap, finding nothing of concern. She reached for it . . . and upon touching it, immediately sensed that it wasn't her copy. A bolt of alarm shot through her, the kind of fear she hadn't experienced since she'd left the battlefields and their many perils. Adsila whistled a question she couldn't answer.

Stearanos knew exactly which book she'd taken and that she'd left one behind. Well of course he did, she chided herself. She'd been overconfident, thinking she'd so neatly outwitted the Stormbreaker, and now he'd lured her into coming into contact with who knew what. He'd replaced her copy of *Dragon Anatomy: From Tooth to Talon* with another. Likely his, given all of his considerable remanence oozing from it, a challenge as palpable as a glove slapped in her face.

He'd left something else in it, too.

She remained frozen, experienced enough to realize she might've triggered some magical trap too sophisticated for her to sense just by touching the book. That's what she would've done, in his position, and Stearanos was powerful enough to have set a trap like that. Since nothing had yet occurred, it could be that any movement on her part—especially letting go of the book— would set it off. Cautiously, she examined the book with her sorcerous senses again, analyzing it every way she knew how.

It seemed completely innocuous, except for the addition of the *something* inside that was not part of the book. The *something* that could be very bad, indeed.

The room grew lighter, the sky bluing rapidly outside the windows, and her sleepers fluttered against the confines of the enchantment holding them. She could keep them asleep indefinitely, but as their natural waking rhythms struggled against the unnatural sleep, the spell would require more and more magical energy from her. She was already running low from her long Dream search. To free herself from this potential trap—or, worse, battle Stearanos if she lost control and he escaped her sleep enchantment—she'd need all the resources possible. And she could not stand there forever, like an insect caught in honey on her kitchen counter, wings shivering helplessly.

She pulled the book from the shelf, her defenses high, her magic ready.

Nothing happened.

Not yet, anyway. Still not daring to release the book, she kept it in her hands and carefully opened it to the page where the foreign object had been inserted. A folded slip of paper greeted her. Innocuous. No magic to it. A different sort of trap entirely.

Setting the book aside, aware of the growing light and the insistent tug of the habitually early risers, she unfolded the simple slip of paper and read the message it contained.

> *Dear Thief,*
> *For thief you are, replacing a rare and unusual book with something I already own, and such a banal text, I can only interpret the substitution as a deliberate insult, in addition to the other injuries you've inflicted, having the temerity to invade my home. I demand the return of my property, which you cannot possibly have any use for. I also demand a forfeit, in recompense for invading my territory and casting unfriendly spells. Whatever game you have initiated with me, I shall be the victor.*
> *Explain yourself on pain of my vengeance.*
> *His Majesty's Sorcerer, Eminence Stearanos*

Oneira, having at first startled at being called thief before realizing that he'd used it generically, not as the irritating moniker given her by the balladeers, nearly laughed out loud. She caught the sound on a choked breath. The Stormbreaker had left her a *note*. He hadn't laid any sort of additional magical trap, he'd simply written a message full of arrogance and bluster. And . . . had invited her to reply, it seemed. Why? She didn't understand his move in this game, perhaps as he intended.

She shouldn't reply. She *should* leave immediately. Lingering at the scene of the crime, knowing she'd already been found out, was foolish to the point of recklessness. Though, reading between the lines, it was clear that Stearanos didn't know who she was or the purpose behind her visit. He was fishing for information. She should leave him to stew in his curiosity and paranoia. Knowing his propensities, the mystery would bother him more than anything.

Still, she found she wanted to reply. That same mischievous impulse prodded her, just as it had prompted her to mess with his shelves in the first place. It had been a strange night, one of feeling all sorts of things she hadn't felt in so long that it seemed like forever. But it was also nice to feel something other than numbness coated over pits of dread, horror, and bitter regret.

She checked her spell yet again—*now who is paranoid?* she chided herself—and verified that the sleepers indeed slept on, captive to her enchantment. Going to his desk, she found that Stearanos had left a sheet of paper and a quill in the center of it. Both completely mundane, nothing magical about them. A trap, baited as an invitation, as seemed to be his method.

Well then. She could evade this snare, also. She wrote her reply.

Dear Eminence,

What a dreadful title you bear. The official one is even worse than "Stormbreaker." So many syllables; such a dull word. I shall call you Em, for short.

I had already brought a better gift, in payment for your book, which I have an exceedingly pertinent need to retain. I can apply practically what you can only contemplate in theory. I'm keeping your book, which—if I'm not mistaken—makes me the victor.

Vengeance will not be yours this day, Em. Alas for you.
However, you may sleep easy. I'm very busy and have no need
to trouble you again.

She hesitated over how to sign it. Naturally she couldn't affix her own name, or any of the equally cumbersome titles that had been laid upon her over the years. She also refused to call herself Dreamthief. It might be accurate, but she'd never cared for the implicit insult. In the end, she left it unsigned, figuring that would bother him more than anything else. Folding the note, she set it inside the pages of *The Adventures of the Beastly Bunny*, whimsically putting it at the same page number as he'd done in the dragon anatomy book.

There—that should appeal to and offend his compulsive and eclectic orderliness. She felt almost a sense of affection for her obsessive enemy.

On impulse, she plucked a leaf from one rosebush, setting it inside the folded note so as not to stain the pages, before replacing it on the shelf where his book on Veredian roses had been. Then she took a bit more time, which she really shouldn't do, but she was engaging in defying all sorts of rules of rationality, and looked for where Stearanos might have shelved *her* copy of *Dragon Anatomy: From Tooth to Talon*.

It required a bit of searching, but she finally spotted a familiar set of books that was the *Basilisk Cycle*, a month-long performance of a Tsarkarian myth. Never mind that a theatrical script in twelve volumes would not be, in any sane universe, shelved with a textbook on dragon anatomy. Stearanos and sanity clearly lacked even a nodding acquaintance, because all the books on that set of shelves had to do in some way with . . . she finally identified the theme as scales and fire.

Shaking her head, Oneira climbed the ladder to the shelf,

found her copy, and replaced it with his. Upside down, just to tweak his nose a bit more out of joint. She'd never laid eyes on the Stormbreaker, but she imagined him with a long, hooked nose that just begged to be tweaked. Beyond the pleasure it gave her, the positioning would serve to inform him that she possessed the basic wit to differentiate her book from his, alike as they might be. Of course, she possessed a great deal more wit than that, but he didn't need to know.

By the time she descended the ladder, the sun had risen, spilling golden light into the library and illuminating all the glorious colors of the thousands of books. The furniture and plush throw rugs scattered around on the polished wood floor were also surprisingly colorful. Ironic that the grim and mathematical Stearanos lived in such flamboyant environs while Oneira's chosen home lacked most color and all frivolity. She preferred the clean simplicity of her white walls.

Didn't she? Of course she did.

Whistling for Adsila, who immediately winged back to her shoulder, she gathered her things and took one step into the rapidly contracting Dream. Too many people were awake now for it to be as robust as it had been, but thank the stars for late sleepers.

Quickly, she severed the thread to the enchantment, allowing her own restless sleepers to awake. Somewhere in the far reaches of the castle, a man bellowed in startled rage, nearly a howl of frustration. "Good morning, Stormbreaker," she whispered, and was gone.

She would not return.

Stearanos nearly threw the book across the room. His own copy of *From Tooth to Talon*, that was—not the slim, worn volume of a children's tale his intruder had left. All of it designed to taunt and enrage him. Whoever this magic-worker was, they'd kept him asleep despite the measures he'd taken. The window had been such a simple trap, he hadn't truly expected it to work, but the invader had nimbly avoided every other trap he'd set, too.

Not only that, but they'd stayed even longer this time, clearly unafraid of him, thumbing their nose by switching back the dragon texts and demonstrating their knowledge of him by returning his copy to its usual place, impudently upside down. And, a deeply concerning development: an avatar of some deity had accompanied them, leaving a whiff of the numinous behind.

It was intolerable.

Forcing himself to relax, he laid out the clues on his desk. The children's book, the insolent note with no signature, and the rose leaf. Picking up the leaf, he sniffed it, but it only smelled green. He knew it for a rose leaf by the pinnately compound oval shape and fine, sharp tooths at the edges. These tooths were longer than on any rose he knew, almost spikes, with a distinctive curve to them. He suspected, deep in his bitterly jealous heart, that the leaf belonged to a Veredian rose.

"I would look it up," he snarled under his breath, holding the taunting leaf up to the light, "but I no longer have *my fucking book!*"

He turned his attention to the battered volume. *The Adventures of the Beastly Bunny* seemed to be an extended poem about a rabbit stealing carrots from a garden. *I had already brought a better gift, in payment for your book*, the intruder had written. He muttered a vile imprecation. *This* was what they considered a better book? Granted, almost anything was more interesting than the dragon anatomy textbook—unless one needed to reference dragon anatomy, naturally—but in what universe would anyone think this volume of nonsensical, puerile babbling was *better*? He suspected an insult, another layer of sneering meant to get under his skin, this thief implying that childish rhymes better suited his intelligence than the challenge of cultivating the rarest species of rose.

A rose that this person apparently had in their possession, the leaf left as evidence of their greater claim to the information in *his* book. Perhaps that had been their simple goal all along—to steal that book—and it was sheer coincidence that he'd been reading it. Not that it rankled any less, especially since he regarded coincidences with deep suspicion.

The little Beastly Bunny book was definitely old and quite likely rare. To be sure, he'd have to consult some of his catalogs, perhaps take it to one of the rare book dealers he frequented. He unquestionably didn't already own a copy, which at least conferred a tiny bit of value. Not really enough to believe the thief was sincere about trading value for value. Of course, he had to read through the thing, partly to determine the theme, so it could be properly shelved, and partly to hunt for clues as to his intruder's identity.

The bit in the note about sleeping easily seemed like a broad hint, though Stearanos had enough intelligence to have already recognized that bit of sorcery, which was hardly unique or exceptionally difficult. Most sorcerers powerful enough to evade wards like his had a sleeping spell or two up their sleeves. Although keeping all eighty humans in the castle asleep required enough power and skill to narrow the field of possibilities. He scrutinized the sappy rhymes of *The Adventures of the Beastly Bunny* to determine if any of it held more significance than a quick scan had indicated. Perhaps theft was an appropriate theme. Had that been an additional joke intended to—

"Eminence Stearanos?" His secretary, James, knocked on the library door, popping his head in as he spoke. "My deepest apologies for disturbing you, but I have a missive from His Majesty."

"I'm on sabbatical," Stearanos replied, attempting to subtract the growl from his voice. Everyone in the castle knew he'd been in a foul temper since—finally—awakening, and had given him a sympathetic and respectfully wide berth. James wouldn't interrupt him if the missive wasn't urgent. Still.

"I'm sorry, Eminence," James said in all sincerity, "but it's marked urgent."

"His Majesty probably discovered a hangnail and can't imagine what to do about it," Stearanos snapped back, closing the little book.

"His Majesty places great value on you, Eminence," James replied neutrally, still lurking in the dubious safety of the doorway.

"Oh, bring it here," Stearanos said, snapping his fingers unnecessarily. Every time James used his title, it reminded him of the thief's impudent promise to call him "Em" for short. James brought the thick envelope to him. It was the size of the man's head. His Majesty never did anything by halves.

"Shall I remain to draft a reply, Eminence?"

"Might as well." Despite the hugeness of the page enclosed, the letter itself was relatively short. The king seemed to be contemplating war, shockingly enough, and required that his favorite sorcerer return early from sabbatical. Something had transpired to create a new urgency.

The possibility of war was never a surprise in their conflict-ridden assemblage of kingdoms, but Stearanos had chosen this time for his sabbatical for a reason. They'd just finished a war, emerging from it if not precisely victorious, then at least with His Majesty's collection of kingdoms intact. The collective stalemate had frustrated both sides, but their enemies had been silent for some time, in some sort of disarray or licking deeper wounds than His Majesty's spies had been able to ferret out.

Briefly, in profound irritation, Stearanos contemplated refusing the summons. A bit of indulgence to imagine he could, but he occasionally fantasized about snapping the leash that chained him.

He'd rue the day he signed that contract with King Uhtric, except he hadn't even been given that much of a choice. It had been signed for him, essentially selling him to the king in return for a vast sum that had paid for his upkeep and training several times over. The academy that had discovered and taught Stearanos had made their fortune on him, the owners even selling the place to retire and enjoy their wealth.

Not that any of it was a new story. The many magic academies around the world had refined their business to a fine art, using contracts based on a blood geas concocted centuries before. When the academies took on a pupil, usually purchased from families willing to take any price to rid themselves of a magical child already causing havoc, they used the child's own blood to fuel a geas, tying the spell to their life force. Initially, the enchantment bound the pupil to their academy, ensuring their obedience to the authorities. Upon graduation, the geas was transferable by contract.

King Uhtric had preempted all other potential clients, using the wealth of his many acquired kingdoms, to buy Stearanos's contract in full.

Any attempt to evade the stipulations of the contract began draining Stearanos to the point of death. Even contemplating refusing the summons nibbled at the edges of his vitality with hints of enervating weakness. There might be some inflection point, where his life force would have ebbed enough to weaken the binding power of the contract sufficiently for him to free himself of it, but that posed a circular problem in that he'd then be too weak to muster the magic to break the blood-borne enchantment.

In his early years, Stearanos had bent all his free time to research ways to break the contract, running countless calculations to find that inflection point. To no avail. The thing had been wrought with wicked cleverness. No sorcerer had ever broken it, though many had tried. His only way free was to earn his way out, which would take so long that Stearanos would be working still for the king's son, possibly his grandson.

Though Stearanos had reduced his debt to the king by leaps over the years, the remainder towered over him like a mountain too high to climb, the air at the summit so thin it would kill him the moment he reached it.

He'd also tried, in his early years, to refuse the king's gifts of jewels, clothing, the castle he lived in, even the annuity to pay the seventy-nine servants necessary to keep the thing running. But it turned out the contract forbade even that. As His Majesty's favored sorcerer, Stearanos must maintain a minimum standard of living. Never mind that the meticulously defined minimum standard eclipsed the budget of a small kingdom.

His Eminence must reflect the status of his employer. All bond-servants should live so handsomely.

Pocketing the slim volume of *The Adventures of the Beastly Bunny*, so he could study it further for clues, he directed James to send the only reply he was allowed to, and mentally prepared for the ordeal of meeting with the king.

But first, he'd leave a reply to his thief, along with a few surprises. They might claim they wouldn't visit again, but Stearanos would be a fool to take this criminal at their word.

Stearanos might be many things, but a fool wasn't one of them.

The imperial palace towered against the sky, by design both impressive and intimidating. Not that Stearanos experienced anything but a sense of weariness at the sight. With the palace atop the highest hill and the city spilling down on all sides to the several bustling ports and harbors, the whole thing reminded him of a hastily decorated, multitiered cake, topped by a confection far more delicately wrought than the rest.

Already he regretted leaving his quiet home with his garden and its serene view of the sea. The city surrounding the seat of the king bustled with so many people that Stearanos had to stop habitually counting them all, lest he exhaust himself. He could consciously control the impulse; it just annoyed him to do it. Like suppressing an itch he shouldn't scratch lest he make it worse.

"Eminence Stearanos!" His Majesty boomed from the throne at hearing the sorcerer's name announced. "Welcome home. You've been missed."

Stearanos set his teeth and assumed a polite, if stern, expression—one much remarked on in court circles—and managed to bow to the king, then nod to the richly dressed courtiers who broke into applause and cheers at the king's greeting. He also set himself into a well-cultivated state of extended patience to endure the pageantry and speeches accompanying his return to the imperial palace. He'd long since learned not to object to being treated as a hero, instead occupying his thoughts with more interesting musings while allowing the empty adulation to slide off him.

In this instance, he found himself pondering the mystery of his thief and, ridiculously, the saga of the bunny stealing carrots from a well-tended garden. James had interrupted him before Stearanos had reached the end of the lyrical and fetchingly absurd saga of the wily bunny and the frustrated gardener, so he had no idea how it ended. Who won their little war—the young rabbit or the old gardener? The book in his pocket seemed to burn against his hip and he nearly pulled it out half a dozen times while the king's sycophants postured and praised. Only the awareness of how people would react to seeing the terrifying Eminence Stearanos with a children's book stopped him.

"Attend me privately, Eminence," the king declared for all the court to hear, a flexing of his authority to command the most powerful sorcerer in all the land, a completely redundant instruction as it was the entire reason Stearanos was there at all instead of in his comfortable library.

He followed the king, and was followed in turn by the king's entourage, into the private council chambers above the throne room. Ringed with windows, the circular room commanded a view of King's City in all directions, and the lands and seas beyond. In the center of the room sat a table with a relief map of the king's currently owned realms, as well as the enemy lands beyond. The color coding differentiating the two categories changed over time with the vagaries of politics and war, an ebbing and flowing tide that lapped at the shores of the metaphorical island that was the current empire.

As the king settled himself in the high chair that allowed him to see the extent of the table and also tower over everyone else, accepting or rejecting the various obsequious offers from his entourage, Stearanos studied the map. No obvious changes had been made to the borders since he'd last seen it. They were as agreed upon following the various accords that served as the denouement to the last war, the tedious epilogues intended to end those tales but that simply served as prologues—or sneak peeks—into the next set of wars. An unending tale that changed only in specifics, reiterating the same plot with mind-numbing repetition.

Just once, Stearanos would love to see a true plot twist.

Finally, mug of wine in hand and feet comfortably propped on a padded stool, the king dismissed his attendants, leaving the two of them alone. Interesting. "There is news from the Southern Lands."

"Oh?" Stearanos asked, not particularly curious, but playing his assigned role of coconspirator.

"The sorceress Oneira has retired," the king announced portentously.

"Good for her," Stearanos replied, not without considerable envy for his—he supposed now former—nemesis.

"Apparently she disappeared quite some time ago and shows no sign of returning. Perhaps she's even dead! This means the Southern Lands are undefended," the king said, excitement lighting his face.

Stearanos never met the sorceress Oneira, as they'd been kept carefully apart by their handlers. He knew her only by reputation, which was formidable, so he seriously doubted she was dead. Only another sorcerer could kill a person of her reputed skill and power, and Stearanos—along with every other magically sensitive individual in all the realms—would've felt the echoes of a magical battle that immense and potent.

Thus, logic dictated that she had somehow managed to pay off her contract and had indeed retired. How had she managed that when the best he'd been able to negotiate was a sabbatical imperiously cut short? That jealousy-fueled bafflement on top of the growing irritation that *this* was His Majesty's "emergency" consumed him. No impending peril had prompted the king to summon Stearanos, only rapacious greed. And Stearanos, with all the power at his command, could do nothing about it. Though that didn't mean he had to be enthusiastic.

"The Southern Lands are hardly undefended, Your Majesty," Stearanos objected, inclining his head to add a flavor of obsequiousness he didn't feel to the contradiction. Was there no end to the man's desire for more and more? He was barely able to govern the lands he'd already conquered, let alone attempt to acquire distant and foreign cultures across the sea. "The Southern Lands field armies at least half again the size of yours."

King Uhtric gazed at him with considerable irritation. Very few people told His Majesty no to anything, even obliquely.

"*Magically unguarded*," the king clarified, enunciating as if the sorcerer might somehow fail to understand the words themselves. "Everyone has always advised me against conquering the Southern Lands in the past on the grounds that pitting you against the sorceress Oneira was considered to be too extreme a risk to the valuable resources we hoped to acquire. You know this, so don't play the fool with me. With the sorceress removed from the equation, there is no reason not to take action."

"I can think of a few," Stearanos replied mildly.

The king's face grew taut, reddening. "You work for me, Eminence," His Majesty reminded him. "I shouldn't need to remind you that the ability to contradict me is not in your contract."

Stearanos braced his hands on the rim of the map table, pretending to study it so the king wouldn't see him gnashing his teeth. For the *n*th time, he cursed that bloody contract. He'd curse the bloody geas that trapped him and every magic-worker alive from early childhood, but he might as well shake his fist at the clouds in the sky.

"How much is it worth to you, Your Majesty?" he asked the map table, grinding out the question wearily. This was what they'd made him: a man willing to decimate innocent people for a paycheck, eternally eroding the rock of his debt, drop by drop.

"Hmm . . ." The king hummed happily. "Well, it won't be much of a challenge for you, with no opposition to speak of."

"The queen of the Southern Lands will have hired someone to take Oneira's place," Stearanos pointed out, his gaze moving to those verdant southern lands he'd only read about.

"As if that harridan could find another magic-worker anywhere near your caliber. No, if anyone else in all the world could defeat *my* sorcerer, I'd have heard about it. At last, my considerable investment in you will pay off. This should be an easy conquest, so I want you to work with my son on the war strategy. You'll report to him for this project and obey him as you would me."

"Crown Prince Mirza?" Stearanos said, raising his head in his surprise, feeling foolish to have asked such an obvious question, as though the king had more than one son. He did have plenty of daughters, though the princesses seldom garnered His Majesty's attention, unless one of them looked to be useful as a trading piece in a negotiation. Several had been married off and now decorated the courts of subsidiary kingdoms under their father's imperial rule. It was fortunate that the crown prince was the clear heir to the throne, as the jostling among the also-rans, such as the husbands of the king's daughters, would likely result in internecine strife and even more war.

The king did not notice the foolishness of the question, nodding in satisfaction. "My heir, yes. You don't have children, Stormbreaker, so you don't know. A father wants to pass on his wisdom to his son. It's only natural." He smiled wryly, as if he and Stearanos enjoyed a long friendship.

"Mirza is restless," the king continued. "I've raised him to be a monarch and he chafes to realize his destiny. I need to give him another throne, lest he become too interested in mine." The king winked. "In exchange for conquering the Southern Lands, Mirza will rule them in my stead. This project will absorb his youthful energies and he can learn from you at the same time, where he might not listen to his old father. And it will be good for you to work together. Who knows, you'll likely be his sorcerer someday," he added with a chortle.

"If I'm teaching the crown prince, then I should be paid double the price of every magical attack we agree upon," Stearanos pointed out with careful neutrality, then studiously did not hold his breath.

Say what you would about His Majesty, the man had not gotten where he was by being unobservant or a lax negotiator. Fortunately, paternal affection and the prospect of the riches of the Southern Lands had the king in a generous mood. "Fine, fine," he replied, waving that off as negligible. In truth, it was. Even at double rate, the fees wouldn't do much against Stearanos's debt. "Do your research, Eminence. I want your strategic plan in a month."

Stearanos bit down on an incredulous repetition of the king's words. *A month?* To plan the conquest of an entire country none of them had been to?

"I'm confident you're up to the challenge." The king, never a fool, pinned Stearanos with a sharp stare. "I know you wouldn't want to displease me," he added, stopping just short of making it a threat.

"Of course not, Your Majesty," Stearanos managed to reply, bowing to hide his expression. *Anything else? Perhaps I should pull the moon from the sky and hang it upon a chain around your neck?*

"You'll set sail as soon as the war council approves your strategy," the king continued, "so include constructing a sufficient armada in your plans."

Better and better. "Anything else, Your Majesty?" he inquired, hoping no sarcasm leaked into his tone.

The king frowned at him, suspicious, but not quite enough to dampen his great, good mood. "When I think of it, I shall summon you, Eminence."

"I'd work best from home, Your Majesty," Stearanos said firmly, hoping the courteous use of Uhtric's title would soften him. "I'll need access to the books on the Southern Lands in my library."

"Yes, yes, whatever you need to do," the king replied, already losing interest in the minutiae. "Just see that it gets done. I shall be remembered for this," he added, with a beatific glow. "My greatest achievement."

Stearanos agreed, taking his opportunity to flee, not pointing out that the king had already forgotten about this war ostensibly being his son's achievement. It mattered not.

All things belonged to His Majesty, including Stearanos.

Y ou look perfect, darling," Zarja, Queen of the Southern Lands, murmured appreciatively. "Come here."

Leskai Orynych took one last look at himself in the mirror. He did look splendid, garbed in the new clothing his queen had gifted him. Never had he owned anything so richly made, so perfectly tailored to his tall, slim form. Even Yelena, the queen's pet sorceress, looked upon him favorably, at least for the moment. Reluctantly, he tore his gaze from his own image and turned to obey his mistress, the queen, she who held sway over him in every sense of the word.

She was beautiful beyond doubt, sensual and mysterious with her ebony hair, light brown skin, and dark eyes. Generations of kings choosing the most beautiful virgins in all the realms they could access had assured this royal daughter perfect bone structure, straight teeth, and lustrous beauty. The attentions of countless handmaidens and the best treatments all the coin in the world could buy had ensured the flawless skin, silky hair, and gestures so graceful the queen seemed to move like water at midnight.

She beckoned to Leskai with that seamless grace, hand outstretched palm up, long, elegant fingers that had never done a moment's manual labor curling him toward her. He went, as instructed, and sank down to one knee at her feet, shuddering with desire as those fingers combed through his pale hair. The thick mass of it waved back from his forehead and cascaded to nearly the base of his neck. The queen had persuaded him to start grow-ing it long, something for her to grab ahold of, she liked to say.

She twined her fingers in it now, dragging his head back so that he must look up at her. Her sensuous, red-painted lips curved in a satisfied smile and she tightened her grip just a bit more, pleased to see his inadvertent wince. She'd trained him well over the last year, preferring that he show no reaction to pain—or pleasure, for that matter—until he couldn't help himself. She loved that part, extracting the sincere response through his attempts at resistance, breaking his poise and self-control repeatedly to demonstrate her power over him.

As if she needed to. Her power was absolute, and he trembled inside at the raw knowledge of it.

"I require a service from you, my darling Leskai," she purred, leaning forward and pulling his head back harder.

"Anything, my queen," he gasped, scraping his obedience through his strained throat, meaning it utterly. She liked to tighten the collar she'd placed on him so that she couldn't insert so much as the long nail of one pinky finger between the black leather and his constrained skin. She tested it then with her free hand, scraping his flesh in an attempt to dig the nail in there. He whimpered and she kissed him, softly and lavishly, holding him helplessly in place. Not that he'd fight her, not without permission. Even then the most she allowed him was token squirming, and then only because it amused her to watch him struggle.

The tightness of his collar should be perfectly adjusted, she'd explained early on—enough to dig into his throat as a constant reminder of her ownership, not enough to restrict his ability to breathe, under most circumstances. When desire rode him hard as it did in that moment, his heart thundering, his body strain-ing against the other bonds she'd placed beneath the fancy suit of clothing to tame him to her will, breath came painfully hard.

"Perfect," she murmured against his mouth, licking his lips with lascivious sweeps of her tongue. She loved his mouth, she often remarked, the plush fullness of his lips unusual in a man. "Will you miss my collar, Leskai?"

He blinked at her in bleary confusion, head swimming with arousal and lack of air. "My queen?"

"As I said, I require a service of you, sweet Leskai. You will have to pretend to be your own man again, where I am sending you. Do you think you can do that, my darling pet?"

Leskai struggled to understand. He almost couldn't comprehend her words, it had been so long since he'd been anything but her toy. His queen didn't like her lovers to think, so that had been one of the first flaws she'd trained out of him. Mindless obedience and seething lust were what she required of him. That and to be beautiful for her. *Sending him.* She was sending him away. Beyond the queen, Yelena smirked, enjoying his panic.

"Have I displeased my queen?" he whispered in aghast horror, desire and terror twining together in agonized delight at the prospect of her punishment. Surely that's what this was: part of a new torment she'd devised for him to prove his abject devotion.

"On the contrary." She tapped his obediently open mouth with a long, sharp nail. "You have pleased me in every way, Leskai. You have submitted to my will more completely and with such heartfelt enthusiasm as I have never found in another man."

Somewhere inside, a fragment of his old self curled in shame. He barely remembered the man he'd been when he arrived at Her Majesty's court, full of ambition and hubris, eager to prove himself, dazzled by the beautiful queen's interest in him. He'd eagerly succumbed to her invitations, perhaps even pretending to himself that she had fallen prey to his seductions, as so many women had before. Flirtation was both a talent and a skill, and Leskai had become very good at talking to women, inserting himself into their trust and confidence. He treated them well, too, knowing how to please them in bed and out of it, always sincere in his way.

The queen had turned him inside out. And yes, it had been easy for her. For her and the lovely Yelena, who sometimes joined them in their games. Vaguely he understood that magic had been used, but he'd been easy to turn. Eager, even. And now the queen was sending him away. "Please don't send me away, Your Majesty," he begged, tears rolling down his face.

Queen Zarja wiped the tears away with her lips, smiling and no doubt leaving smears of her lipstick on his face. "I have a very important job for you to do. Once you complete it—to my satisfaction—then you may return to me, and I shall reward you beyond your wildest dreams."

"I want only this," he begged her with urgent sincerity. "I need nothing more than to belong to you."

The queen straightened, a single line between her elegant brows marring her otherwise smooth forehead. "Leskai." She spoke his name sternly, with disappointment. "What about what *I* need? Are you so selfish, so self-absorbed that you care nothing for what I want and need?"

He struggled against the sobs of protest, wanting to prostrate himself and beg her forgiveness, but she still held him in place. "No, my queen," he gasped. "Whatever you ask of me, I'll do gladly."

The line vanished as if it had never been and she smiled radiantly, before bestowing another lavish kiss on him. "I knew I could count on you, my darling, my precious. You know you mean more to me than any of the others, yes?"

He didn't know, but he wanted it to be true. He also knew better than to answer that question. "What would you have me do, Your Majesty?"

She finally released his hair, patting him on the cheek. "Stand up. Have some dignity." She waited for him to obey, to attempt to compose himself. The collar was terribly tight, the rest of his body throbbing and swollen, straining against the bonds under his clothing, with no relief in sight. "I want you to travel to the fastness of the sorceress Oneira and convince her to come work for me again."

"Oneira?" he echoed, searching his muddled brain. He'd heard the name before, but no face came to mind, even as he thought through the many magic-workers the queen employed. "Have I met her?"

"No." The queen tapped her glittering nails on the arm of her throne, irritation glittering just as sharply from her dark eyes. "She departed before you arrived in our court, which gives you an advantage: she will not recognize you as being one of mine."

"I see." Though he didn't, not yet.

"You will go to her fastness. It's well-warded—nothing can get in or out without her knowledge and permission—so you will have to use your considerable charm to convince her to allow you in." She fixed him with a stern look that made his knees weaken. "This is something you know how to do, Leskai, charm powerful and lonely women, remember?"

"I remember," he answered through dry lips. Had the queen seen through him all along? Perhaps she'd been using him, twisting his confidence back on itself, making him into a tool from the beginning. He put a hand to his head, feeling a sudden pain. In a moment, Yelena was beside him. She laid cool fingertips to the stabbing ache and it immediately subsided, the disturbing questions receding like an ebb tide.

"Have a care, Your Majesty," the sorceress said over her shoulder. "Leskai works so hard to please you that he will dredge up memories if you ask it, which creates dangerous cognitive dissonance."

She focused on Leskai, her eyes a blue as pale as ice. "There, darling, that's better."

He couldn't recall what it was better than, but he felt good, invigorated, ready to do what his queen asked of him. "I shall find a way to be invited inside the fastness of the sorceress Oneira, but I don't know how to find where she lives."

"We know," Yelena said with satisfaction. "I will give you a map."

"And I'll go there." Leskai didn't like it, but he truly wanted to please his queen. "As a traveling poet?"

"Yes, exactly as you came to me," Queen Zarja answered with a contented smile. "You will become her friend. She will disguise her power and you must never reveal that you know who she truly is. Then, when I send for her to take up her duty to defend the Southern Lands against invasion, you will convince her to accept."

"I beg your pardon, my queen," he said, some older, canny part of his mind kicking into motion. Once upon a time, he'd been good at political machinations. "May I know why Your Majesty hasn't simply asked to hire her?"

The queen pursed her lips in irritation, not at him, however. "She refuses all correspondence. No one can get to her. She declared that she was retiring and would no longer accept any more jobs, from anyone, ever again." She made a decidedly unroyal sound of utter disgust.

"Her academy set Oneira's price too low," Yelena observed, "or she'd never have paid off her debt so soon."

"Yes, or we paid her too well, along with all those side jobs she took," the queen replied with weary resignation. "And now I am left with no one to guard my shores while the king of the Northern Lands points the Stormbreaker at my throat."

"I wouldn't say you have no one, Your Majesty," Yelena said, moving away from Leskai, sounding cold and annoyed.

The queen speared the woman with a long, dark glare. "Is that so, Yelena? It seems your hubris has grown considerably if you think yourself capable of facing the great Stearanos in battle. Be careful, or I shall pit you against him just to see what happens. It might prove instructive to my other tame magic-workers who might begin to think too highly of themselves and their influence in my court."

Yelena visibly blanched, lines bracketing her thin mouth, lending an expression of stark pain to her thin face. "Your Majesty . . ." She trailed off, apparently searching for words, and Leskai experienced a surge of pleasure as the woman struggled.

"You have something to say to me, Yelena?" the queen crooned. "An admission of your self-acknowledged limitations wouldn't be amiss here."

Yelena bowed her head in defeat. "I could not stand against the Stormbreaker, Your Majesty, I admit. Not alone. But if many of us worked together, perhaps—"

"It's been tried," the queen snapped. "Have you forgotten Dridma and what the Stormbreaker did to their coalition of mages?"

"No, but they didn't—" Yelena broke off and bit her lip. "I apologize. Your Majesty is wise and I am foolish."

"Indeed." The queen examined her nails, then fixed Leskai with a cruel smile that made him tremble anew with desire and terror. She could do that to him, with a single glance. "I have possessed the wisdom to spend the time since Oneira abandoned me preparing for this moment, knowing this day would arrive. Uhtric is nothing if not predictable. But I have not been idle and Leskai will not fail me. Will you, pet?"

"Never, my queen," he averred, wanting to drop to his knees again but remaining obedient to her most recent command to stand and be dignified. "I will charm Oneira, become her friend, and convince her to accept your invitation when the time comes."

"The time will come sooner rather than later," the queen warned him. "You will not have the luxury of dallying."

"I understand."

"You must not disappoint me. Think back to the last time you disappointed me."

He swallowed hard. Enduring her disappointment had nearly broken him. *Had* broken him, in truth, until she deigned to build him up again with her mercy and terrible attention. "I will die before I disappoint you again, my queen."

"You will *succeed*," she specified, pointedly.

"Yes. Yes, I will succeed," he promised with fervent desperation.

"Good," she purred, then held out a hand. He took it, helping her down from the high throne. "Come with me, darling pet, and I shall give you a reward to remember me by." She drew a sharp nail down the skin bared by his parted shirt, making him tremble, though he dared not emit the slightest sound. "And in the morning, you shall set out, an itinerant poet, carefree, seeking a wealthy patroness like the last one, who gave you such a pretty outfit. Only you and I will know who holds your leash." Timing the action with her words, she clipped a leash to his collar. "Hands and knees, sweetling."

He dropped to the floor with a whimper, his body an ache of desire, kissing the hand that held his leash. He would do exactly as she bade, and then he would return to her, the only woman he truly craved, the only one who could make him happy.

Somewhere deep inside, that part of him that curled in shame wailed in despair, pounding his fists against the will of she who had imprisoned him.

Yelena watched him crawl at his mistress's heels, and smiled. The much-touted Oneira, with all her fabulous power, disdained the smaller, subtler techniques of psychic magic. Mentally derived phenomena didn't operate in the same way as other magic, and it was the careless sorcerer who failed to account for that possibility. Yelena had observed Oneira for a long time and, for all of the senior sorceress's caution, she was also overconfident, as the powerfully talented always were. In this small way, Oneira was careless.

The queen wasn't the only one to play the long game.

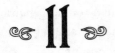

O neira spent hours digging the new bed for her roses. Bunny tried to help, but his "assistance" tended toward wildly scrabbling with his taloned paws, sending great gobs of dirt flying willy-nilly. Besides which, as Bunny was a magical creature, Oneira didn't want to skirt the boundaries of what the ancient gardener had instructed by allowing him near. She firmly banished Bunny, making him stay a good distance away, where he lay with his head morosely on his filthy paws, watching her with reproach.

Moriah ambled by, looking amused by Oneira's labors as only cats can, full of supercilious condescension, and not remotely interested in assisting. She leapt easily to the top of the nearby high wall, sunning herself lazily. Adsila came to observe also, perched on an overhanging limb, head cocked from side to side, obsidian gaze alert with interest.

Oneira—sweat-soaked, grimy, crimson hair falling in damp, brick-dark snarls around her face and neck where it had fallen from the knot and she hadn't wanted to pause to put it back— nearly told them all to go away. She didn't need an audience for her humiliating struggle to do something so simple.

It had been humbling to discover exactly how little she could accomplish without resorting to magic. All of her experiments with gardening and housekeeping, of which she'd been rather proud, doing for herself without servants and support staff, now showed themselves to be false and flimsy, not truly the work of her own hands.

Those hands had grown sore, blistered, rubbed raw and bleeding from gripping the shovel. She knew she should be using her feet to leverage her weight as the ancient gardener had demonstrated, but she couldn't seem to quite get the knack of it. She also lacked the proper footwear; the boots she wore for hiking the mountains or descending the steps to the sea were decidedly awkward in this circumstance. The slippers she wore inside were even worse. She could magically modify some, but that might be again skirting the no-magic rules and she was determined to do this by the book, as it were.

In the back of her mind, she relished the pain and sweat as a sort of atonement. This small and transient suffering of course paled compared to what she'd caused others, but at the same time, the part of her that wished to be washed clean—or whatever metaphor *did* work—nursed the fragile hope that this task had been given to her as a sort of test, a trial as in the tales of old, whereby she might at least prove her sincerity, much as she lacked anything resembling purity of heart. So she scrupulously adhered to using no magic at all in the digging of the new rose bed.

She'd referenced the Stormbreaker's book to identify the perfect location. She carefully paced out the precise distance for the roses—resting in the shade, their rough-fabric sacks moistened—to be separated from one another. They could survive for some time uprooted, the book explained, but then cautioned that too long out of the ground could jeopardize their ability to adapt, especially to a foreign environment. On top of which, spring had suddenly turned intensely warm, galloping toward high summer with reckless disregard for the stately progression of seasons. If she delayed, Oneira would potentially miss the perfect window for planting the finicky roses, and she could not see herself returning to the ancient gardener, tail between her legs, asking for more rosebushes.

No, if she failed to make these live and grow—that is, she mentally corrected herself, if she failed to properly nurture these plants and coax them into flourishing—then she'd have to abandon the project. Every time she imagined that failure, an image of Stearanos looking down his hooked nose, gloating smugly, filled her mind. Ridiculous, as he'd never know who she was, much less that she hadn't succeeded. Somewhere along the way, she'd begun to see this as a personal competition with her enemy-in-theory.

She kind of wished there had been a way for her to linger in his library, to observe his expression when he found the rose leaf and read her reply to his arrogant missive. Pausing to drag her sleeve across her forehead, wiping away the dripping sweat that had been falling to sting her eyes, leaving a trail of prickly grit behind, she indulged in picturing the moment, smiling in imagining him jumping around in a fierce tantrum, frothing at the mouth.

It was tempting to return to his library to see if he'd left her a reply. What had he thought of *The Adventures of the Beastly Bunny*? Perhaps he'd taken the book's youthful simplicity as an insult. She hadn't explained in her note why she'd picked it for him, figuring it wouldn't matter, to either of them, in the long run. Although the story of the bunny evading the gardener had been a bit of a clue, Stearanos couldn't possibly have enough information to follow that clue to the riddle's solution. Still, she'd given him a glimpse of herself, which had been only fair play after she'd gleaned something of his inmost heart from his dreams.

The two of them were nothing alike, and yet she shared an odd affinity with Stearanos. Yes, she'd borrowed his interest in the Veredian roses, but she'd also immediately understood his fascination with them, beyond her own personal connection. Also, the way the Dream swirled around him, the darker elements of regret, bitterness, despair, and guilt that sharked through his dreaming self, attracted to the blood trail that waked behind him . . . Well, she understood that, too.

Although she'd written in her note that she wouldn't return to his library, she very much wondered if he'd left a reply anyway. As she resumed digging, extracting more rocks from the soil for the growing pile nearby, she distracted herself by imagining what that note—the one he'd surely never written—might say to her. She composed and revised his words in her imagination, ending up with a message so vivid in her mind that she also framed her own reply.

By the time she'd finished digging the rose bed, the sun was sinking and Oneira had constructed an entire fantasy correspondence with this man she'd never met and never would.

She went inside to bathe, washing the embedded dirt from her bloodied hands. Honest blood this time. Not the blood shed by innocents, but her own, given freely in service of this effort. All right, fine: it was hardly a selfless task. Oneira recognized her own pride in her determination to make these roses grow. That is, to discover the way to nurture them into flourishing, she mentally corrected herself, for the nth time. Nevertheless, regardless of her self-interest, this project was in the service of creation, of adding beauty to the world, propagating something rare and precious.

It wasn't about destruction and waste and death. That was the point.

She bandaged her hands and reheated soup, toasted some bread, deeply grateful that she already had both made, as every bit of her ached with exhaustion. It might not have been the wisest choice to work all day digging this rose bed after walking the Dream all night. At least, she'd sleep hard.

That would be good, as tomorrow night she needed to enter

the Dream to obtain the soil amendments the book listed as necessary before planting. Hopefully that didn't count too strongly as using magic, as she had no other way to gather them, not without mundane travel back into the world of men, and she wouldn't do that for any reason. No, she'd have to go via the Dream and pay with coin. Tomorrow. Even she wasn't so arrogant and cavalier as to venture into the Dream in such a worn-out state.

An oneiromancer who lost themselves in the Dream, either in their body or severed from it, became part of the fabric of the Dream. Oneira's teachers disagreed in principle, certain that only actual dreams contributed to the soup that was the Dream, not entire beings. They didn't know the Dream as thoroughly as she did, however.

The Dream subsumed all sorts of elements into itself that weren't strictly the dreams of animals and people. Once, when traveling the Dream, Oneira had come across a person trapped there. He was real—or had been, at some point—and not a construct of some dreamer. She'd thought so because he looked different. He hadn't born the hallmarks of dream beings, disproportionate in some way or oddly colored, not shifting in the mutable way of people in dreams, wearing first one face, then another. When he saw her, he'd tried to speak to her, she'd been certain.

At first he'd stared at her, likely recognizing the same aspects of her relative reality, then he'd yelled, waving his arms, desperately trying to reach her. But the Dream responds to dreamers and oneiromancers, not ordinary people, and the currents of a purple wave carried him off, still screaming for help. Or so she supposed, as he hadn't used any words, his mind distorted by the Dream. No one could live in the Dream for long, the reality eroding away, until they became just another fragment. There was nothing she could have done for him. Even if she'd extracted him from the Dream, he wouldn't have survived in the waking world.

No amount of magic could have restored his living body—if he didn't have one out there already, gradually dying.

Sometimes, when Oneira fantasized about laying herself down upon the bier she ritually prepared every morning, she thought she might simply sleep and step into the Dream forever, severing her connection to her body. It would be a kind of death, and a realm far more familiar to her than actual death, which was a foreign land to which she could not pay an exploratory visit and from which she could never return.

Who knew? Perhaps stepping into the Dream for all time would be the next and final phase of her self-exile. As a skilled oneiromancer in the Dream, she might be able to retain the integrity of her mind and spirit. She could move about and through the dreams of others. Stearanos, for example. It might be fun to meddle in his dreams, extending the game they'd begun.

And why did her thoughts keep returning to him?

Banishing the Stormbreaker from her mind, she stood, taking her plate with her, and discovered Adsila, Bunny, and Moriah all watching her from various poses of rest, their gazes as keen as if they still observed the digging of the rose bed, something of accusation in them. Ah, yes. If she stepped into the Dream forever, they could not follow. Well, perhaps Adsila could, but then the kestrel could never return on her own.

"I wouldn't take that step without giving you notice," she reassured them all. "And in that case, the house would be yours."

They seemed unimpressed and Oneira shrugged it off. She hadn't asked for any of them to join her behind her white walls. All she'd wanted was to be left alone. That was *still* all she wanted, which was why she would not indulge in this insane impulse to visit Stearanos again. There would be no correspondence such as she'd constructed in her imagination. If she went to look, he wouldn't have left her a reply anyway. Why would he, when she'd explicitly said she wouldn't return? Which she wouldn't. So, if he had replied, she would never know.

There, that should put that line of thought to bed, which she did, along with herself.

And yet.

And yet, the next night as she readied her list of supplies for the rose bed, she found herself contemplating a visit to the Stormbreaker's library, also. Just to see if he'd left a reply. Her old friend curiosity prodded her relentlessly. Despite the dreary adages about curiosity leading one into trouble, Oneira had never been able to regard her insatiable curiosity as a failing. Following her curiosity had led her down the most rewarding paths of her life, including the most recent excursion into the realm of Veredian roses.

Her rosebushes seemed to be all right, still. Following the book's instructions, she hadn't disturbed the soil around their roots, only dampening their sacks and rotating them where they stood in a sheltered nook, so all sides could receive sunlight. With the help of the ancient gardener, she'd marked on the swaddling where the bushes had faced due south in their former home, and she checked to be sure those marks hadn't washed away. When she planted the roses, she'd set them in the ground at the same orientation.

Other than checking on the roses and refreshing the bier with some spring blossoms, she'd spent the day resting and puttering at small tasks in the garden and kitchen. She'd made more soup and bread, enjoying the regular rotation of kneading, allowing the dough to rise, and punching it down again. Not unlike the pattern of life, she often reflected, though she'd yet to decide what the metaphor would be for the final stage of baking. The crucible of eternal torment, perhaps? Except that one didn't emerge as a baked loaf from that.

Foolish ruminations, anyway.

Giving herself plenty of time to fulfill her long list of gardening needs, Oneira stepped into the Dream well before midnight. She should be able to find her supplies relatively nearby. What she hadn't expected—though likely she should have—was that she'd find everything she needed all in one place and not far away at all. It made sense: other gardeners in her general region would need the same soil supplements, and would want them all in one errand, also.

She loaded up the various bags and boxes, sent them all back to her house to await her return, and left coin to pay for them. The vendor also managed a small greenhouse, rich with the scents of moist soil, green, growing things, and the higher, sweeter notes of night-blooming flowers. The place reminded her of that other nighttime garden and how she'd longed to explore it. So, she strolled the aisles, the waxing moonlight filtering through the glass above, and examined the plants, reading the informational signs that accompanied them.

In the end, she found several she wanted to take home and plant in her own garden, so she left more coin—probably far too much, as she had no idea of their prices, but better that than far too little—and took her prizes back with her. Laden with her new guests, she stepped out of the Dream and into her own garden, setting the plants next to the Veredian roses, so they could all become acquainted.

Now what? She wasn't tired, having slept and rested so much. She could read, she supposed, but she still had read every book she owned, now including the Veredian rose cultivation guide. A visit to the library might be just the thing. She wouldn't be yielding to the impulse to see if Stearanos had left a reply, because he wouldn't have. She simply needed to borrow a book to read. One she'd return as soon as she finished, with no teasing or other shenanigans. Really, she could do this without tipping him off that she'd been there, as she should have done to begin with.

Her impulse duly rationalized, she stepped into the Dream and followed the path that led to Stearanos.

12

His thief had not returned.

Though Stearanos made it back home early enough the following day, easily in time to sniff out any lingering trace of the nocturnal intruder, no hint of their magic remained. None of the castle denizens had been aware of having been enchanted asleep on the two previous occasions, so they wouldn't realize if they had been tampered with again. A few had remarked on sleeping in unusually late that one morning, especially the kitchen staff who rose early to prepare breakfast. They'd worried about their lapse until Stearanos told them not to fret about it, a command given in no uncertain terms, but which reassured them regardless.

But Stearanos knew they hadn't been enchanted asleep again. The moment he stepped across the threshold, sorcerous senses eagerly threading ahead of him to suss out any new evidence, he knew that the thief had not returned. They'd said they wouldn't, and they hadn't.

Still, he went directly to the library anyway, going to the book he'd left in place of *The Adventures of the Beastly Bunny*, finding it undisturbed, the note he'd left inside in its original creases. Wrestling an odd disappointment where he should be feeling relief, he put the book back and went to sit in his chair. Triggering the wards on the window frame with a thought, he sent the window flying open, needing the fresh ocean air to cleanse his mind.

Ridiculous that he'd had some sense of—what?—looking forward to the next round of taunting and nose-thumbing from the impudent intruder. The invasive interlude had been a break in the sameness, the dreary, infinite round of over and over his life had become. No, that it had always been. That was the only reason this excursion from the ordinary had captured his attention and anticipation. He resisted the insidious notion that he'd somehow ruined it by leaving, by missing a night. His thief might have come and left again, disappointed by his absence.

Heaving a sigh at the fanciful notion, something completely out of character for him, Stearanos pushed himself up again. He should be delighted and relieved that the criminal hadn't returned. No one expected a sneak thief in the night to have the integrity to keep their promises, but apparently he'd been mistaken. Never mind that it hadn't been phrased as an actual promise, more as a reassurance, albeit a provoking one.

He should be happy that nothing more had been tampered with, even if he was still missing his book. While in the imperial city, he'd taken the time to visit a few of his favorite rare book dealers. No surprise—none of them possessed a copy of the manual on growing the excessively rare and fragile Veredian roses, nor did they know of anyone who did. It had taken years to locate the copy he'd only recently acquired. He'd set them all on the quest to locate another for him, paying in advance. The bookseller who'd found the original copy for him had spoken promisingly of her ability to locate another, thinking perhaps her source might be able to access the same connection, but he wasn't hopeful.

In the meanwhile, Stearanos had an assignment to execute and delaying would yield him nothing, except perhaps the displeasure of His Majesty. Stearanos would be paid according to his success in this ill-advised conquest, so the more he researched the Southern Lands, the better he'd be prepared. Besides which, it simply wasn't in him to do less than his best. Much as he hated

NEVER THE ROSES · 109

Uhtric and his wars of acquisition, Stearanos still strove to outdo himself in winning them. More than once, he considered the propensity might be a curse. Although, if he had any chance of freeing himself from debt, it lay in those victories, not in losing.

Counting the books in his mind, he moved from shelf to shelf, theme to theme, pulling every one that had anything to do with the Southern Lands. This part of the process, at least, would be interesting. He could bury himself in the research, making notes and formulating an idea of that realm. In the exercise, he could forget for a while the ultimate purpose in collating this knowledge.

As he went to a shelf in a more distant, shadowed corner, his boot ground against something gritty. Odd. Stepping back, he scanned the polished stone floor at the verge of the colorful rug, then knelt to run his fingers over the brown stuff there. Dirt. Most unusual, as his housekeeper commanded her army of cleaners with military precision. They cleaned every room in the castle on a rotation reliable as clockwork. The library had been last cleaned three days before, so this dirt incursion was new since then, which meant only one person could have introduced it: his thief.

Excited about this newest clue, Stearanos retrieved a glass vial and a small brush from his desk. He would analyze this sample for its origin and perhaps learn at least what region of the world his intruder hailed from. From there, he could follow a path of logic and reasoning to uncover their identity, and then . . . Victory would be his, eventually. He didn't mind his vengeance being served cold. Back on hands and knees, he scoured the area for every grain, his nose nearly to the floor as he scavenged all available clues. "Made a mistake, didn't you?" he murmured, feeling almost a sense of affection for the unknown magic-worker, as he placed every grain of dirt into the vial before securely corking it. "Happens to everyone, thief. The gods are in the details."

Evidence duly gathered, Stearanos stowed his prize for alchemical analysis later and returned to his task, humming a tune now as he gathered the remaining books he needed. He took those to his desk to stack with his new acquisitions.

While visiting the booksellers in King's City in the vain search for another copy of the book on Veredian roses, he'd also acquired a few additional relevant tomes on the Southern Lands, placing orders for still more. Good to have an excuse to buy new books, especially on His Majesty's account. Keeping the new and uncatalogued books separate, he sorted the others into piles, categorizing by relevance and potential usefulness, the most salient to his research on top.

He'd begin there, with the books he'd already read and which he knew contained important material, refamiliarizing himself with that information. That would allow him to outline what he already knew about the Southern Lands and thus identify gaps in his understanding.

At that point, he'd delve into the new books he'd acquired, flesh out a summary of those, and then identify any further information needs. After that, he'd have to find more books or even resort to using His Majesty's spy network. He had little trust in spies, as it meant relying on the observations of people who were sneaky by nature, with none of the scholarly discipline one could depend upon in authors of books. His own sorcery, however, didn't adapt itself well to spying. Still, other sorcerers in the king's stable had various tools at their command and wouldn't necessarily be useful on the actual battlefield, so Stearanos might as well take advantage of them. Probably a number of them had been spying already, which was no doubt how His Majesty had discovered Oneira's retirement.

Now there was an interesting riddle. The sorceress so powerful that her name was used to frighten children into good behavior—not to mention rapacious monarchs—abruptly washing her hands of it all. It seemed dramatic and out of character, but then Stearanos knew little about her beyond her fearsome reputation, which had leaked across the sea in dribs and drabs, tantalizing clues that washed up on their shores. Most of it had come from either those untrustworthy spies or those most ridiculously unreliable of creatures: poets. Those tellers of tales thought nothing of fictionalizing to please an audience, so Stearanos dismissed most of the ballads about Oneira as utter nonsense.

At one point, he had been given a file detailing what had been verified about her abilities, should he need to face her in combat. They called her Dreamthief and she could manipulate the world of dreaming like no other, calling anything forth from it. The poetic sagas focused heavily on the monsters and night terrors she could unleash, devastating magical and mundane opponents alike. Because Stearanos had insisted on verifiable facts only, the documents had contained little about her as a person. Red hair, no spouse, no children. A fiery temper to match the hair. That was about it.

He snorted to himself. Even if he had asked to know more, no doubt no one in her realm cared about her as a person any more than Uhtric cared about Stearanos. They were both tools—born with terrifying power and meticulously trained to harness it to be of service to the power base rather than upend it. He was more than a little shocked that they'd let her escape the leash.

Most likely she'd grown old and feeble, not wanting to spend her dotage fighting wars. Perhaps her powers had weakened with age and she'd reckoned it the better part of valor to retire from the field of battle rather than risk an ignominious defeat. That's what he would do.

Regardless, she had somehow paid off the debt of her early

training, or the Queen of the Southern Lands would never have released Oneira from her blood contract. Stearanos could live his lifetime thus far over again and then some, and still not be free of his debt, so he could only imagine how ancient this Oneira must be. But even doddering sorcerers have their uses, so they'd have kept her in harness if they could have.

In the end, and despite his rather desperate envy, he wished the ancient lady well. He could allow that indulgence, as they'd never face each other in battle now. He hoped she lived long enough to enjoy some of her retirement. One less enemy in the world for him to worry about. Perhaps someday he'd be able to follow in her footsteps.

The matter settled in his mind, he set himself to taking those initial notes to create the outline he'd have James transcribe into a more legible and orderly document, the scholarly focus giving him a bit of reprieve from thinking about the no doubt horrific war to come. The project also occupied his attention enough that he barely gave thought to his nocturnal intruder—now there was an effective spy for you—and whether they'd ever return.

Though, how had they come to leave dirt behind when they were otherwise so scrupulous about leaving no trace? Muddy boots, perhaps, but that seemed unlikely. Any thief who neglected to clean their shoes couldn't have come and gone with so little impact. There would have been other evidence.

The answer nearly slapped him in the face: the roses.

The thief had had a rose leaf with them. Had they had an entire rosebush? A Veredian rosebush, if he didn't miss his guess. In that case, the dirt might've been deliberately left behind, just to rub it in that a Veredian rosebush had been right here, in this very library, and taken away again. Infuriating. The quill pen in his grip snapped, digging shards into his palm and yanking him out of his unproductive thoughts.

Taking a deep breath, calming himself, he set the broken quill aside and took up a new one, holding it in a deliberately gentle grasp. He would not allow this imp of a thief to distract him from his work. It couldn't be a coincidence that this intrusion had occurred in concert with His Majesty deciding to declare war on the Southern Lands. Stearanos had to keep strongly in mind the subtle tactics of many sorcerers and that this one likely sought to sabotage him before they even began.

His gaze going to the book he'd left on the shelf for his unwelcome visitor, he contemplated the note he'd put inside, considering how he might redraft it in light of this new insight. But no . . . He would leave it. Better to have a message out there that came cleanly from a state of his not knowing about the dirt, about the actual roses, the ones he'd longed for, having been right here in this very library.

Besides which, if the invader's aim was to distract him, then he'd thwart them best by remaining focused. With renewed will, he put the thief firmly out of his mind and concentrated on his research.

But, in case his tormenter returned and these apparently innocuous visits were connected to Uhtric's plans to invade the Southern Lands, Stearanos knew just the thing to draw them out. A bit of a wink and a nod. Then they'd see what happened next.

13

Oneira stepped out of the Dream and into the darkened library. Darker than usual. Was there a storm or was it overcast, to block the moonlight? No, she realized, as her eyes adapted. All the heavy curtains had been drawn over the windows, eliminating all ambient light. What new game was this?

Though she'd told herself she'd only come to borrow a book to read, a little thrill of anticipation ran up her spine, looped through her imagination, and settled into her heart, which fluttered unexpectedly. Stearanos had anticipated her return, either thinking her a liar or unreliable in her guarantees of not returning. Both were more or less true, in the end, she had to acknowledge with chagrin. She would have to be careful to cleave to the truth from now on, as prevarication held many pitfalls for the unwary sorcerer.

But she'd only come to borrow a book, nothing else. Here and gone again. She'd return it as soon as she was done, to its proper spot, with no mischief. She would need light, however, to select the book, which had to be what Stearanos would expect. He could have laid some sort of trap triggered by illumination— either from summoning fire to the wicks in the lamps around the library or creating light via magic. Or it could be triggered by an attempt to open the curtains and allow the moonlight in.

She remained carefully in place, quite certain that she'd not yet triggered any traps by her arrival. Out of long habit and an abundance of caution, she never stepped from the Dream into the exact same spot. She also checked the sleep enchantment she'd laid over the castle. All was well . . . But was *that* a trick, an illusion? Invigorated by the challenge, Oneira thought through the puzzle, reversing perspective to consider what she would do to thwart an intruder of unknown purpose and origin, who somehow evaded her wards to appear inside her walls.

Of course, Oneira—as a powerful and experienced oneiromancer—also protected her home against anyone arriving via the Dream. She did that from the Dream side, a task well within her abilities. No one could enter a place from the Dream except via a dreamer. It was simple enough to shield her own dreaming self so that no one could insert themselves into her dreams. She'd learned those skills as a child as part of the early lessons in protecting the world from her dreams, and other dreamers from her unconscious mind, so she'd never again inadvertently pull the Dream into the waking world.

She could and did also shield the dreams of Moriah, Bunny, and Adsila, just as an extra precaution. She could not, however, realistically shield all the dreams of any creature that passed through or near enough her home to create an avenue through her wards. Someone would have to know exactly where to look for her, but Oneira hadn't survived this long by neglecting remote possibilities. Instead she thickened the Dream in a bubble around her physical location. Not enough to prevent the natural flow of the Dream, but sufficient to deflect any but the most powerful oneiromancers from making their way through. As she was the most powerful oneiromancer in existence, that meant no one could get through that way.

Stearanos had to be plagued with curiosity—and perhaps some of his infamous paranoia—trying to figure out how she got in. Everything she knew about him pointed to his love of knowing, of controlling, categorizing, and quantifying. He also loved to win, and was accustomed to being the victor of every battle. Just as she was. "Not this time, Stormbreaker," she murmured, pondering what measures he might have taken.

He'd clearly thought she came in the windows, so the curtains would be a trap. Or they set the stage for the real snare, as he'd know she'd need light.

In his place, she might have rigged the lamps to burn her if she lit them, perhaps with a blaze hot enough to kill her. They were, after all, enemies. Even if he didn't realize exactly who she was, he regarded her as a thief and invader, rightfully so. It would be difficult, though not impossible, for him to set a spell triggered by a very small use of magic, such as to summon a lick of flame. Any spell like that, however, should have gone off already in response to her oneiromancy, and all remained quiet.

It was a risk, but a small and exciting one. Oneira created a ball of soft green radiance and rested it on her palm. A child's trick, requiring minimal magic and yet producing enough light to see anything up close. Her magic coiled, resting lightly on the sliver of a portal she'd opened to the Dream. It gleamed with its own iridescence, shedding light from the single, thin vertical line, as she waited for anything to change, however minutely. Nothing did.

Smiling, pleased with the initial victory in this round—she was well ahead in this game with the Stormbreaker—she moved to a shelf she'd previously noted with books themed around air and flying. With her recent ruminations on what it might feel like to fly, she craved a book with wings involved. Running only her gaze over the spines, she looked for fiction, letting go of the burr of irritation that Stearanos couldn't arrange his books in a more logical fashion. Even within the theme, novels weren't grouped together, instead organized according to some arcane system she'd yet to fathom. The sorcerer's mind was truly a labyrinth where logic lurked only in the dead ends and alleyways. Finally selecting a book that looked interesting, she slipped it into the pocket of her gown and prepared to leave.

In and out again, only borrowing a book, she reminded herself. Yet, she hesitated, tempted to go to the shelf where she'd left *The Adventures of the Beastly Bunny* and her reply to his first note.

She *so* wanted to look. For the first time, she considered that her curiosity could indeed lead her into real trouble. The Stormbreaker was certainly trouble, by any definition, and this enticing game they played had already tempted her into risky behavior.

What real risk, though? She'd built herself a bier, for stars' sake. As much as the romantic image of laying herself upon the bier to die appealed to her, the underlying fact remained that she hadn't cared if she lived or died for a long time. Justifying it to herself that way—ignoring the niggling voice that suggested she had, in fact, recently discovered several reasons to want to live—she went to the shelf.

The Adventures of the Beastly Bunny was gone.

In its place sat a thick volume that appeared at first glance to be about gardening. Intrigued, she slipped it from the shelf—after checking it for magical traps; she wasn't that careless—observing that a folded note had been left inside. He'd written to her again, something that should not give her such a thrill of pure exhilaration. Prolonging the anticipation, she opened to that page and examined the chapter heading in the soft green light, a laugh escaping her as she saw the title: *Chapter Twenty-Two, On Rabbits and the Various Methods for Protecting Vegetables from Their Incursions.*

Delighted with this escalation in their game, she pocketed that book, also, and unfolded the note.

My Dearest Thief,

I cannot fathom why you imagined I'd find the torturous tale of a persistent, disagreeable lagomorph and its willful destruction of an innocent gardener's sustenance a subject of amusement. Perhaps you imply that I should be infuriated by the gardener's hapless and ineffectual efforts to combat the creature. Am I to suppose you are the adorable bunny in this scenario and I am the excessively stupid gardener? I assure you, I am no such thing.

Stop taking my carrots or you shall be rabbit stew.

Em

Oneira read the note three times with rising levels of astonishment and furtive glee. Was she mistaken or was he being . . . playful? He'd actually read the epic poem of the bunny and the gardener and taken it seriously enough to reply with barbed commentary, to the point of locating a book with the apparent intent of educating her on the topic. Which she intended to read, as her canine Bunny had only minimal devotion to his duty and the tender shoots of new lettuce were suffering from his inattention.

Most interesting was that Stearanos had signed it "Em."

She studied that bit assiduously, bringing the light very close to the page to be sure that he hadn't started to write "Eminence" and had broken off or failed to finish in some way. Blowing out a breath, she took a moment to ponder, folding the note and putting it in her pocket. She had to think about this and not dash off a similarly playful reply. Stearanos couldn't possibly be *flirting* with her, could he? Her own fascination came from having an idea of who he was, at least on the surface, catching glimpses of his life and dreams. And from their long relationship, distant and manufactured as it had been. Still, they'd been colleagues of a sort.

Well, and his library was terribly seductive.

But for all that Stearanos knew from his side, she could be anyone at all. A lethal enemy, even, though she hadn't attacked him directly, not beyond a little extra sleep inducement. Still, he couldn't know she wouldn't escalate as she continued to evade his defenses.

Reconsidering, she mulled the possibility that the note's apparent playfulness was a subterfuge to lure her in, to lull her into lowering her guard and yielding clues that would reveal her identity. Stearanos had a reputation for being a master strategist, a puppet master beyond compare, so she needed to consider her reply very carefully. *If* she replied at all, which she shouldn't. Truly, if she were being smart, she would nip this in the bud now, leave both books behind and never return.

Still, even given that, she could leave a quick note, a thank-you for the books—she still had coin in her pocket, she could leave payment for all of them, which ought to stick in his craw—and end this odd "correspondence" forever. Resolved on this course of action, the wise thing to do, she went to his desk for the paper and quill he'd surely left out for her.

Only to find the desk piled high with books. This wasn't like him, to leave books out and unshelved, an untidy monument to the chaos he loathed. Why would he depart from habitual behavior now? Unless this too was a message.

Perplexed, intrigued, perhaps a bit nervous, she held the light close to examine the spines. And gasped aloud in horrified astonishment.

They were all books on the Southern Lands. Her realm, where she'd dwelt and worked all her life. Did this mean Stearanos suspected her identity, that he'd piled up all of these tomes as an accusation, a mocking hint to show that he'd found her out?

But that made no sense. If he had an idea of who she was, he could have gotten an oneiromancer to ward his dreams. It wouldn't have worked to keep her out, but she would have noticed the warning.

Or, more likely, and a smarter move for him, he could have learned of her location. It would be simple enough for a sorcerer with his resources to find out. Where she'd chosen to build her house was discoverable information, if only because she'd warned everyone to stay far, far away from it.

Early on in her plans to walk away, she'd contemplated keeping her location secret, but ultimately decided it would be more work to disappear and stay disappeared than to simply make an unassailable fortress and promise annihilation to anyone who tested her boundaries and patience. She was a battle sorceress, after all, with a fearsome reputation. Her strengths lay in intimidation and the threat of violence beyond imagining, not secrecy and vanishing.

And yet, the Stormbreaker hadn't come after her. The thought of him appearing on her doorstep—perhaps invading her home as she had his—had her heart hammering.

He hasn't, she reassured herself mentally. *If he knew who you were, he'd have come after you, and he didn't. Therefore, he doesn't know. He's only guessing.*

Even though it couldn't be an accident or coincidence that he'd collected books on this exact topic and that he'd left them out for her to see, an obvious wink at her. Hastily, she revised her estimation of him—hadn't she cautioned herself not to underestimate the man?—along with her plan of action. Removing her remanence from it, she left the new gardening book on top of the nearest pile, so he'd know she'd been there. She was too flustered, too caught off center to choose which book or pile.

She would reply to him. Oh yes, she couldn't leave this unanswered. But she needed to muster all her wit to do so. Sadly, none of her imagined correspondence with him could be repurposed.

He'd surprised her too entirely. She couldn't be flip or clever in that moment.

She would borrow the novel, read it, and take her time composing a reply with diligence and cleverness. Stearanos could never have bested her on the battlefield and he wouldn't best her now. Certainly he wouldn't send her into hiding, afraid to even meet his note with her own.

No, she would answer this sally with something better. She would give him words that would suss out his strategy. Two could play this game of pretend flirtation. Perhaps she would even deliberately mislead him, offer him clues that would point him at someone else entirely. She'd have to decide which of her enemies most richly deserved to have the unwitting wrath of Stearanos turned upon them. Fortunately, that was a long list.

Satisfied that she retained the upper hand, and that she would indeed best him, Oneira lifted the enchantment from the castle, allowing its denizens to slide into a more natural sleep.

Except for Stearanos.

As she stepped back into the Dream, Oneira couldn't resist poking at him just a little bit more. Lightly touching his dreams, she inserted a bunny holding a book in its mouth, rabidly chewing it up with sharp, pointy teeth, froth and paper fragments flying in a blizzard.

Let him make of that what he would.

14

Of course, she immediately regretted her impetuous move. Even before she stepped out of the Dream and back into the safe confines of her white walls, she was kicking herself for succumbing to that wild, irrational impulse. Inserting an image into his dreams, of all the stupid ideas.

"What is *wrong* with you?" she muttered to herself, speaking her thoughts aloud as she almost never did. Clearly she was losing her mind. Perhaps this was the next stage in her decline. First, her sudden and shocking retirement, then the crazy behavior in building her fastness with a decorated bier at the fulcrum, then stalking her ex-enemy and wandering about the Dream in search of extinct roses that bloomed only when no one could see them, and finally *this*.

Whatever *this* was.

It certainly wasn't any kind of calculated strategy. Quite the opposite in that Stearanos should be sorcerer enough to know that the scene she'd inserted into his dreams hadn't been anything that came from himself. An ordinary person, yes, might assume the book-devouring monster bunny had morphed from their recent experiences, but most magic-workers, let alone a sorcerer of his caliber, would be alerted by the peculiar vividness of a scene inserted by an oneiromancer.

"Stupid! Stupid! Stupid!" she railed at herself, stomping around the midnight garden, kicking up clods of dirt and detritus left over from the precipitous snowmelt. At least she retained the presence of mind to stay clear of the new rose bed, careful not to adulterate her hard work with contaminants she'd just have to dig out again. Her tantrum exhausted, she sank to sit on the roots of a tree, the chill damp of the sodden ground immediately soaking through her skirts. She remained where she was, knees drawn up, back against the tree, gazing up through the spider-web of still bare branches at the star-smattered sky beyond. The moon had set in her part of the world, leaving the stars to shine with uninhibited radiance.

Briefly, Oneira considered going back. She could extract the dream from Stearanos's mind again. People, even sorcerers, re-membered dreams in fragments anyway. It would be easy for her, and he would never know the difference.

It was also something she'd sworn never to do.

Taking away people's memories was a violation of the most extreme and intimate violence. She would—and had—killed people before she'd consider cutting away a piece of themselves like that. Oneira had no perspective into the realm of death; she knew no more than anyone else. Despite the tales and poems that depicted dreams and death as intertwined, they were not.

The Dream was a place of the living, generated and perpetu-ated by living creatures. If the dead dreamed, then their Dream was entirely separate. Still, Oneira felt certain that the death of the mortal body wasn't an end, but a transition. For all she knew, people carried all of their memories, which formed the core of the selves they'd built over that lifetime, into the next realm.

Causing someone's death was a grave transgression, and she would bear the guilt of the deaths she'd caused for all eternity. But taking away a piece of their essential, immortal selves forever . . . That she would not do.

No, she'd put that image into Stearanos's dreams and she

could not take it back. She could only hope he somehow wouldn't notice. A vain hope, indeed. This could be the end of her, and she'd brought it all upon herself. Foolish and careless.

The black cat Moriah manifested out of the night, first a darker outline, soon filled in with languid feline movement, her emerald eyes gleaming with what could only be reflected starlight. She sidled up to Oneira, rubbing a long, slow, body-long caress of affection, then sighed into a sprawl, back against Oneira's hip and feet. The sorceress combed her fingers through the plush fur, smiling despite everything at the purr welling up and thrumming into her with the deep vibration of healing comfort.

"I don't know what's wrong with me," Oneira said aloud, repeating herself more than speaking to Moriah, who never answered anyway. Her words hung in the still night air, then faded, leaving only the sound of the distant surf against the cliffs. She hadn't been able to hear the sea through the window in the Stormbreaker's library, the irrelevant thought occurred to her. Either the sea there was as tame as it looked, or his castle sat too far above it.

"Even the sages do not know how the heart heals."

It took Oneira a long moment to realize the voice was Moriah's, the tenor velvet-soft as her purr, the words heavily accented by a language Oneira couldn't identify. It took her even longer to parse what the cat had said to her.

"My heart isn't broken," she finally replied, pondering that this should be the subject of the first—perhaps only?—conversation she'd had with the keeper of spells and wisdom.

"Isn't it?"

"I have never been in love, thus my heart is intact."

"Is that the only way hearts are broken?"

"One must have loved to have then lost. I have never loved." Or been loved, she acknowledged with an abstract ache, a distant part of her surprised that she still felt pain over that.

"Again, I pose the question."

Oneira let her head fall back against the tree, giving the question due consideration. "I suppose hearts can be broken in all sorts of ways. We are fragile creatures, so easily damaged. But, though I have dealt suffering, I have not suffered, myself; therefore my heart is intact."

"Haven't you suffered, Oneira?"

It just figured that the voice of wisdom spoke primarily in questions, not answers. Though she'd been seeking a question, hadn't she, when all this began. She'd first gone to the Stormbreaker's library on instinct, following her intuition—and a mischievous impulse—to discover a question worth pursuing, and she'd found the book on roses. An answer and question in one.

"My suffering is all secondhand," she said to Moriah. "I dispensed suffering freely, like a spring maiden showering petals of pain, destruction, and death over a thronging crowd, indiscriminately and with grotesque generosity. Feeling bad about what I've done doesn't register in the same category."

"Suffering isn't quantifiable. It cannot be counted and weighed and totaled up to be compared to another's. Suffering is personal and we all suffer in our own ways, struggling under the burden of it."

A surprisingly long speech. Oneira very nearly didn't ask her burning question, but her curiosity got the better of her. "Have you suffered, Moriah?"

The cat was silent for so long Oneira had decided she wouldn't answer.

"We all suffer in our own ways," Moriah finally said.

Oneira took that as a yes, bemused that an ancient and powerful creature would acknowledge such a thing. "So, you're saying what's wrong with me is that my heart is broken. *I* am broken, so I'm behaving in broken ways."

Broken, broken, broken—third time's the charm, as the elementary school saying went.

Moriah said nothing more. She didn't really need to.

❧

Though Oneira had resolved—definitively, definitely, and without a doubt—that she would not return to the Stormbreaker's library, she mentally composed her reply regardless.

She couldn't seem to help herself. All the time she measured the soil amendments and worked them into the new rose bed, lines of dialogue circulated through her mind. She found herself in imaginary conversations with Stearanos, where she sometimes explained herself, other times eviscerated him with her wit, and at still others demanded an explanation from him.

Why was he studying those books on the Southern Lands? If he knew who she was, why hadn't he attacked? In the time-honored fashion of all sorcerers, whether engaged in overt or passive wars, he should have sent a missive or done some small thing to inform her of his knowledge and intent to destroy her. She'd engaged in duels before, either personal or at the behest of another, so she understood how the escalation worked. Stearanos had dropped the ball, for some unknown reason.

Unless this was his strategy, to make her stew in anxiety, waiting for him to strike.

That would be just like him, puppet master and tormenter.

By the end of that day, her roses were planted in perfect orientation to their previous lives, every instruction followed, and even part of the novel she'd borrowed from Stearanos had been read. She liked it and would *not* be returning it, especially since she'd resolved not to visit his library again, under any circumstances. Still, though he'd never read them, the words of her mentally composed reply burned so determinedly in her mind that she had no choice but to write them down.

She would write the letter, but not send it, she decided. That would purge the conversation from her thoughts. She would burn the letter, consign the words to the air itself, the ashes to scatter over the sea. The furious passion she applied to writing the note failed to match the flip tone she wanted. Even with it mentally composed, she went through several drafts before she was satisfied. Not that it mattered, as she fully intended to burn the cursed thing when she was done. She definitely would *not* take it to his library and leave it.

She surveyed her final missive with satisfaction and carried it out to the cliff's edge, pulling a lick of flame from the Dream to rest on the tip of her finger, ready to send the ashes on the winds.

Poised there on the precipice, she couldn't quite seem to set the letter aflame. Marveling at her own recklessness—where was the meticulously methodical sorceress who'd exercised caution above all?—she knew she couldn't do it.

She had to deliver the note.

She supposed that *was* like herself in that she'd always had to have the last word.

🌿

Oneira stepped out of the Dream and into the library. As she crossed the threshold from the shifting, lurid colors of the Dream landscape, the waking world blinded her.

Lamps blazed, lighting the library. Already tense, she nearly panicked, certain an attack arrowed toward her, and readied a nightmare to fling at Stearanos—

But he was soundly asleep under her enchantment. As was

128 · *Jennifer K. Lambert*

everyone in the castle. She hadn't made a mistake. At least, not of that variety.

Because she'd failed to note that the Stormbreaker wasn't in his bed.

He was right there, slumped over the desk, head on the parchment he'd been inscribing, his quill pen dribbling ink in a wayward line. Arrested, heart slowing from its frantic pace, Oneira stared at the slumbering sorcerer, feeling as caught out as if she were a child discovered filching cookies from the academy kitchen. Even though she knew her spell held him fast—she checked yet again to be extra certain—she still somehow expected him to rear up and accuse her, perhaps hit her with that devastatingly lethal attack she'd been braced for.

Or for the trap he'd surely set. She waited, ready for it to spring. Perhaps in the next moments she would die.

She'd always wondered if she'd know when she faced death. Would her life parade before her eyes in all its terrible glory? More likely that was utter nonsense and death came as a complete surprise. And yet, she'd always taken the absence of that parade of her past as a good omen, that her day to die had not yet arrived.

No past paraded through her mind. The Stormbreaker slept on.

Gradually, sensing no imminent danger, Oneira relaxed, daring to take a few steps closer. She recognized the sorcerer, to her mild astonishment. Naturally, the man sleeping on the desk in the Stormbreaker's library and radiating magic even while asleep, like the sun burning through a thin overcast, had to be Stearanos. He could be no one else. Even so, had Oneira met him in a different context, she felt sure that she would have recognized him regardless. Perhaps she knew him from his dreaming mind. Perhaps in some other way.

But he was familiar to her. Like an old friend would be, except she obviously had no old friends. Though, she supposed Stearanos came as close as any, as she'd known about his existence out there in the northern part of the world before she even graduated from the Hendricks Academy for Sorcerous Pursuits.

Drawn, confident that he slept deeply under her spell, she moved even closer, fascinated despite her better judgment. She should drop the note she'd written on the floor—her entire and only reason for being there at all—and escape back into the Dream. Instead, she drew close enough to touch him.

The Stormbreaker was a stern-looking man, no surprise there, with the care of years inscribed in lines that didn't fade from his face even in deep repose. It didn't help that his visage had little extra flesh beneath the skin, his nose the hawkish protuberance she'd expected, beneath dark and bristling brows. Even his lips were thin, slightly darker than his weathered skin, pressed together in a disapproval she suspected was a permanent expression, his resting frown enhanced by a few white scars that jagged here and there. Another surprise: he wore his hair long, the dark threaded with silver, though not much, woven into a multitude of thin braids he'd bundled together and tied with a cord.

Tall, lean, with broad shoulders and more scars across the backs of his hands, the man looked more like a battle-hardened warrior than a soft-skinned and pampered sorcerer. How interesting, and not at all how she'd imagined *His Eminence*. The man bearing that title should be soft from rich foods and dressed in purple velvets, not scarred and wearing quite plain clothing. Though he did look like the Stormbreaker.

How did he come by those scars? He looked as if he'd walked through a plate of glass, which wasn't the usual sort of attack a sorcerer faced.

Perhaps this unexpected physical toughness of his contributed to the sorcerer's uncanny ability to evade defeat. Many times his death had been rumored and then disproven by his continued existence. Confident in her power over him, Oneira peered closely at the scars on his hands and face, trying to discern what had caused them. Unaccountably, she wanted to touch them, to determine if they stood out in fine ridges or blended with the texture of the man's skin. She didn't dare do any such thing, no more than she'd put her head in a basilisk's mouth, but she could look all she pleased.

Even close-up, the scars still looked like thin slices to her, all apparently identical in length and depth, as if they'd occurred all at once, except they seemed to be all over him—unlikely in any scenario she could envision. Nevertheless, whatever had caused them, they looked painful, and she winced in sympathy before recalling that he was her enemy and not deserving of care from her.

Dark smears of ink stained his fingertips, sinking into the lines of his calluses, and dirt made crescent moons under his nails. She knew those moons well, having scrubbed them from her own hands in recent days, the inevitable wages of gardening. Stearanos wouldn't do his own digging, however, she imagined. Perhaps he simply had terrible hygiene. Though the rest of him looked clean enough and he didn't stink. She'd been around enough warriors, and courtiers too lazy and self-indulgent to bathe, that she recognized the reek of the unwashed. Stearanos smelled clean, an undertone of some spicy soap or oil to him, probably for his hair or from shaving, given the clean line of his jaw.

And what on earth was she doing, standing there inhaling the scent of her sleeping enemy? She'd lost her mind. That had to be it. Moriah's hints about Oneira being broken surely meant that. Not a broken heart, but a broken brain.

She would leave her note and go. The now-familiar urge to mischief seized her and she decided to tuck the note in his hand, so he would wake knowing just how very vulnerable he'd been to her. As she bent to do so, her gaze snagged on the words he'd been writing, the quill lying at an angle in his lax grip.

Cowardly thief! Wake me from your spell and face me li. . . .

She blinked at it. He'd written her a note. In the moment, that was, as opposed to composing them in her absence. Sensing the encroachment of the sleep enchantment—which, a normal person wouldn't have been able to feel, but this was the Stormbreaker, so all bets were off—he'd scrawled that message, not quite able to finish before he succumbed. And called her a coward.

She liked the notion that he'd attempted to fight off her spell and failed, even though he'd clearly stayed awake in a deliberate effort to await, and possibly to thwart, her arrival. A good lesson for him that he couldn't withstand her power. But she didn't at all like being called a coward. She'd thought he'd at least have the wit to respect his wily intruder. It stung unexpectedly to be dismissed that way.

He was the one broken in the head if he thought his challenge would compel her to wake him. She could lose the upper hand with remarkable speed if she did that. Oneira knew her strengths, and sneaking in via the Dream gave her the greatest advantage in a myriad of situations. Stearanos wasn't the strategist he imagined himself to be if he thought such childish taunting would draw her into being careless.

You're already being careless, her inner voice reminded her, *just by being here, which you'd resolved never to do again.*

And this would absolutely be her last visit. Stearanos already knew too much about her. He'd clearly realized that she'd been casting sleep spells, but most magic-workers worth their contracts could do at least low-level enchantments to encourage slumber. She still retained a smidgeon of hope that he hadn't connected his dream image of the bunny to her. And there was still the remote possibility that this research of his into the Southern Lands—well underway by the look of it—had nothing to do with her.

Regardless, this time she truly would not return. She tucked the note between two of his knuckles, then slipped the quill from his other hand. It was warm from his touch. She refused to allow herself to be distracted by that.

She really wanted to write "in your dreams" or "dream on," but apparently her recklessness hadn't quite exceeded her better sense and discretion. A threat would be better. She quickly wrote it and left, canceling the sleep spell behind her as she vanished into the Dream.

❧ 15 ❧

Stearanos jerked awake, fingers convulsing on empty air, the quill no longer in his hand. The thief was there.

Shoving himself upright—mentally cursing himself for succumbing yet again to the sleep enchantment despite the precautions he'd taken, ones that clearly had failed to work—he mustered his magic and gazed wildly about the library.

Correction: the thief had been and gone. Looking down at the note he'd ignominiously failed to finish as the other sorcerer's magic overwhelmed him, he saw they'd written an answer. Incredulous, shrinkingly aware that his enemy had stood at his shoulder, had plucked the quill from his hand and used it as he slept like a babe in arms, he read their reply.

I could have killed you while you slept, Em. Don't push me.

"Oh, I don't think so," he muttered. "If you believe I'm so easy to kill, you're not even half the sorcerer you think you are, you coward."

Who was this sorcerer that they'd refused a direct challenge? They had the brass to repeatedly invade his library and steal his books. He had yet to decide on the significance of the novel they'd stolen, this time leaving nothing in its place, the message there unclear to the point of driving him to distraction. And yet they shied from confronting him directly. And then to hide behind their cowardice and taunt him!

He'd about had enough of this nonsense. Clenching his fists, he became aware of the folded note between the knuckles of his other hand. Another sly joke at his expense, that he'd been sleeping so hard, so vulnerable that they could have simply put a knife in his back as easily as the note between his fingers. Not left between the pages of a book this time, they'd given their reply directly.

He should throw it in the fire, but—who was he kidding?— the consuming desire to know what reply they'd composed ahead of time and come here to deliver would never let him destroy the missive unread.

> *My Dearest Em,*
>
> *I'm concerned about your obsession with rabbits, and carrots, and gardeners. It seems rather puerile to create an extended analogy from a children's tale. Some things are random, including most of life. I'm surprised a sorcerer of your advanced years doesn't know that.*
>
> *You may save your blustering and empty threats—rabbit stew, really?—as you clearly lack the power to stop me from taking whatever I wish. It's your great, good luck that I only wish to borrow from your library. Such interesting books you have. I wonder what you're up to with those piles on your desk.*
>
> *Your Thief (a misnomer, as I only borrow . . . so far)*

He read it again, torn between amusement and frustration. *Rabbits, and carrots, and gardeners.* Yes, he was apparently obsessed, to the point that he'd even dreamed—with extraordinary vividness—about a fanged bunny chewing up his books.

And *advanced years?* He snorted, wondering if this could be some young sorcerer testing their mettle against him. It wouldn't be the first time in history. Young people tended toward overconfidence, and young sorcerers even more so. Usually their teachers and academies restrained them from such bold and foolish actions, often forcibly, careful to protect their expensive investments from getting themselves swatted by an irritated magic-worker out of their league.

Every once in a while, though, an especially clever kid evaded the fences erected to protect them and managed to find their target. The histories held several notable examples of those cautionary tales. It should come as no surprise to anyone that the juniors always lost—and usually died, unless the senior was in an exceptionally tolerant mood.

Still, this invader was no kid, of that much Stearanos was sure. The temerity matched that model, but not the thoroughness, the meticulous attention to covering their tracks. No, this person didn't make mistakes and that spoke to the confidence of experience. His thief didn't act out of bravado or impulse. Except . . .

His gaze went to the scribbled reply to his challenge. The notes they'd written previously displayed the perfect, even artful, lettering expected from any magic academy graduate.

Not every sorcerer's greatest skill lay in runes or other inscribed spells, but any magic-worker worth their certification could employ at least rudimentary rune magic, and that required perfect handwriting. That was a disadvantage of using runes—unless you had them prepared ahead of time, they weren't so useful in the heat of battle or other fast-moving attacks. Even if the sorcerer possessed a stone-cold character that enabled them to trace runes with fire raining around them or monsters tearing at their throat, there simply wasn't flexibility to meet a changing attack. One couldn't pivot fast enough. Still, runes were useful for other, less time-sensitive workings, and every graduate learned them.

In contrast, the reply the intruder had written on the spot showed signs of haste, the lettering not so meticulously rendered. It smacked of rare carelessness. His gaze drifted to the quill discarded to the side, askew from where they'd dropped it. Dared he hope?

If the thief had forgotten to erase their remanence from the quill, then it would hold valuable clues. He would not squander this perhaps singular opportunity. The dirt in the vial hadn't told him anything, even after hours of alchemical manipulation, except that it was from a place he'd never been, which only increased his frustration.

Gathering his tools, he used a neutral set of glass forceps to lift the quill and deposit it on a sterile glass plate. He carried it to his work bench on the far side of the library, where he kept a second set of scrying instruments. Truly, he should use his best set, but those were in his arcanium and he didn't want to take the time to climb to the tower room. Remanence faded naturally with time and his best information would come with the thief's touch the freshest.

Calculating the surface area of the quill, its composition, the volume of the empty hollow within, Stearanos reached through the numbers, delicately applying his magic via the equations running through his mind. He might be weak at psychometry, but the wonderful thing about magic was that there were multiple ways to get at any given problem, and he was strong at math. Any time he could apply numbers and quantify his analysis, he could win. This saucy thief would find out who was pushing whom.

Numbers and equations seemed to sparkle through the air around him, though he knew they were visible only to him, an artifact of how he perceived his own magic. A sense formed in his mind, excitement building. Oh yes, they had indeed carelessly left their remanence on the quill.

No . . . *she* had left her remanence there, a deeply feminine resonance to the magic. Startlingly powerful magic, too. So much so that it amazed him that she'd been able to erase her presence as much as she had.

Sorcerers of her level tended to leave pools of magic in their wake, like bloody footprints in the snow. Her magic was as potent as his own, perhaps more so, since he doubted he could erase his trail as effectively, given the same circumstances. In truth, he'd never tried as sneaking about wasn't his forte, not like it clearly was for her.

He concentrated on qualifying her exact magic, which was difficult to discern, occupying an entirely different realm from his. Almost as if she were the flip side of the coin, death to life, though there was no stink of necromancy to her. That would've been beyond unlikely as necromancy had been declared taboo centuries before and any child manifesting that flavor of magic had it burned out of them before it could take root.

Or they were killed, if it already had.

Still, this wasn't death magic. It was . . .

He shot upright, dropping the glass dish so that it shattered against the polished granite surface of the workbench, the quill bouncing away. None of that mattered now. He knew the identity of his thief. It wasn't death magic to his life. It was dreaming to his waking.

The Dream.

His dreams, that fucking fanged bunny chewing up his books, so unnaturally vivid. *She* had put that in his dreams. And the powerful sleep enchantment he'd been unable to fend off, no matter what spells he used to ward it. He kicked himself for being a fool, for missing the many and obvious clues. Only one sorcerer could do what she had done, so easily and with such skill and insouciance, uncaring about the potential backlash of her actions. Only an oneiromancer could step inside his wards, as the Dream was everywhere and nowhere. And only one oneiromancer in existence possessed this kind of power.

Oneira. Fucking Sorceress Oneira.

Stunned, he found himself looking wildly about the library,

as if the infamous sorceress might suddenly appear again. Like a child, he wished for daylight, for high noon, when the potency of the Dream faded with so few dreamers to feed it. No wonder she came at night, in the early morning hours, at the height of her abilities. He supposed he found that vaguely reassuring, that she dared his domain only when she felt strongest.

Don't push me.

That had been no idle boast. She *could* have killed him while he slept, a dozen times over, and him helpless as an infant to defend himself. And why hadn't she? They were enemies, held as threats one against the other for as long as he could remember. All this time he'd rested easy, thinking his much-vaunted wards had prevented just such an assassination. If she could have dispatched him so expediently all these years, why hadn't she? There had to be a reason.

More pointedly, why had she come to his library now?

She'd retired, that's what His Majesty had said. Walked away from it all and vanished. That, however, could be a subterfuge. It would be a brilliant strategy, he had to acknowledge. Create the fiction that his nemesis had stepped off the field of battle and make it appear that the Southern Lands had lost their most formidable defense, thus luring the king into the exact conquest he now contemplated. Stearanos sat in his chair by the window, propping his elbows on his knees and clutching his head in his hands, mind spinning with the implications. A trap. This could all be a massive trap.

If so, however, why would Oneira tip her hand in such an egregious manner? Viewed in this light, her actions in invading his library, engaging in this correspondence, looked utterly irresponsible. And Stearanos didn't think the sorceress would be.

Ruthless, yes. Devastatingly powerful, able to twist minds back against themselves. One well-documented tale in her file detailed how she'd put an entire city—albeit a small one—to sleep, allowing the invading army to sweep in and kill them all while they lay as defenseless as he had. Having experienced her enchantment himself, he didn't doubt a word of it. Purportedly every person had died in those early morning hours, down to the newborn infants, a level of cruelty shocking even to him.

Difficult to reconcile that with the woman who'd left a well-worn children's book as a trade. Or the woman who'd stolen a book on the cultivation of rare roses. Why would the fearsome and loathsome Oneira want Veredian roses?

Unless it was all a deeply crafty method for twisting up his mind. As he'd thought that first morning, she could be under-mining the enemy before he arrived on her shores, making him doubt himself, demonstrating just how vulnerable he was to her least whim. She'd taken what she thought mattered to him. No doubt she'd discerned that he'd been reading that book on rose cultivation, perhaps read his desire for those rare and beautiful blossoms in his dreams, and focused in on that. She wanted him to see himself as a child compared to her, vulnerable, easily ma-nipulated and murdered.

Perhaps she meant to scare him off before the conquest began. Perhaps they meant to invade his own lands. Still, why tip her hand? She could have sprung this trap without baiting him, so there must be a deeper agenda, something he hadn't thought of yet.

Not yet, but he would. She might possess the power of dreams, but he knew strategy. He'd become His Majesty's Eminence for his keen intellect and understanding of war, even as a young man, as much as for his sorcery. He could outwit the oneiromancer.

He knew her identity, his first and best advantage. She'd taken pains to hide that from him, except for that one, telling mistake. Oneira possessed a fiery temper and he'd tripped it with his challenge, annoying her enough to respond hastily to his insult. But would she realize she'd made a mistake?

No, he thought not. She had underestimated him, thinking herself the superior magic-worker, waltzing into his home and taunting him with taking for herself what he dreamed of having, making it clear she thought of him as a child. *You lack the power to stop me from taking whatever I wish.*

She'd also made note of his research, probably laughing at the evidence that he was blithely walking into the trap they'd set.

How to proceed from here? His Majesty would be unlikely to listen. Or, if he did, Uhtric would be that much more determined to wage this war. It would infuriate him to discover that Queen Zarja of the Southern Lands and the sorceress Oneira might have played him. He'd want to show them he couldn't be tricked or cowed. And Stearanos would end up facing Oneira in battle, which could not end well, for anyone.

Before he went to the king, Stearanos needed information. He had to know what Oneira was up to, if she'd truly retired or if this was all a game. He might not be able to travel via the Dream as she could, but he had his ways of finding people. He could locate Oneira and, though she'd likely have warded her home, he'd stake his reputation that he could outmatch any ward she'd created.

Enough of waiting for her to come to him. He was going to her.

16

Oneira tried to focus on reading the novel and couldn't. It felt too much of Stearanos, his presence sifting from the open pages in a slow-moving mist until the sense of him filled the dome. She could only read the thing outside, lest her head fill with *him* instead of the story. Unfortunately, it was pouring rain. Too bad, because she very much liked the novel, a haunting retelling of a princess in hiding and her flying horse. Stearanos might be infuriatingly insulting—calling her a coward!—but he had excellent taste in books. No wonder his library held the reputation it did.

Tossing aside the book with a sigh, she stood, her three companions lifting their heads in harmonious inquiry. They'd all joined her in the dome, the spring storm off the ocean lashing against the crystal in impotent fury. Even Adsila didn't want to fly, tucking her head under her wing and snoozing the afternoon away.

The storm made for quite a show, the rain pounding on the transparent surface of the dome, running in rivers over the curve and falling in a circular waterfall from there. Every once in a while the lowering clouds parted, revealing the rainswept, terribly green landscape and the roiling blue-black sea beyond.

Oneira fretted over her roses, the ghost of Stearanos and his inevitable disapproval hanging as heavy in the air as the dark-bellied clouds. Ridiculous that she should feel any sense of obligation to him. Whether she succeeded in making those roses live—encouraging them to thrive, that was—had nothing to do with Stearanos and his interest in them. "Let him get his own roses," she told the three animals, though they'd all gone back to napping and ignored her.

Moriah hadn't spoken to her again, though Oneira had tried to coax her into it, oddly missing conversation all of a sudden. Bizarre that she'd gone for so long without uttering a word, even to herself, not having the slightest inclination to give voice to her thoughts, and now she craved speaking with another person.

She'd even considered going to visit the ancient gardener, just to satisfy that urge for company, but the gardener would ask after the roses and Oneira had little to report yet. In truth, the roses had begun to look a bit shocked and bedraggled. The book had predicted this, that initially the bushes would droop due to the trauma of transplantation, but Oneira still worried. She couldn't face the gardener until she had good news. Besides which, she hadn't been invited, and Oneira hesitated to trespass again.

Also, the person she really wanted to talk to was the one person she didn't dare go near, ever again. At least she'd stuck to her resolve not to return to the library and its intriguing owner. It had helped to realize that what she'd thought was a playful, even flirtatious interchange, had been in deadly earnest for him. Not that she blamed him—sorcerers were a paranoid lot for good reason and Stearanos famed for his justifiable caution—but calling her out as a coward had been a bridge too far.

Oneira was many things, and many of them she regretted, but she was no coward. In fact, her teachers had often cautioned her about her fearlessness. She tended to go into every situation wholeheartedly, full of blazing confidence. She'd earned that confidence, too, never—all right, rarely—verging into the realm of arrogance, always employing suitable care to guard against errors. Stearanos had no idea whom he'd accused of cowardice.

That much soothed her: he literally had no idea who she was.

She'd held her mental breath that first day, wondering if he'd realize she'd tampered with his dreams and that only one magic-worker in the world could accomplish that feat. Then nothing had happened. She didn't know exactly what she expected, but nothing had and—

Something bumped against her wards.

She immediately stilled, clearing her mind and sharpening her sorcerous senses. Her magic coalesced at full power, a distinct advantage of having not spent it on traveling the Dream. Someone was out there, on the road to the world of men in this blinding storm, attempting to penetrate her wards.

Her heart simultaneously leapt with anticipation and sank in dread trepidation. *Stearanos Stormbreaker.* He'd found her. And he'd come to . . .

No. It wasn't Stearanos, she realized with a crash of what she refused to acknowledge was disappointment. She knew the feel of Stearanos—after all, the miasma of him was all around her, just from one of his books—and no matter what guise he wore, she'd recognize him. This was someone else. A man, weak and injured. No surprise, given the elements.

Bringing her far-sight to bear, she *looked* at him. He stood calf-deep in the mud on the road—which was practically a river, water streaming down the middle in a torrential flood—his sodden horse standing nearby, head down in misery. The man, similarly drenched, his hair blackly sleeked to his scalp, beat the meat of his fists against the invisible barrier of her wards.

"Fool," she murmured. The signs were clearly posted, warning all away from the private property, promising dire retribution to trespassers. He'd have had to pass them all to reach this far. Well, he could die on her doorstep. She didn't care.

"Please!" he shouted against the storm, as if he knew she could hear him, which he couldn't possibly know. "I'm injured and so is my horse. We cannot go back. We'll die out here. I am but a lowly scholar and poet. All I ask is shelter from the storm."

Arrested, Oneira splayed her hands against the cool crystal of the dome, her eyes unfocused as she *looked* and *listened* to the distant plea. The man spoke with a familiar accent, one peculiar to the realm she came from, a small and remote principality. She saw then that he spoke the truth about his injuries, bleeding from his thigh on the same side that his wretched mount showed deep, bloody furrows on its haunch, the relentless rain washing it pink down the horse's leg to join the torrent down the road.

"Please," the man cried again, weakly, sagging to his knees. "My horse is an innocent beast. At least let him in."

Oneira pulled back her attention, glancing around to her three companions, all alert and awake now, gazing at her with intent interest. Tipping back her head, Oneira studied the sky she couldn't see, seeking an answer it didn't have. She loved animals. Always had, and had always gone to pains to spare them in wars whenever possible, which admittedly wasn't often.

And the man, himself, was likely harmless. No magic to him at all. A mere mortal, mundane man could hardly do a thing to harm her, and hadn't she just been wishing for company? A scholar and poet, too. He'd have tales she hadn't heard, possibly books in those bags, saving her from having to visit bookshops or the temptation to raid the Stormbreaker's library again. Or the temptation to have a conversation with the sorcerer.

Having this young man visit, however temporarily, would be the distraction she needed from thinking about the Stormbreaker and his scent, wondering about his scars and his thoughts and what his voice might sound like. That was all loneliness acting upon her, and giving the wayward poet shelter for a night, patching up his wounds, wouldn't give her any trouble. One good deed wouldn't stack up against the many terrible things she'd done, but it was a small step.

And it was surprisingly good to hear the musical accent of her childhood again.

She could let him stay one night and then send him on his way. He'd never even have to know who she truly was. Plenty of recluses employed magical wards like hers. She could play the wealthy and eccentric hermit. Her determination to live a semi-humble life, making her own food and so forth, would add to that appearance. He would stay one night and leave again, never knowing she was the dread sorceress Oneira.

Still, she wasn't past all caution. She took a moment to open the Dream, seeking the vestiges of dreams connected to the man. They were tattered and faded, barely clinging to his waking mind, but what she found revealed nothing untoward. He was exactly what he seemed.

With a thought, she pulled aside the ward on the road like a curtain, the man suddenly falling forward and catching himself on his hands. He stayed there a moment, shaking, on hands and knees. Oneira very much hoped she wouldn't have to go out into the storm to help him. To preserve her cover story of being a simple woman who lived alone, she wouldn't be able to use sorcery to keep herself dry. Good deeds were one thing, but a service of that sort would be a whole other level of selflessness. She was already acting out of character. If she went too far, who knew what would happen?

To her relief, the man's laden horse stepped forward, nudging him, and he grabbed ahold of the gelding's tack, using the support to drag himself up, weeping. Oneira had seen men cry before, but usually in the extremity of war, seeing their homes and families destroyed. To witness a grown man weeping over a relatively minor rescue took her aback, and also reassured her that she'd made the correct choice. No such man could pose a danger to her.

She waited for him to walk past the boundary, holding on to the horse for support with every step, then sealed the wards behind him. From there it wasn't that far up the path to the gate in her walls, though it took a while at the man's pained pace. While she waited, Oneira added a guest room onto the far side of the house, quickly furnishing it with things simple enough to pull from the Dream without her needing to modify them extensively. It would be spare, but that fit the image she wanted to portray.

Pulling on an oilcloth cloak, she drew the hood deeply around her face, hiding her visage just in case. Far-seeing was useful, but didn't substitute for evaluating a person with her own eyes and sorcerous senses. If she recognized the man, she didn't want to be recognized in turn. She also readied a portal to the Dream, poised to summon a night terror to strike at him if anything seemed off, and went to meet him at the gate.

Keeping to her assumed role, she peered through the loops in the wrought iron, as if uncertain and perplexed. "Who are you?" she asked, pretending to be surprised.

"A simple scholar, poet, and traveler, madam," he answered in that so familiar accent. "Seeking shelter." He had very dark eyes, both soft as a deer's and penetrating. Unlike Stearanos, this man had soft lips, almost plush, and a graceful mien. No scars on his pale skin. "I can pay," he added, gaze wandering up to the white house rising above the garden walls, the tower above, his expression creasing with uncertainty as he realized that might not be a persuasive argument. His dark eyes returned to hers and he offered a crooked smile, a sensual cant to it. "In whatever coin my lady desires."

Bunny appeared at Oneira's side—he must have come through the tunnel—and pressed against her legs, baring his fangs in a canine grin at their visitor, forked black tongue flicking out to taste his scent.

The man visibly startled, blanching even paler under his already fair complexion. "What *is* that?" he breathed in stark terror, though retaining enough presence of mind to hold on to his horse's bridle as the gelding shied, trying to jerk away.

Oneira set a hand on Bunny's shoulder. "My dog. He won't harm you."

"Your *dog* . . ." The man's gaze rose to hers, gratifying admiration in them. "Who are you that you command such a fierce creature?"

And that was him unable to recognize the dark magic that formed the *scáthcú*'s very being. Wait until he met Moriah. "A simple woman," she replied. "Bunny, off with you. You're frightening our guests." With a reproachful look, Bunny trotted off.

"Bunny," the man echoed with a bemused smile.

"I will offer you hospitality." She pushed open the gate, remembering at the last moment to do it manually. This would be a good exercise for her to become more aware of the small ways she still used magic out of habit. "Welcome."

He stepped through the gate and into the rain-drenched garden, looking about in wonder, the first human besides herself to see the place. "It's so beautiful."

"Thank you." She was remarkably pleased by the praise, wanting to tell him she'd made it herself, though, naturally, she couldn't.

"Is there a place to stable my horse?"

Kicking herself for forgetting such a basic aspect of mundane life, Oneira gestured vaguely toward the back of the house. "I can take care of your horse," realizing as she said the words that she had no earthly idea what that entailed, and that a lady of her apparent status wouldn't make that offer.

He shook his head and smiled. It was a sweet smile, almost

boyish. "I couldn't possibly stand by and allow a lady to do such work in my stead. I'm not so injured that I can't care for my steed."

While he was talking, Oneira hastily found a small stable in the Dream and pulled it onto the back of the house, hoping it would be more or less right. She hadn't actually ever been inside of one, but how complex could they be? It should have hay, probably. Also horse brushes. Did she have any books on equine care in her collection? No doubt Stearanos did, and probably shelved under something absurd like grooming long hair or vegetarian diets. "Mine is quite simple," she told him, "and has never been used, so please let me know if it lacks anything."

He cocked his head, curious, raindrops beading from his soaked hair and running down the soft skin of his handsome face. "You don't keep a horse?"

"I never go anywhere," she answered.

His gaze roved over the house, taking everything in, then he bowed, all grace and courtesy. "I am Tristan. Well met, Lady . . . ?"

Ach. She needed a name, and not the infamous one of a dread sorceress. "Lira," she answered, figuring it close enough in sound that she'd answer to it.

He extended a hand and she stared at it, bemused, then recognized it as a courtly gesture. People had not ever used it with her, always superstitious of touching her, as if she could send them into the Dream in a moment. She could, of course, but she didn't need to touch them to do it. Extracting a hand from her cloak, she laid it in Tristan's, momentarily taken aback by the feel of his skin, as soft as it looked. How long had it been since she touched someone? Forever. Since long before she retired.

He bent over her hand, kissing the back of it, a velvet caress even more stirring. "I am your servant, Lady Lira."

She found herself flushing. Had anyone ever touched or spoken to her so? Never. She both wanted more and shied away from the stirrings deep inside. Withdrawing her hand from his, she said, "Stable your horse and come inside."

She turned and went into the house, feeling his gaze on her back and suspecting that she hadn't carried off being ordinary very well. Alas for that, and alas for the normal woman she'd somehow never managed to be, in any lifetime.

17

Oneira hung up her sodden cloak, grateful to be out of the storm, and oddly flustered by the interaction with Tristan. She smoothed her hair, wondering how she looked, and turned to find Moriah observing her with a canny expression. "I have offered the man, Tristan, hospitality," she informed the big cat. "Please do not make a liar of me."

If a cat could raise her brows, Moriah did. Then she ambled off, no promises made. Oneira checked the fire, then remembered to make it real and not magical, and added wood for it to burn. She put some towels and a robe in the vestibule, leaving them for Tristan. Satisfied she'd fulfilled human-hostessing expectations, she went to the kitchen to heat soup. She'd baked bread that morning, so it was warm and fresh, filling the kitchen with homey, yeasty scents. Tristan should like that—and then she wondered why she cared about pleasing Tristan.

He's a handsome, vigorous young man who thinks you're but an ordinary, lonely woman. And you've been alone too long.

She'd had lovers, here and there in her life, but those sessions had never gone well. The men had always been either frightened of her and irritatingly subservient, or determined not to be frightened of her and obnoxiously overpowering. Neither type had provided much pleasure and she'd given up the entire business as more of a waste of time and energy than it was worth. Perhaps it would be different with a man of her same status, but sorcerous types didn't consort with one another, for obvious reasons.

With Tristan, however, with his knowing nothing about her,

perhaps it would be different. Again she found herself blushing and rolled her eyes to the ceiling, hung with dried herbs from her garden. The handsome poet was likely half her age, or even a third, considering how long she'd lived. She might not look it, but she felt every year inside. In truth, she'd thought that part of her had died, but apparently it had only been slumbering, awakening at the brush of Tristan's kiss and soft skin. *Desire*. Something she'd never imagined feeling again or wanting.

Would it be wrong to have him? He would be gone again soon enough and it wasn't as if men flocked to her gate—entirely her fault, what with the wards, but still—and Tristan was so harmless. Charming. Sweet. And those full lips that—

"Smells good."

She jumped, so preoccupied with her prurient thoughts that she hadn't heard him enter the kitchen, nor had she sensed his presence. Harmless he might be, but that was no excuse to have her guard so utterly lowered. She'd grown lazy and comfortable, being alone so long, so that her once-reflexive and constant scanning of her surroundings had faded away over time. *Bad sorceress*, she scolded herself, before turning with a warm smile to greet her guest.

He'd toweled his hair dry and it stood in disarrayed waves, not dark at all, but a lovely silver-blond shade, paler than his skin and setting off his dark eyes with seductive contrast. Smiling crookedly at her, he plucked at the robe, then gestured toward the front door. "I left my clothes in the vestibule. They're soaked and filthy, so I didn't want to bring them any farther inside. My packs are there, too, as I wasn't sure where to . . . ?" He trailed off, smile abashed and hopeful. She wanted to kiss those tempting lips and comb her fingers through that thick hair. This man, she could touch without fear.

"Leave the clothes," she replied, finding herself smiling back, a giddy stretch of her warm cheeks. "I'll show you to the guest room so you can stow your bags. I imagine you'd like a hot bath?"

"I want to say I'd kill for a hot bath," he replied, grin widening so his dimples showed, "but I don't want to frighten my beautiful hostess." He paused, gaze traveling over her. "I couldn't see you before, in that enveloping cloak, but you are astoundingly lovely. That crimson hair . . ."

Oh, how she blushed, ducking her head to hide it. This was really too much for her to handle. She felt like an awkward girl again, singularly unequipped to handle a man's attentions. Had it really been so long since anyone flirted with her? Yes. Yes, it had. Which was likely why she'd read flirting into the notes Stearanos had left her. And why she'd behaved so recklessly.

"I apologize," Tristan said ruefully into her extended silence. "I am clearly off my head from all that's happened. I usually have better manners than this."

"No," she replied hastily, prodding herself to have some composure. "I should apologize, keeping you standing here when you're exhausted, cold, and injured. Come this way." She led him through the house, none of the animals in evidence. He limped a little as they went. "Once you wash, I can bandage your wounds, if you like. I have a salve that heals and numbs the pain."

"I would be eternally grateful for that, my lady." He paused as they passed her bier, giving the wilted spring blossoms from the day before—she hadn't gathered new ones due to the rain—a curious look. "Is this an altar?"

"Of a sort, yes." She swept past the bier, slightly embarrassed that he'd noticed it and grateful that he'd offered an alternative explanation for it. "You can put your bags in here." She stepped aside so he could enter the guest room, giving it a last once-over. It seemed like the expected things were there.

"Beyond expectations," he said, giving her a long look that made her wonder if he meant more than just the room.

"The bathing chamber is this way." She'd indulged herself mightily with the bathing room, building a deep soaking pool from various happy dreams, along with a heated brazier that could be sprinkled with water to make steam. This was one luxury from her former life she was unwilling to forsake. So many times, after terrible battles and grueling duels, she'd soaked away the blood and horror in baths like this. All the nobles had similar facilities, and she'd ruthlessly used her position to claim first and exclusive access to them.

Tristan whistled in appreciation, taking in the elegant chamber. "I feel as if I've stumbled into an old tale—the palace with every comfort, fine food, and the most beautiful woman I've ever seen offering to tend my wounds." The smile he gave her was almost shy, making her feel both delighted and tender toward him.

"Soak as long as you like," she said. "I'll tend to your horse's injuries in the meanwhile."

"Thank you." His voice, that lovely lyrical accent she hadn't heard in so long, resonant with sincere warmth as he bowed to her. Straightening, he ventured a slight smile, meeting and holding her gaze. "I don't suppose you'd like to . . ." He gestured toward the steaming water.

She would like to. Very much. Too much. She'd only just met the man. If she decided she wanted him enough to take him to her bed, there was time to come to that conclusion. She would not be hasty. Backing up a step, she shook her head. "I'll look after your horse and see to the soup. After a while, I'll check on you."

"Of course, my lady." He blushed with self-effacing charm. "I don't mean to keep you from your accustomed activities. A lady of your stature no doubt has far better things to do than waste time keeping company with a scraggly wanderer the likes of me."

She almost corrected him, nearly said that she couldn't think of anything else she should be doing, but the horse—yes, the horse needed tending and she needed time to reflect, gather her thoughts, and reason logically. "I'll be back."

"I'll be counting the minutes." He shrugged out of the robe, letting it fall, and stood before her naked. Tall, lean, with finely formed limbs, he was gloriously handsome, his skin smooth and free of scars, except for the deep scratches on his left thigh. They'd scabbed over, bleeding only lightly now.

Oneira tried to look only at the injury, and not his long cock. It wasn't erect, but it wasn't entirely soft either, head nestling out from his foreskin, his scrotum heavy and darker, all of it free of hair. "The injury doesn't look too bad," she observed, in part to maintain the fiction that she wasn't ogling him like a fancy pastry. "Are you in pain?"

She raised her eyes to his and found him watching her with his dark gaze, his sensuous lips serious, as he posed for her. "Barely at all. You could . . . examine me more closely."

"Later," she replied, quickly averting her gaze.

"The offer is open, beautiful Lira," he murmured.

Abashed, Oneira fled, face hot and blood stirring hotter.

Working with the gelding calmed her agitation. Tristan had set the tack aside and groomed the horse to gleaming, another example of the young man's thoughtfulness and diligent care. The horse happily munched the fragrant hay Tristan had placed on the floor for him. Oneira would have to obtain some real hay for the creature, lest he starve on the Dream variety. At least it seemed to taste good.

NEVER THE ROSES · 155

As she ran her fingers over his glossy hide, examining the scratches, which were not so deep as she'd originally supposed, Oneira imagined Tristan grooming the gelding—and how those long, clever fingers would feel on her body.

The offer is open. And he'd called her beautiful, more than once. She knew herself to be comely enough, though even as a young woman, no one would've called her pretty. As she'd matured, she'd grown into her rather strong-boned face and vivid coloring. Still, physical beauty had never mattered much to her, especially amid the courts of men, where fawning flattery made every compliment sound insincere and like a path toward losing her better judgment. Besides which, beauty only goes skin-deep, and she was horrifically rotten beneath it all.

But Tristan didn't know that about her. Innocent to the point of naïveté, he looked at her and saw . . . if not true beauty, then something that attracted him. The way he looked at her made her *feel* beautiful, believing in the possibility as she never had before. It would be an indulgence to have him, but fate had also dropped him in her lap, perhaps for a reason. *Even the sages do not know how the heart heals,* Moriah had said. It could be that taking this lovely, charming young man to her bed would be healing. She would maybe feel, if not pure or innocent again, then at least like this woman she might have been. In Tristan's arms, enjoying his caresses and ardent words, she could pretend to be young and carefree, the sort of easy and open woman who enjoyed her lovers.

Not a murderess and destroyer of realms. If only for a little while.

The horse's scratches salved, Oneira returned to the house, made sure the soup remained on low simmer, then went to check on Tristan. Outside the bathing chamber door, she hesitated, smoothing her skirts with damp palms. Knocking lightly—why, as Tristan clearly wasn't modest? Quite the reverse—she opened the door and peeked in, half expecting him to be asleep in the steaming water. Instead he'd turned his head, giving her a wide and happy smile, stretching his finely made arms along the rim of the tub.

"This is glorious, Lady Lira," he said, gaze caressing her. "I can't thank you enough."

"No need for thanks," she replied, blushing as much as before. Was she seventeen years old again? She certainly felt that way.

"How is Galahad?"

"I beg your pardon?"

"My horse," he explained with a sweetly chagrined wince. "Over the top, I know, but I'm a poet, so I can't help myself." He shrugged. "Everyone, even horses, should have important, meaningful names, don't you think? What does Lira mean?"

"I have no idea," she answered with perfect honesty. So far as she knew, the hastily concocted name meant nothing. "And Galahad is fine. I believe the scratches will heal cleanly, though I have no talent for healing. I do have the salve, however." She held up the tub of ointment she'd used on the horse, a salve she'd acquired to treat her own scratches, mostly from the rose thorns. "I can leave it here for you. And these bandages."

"I'd hoped you'd tend me," Tristan said with a searching look. "Unless you'd prefer not to? I promise to be a perfect gentleman. Or if you're too busy . . ."

"Not at all," she assured him. "I can come back."

"No, I'll get out." He made a show of moving lethargically, standing in the waist-deep water and stretching with languorous sensuality, drawing and holding her gaze as water sheeted off his long, lovely form. "Such a luxury to soak like this. How do you keep the water hot?"

Oneira turned away, busying herself with organizing the

bandages and not only because he'd started climbing the steps, revealing his glorious nakedness, and she didn't trust herself not to gawk. She also needed to hide her face in case her irritation at her laxness showed. Oh, how she'd congratulated herself on not using magic and here it was everywhere in the simplest conveniences. "Geothermal," she said, excitedly hitting upon a plausible answer.

"Here, on a cliff above the ocean?" Tristan asked from much too close. But he also picked up the robe, his hand reaching past in her peripheral vision, so soon he'd be safely covered up.

"The house was built on top of a hot spring," she answered with a shrug, simply a rich recluse who took things at face value, who didn't need to know how things worked, just so long as they did. "So I was told when I bought the place," she added, to forestall further questions.

He sat down on the bench, wiping his face with a towel. "A puzzle, to be sure." Drawing aside the robe, he bared his lean thigh, lightly furred with silvery-pale hair, the angry furrows marring his otherwise perfect form. "What do you think?"

Oneira swallowed back any number of answers to that question, kneeling down and ignoring that Tristan had opened the robe more than necessary, giving her enticing glimpses between his slightly spread thighs, tempting her to slide a hand into that warm crevice. She made herself focus on the scratches and nothing else. The soaking had taken most of the blood away, leaving the skin pink, the edges of the shallow scratches even and not ragged. Galahad's had been the same. "How did this happen?" she asked, running a light finger along the edge of one, enjoying the way he twitched under the touch.

"A mountain cat. It leapt out of nowhere, catching my thigh with one paw and Galahad's flank with the other."

She frowned, puzzled. "They're so shallow for an attack like that."

"We were lucky," Tristan replied fervently, as if agreeing with something she'd said. "I am lucky that Galahad is so bold and fast, that he outran the beast. But then, in that headlong flight, we must have taken the wrong fork. I was terrified," he confided, "and not paying attention as I should have been, imagining those claws sinking into my back at any moment. By the time I realized we were lost, the storm hit and I couldn't see past Galahad's ears. I think we walked face-first into your wards." His voice softened to a purr. "Did I mention lucky?"

She glanced up at the change in tone, finding those dark eyes fastened on her with artless admiration. He picked up a strand of her hair where it streamed over her shoulder, lifting it and running his sensitive fingers down the length of it. "Your hair is such an extraordinary color; I've only seen this shade once, back in my home realm. I haven't been back in years, but I remember it vividly. It turned up regularly in certain families."

"Where are you from?" she asked, knowing the answer and also knowing that would be the logical question.

"A very small kingdom that no one has ever heard of." Tugging lightly on the lock of hair, his smile went teasing. "Perhaps one of your ancestors came from there."

"Perhaps so." She made sure to sound like she didn't think it likely. Drawing her hair from his light grasp, Oneira reached for the salve. "I think your wounds are clean enough from the soaking. I'll just apply this salve and bandage lightly. As you noted, you were lucky."

"I know," he said, leaning back a little as if to give her more room, parting his legs farther. "You have a lovely touch."

She tried to ignore his distracting nearness and her near-constant blushing, brushing the salve lightly over his wounds so as not to hurt him. To keep her thoughts on healing, she attempted to think of it as just like putting the salve on Galahad, but that led her straight back to the fantasies she'd brewed in the little stable, imagining Tristan's hands on her, which only worsened her growing desire. It felt so good to touch another person, his skin hot and steaming in the bathing chamber, his breath increasing as he responded to her touch in return.

Done with the salve, she wrapped the bandage around his thigh, mostly to keep the wounds clean. Deftly, she tied the knot, then looked up. He watched her with that same disarmingly rapt expression, a bead of moisture caught on his full upper lip that she badly wanted to kiss away. "There," she said, trying to sound brisk. "That should hold."

"You're good at this," he replied with a note of surprise. "I thought you said you didn't know healing."

No, she'd said she didn't have a talent for it, meaning her magic didn't lie in that arena and which had been careless of her. Still, she'd spent most of her life on one battlefield or another. When her magic ran out, she'd still wanted to be useful, and had picked up a few tricks from the always overworked healers. "We are plagued by endless wars. It's good to know basic field dressing."

"True." But he frowned. "Still, a lady such as yourself . . ."

"Even wealthy ladies like to be useful now and again."

"I didn't mean to offend."

"You didn't," she said with perfect honesty and stood. "Shall we eat? I'm sure you're hungry."

"*Starving*," he replied, also standing and testing his leg. "It feels so much better," he observed with a note of wonder. "Thank you."

"You're welcome," she said with equal gravity, aware of how close they stood, that delicious-looking mouth so near her own.

"How can I repay you, lovely Lady Lira?" he asked throatily, raising a hand to touch her cheek. "It's traditional for a damsel in distress to offer a kiss to her rescuer, but . . ."

But. Her mouth was dry. Her body throbbing with longing.

Did she dare? What harm was there in a kiss? She was playing by old rules that no longer applied, and there was no earthly reason why she shouldn't have this. "A kiss would be nice," she answered, her voice hoarse.

He didn't smile, eyes flaring darkly, face solemn with desire. Raising his other hand, he threaded his fingers into her hair at both temples, combing them through until he lightly cupped her head, bending to lower his lips to hers. He brushed her lips with his, soft as silk, hot as a brand burning through her. Something that was clenched inside her released, loosened, and billowed into being like a rose blooming from a tightly locked bud. She melted, daring to put her hands on his shoulders, then slid them up his neck and into his hair, so thick, slick and textured in her hands.

After a long, lingering kiss, Tristan pulled back and took her hand, smiling with playful delight. "We're not standing here kissing in this steam room. There's time for more kisses, if you want them, lovely Lira."

She did want them. More and more and more. "And you are hungry."

"Oh yes," he breathed. "And also I need food. Come on." He tugged her hand, pulling her to the door.

Laughing, light and delighted and carefree as she'd never been, Oneira went with him.

18

Perhaps this was indeed how the heart healed, Oneira reflected, as she sat eating the simple meal across from Tristan. At his suggestion, they'd pulled over a small table to sit in front of the fire, and the warm flickers shone rosy in his silver hair, gilding his fair skin. With the rain drumming on the roof and the wind howling like a pack of *scáthcú* beyond her white walls, it was cozy, even intimate, sharing the meal with him. An entirely new experience for her.

He'd asked if she had any wine. Naturally, the wealthy woman she pretended to be would have, so she pulled a few bottles of a rich red from the Dream, hoping it would at least taste right. Apparently it was real enough to have alcohol content—thank you, vivid dreamers—and she was slightly tipsy, warmed from within by the soup and wine, and from without by Tristan's lavish compliments and scintillating company.

Quickly discerning she had no interest in hearing about politics or other events current in the world of men, Tristan entertained her by reciting poetry and relating epic tales of bravery and foolishness. He held her rapt with fascination, then had her helplessly giggling. *Her*, actually giggling. If only her detractors could see the dread sorceress Oneira in that moment. Would they call her the cruel, ruthless ice queen now? Or would they sneer at her giddiness, not understanding what this meant?

She didn't care either way. For once in her life, she was living in the moment, relishing Tristan's unsubtle courtship. He seemed to know just how to tease her to draw her out and when to back off, noticing when she grew nervous. Sometimes he picked up her hand where it rested on the table, gently toying with her fingers and holding her gaze, that stirring intensity in his. Then he backed off, giving her time to adjust to her changed circumstances and the sometimes alarmingly potent sensual charisma he exuded.

After a time, they'd eaten all they could hold, and sat back, sipping wine. "You have an excellent cook," Tristan sighed happily, patting his flat belly. He still wore the robe and it parted over the hard planes of his chest, silvered with small, silky-looking hairs.

"I *am* the cook," she replied with a smile that felt smug even to herself. After her many early failures, she felt justifiably proud of herself for her hard-won skills, enjoying Tristan's praise for the perfectly crisp crust and meltingly tender interior of her fresh bread, the delicately seasoned vegetable soup, hearty and tasting of high summers past, as much as his comments on her loveliness. She realized her misstep when he raised his brows in surprise.

"You have no cook?" he asked, looking around as if he expected one to appear. "I thought perhaps she was caught in town in the storm."

That would've been an excellent excuse, had Oneira thought of it. Too late now. Besides which, there was no town within leagues, part of why she'd picked this particular spot. "I have no servants. I prefer it that way."

"You live totally alone." He made it sound tragic.

"I'm not alone," she replied, a bit tartly. "I have my animals." Who had not put in an appearance since she'd let Tristan into the house. Perhaps they were sulking. "And I like the solitude," she added.

Tristan watched her closely, solemnly listening. "It sounds like a lonely life to me, but you must have your reasons."

She did, of course, and all of those reasons welled up in a roar, a cacophony of suffering and blood and death that forced tears to well up in her eyes, and she looked away so he wouldn't see. Too late.

He took her hand, rubbing a thumb softly over the back of it. "I'm sorry," he said softly. "I didn't mean to make you sad, lovely Lira."

"You didn't," she lied, dashing the tears away. She was more than tipsy; she was drunk. "I should clear the dishes."

He let her go without protest and she stacked their plates and silverware, carrying it all to the kitchen. Rain still lashed against the windows, driven by the gale howling off the ocean, invisible out there in the night, but making itself known in all its ferocity. When she returned to the fire, Tristan was standing before it, casually holding his mug of wine and studying the coiled hank of yarn she'd made of Bunny's fur. Flushing with embarrassment, Oneira wished she'd hidden the ugly thing, or burned it, as there was no reason to have kept it.

Hearing her approach, Tristan glanced over his shoulder, then indicated the yarn on the mantel. "Is this an artwork? It's so unusual." He grinned. "I'm betting on a gift from someone you didn't wish to offend. Otherwise, why keep something so ugly?"

Why, indeed? "I find it interesting," she answered, which was mostly true.

"She is as mysterious as she is beautiful," he observed without rancor. Setting aside his wine, he came to her, taking her hands and lacing their fingers together. "Now what?" he asked quietly.

The question needed no further elaboration. Did she want to take him to her bed? She did and she didn't. She wasn't sure and it seemed that she *should* be sure. Still, this choice wasn't about a critical strategic decision point in a war. It was about a night of pleasure—hopefully, anyway—and simple joys that she should be able to grasp without making it into a referendum on her entire life. One night with a handsome, wandering poet who *wanted* her. When would she have another opportunity like this? Probably never.

Still, it felt like a turning point and Oneira had never been one to take risks. Not until recently. Still, that's what this was, no matter how she talked herself around it: she would be risking something here, her inner voice warned, even if she couldn't identify what it might be.

"Not tonight," she heard herself saying. "Not yet."

Instead of disappointment, a pleased smile quirked over his sensual lips. "Not tonight, not yet, but . . . maybe later?"

"Maybe later," she confirmed, relaxing in the knowledge that he wouldn't push. "Maybe tomorrow."

"Then I can stay?" he asked hesitantly. "A day or two more, though we agreed that I'd impose on your hospitality for only the one night, and I know you value your solitude."

How refreshing to find a man who listened to her, who paid attention to what she cared about. "I would like you to stay."

He grinned radiantly and lifted her hands, bending over to kiss the backs of her fingers, then looking up at her. "And I would love to stay. Good night, my lovely lady."

"Good night."

Giving her a last, softly chaste kiss, he stepped away and bowed, then walked off to his room, humming a tune, taking his full wineglass with him.

Oneira watched him go, telling herself she'd made the smart decision, that there would be tomorrow. That she wasn't disappointed with his easy capitulation.

She woke in the morning to silence, clear-dawn skies beyond her crystal dome, and a triad of animals looking at her. They didn't say anything, of course, and Oneira told herself she imagined the accusation in their eyes. What could they possibly castigate her for? Perhaps they didn't care to have *their* solitude interrupted.

Well, they didn't have to put up with Tristan, if they didn't want to. This was her house and she hadn't asked any of them to come live with her. Feeling cranky and realizing that overindulging in the wine had left her with a dull headache and foul taste in her mouth, she groggily crawled out of her pillow nest and went down a level to refresh herself and dress. To her annoyance, she discovered that her menses had chosen that opportunity to present itself, soaking through her undergarments in bloody glee. Just as well she hadn't shared a bed with the tempting Tristan. Living alone, she hadn't much bothered to keep track of her menstrual cycle. It came and went regularly—she'd never been one to suffer much pain with it—and it didn't really matter either way.

The appearance of it now provided a salient reminder, however, that she hadn't given any thought to the possibility of conceiving a child with Tristan, had she succumbed to temptation the night before. Always in the past, she'd been in the courts of men, and men at court were eternally concerned about not being saddled with children to support, even gotten on a sorceress worth more coin than they would ever see. Perhaps Tristan had thought of it, but it didn't speak well of her own state of mind that she hadn't.

For a moment, as she brushed out her hair, watching herself thoughtfully in the one mirror in the house, she considered that she *could* have a baby at this juncture in her life. Her body was clearly still capable and she had nothing but free time to devote to raising a child. Or children. She didn't delude herself that the itinerant Tristan would stay forever. In truth, she caught herself frowning at the prospect of him staying forever. That would require her to confess her actual identity, at which point everything between them would inevitably change.

But there was no reason she couldn't keep his child. She doubted he would care. Men didn't, so long as they were absolved of responsibility, and Tristan struck her as the type happy to be absolved of any and all responsibilities. It was part of his charm. Setting the brush down and turning her face side to side, she imagined herself as a mother. Not an idea she'd tried on before, but why had she retired if not for something like this? Perhaps *this* was the question she'd been looking to answer. Having a child would certainly stave off boredom.

Turning her body profile, she smoothed her hands over her flat belly. Never voluptuous by any stretch, she'd lost weight during her exile, eating nothing but bread, soup, and roasted vegetables. Tristan had asked about dessert the night before and she'd been nearly startled by the concept. She'd had to tell him she had none, with no opportunity to seek some out in the Dream for him. Just as well—if dreamers dreamed wine accurately, they tended to dream sweets all wrong, making them all appearance and lacking substance, not unlike books. Perhaps she could learn to bake cookies. Children liked cookies, didn't they?

Plucking the loose folds of her gown, she held it out, mimicking a pregnant belly, then huffed a disgusted breath. She knew nothing about babies and children; she knew only dealing death, not creating life. Maybe if she could keep her roses alive . . .

As she descended from her tower, a song made its way through the silent house. Tristan, singing in an off-key tenor. It made her smile and she picked up her pace, eager to see him. She found him in the kitchen, the place entirely in disarray with all the things he'd pulled out and heaped on the counters. She'd left the kitchen clean and orderly the night before. It irritated her unreasonably to see it in chaos.

Seeing her come in, Tristan gave her an abashed grin, shrugging boyishly. "I was looking for eggs. Maybe some bacon? Or ham."

"I don't have any meat," she told him. "There's bread and honey. Or I can make a porridge of grains."

He made a face. "I had my heart set on bacon and eggs."

"Your heart will have to set on something else." Not even to please him would she bring death inside her white walls. Too much of it hung about her shoulders, invisible and reeking like a charnel pit, for her to add to it.

"I apologize," Tristan said, wincing and coming around to set his hands on her hips, giving her a winning smile. "I woke up ferociously hungry and I thought I'd make you breakfast, that it would be romantic. Let me start over. Good morning, lovely Lady Lira. You are as beautiful as the dawn over the ocean."

He did have a knack for being pleasing. She relented, aware of her own crankiness. She'd lived alone so long that she'd grown used to the simple pleasure of things remaining exactly where she'd left them. "Thank you, and no apologies necessary. I have a bit of a wine headache myself. Let me make us some tea."

"No coffee?" he inquired hopefully, hitching himself onto one of the stools at the overburdened counter.

She shook her head, then regretted it as a bit of dizziness swirled up. "Tea," she repeated, filling the kettle on the stove from the jug she kept there. She'd have to fetch more water from the stream. She lit the fire under the silver kettle with matches, then surveyed her dried herbs. "I have thyme, bergamot, chamomile, or tansy." Deciding on a soothing combination of bergamot and chamomile for her uneasy constitution, she drew those bunches down.

Tristan was watching in consternation. "I don't know what those are."

"And you call yourself a scholar."

"Mostly a poet," he clarified.

"Herbs. I grew them myself."

"I'll have what you're having then." He didn't sound thrilled, but so it went. No more pulling edibles from the Dream. That could explain the effects of the wine. Though Tristan seemed untouched, so probably it was simply that she hadn't drunk any in so long. And being off-balance from her menses beginning, too. "You live in an odd mix of magical conveniences and manual labor," Tristan commented, breaking into her thoughts.

"Hmm." She made the sound noncommittal to discourage further discussion, opening the windows and glass-paned doors to the lovely morning, allowing in the rain-washed air and the purring of the surf, quiet now, having spent the storm's energy. She put away the food and pans Tristan had gotten out. Restoring order soothed her, calming her irritation, making her wonder if Stearanos had developed or indulged his own obsessiveness for this reason. The two of them might be a horrible mess inside their heads, but at least their surroundings could be peaceful.

"You have those extraordinary wards," Tristan continued blithely. "And the bathing chamber—one of the fanciest magical conveniences I've encountered. But then you live without servants, growing your own food, baking your own bread."

She nearly asked if there was a question in there somewhere, but that would be aggressive and she didn't want to be unkind. His curiosity about her was natural. She'd have been surprised if he hadn't wondered. It would be paranoid to interpret the remarks as him digging for information. "Thermal pools," she reminded him, sticking to her previous lie. "The wards were expensive, yes, but I am a woman alone."

"True," he said, though his gaze lingered on her as if he thought to say something else.

The tea kettle whistled at that point—a sound like a cardinal's fluting call, the entire reason she'd acquired that particular one from a vivid dream—and she poured the steaming water into their cups, setting one before him where he sat. "Let it steep a few minutes," she advised, following her own advice and finishing putting everything away while she waited.

Deciding upon porridge, she set the grains soaking with the remaining water in the jug, then sliced the last of the bread for toasting, to tide them over while they waited. Thinking ahead, she started dough for more loaves. Tristan was chattering on, talking about various magical conveniences he'd encountered, detailing how they worked. She listened with half an ear, as he was explaining things she already knew, and far better than he did, though he couldn't know that about her. He was harmless and her tea tasted good, calming her unsettled system as she'd hoped.

"Bread and honey?" she asked when he paused for breath.

"Sure." He sipped his tea finally, wrinkling his nose a little.

"Not to your taste?" she inquired, smearing a generous portion of honey onto the toasted bread. If she got the bread at the right temperature, the honey warmed and formed a lightly crunchy border where it met the bread. A quiet delight she never failed to enjoy.

"Do you have sugar?" he asked.

Finishing with the toast for herself also, she put the honey pot next to the plate she set before him. "Honey," she said with a smile, reminding him.

"Sweetheart," he said with an answering smile, reminding her of all she found charming in him.

She added last autumn's dried berries to the stewing grains so they would soften and add their sweet redolence to the porridge, then took a bite of her honeyed toast, closing her eyes in pleasure. Perfect. Followed by a sip of the flavorful tea, she relished this simple joy.

"You look so sensual right now," Tristan said softly, reminding her that she had an audience.

Opening her eyes, she gave him a smile, noticing he'd already wolfed down his own toast. Young men. "Would you like another?"

"You know what I would like?" He stood and came around the counter and took the cup of tea she'd been cradling in her hands, setting it aside. Leaning back against the counter, he gently drew her into his embrace, bending his head to kiss her. The caress of lips sent a flutter of sweet desire through her. More familiar to her this time, she savored the soft sensuality of his lips, the expert stoking of passion. "Mmm," he murmured against her mouth. "You taste like honey."

With a mischievous quirk of that clever mouth, he reached for the pot of honey, dipped in the tip of his finger, and drew it across her bottom lip. The sticky honey contrasted with his smooth finger, sending sensations all through her, her body warming further, her sex blooming and aching to be also touched. Tristan put his honeyed finger in his mouth, pursing his full lips around it as he sucked, and she'd never seen anything so innocent and blatantly sexual at the same time.

He lowered his mouth to hers, kissing her lightly, then licking the honey from her lower lip, before drawing her lip into his mouth, sucking on it with growing intensity. Moaning, she let herself melt against him. Never had she experienced this sort of slow seduction—and the attendant arousal. No one had taken the time to savor her mouth as if she were delicious.

Tristan nipped her lower lip, catching it in his teeth teasingly, so that she shuddered with need, then released it. Skimming a hand up her waist, he cupped her breast, grazing her taut nipple with his thumb, his mouth feeding on hers with warm, lingering kisses. "Delicious Lira," he purred, "would you come to my bed?"

Her mind bleary, she considered the question. A hot surge of moisture between her thighs reminded her. It could be her arousal, but it might also be her menses. Some men minded that. "My menses began in the night," she told him, watching him carefully. "I'm a heavy bleeder. I don't mind, but if you do?"

And there it was: a flicker of disgust, quickly hidden. "Bad timing," he replied ruefully. "But perhaps this means I can stay a few days longer? In the meanwhile, we can indulge in other ways."

He kissed her more, teasing her tongue with his, then slid his thigh between hers. Holding her by the hips, he lifted his thigh until she was riding it, the pressure such an intense sensation that she gasped, clinging to his shoulders, digging her nails into his bare skin. He still wore the robe with nothing beneath, and it had parted considerably during their play, falling off one shoulder entirely. Kissing her deeply, Tristan rocked her on his thigh, the climax building in her with astonishing rapidity.

She came with a cry that sounded agonized, the orgasm wrenching and wringing her, a purging wave unlike anything she'd experienced before. As if a lifetime of tension, stress, and the dregs of violence had built to a pressure point within her and burst forth. Oneira laughed then, throwing her head back and releasing that, too, a cascading riff of release. With effort, she trawled back the magic wanting to burst from her before it could sparkle in the air, making itself visible even to Tristan's mundane eyes.

Gathering herself, she pulled her gaze to Tristan's face, ready with some explanation. But at that moment, something hit her wards.

Hard and fast.

19

As Oneira staggered from the force of it, Tristan steadied her, nuzzling her neck, taking her hand and drawing it inside his robe. "That was a lovely start, now how about—"

"Shh!" She cut him off with abrupt impatience, struggling out of his oblivious, clinging embrace. She was a fool to have lost her head so completely, to have been so complacent. Her wards had held, but they wouldn't continue to do so without her full attention. Even then, judging by the force of the blow, they might soon crumple.

Tristan still held on to her wrist, trying to tug her back, laughing playfully.

"Stop," she told him, twisting out of his grip. "Something is testing my—the house wards."

He looked around at the sunny kitchen, birdsong and distant surf flowing in. "How can you tell—is there an alarm?"

"Yes," she answered, figuring she could concoct one later. "Be quiet, in case they knock again. I need to pay attention."

He shrugged, then helped himself to the rest of her uneaten toast. "Let them in. I don't mind."

She cast him an incredulous glance. "The wards are there for a reason."

"You let me in."

"Because you were harmless." She said it without thinking, her thoughts far away, traveling from ward to ward, seeking the source of the attack. It had come from everywhere and nowhere at once.

"Harmless, huh?" he muttered, sounding sulky, and slinking over to the porridge. "This looks done."

"Eat it," she told him, and left him there, stepping outside to the quiet of the garden so she could concentrate.

Adsila landed on the branch of a flowering apricot tree as Bunny galloped up from the steps to the sea, dripping saltwater. Moriah sifted out of the shadows of the grape arbor, winding around Oneira's legs. They'd all sensed the hit.

Oneira waited for the next blow, senses resting lightly on the web of wards, magic coiled into a sliver of a portal to the Dream, ready to unleash defenders should her wards collapse. Which they would, that much was clear. This was no simple knocking at her wards as Tristan had on the road. Also, having her wards go off twice in two days was quite the coincidence, which she knew better than to believe.

If she had to reveal her true nature to Tristan, then there was no help for it. Better to possibly drive away a potential and very temporary lover than meekly allow herself to be destroyed. No, this testing of her wards had power behind it, the might of a sorcerer. The wards still resonated with the force of the strike, echoing like a bell rung and humming in the waiting silence. Despite that force, Oneira knew in her bones that the first hit had been only a test. Whatever or whoever it was had withdrawn just enough to muster sufficient power to drill through her wards or determine a weak spot, to maximize their chances of breaking through. She could reassure herself on that point: her wards were solid, cohesive, intertwined with dream magic to a smooth defense. There were no weak spots.

However, she was no wardmaker. As a sorceress who traveled

via the Dream, her best weapons and defenses lay in mutability. She could move in and out of the Dream, evading attack and attacking in return from a place that reached everywhere. Against a known enemy—usually one hunkered down in a fixed location—she was unstoppable.

But in this situation, she had become the sitting duck, not knowing from which direction the attack might come. She could flee into the Dream, but only as a last resort. Whoever had found her home would pursue, if not into the Dream, then to wherever she emerged. Her best chances lay in destroying them now, while she was at the pinnacle of her power, before they harried her into exhaustion, using fear and intimidation to put her off her game.

The animals held vigil with her, a mental clock silently ticking the seconds away. She held herself coiled like a venomous snake, relaxed and in position, poised to strike at—

There. She lunged at the tap on her wards, calling lightning from the Dream to fry it—only to stagger as five more points lit up, all around her perimeter, in sequence. Nothing could move that fast. She was being played, drawn into attacking at nothing, exposing her back. She'd been through this sort of duel before, but never with a sorcerer this proficient. They were everywhere and nowhere, stabbing at her wards with tiny needles of power, just enough to sting and draw her attention, so fleeting she couldn't muster a counterattack before they were gone again.

Recognizing how quickly she could burn through her focus this way, not to mention drive herself into an unreasoning frenzy trying to swat every gnat in a stinging cloud, she forced herself to pull her attention back from the wards, as wrong as that felt.

That was what they wanted, so she wouldn't give it to them. She coiled back again into resting position, widening the portal to the Dream, but holding back the nightmare denizens she'd summoned through force of will. She'd have one chance if they managed to break through. No matter how powerful the sorcerer, they couldn't physically be in more than one place at a time—unless they possessed abilities she'd never heard of, in which case she was already dead—and they'd have to come through her wards in person at a single location. There would be a brief moment of vulnerability when she would have the advantage, when they'd be momentarily low on power from punching through, orienting themselves to their changed physical location, when she would strike.

So, she watched, senses alert, and waited for her opportunity.

Her animals waited with her. Adsila half-mantled, ready to launch into the sky. Bunny's nose high, sniffing the air. Moriah lithe and ready. Oneira hadn't asked for them to come, but they had, and they stood by her side. She found herself moved by their unasked-for loyalty, might have grown a little misty over it, had the circumstances been less dire. For the moment, she locked her emotions down tight. There was no room for sentiment in a sorcerer's duel.

Boom!

The attack came like an exploding star. Searing a hole in her wards, the sorcerer flared like the sun, hot, brilliantly powerful, so bright they burned her senses. Oneira held on, snapping her own attack into action, shooting a night terror at the intruder, who staggered . . .

But they instantly recovered and deflected it, dissolving the creature before it fully resolved into the waking world, as if they'd been prepared for it. The remainder of her wards collapsed against each other, like game tiles tipping one into the next, the weight of each increasing the pressure on the one following, until they all *poofed* into an invisible smoke of residual magic, the imagined scent acrid as her fear.

Curse it all. She'd lost that temporary advantage. Whoever this was would require everything she could muster to defeat them, and she wasn't sure she had it in her. She'd also never engaged in a duel without knowing her opponent's strengths and, most importantly, their weaknesses. Worst of all, they knew her, and had chosen the timing of their attack well, at midday for her location, when most dreamers had awakened, and before many had begun to truly dream on the other side of the world.

Bracing for the counterstrike that would surely come, she looked around at her animals, all gazing at her with full trust. "You should flee," she told them. "Save yourselves."

If animals could roll their eyes, they would have. Instead, Adsila dropped to her shoulder, steadying with light talons. Bunny came to stand at her side, Moriah languidly sprawling before her, like a threshold to be crossed. Dropping her hand to rest on Bunny's shoulders, Oneira briefly wondered what had become of Tristan. Yes, the conflict had raged silently, beyond the ken of mundane senses, but some time had passed. Hadn't it occurred to him to check on her?

Ah, well—perhaps it was for the best. If she should perish, the invading sorcerer was unlikely to harm a wandering poet and scholar, no more than she'd been inclined to. Most magicworkers didn't like killing normal people, only each other.

She widened the portal she'd opened, summoning everything the thinning Dream could muster, braced for the killing strike that would surely come . . .

That didn't come.

Instead, the invader seemed to be coming toward her. Not from the road that led to the world of men. She'd been too rattled previously, too focused on triangulating the location of the attack to pay attention to where in the physical world they'd entered her domain. They were coming from the steps to the sea.

The thought of some intruder's feet violating her pink-pebble beach, climbing the steps she'd painstakingly carved into the cliff—if not precisely with her own hands, then with magical precision—all of it stuck in her craw, sour and bitter. Briefly she considered bringing down her beautiful house, shattering the white walls, so they couldn't have it. If not for Tristan innocently vulnerable within, she might have done it. But none of this was his fault. He was only here through unhappy accident, her charming and hapless poet.

The four of them faced the edge of the cliff, waiting for her enemy to come into view. Adsila chirped at the same moment the vague sense of familiarity focused into Oneira's own recognition. In disbelief—though really, she should have guessed, should absolutely have known—she kicked herself internally as the tall form appeared, then stepped onto the terrace facing the sea. He had his long braids tied back, a grim smile on his stern lips, and fireballs spinning on his fists, clenched by his sides.

Stearanos Stormbreaker.

Of course it was Stearanos, and she had only herself to blame for this. Through her recklessness and cavalier disregard for common sense—not to mention the healthy respect she should've had for his reputation—Oneira had tweaked the lion's nose and brought him to her very doorstep.

"Dreamthief," he greeted her, genially enough, though with iron in his voice. "I have no doubt you recognize me."

"Stormbreaker," she acknowledged in turn, unmoving. "To what do I owe this dubious honor?"

"Oh, I think you know," he grated out, advancing on her step by step.

She refused to back down. He could kill her, and likely would, but she wouldn't go down without a fight. She wouldn't beg for her life or offer to become his slave-in-magic. Too many magic-workers went down that way, sacrificing pride in their ultimate terror, only to discover that a slow death became a torture that made them long for the quick one they'd avoided.

"Let's not have any pretense between us. You've been a naughty thief, in more than just dreams, Sorceress Oneira," Stearanos continued, thin mouth flattening further at her lack of response, his braids lifting in the wind of his billowing magic. "You have something of *mine*. You are going to return what you've stolen from me and you're going to pay the price for your insults and injuries."

20

Oneira Dreamthief faced him without flinching. Far from the ancient sorceress he'd expected, she was young, possibly younger than he. That only added to the galling fact that she'd paid off her debts when he hadn't even come close. He'd fully expected to be justified in all of his assumptions about her, including that she deserved his hatred. It pissed him off to discover otherwise.

He also hadn't expected her to be beautiful. And he found himself unreasonably angry about that, too. Her exterior should be as corrupt as the charnel house of her soul. But then, his own internal monstrosity didn't show on the outside either, for the most part. Her hair—an extraordinary shade of crimson that should have made it into the tales about her, instead of being called "red"—hung long and loose like a cloak about her tall willowy form, stirring in the ocean breeze. She had the fawn-colored, lightly freckled skin of that hair type, her eyes a gray so light they looked almost silver. With her strong cheekbones, firm jaw, and high-bridged nose, she wouldn't have been pretty as a girl, but as a mature woman, her unusual features catapulted her beyond striking into breathtakingly gorgeous.

The luster of magic only added to her imposing presence. She stood there, in a plain gown, wearing her animal companions as a court lady might accessorize with jewels. Stearanos narrowed his eyes, studying the creatures, all appearing as relaxed as the Dreamthief herself, none of them fooling him. The huge cat, a glossy obsidian with scintillating emerald eyes, gazed at him unblinking, a hint of unsheathed claws peeking from the fringe of her great paws, no doubt poised to eviscerate him, given half the chance. Though he'd only ever read about her, he recognized the cat immediately.

"Moriah, Lady of Night," he said, bowing courteously, ratcheting back the fireball spell a notch. "I have no quarrel with you."

If Oneira was surprised that he knew the cat, she didn't reveal it. In truth, the sorceress's coldly composed face showed nothing of her thoughts. With a queasy sense of uncertainty, he considered that this could be part of the trap she'd devised, that—instead of him taking her by surprise with his sudden attack—she'd deliberately lured him here, to her home territory, to somehow sabotage his ability to fight the coming war, or to do away with him entirely. He readied himself to throw the fireballs, just in case, running the calculations in his mind on velocity, trajectory, and heat yield to soothe his building anxiety.

It had been a risk, coming after her. Perhaps a fatal one.

"Eminence Stearanos," Moriah replied in a smooth, purring voice, astonishing him so much that he might've missed Oneira's quick, startled glance at the cat, if he hadn't been watching her so closely. "If you quarrel with my friend, you quarrel with me."

Stearanos covered his own surprise. Legend said Moriah could speak, but legends made many outrageous and untrue claims. "Even if your 'friend' crossed the line with me first, casting spells upon me and mine, stealing from me?" he demanded.

"Even so," she replied placidly, a hint of a hiss on the final word.

"Enviable loyalty," he commented to Oneira, who watched him again, as coolly as the cat. His gaze went to the kestrel on her shoulder, taking in the rust-and-sapphire plumage, the hint of the numinous showing in the bright-gold ring in its otherwise black eyes. This was the avatar he'd sensed in his library, the whiff light as a night-blooming flower wafting on the sea breeze from far away. His sense of unease grew. Who was Oneira that a goddess had gifted her with this avatar? Was She Who Eats Bears on the side of the Southern Lands in this ill-advised conquest? This began to look worse and worse.

"Adsila," he said, identifying the bird with a sense of satisfaction. Not being able to previously had gnawed at him the way trying to recall a once-familiar name did. "Avatar of She Who Eats Bears. I have no quarrel with your goddess either."

The kestrel did not acknowledge him beyond fixing him with the keen gaze of a predator.

Not caring for the feeling of being nothing more than a mouse, Stearanos put his attention on the giant, white wolf, apparently fabricated whole cloth from magic. He couldn't place the creature in any particular tale or mythology, except that it had to be one of the *scáthcú*, rumored to run wild in the high mountains of this realm. "I apologize that I don't know your name, *scáthcú*," he said, "but I have no quarrel with your kind either." The wolf bared daunting fangs at him, flicking out a forked, black tongue, and growled.

Oneira soothed the beast, her hand on its shoulders where it stood at her side, as high as her hip, even with her height. Her long, golden-pale fingers combed through the creature's fur, a casual display of affection. "He came to me without a name," she said, her words nearly as much of a surprise as Moriah's at this point. Stearanos had rather thought she'd determined not to speak another word to him, quiverful of silent and accusing arrows in her arsenal. "I call him Bunny," she said, raising one brow at him, clearly expecting him to make the connection.

He stared at her, more than a little flabbergasted. Was that a hint of humor? She was toying with him, if so, not behaving at all as if he'd just toppled her wards like a child's building blocks.

"Bunny," he repeated, thinking of the epic tale of the beastly little bunny in the children's book and the fanged, ravenous rabbit she'd inserted into his dreams. If this was another trick to twist up his mind, she was master-level genius in her subtlety. He should have expected that of the Dreamthief.

She was bold, he'd give her that, rather admirably so, since he should have her more or less at his mercy. He'd timed the attack carefully, aiming for midday when the Dream should have less power. Not that he expected her to be without resources, just with her most powerful weapon weakened. The fact that she showed no fear at all had him wondering if he'd been overconfident, if she knew something he didn't, something like the potential trap that worried him.

In truth, he'd expected to find her gone into the Dream when he arrived on her doorstep, and added grudging respect for her courage and tenacity to the list of things he didn't want to like about her. To make up for both his attraction and his concern, he advanced on her, amping up the fire in his fists, willing her to flinch, to give evidence that she knew he had the upper hand here. "Surrender to my demands."

She only raised her chin defiantly.

"Cat got your tongue?" he chided.

Bizarrely, a slight smile bent her lips, a trace of nostalgia in it. "Is that a common turn of phrase in your realm?" she inquired, as if they were having tea instead of squaring off for a duel of epic proportions, the sort the bards would sing of for centuries, if only there were witnesses. "Someone else from your general part of the world recently asked me the same question," she explained.

"Clearly you have a habit of silence," he retorted.

"Clearly," she allowed, and said nothing more.

The sound of the sea filled the quiet that fell between them, thick and fraught with the potential for disaster.

"I want my books back," he told her, regretting the words the moment he spoke them. Bad strategy to repeat a demand—it made it clear to both parties that the terms had been implicitly denied once already, casting him as the weaker of the two.

She waited a beat, punctuating that she recognized his misstep. "So you already mentioned."

He waited the same beat, then put his threat on the table. "I broke your wards. I can break you."

"Over a novel I promised to return?" She posed the question so lightly that she made him sound absurd.

He clenched his fists, magic boiling in his frustration. "Don't play stupid, Dreamthief. You took more than a novel. Besides, you and I both know that your theft is merely emblematic. You wanted this confrontation or you'd never have violated the sanctity of my home. You picked this fight; now you have it."

Oddly, she smiled at that, still seeming bizarrely amused by the whole exchange. "In truth, Stormbreaker, I didn't."

He waited. She gazed back at him, adding nothing more. "I don't understand," he finally said, even though the admission struck him as unwise, as potentially playing into her hands.

"Neither do I," she replied, as if confiding a secret.

This was going nothing like he'd expected. Neither of them moved; only the twitching tip of Moriah's tail disturbed the tableau. A droplet of drool fell from Bunny's fang. Behind Oneira, a spring garden blossomed, incongruously pretty, flowers bobbing in the sea breeze. Absently, habitually, he counted the varieties, naming them to himself, placing a mental pin on the ones he didn't know. "Give me my books, thief," he said on a sigh, "and I won't kill you."

She cocked her head, mischief in her gaze. "Oh, Em. You with your threats. If you're so certain you can kill me, why not do it and take all of my books? Instead, you stand here chatting in my garden, your hands aflame and unused."

184 · *Jennifer K. Lambert*

Why not, indeed? Because he didn't want to kill her, much as he was supposed to want that. That was the bald truth of it, along with how he now felt vaguely foolish with his fireballs prepped. If he reported back to His Majesty that he'd destroyed the sorceress Oneira, he'd be greatly rewarded. Not enough to ensure his freedom, however, as the king would never allow that. The thought gave him pause, making him want to kill Oneira even less. In fact, electing not to do so would thwart His Majesty in a way Stearanos found deeply appealing.

Not to mention that Oneira was the most fascinating—and alluring—person he'd met in a long time, possibly ever, and he didn't want her gone from the world. Of course, saying so would put the ultimate weapon in her hands, if this truly was an elaborate trap. Still, her use of the impudent nickname she'd devised struck him as strangely welcome, giving him a feeling of . . .

He shook away that thought. All, no doubt, part of her plan to make him lose his mind. "Because I want to know your purpose in stealing from me," he answered, reminding himself of his own plan in coming here, not just to put an end to her spying, but to discern her agenda.

"My purpose should be abundantly clear. I wanted your books."

"That can't be the only reason!" he exploded, losing his own fiery temper in the face of her cold composure, the fireballs on his fists sending sparks in his agitation.

"Can't it?" she asked, tracking the trail of sparks with idle interest, completely uncowed.

Oh, this was a trap, for sure. No one could possibly be this disingenuous, especially not Oneira Dreamthief, Destroyer of Kingdoms. "Who are you working for?" he demanded, abandoning strategy in his frustration and taking another step closer to her, raising his hands in implicit threat.

The *scáthcú*—who could not possibly be named Bunny—

growled, and Oneira petted his big head, murmuring something to the wolf that Stearanos couldn't hear, even close as he was. She raised her gaze to his, the crimson lashes fringing those unusual silvery eyes like fire around a frozen lake, cool and calm, not at all concerned with his threats. If he hadn't known she was a powerful oneiromancer, he'd have recognized her as one in that moment. She possessed a dreamy quality to her, a quirky restfulness that belonged to a realm beyond their reality.

"I work for no one, *Eminence*," she answered, stressing his title along with its significance, that he *did* work for someone, for a king who could not be denied. "I have retired. Perhaps the news hasn't made it to your part of the world, though it was some time ago."

"Oh, we heard," he retorted with a scoff. No sense allowing her to think their reconnaissance was inadequate, although His Majesty's spies had apparently been well behind on the news. "No one believes it."

"No?" She glanced about, the white walls of her house rising behind her, the colorful garden ringing it. "I should think you would believe now, having seen with your own eyes. I am not at court. I live here alone, minding my own business."

"I don't live at court either," he shot back, "as you well know, and that proves nothing."

"True," she allowed on a sigh. "And you're hip-deep in it all, aren't you? Planning a conquest of the Southern Lands for your king."

"Aha!" He stabbed a finger at her, the fireball flaring into a crackling aura. She still didn't flinch, even when sparks flew her way. "How did you know *that*," he continued, "if *you* are no longer in service to your queen?"

She gave him a pitying look. "I saw your research, Stormbreaker. Books piled high, all on the same topic. You must have wanted me to, or you wouldn't have left them out for me to see. You're otherwise so *organized*."

She spoke the last word with such a taunting lilt that he knew she meant to poke him about his somewhat obsessive tendency toward neatness. Well, he would not be provoked. "So that was your purpose in my library, to spy on me."

"No. I don't care what you or your king does." She met his gaze calmly, no artifice in the calm lakes of silver. "I don't care what the queen does. She is not mine and, more importantly, I am not hers. I've washed my hands of it all. I'm done with war." Her voice resonated with deep conviction. He almost believed her.

"Then why invade my library?"

"I was . . . curious." She said the final word ruefully, gazing out at some distant point, then meeting his eyes again with a click, that glint of amusement flickering in them. "Just like you are."

Thoroughly taken aback, feeling caught out and acutely vulnerable, he searched for a reply that would be more intelligent than "nuh uh."

"Eminence Stearanos," she said, almost gently, "if you were truly bent on killing me, you would have done so immediately. Instead you've engaged in verbal fencing with me."

"I've been assessing your strengths and weaknesses."

She actually laughed, a harsh, scornful, scoffing sound, one that made her sound as old as he'd expected her to be, and far more bitter. "Oh, please. You knew everything about my strengths and weaknesses already, Stormbreaker. Just as I know everything about yours. Don't pretend that you haven't been prepared to fight me your entire career, just as I've been thoroughly educated in how to defeat you. We've been held at each other's throats, a dual-sided dagger that would assure mutual destruction. You knew exactly how to hammer through my wards, and to arrive at the time of day when the Dream would be weakest. The only reason you've been standing here chatting with me is because it's the most fun you've had in forever. The same reason you exchanged notes with me when I was only your mysterious thief." She smiled briefly, then sobered. "I see through you, Stearanos."

He opened his mouth to counter. Came up with nothing. So much for her habit of silence. He almost preferred that to her scathing insights. "If you're so certain I won't kill you, why haven't you tried to kill me? I broke your wards and invaded your home." He held up the fireballs. "Threatened you."

"I told you," she answered, a bit wearily. "I'm done with all of that."

"You wouldn't even defend yourself?" he asked incredulously.

"We don't know, do we?" she countered. "As I haven't needed to. All you've done is bluster and wave your little fireballs about."

"They're hardly little, Oneira," he said, having nothing else.

She actually smirked. "I'm sure they're much bigger than anyone else's."

To his great consternation, he actually struggled not to laugh. He released the spell, allowing the fire to go out. "What are we even doing here?"

Cocking her head, she considered the question as if it deserved an answer, rather than being an admission of defeat. "Continuing a conversation that began in your library, I believe."

He didn't know what to make of that. "Just give me my books," he conceded wearily. "You can keep the novel, but I want the rose cultivation manual."

"I'm not done with it yet," she replied, almost lightly, perhaps even teasing him, yet again. "You've come all this way," she added, with the barest hesitation, "would you like to see what I've done with your manual?"

Arrested by the possibility, by the improbable invitation, he searched her face for signs of a trap. "You have the roses," he said, not a question. After all, he'd known since she left him the leaf.

She nodded, a genuine smile blooming across her face as rare and beautiful as a Veredian rose was purported to be. "I'll show them to you, if you like."

He did want to see them. Badly. And, worse, she knew it. Still, even if that was the trigger that would spring the trap, she'd baited it well. He couldn't resist. "Fine," he nodded curtly. "But no tricks."

"No tricks." She held up a hand in solemn vow. "I offer you the hospitality of my home, Eminence Stearanos, for the duration of this visit, if you agree to guest rules."

A full détente between them. How fascinating. He held up his own hand. "I accept the hospitality of your home, Sorceress Oneira, for the duration of this visit, and agree to abide by guest rules."

"Excellent. Repair my wards—since you were the one to break them and you're better at wardmaking, anyway—and come inside. I'm baking bread and making soup, perhaps a spring salad. We can discuss more over a late lunch, and then I'll show you my roses." She turned and walked away, Adsila on her shoulder, Bunny by her side. Moriah remained where she was, as if assigned to supervise.

Stunned that she'd dared to turn her back on him, Stearanos watched her go. Had she really invited him to stay for lunch and a tour of her garden? Apparently so. And, his stomach reminded him, he was hungry. Bemused, at himself, at her, he put his mind and magic to reconstructing her wards, fully aware that he hadn't done anyone's bidding who wasn't paying him to do so in decades.

It made no sense that he felt cheerful about it.

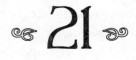

Keenly aware of the Stormbreaker's acute gaze drilling between her shoulder blades, Oneira made herself stroll casually through the kitchen garden and into the house, blowing out her exhalations at twice the count of her inhalations. Her heart rabbited in her breast and a cold sweat trickled down her spine, but she'd made it through the confrontation. More, she'd *bluffed* her way through it.

She'd even instructed His Eminence, the great and terrifying Stearanos—who was even more intimidating awake—to repair her wards. Her own temerity astonished her, and she actually giggled in shocked relief.

"Who is *that*?" Tristan demanded, popping up from behind the counter and startling an undignified squeak out of her. She was still on edge from being ready to defend her life and the lives of her animals, braced for the blow that never came—she could swear her eyebrows had singed from the sparks from those fireballs— and she'd somehow forgotten about Tristan's existence entirely.

"Where have you been?" she demanded in return.

"Hiding," Tristan answered quietly, flushing in embarrassment. "Under the kitchen table."

"All this time?" she asked incredulously. The standoff had taken quite a while.

"I'm not a fighter and I didn't know what else to do," he replied defensively. "Were those *fireballs*?"

Oneira sighed. "A trick of the light," she told him, thinking she could slip something like that into Tristan's dreams as he slept that night, to reinforce the idea.

Adsila flew to her perch and Bunny flopped down where he was. Tristan eyed both uneasily. She didn't blame him for being afraid, then or now, particularly of the *scáthcú*, but she was still sorting through the astonishing fact that not only had Stearanos *not* been afraid, he'd known Adsila and Moriah for who they were. Of course, so had she, but still. It was strikingly odd to be around a sorcerer so much like herself. They were a rare breed and not convivial for obvious reasons. Sorcerers, as a rule, only encountered each other as enemies. Now she'd invited one for lunch.

"That's a big dog," Tristan said, eying the cheerfully panting Bunny uneasily. "Or . . . a wolf?"

"He won't harm you."

"And you have a hawk?" Tristan asked. "A tame hawk without jesses."

"Adsila is a kestrel," she corrected, not bothering to tell him more than that. Better that he not know. She'd have to weave several threads into Tristan's dreams to ease his concerns.

"And the gentleman outside is an old friend." She decided upon the word as she said it, amused with herself. Everything she'd said to Stearanos had been absolutely true—and she'd seen through him because she saw herself in him. That conversation, even worrying that he might throw one of those fireballs at any moment and being unsure if her planned countermeasure would work, had been the most fun for her in . . . probably ever.

"That one, whoever he is, is no gentle man," Tristan scoffed.

"His name is Em."

"A lover?" Tristan asked, sounding displeased. "I thought you said you live alone."

"I do live alone." She punched down the dough she'd set to rise

NEVER THE ROSES · 191

earlier, restraining herself from bruising it in her nerves. "Em is merely visiting."

"Huh." Tristan was clearly unconvinced. "For how long?"

"What?"

Tristan came up behind her and set his hands on her hips, drawing her bottom back against him as he nibbled on the side of her neck. "I apologize, lovely Lira. How long is this Em visiting? I have plans for this beautiful body." He slid one hand up to cup her breast, thumbing the nipple expertly, and adding a sharper nip to her earlobe.

"Stop that," she said, bumping him away, though it was like trying to dislodge a constrictor, his hands returning to roam further with renewed tenacity. "And I don't know. I—"

"Am I interrupting?" Stearanos loomed in the open doorway to the garden, taking up all of the space with his broad shoulders, obvious annoyance, and potent magic. "I didn't realize you had another visitor," he said to Oneira accusingly, behaving as if they had been amiably chatting outside instead of pondering having an all-out duel.

"I didn't think the information was relevant," she answered lightly. "Tristan, off. I mean it." Tristan gave her a wounded look and she realized she'd spoken to him as she would to a mud-covered Bunny. "For now," she added, giving what she hoped was a look of sultry promise, sharply reminded of why she'd never been good at having a lover.

Once Tristan begrudgingly stepped away, giving her sad-puppy eyes, she said, "Em, this is Tristan, a poet and scholar who lost his way in a storm. Tristan, my old friend, Em. He's staying for lunch." She caught the Stormbreaker's gaze and held it meaningfully. The sorcerer was no fool. He wouldn't want a wandering tale-teller to tell this particular tale of Stearanos being in a part of the world where his very presence amounted to a declaration of war, Oneira's retired status notwithstanding.

Stearanos made a sound like a low growl, but inclined his head to Tristan. "Well met, poet."

"I hope you brought your own meat," Tristan said, sounding more than a little put out. "There's none in the house."

"Can't abide the stuff myself," Stearanos replied, but with his gaze on Oneira, a light of interest in them. "Too many battles."

She nodded faintly in agreement, understanding humming between them.

Stearanos waved a hand at the array of vegetables on the counter. "Can I assist?"

She looked over the pile she'd made, thinking he might mean something else. "Do you know how?" she asked, regretting the foolish words immediately. "That is—"

"If you trust me with a knife in your kitchen," he answered with a wolfish grin that transformed his stern face, plucking a chopping blade from its slot, "then yes. I know how to chop vegetables for soup. Or a spring salad. I've spent time on the campaign trail, too," he added, sliding her an opaque glance. "As you well know."

She nodded slightly, realizing he likely understood things about her, too, but taken aback by the offer nonetheless. "Thank you, then."

"What should I do, lovely Lira?" Tristan asked, giving Stearanos a defiant glare.

Naturally, the first time Tristan offered to help was to compete with another man. Oneira nearly rolled her eyes, then caught Stearanos's questioning glance.

"Yes, *Lira*," Stearanos said, emphasizing the false name, "shall I share the chopping? I also know how to pick lettuce, another refined skill of mine."

"Any fool can pick lettuce," Tristan scoffed.

"Then you're just the man we need," Stearanos noted, giving the young poet a wink.

She narrowed her eyes at Stearanos, who gave her a look of blithe innocence that did not sit well on his stern face. "And strawberries," she told Tristan, handing him a bowl.

"Anything for you, my Lady Lira," he said, snaking an arm around her waist and giving her a kiss that she cut off before he did. Tristan threw a smug glare at Stearanos before marching out to the garden.

"Young for you, isn't he?" Stearanos inquired with a mildness that didn't fool her, his blade flashing as he did indeed efficiently chop his way through the mounds of vegetables.

"He isn't anything for me," she answered crisply. "I'd never even met him until he showed up yesterday. I simply treated his injuries, gave him food and shelter."

"And fucked him," Stearanos observed, intently chopping. "Is that part of the standard hospitality you offer?"

"Ha ha. You wish."

His gaze snapped up, catching hers with smoldering intensity that took her aback. About to say something, he seemed to reconsider, shaking his head slightly, then saying, "I'd think a *lady* living alone would be more careful of prettily wrapped gifts deposited on her doorstep."

"Deposited by whom?" she asked in exasperation, covering the unexpected heat stirred by the sorcerer's intent gaze. No sex in ages and now she seemed to think of nothing else. "I'm not easily found, and everyone knows not to bother me, besides."

"I found you," Stearanos said, pointing out the obvious even as it occurred to her.

"Yes, about that. How *did* you find me?"

His sere face broke into that wolfish grin. "Trade secret."

"Fine, don't tell me." She formed the dough into a loaf. "But you are unique in the world, Em. Just because *you* can do a thing doesn't mean anyone else can."

"Why, darling, what a lovely compliment. I had no idea of the level of your admiration."

She snorted. "It's wise to know one's enemies."

"True," he acknowledged, saluting her with the blade. "To return to the point, sneaking a sweet young thing into your bed would be a fine way to get to you."

"As if I can't handle a harmless young poet."

Shaking his head, he resumed chopping. "*If* that's all he is."

"I've heard tell of your legendary paranoia. I'm not plagued with such anxieties."

"No, your problem is overconfidence."

Opening her mouth to deny it, she found she couldn't. They knew far too much about each other for that. "Justifiable confidence," she corrected. "Besides, I *haven't* taken him into my bed, not that it's any of your business."

"The boy is awfully handsy for one who's been refused your bed," Stearanos noted in a neutral tone. "And lipsy."

"That's not even a word."

"Then I shall write it into a book and it will be."

Tristan returned, bowls full of lettuce—torn up by the roots, she noted with a mental sigh—and a few strawberries, not nearly as many as Oneira knew had ripened. The smudge of red juice about Tristan's lips spoke of the fate of the rest. He extended the bowl to her, then pulled it away as she reached for it, leaning in for a kiss. "My reward, first, my lady."

With an audible sigh this time, and mostly to annoy Stearanos, who was far too interested in whether or not she'd bedded the pretty poet, she gave Tristan a kiss. His lips tasted of strawberries, confirming his illicit feast. He perched on his stool at the counter, telling of his travels when Stearanos questioned him, observing as she and the sorcerer compiled the soup. It was almost companionable, Stearanos recognizing her dried herbs for the most part, interested in testing the ones not native to his realm, and making such innovative suggestions to augment the concoction that she delegated the seasoning to him entirely.

Tristan seemed blissfully unaware that Stearanos was actually interrogating him, probing for signs that the poet wasn't who he seemed, happily chattering on about all he'd seen and done. None of it suspicious or untoward. Oneira gave Stearanos the occasional blandly triumphant glance and he scowled back, unconvinced, their ongoing conversation entirely silent and perfectly clear.

Once the soup was simmering, Oneira washed her hands, bemused at how little time the preparation had taken with the extra pair of hands. She excused herself, to change her cup and make sure no blood had leaked through. By the time she returned, Stearanos had finished putting away the remainder of the supplies, easily discerning where most of it went. He only asked for input on a few items. If he'd straightened things in her cooler and on her shelves as he went, she considered it the price of his assistance. Besides, his quirks amused her, and order was always welcome. "You do know your way around a kitchen," she observed.

He cocked a brow. "I'm not an idiot," he replied, glancing at Tristan, who didn't notice.

"Don't you have servants still?" She knew he did.

"Of course, though some sleep on the job," he answered with narrowed eyes and a hint of accusation. "But I find working with my hands soothing," he added, almost a question. "It's a welcome change from my usual work."

"Yes." She nodded, meeting his gaze, answering the question he hadn't quite asked. "Healing, in a way."

He let out a long breath, matching her nod. "Yes."

"I'm careful of my hands," Tristan put in, holding up his soft, elegant fingers. "The tools of my trade, as it were. I treat them like the treasures they are."

Stearanos opened his mouth to say something scathing, no doubt, and Oneira jumped in. "Shall we have that tour of the garden?"

"I am in suspense of this promised tour," Stearanos conceded, meaning it utterly, she knew, though Tristan gave him a perplexed look. "Lead on, lovely Lady Lira," he added, grandly gesturing to the doorway to the garden.

When she gave him a fierce glare for his sarcasm, he only grinned, and—shocking her completely—playfully tugged at a strand of her hair.

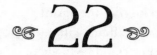

22

Stearanos exercised his patience, following along as Oneira gave him a painfully thorough tour of the garden. She was deliberately stringing him along, building suspense, knowing what he most wanted to see and making him wait for it. That was fine: two could play that game. Besides, the academy he'd attended drilled patient stoicism into every student. The magic-worker who couldn't silently observe while waiting on a glacially slow alchemical reaction, or who couldn't make a still pond of their mind to allow for the perfect clarity required by meticulous spellcasting, would never reach the highest echelons.

Oneira would know that about him, so this was all an elaborate tease, more of her subtle flirtation. For flirtation it was, he was sure of it now. From the first taunting theft, the first cryptic note and exchange of books, she'd been sniffing him out, knowing full well who he was and curious to know more. Perhaps despite herself, but she was as fascinated by him as he was by her. So he could bide his time and see where this went.

What he didn't understand was what she saw in that pretty puppy of a poet. He snorted to himself. See? He could string words together, too. The young man was charming enough, Stearanos supposed, and handsome in the traditional way the court ladies seemed to like, but he wasn't worthy of a woman like Oneira. Stearanos couldn't quite fathom the attraction for her.

Or, perhaps he could. After all, women were no different from men that way. Oneira had been alone, for longer than she'd been retired, if her life was anything like his, and he'd bet a chest of gold he couldn't afford that it was. The opportunity for uncomplicated affairs with admiring lovers who had no idea how easily they could be incinerated or stranded eternally in the Dream didn't come along often. In truth, Stearanos couldn't recall the face of the last lover he'd bedded. She'd ended up afraid of him, he remembered that, the stink of her fear overriding all else that he could recall about her.

Oneira wasn't afraid of him—even when she should have been—and that made her excruciatingly attractive. He wanted to swat away that annoying gnat of a poet, simpering at her, completely ignorant of the dragon beneath Oneira's attractively freckled skin. But he bided his time. He could be patient.

He could also find out everything about the lad, as he still didn't trust that *Tristan*—there was a name for you, and surely not one his parents had thought to bestow on him—had ended up at Oneira's doorstep by accident. Still, after he'd questioned and probed, even Stearanos had to admit that Tristan was exactly what he seemed. Not terribly bright, full of tales and youthful artlessness, intent on seducing Oneira. The worst sins Stearanos could lay at Tristan's feet were that he was likely as attracted to Oneira for her lonely wealth as for her beauty, and that he was dreadfully silly.

In his favor, Tristan was clearly bored by plants, easily distracted by pretty much anything else, which left Stearanos plenty of opportunity to dazzle Oneira with his own knowledge. Or, if not dazzling her, precisely, at least connecting over their shared interest. When they reached the new rose bed, Oneira turned to Stearanos with glowing excitement he knew he reflected. He felt as if he'd come to a sacred site, greedily taking in the sight of the three rosebushes. Veredian roses, as he lived and breathed. He'd nearly despaired of ever seeing any alive for himself.

"They haven't quite recovered from the transplanting," Oneira explained, lacing her fingers together and actually wringing them, the first sign of real concern he'd ever seen from her. "And with that storm . . ."

"They'll recover," he assured her with confidence, quantifying and qualifying them from where he stood. "Their vitality is excellent."

"You know that?" she asked with what he could only call professional interest. She clearly wanted to ask more, but couldn't with Tristan lurking nearby. He simply nodded, allowing her to see the faint sparkle of magic in his eyes.

"They're ugly things, if you ask me," Tristan put in, and Stearanos had to stop himself from saying that no one *had* asked him. "More sticks, twigs, and thorns than anything. Where are the roses?"

"They bloom only at the winter solstice," Oneira informed him, her obvious delight overriding all else. "That's part of what makes them special. When all the rest of my garden is sleeping, these will bloom for a few days only, on the longest nights of the year, bringing scent, color, and life to a dark and frozen world."

Stearanos caught the longing in her voice and wondered at it. What plan did Oneira have for this retirement of hers? Or was it less of a retirement than a full retreat from a life she could no longer bear to live? He suspected the latter and, more, fully understood the impulse. Lucky her that she'd found a way to do it. He longed to ask her more about how she'd obtained the roses, though now that he knew his thief for an oneiromancer, that answer was obvious. She'd used the power of the Dream to travel to distant Vered. He still wondered what technique she'd used to take them. The rose bed had no magic to it—he double-checked, assessing it every way he knew how—so it must have been she'd done everything manually. He very much wanted to know if she'd gotten advice not to use magic. The book hadn't said so, but why else make that choice? But, with ignorant Tristan thinking his lovely Lira nothing but a wealthy, lonely recluse, Stearanos could hardly introduce the topic of her using magic or not.

They went back to the kitchen and ate an excellent lunch, the freshly baked bread fragrant with rosemary from Oneira's garden, all of the fruits and vegetables bursting with liquid sunshine. Stearanos couldn't remember the last time he enjoyed a meal so much, even with talkative Tristan dominating the conversation, now that the dull topic of gardening was out of the way.

Finally, Stearanos said that he must go, Tristan halfheartedly protesting and practically shoving him out the door. Oneira offered to walk Stearanos to the beach—and pointedly suggested that Tristan go check on his horse. Stearanos was greatly relieved by this, as he didn't trust himself not to pitch the poet off the cliff if he tried to tag along.

"Did you make these steps?" he asked her as they descended, and she gave him a surprised glance.

"I didn't think that would be your first question once we were alone," she said. "Yes, I did, with magic, of course."

"Of course. Spectacular work."

She gave a slight smile. "Something I dreamed up."

"And the pink sand beach?"

Gazing out over it, she huffed out a breath. "Another bit of whimsy—though it was easier. I used bits of shell already here, colored them with a particularly vivid dream I borrowed, and simply . . . concentrated the two together."

"'Simply,'" he echoed.

"Well, you would know that 'simple' is a relative term," she allowed.

He waited a beat, for decorum's sake. "And the roses?"

"Now *that* is what I thought would be your first question."

She flashed him a wider smile, that glow in it that she got when talking about the roses. He couldn't help returning the smile, the expression stiff on his face, making him realize how little he'd used those particular muscles in recent years. It also struck him how bizarrely companionable the moment felt, especially given how they'd begun. But then again . . . perhaps not. They'd truly begun this strange relationship when Oneira stepped out of a dream and into his library and took that particular book solely because he was interested in it, as she explained.

As she related the tale of using the Dream to find the roses, the ancient gardener she encountered, how she'd followed the instructions on using no magic to cultivate the roses, he let her enthusiasm wash over him, like a freshwater shower taking away months of campaign grime.

It was good to talk about these simple things like roses— however rare and extraordinary—and gardening, to have made soup together, to be in her house, with its peace and silence. Even with Tristan's chatter, the essential quiet of the place had permeated everything, settling into the core of him. It made him believe in something, though he couldn't quite grasp what it would be.

Still, listening to the details of Oneira's quest for the roses, he found he no longer minded that she insisted on keeping the book. Of course she should have it. And, also of course, he was desperately jealous of her roses, wanting them for himself. Wanting her for himself, too, if he was honest. Two things that could never be.

"You say that the gardener knew who you were?" he asked, focusing on the academic, the quantifiable aspects of her story, not this odd mutual love of these exotic, nearly unobtainable roses that were indeed undeniably ugly for most of the year.

"Not me specifically," Oneira answered with a frown. "Or, if she did know my name, she didn't speak it and she didn't offer hers." She slid him a wry look. "As seems to be traditional for this sort of thing in the old tales."

He nodded knowingly, having encountered such oddities himself. For all that they spent so much of their lives being educated in the precisions of magic, how to refine their natural inclinations into skills to produce the most reliable results, so much of what they did, of what the magical world held, remained deep beneath the surface, emerging on occasion to remind them of their transience and ignorance. They were but human, in the end.

"She did know and correctly name Adsila," Oneira added.

"Even more interesting."

"But then, so did you."

"I imagine you did also."

"Yes, of course."

They descended a steep winding section, suspending their conversation to go single file, that sense of companionship persisting. Perhaps it was only because he'd had so few conversations with his sorcerous colleagues. Or perhaps it was something more.

"I know you took Adsila with you into the Dream . . ." he said when he drew up beside her again, and rather before he knew what he was going to ask, trailing off as he realized exactly where his yearnings were pulling him. Uncertain territory.

"Yes," Oneira answered, as if he'd finished the question, then slid him a canny look. "And no, I can't take just anyone into the Dream, if that's what you're asking. Adsila is the only one who has accompanied me into that realm and it's been entirely of her own initiative. I suspect she can do it because of her numinous nature. As an avatar of the goddess, Adsila isn't bound to the rules of our reality."

That made him somewhat uncomfortable to contemplate. Stearanos knew himself to be a man of their reality, not only bound to those rules, but taking comfort in their solid reliability. Still, he chafed at the restriction of being unable to go where she'd gone.

"If I said I could take you into the Dream to meet the gardener, would you ask me to?" Oneira inquired, clearly following his thinking. Her silver eyes sparkled with knowing mischief.

"Would you say yes?" he countered, quite certain of her answer.

"It would be unwise of me," she pointed out, obliquely referencing their implicit conflict. She would be vulnerable to him in the Dream, inside her magic, potentially revealing her secrets.

"That doesn't answer the question."

She shrugged. "It's a moot point, regardless, as I can't. I don't think I could do it with a mundane human. I wouldn't attempt it even with Moriah or Bunny. With another sorcerer, especially one of your power . . . Well, I think your magic would fight mine and I'd likely lose you in the Dream. I don't think you'd care for that fate."

He shuddered at the prospect of being lost in dreams for all eternity, no hope of waking, no rules to cling to. He'd go insane and become some sort of wandering nightmare to plague others with all that haunted him. Firmly turning his thoughts away from that bone-watering idea, he caught on to the significance of what Oneira had said. "That's why you didn't escape into the Dream when I broke your wards," he proclaimed triumphantly. There were few things he loved better than solving a problem or answering a persistent question. "You couldn't take Moriah and Bunny with you."

"They can take care of themselves," she said, gazing out at the sea and not even trying to pretend she wasn't ducking the question. "They did long before they came to me."

"Then you were protecting Tristan." He sounded sour.

She snorted. "You wouldn't have hurt him."

"Don't be so sure," Stearanos muttered ungraciously. "The boy is a fool."

"And thus not deserving of your attention, much less injury or death at your hands," Oneira returned placidly, raising a brow at his surprise. "What—did you think I would argue? I don't agree that Tristan is a fool. He's quite intelligent, in a thoroughly bookish way. And he's obviously not a boy, though I can see how he would seem that way to a man of your years and—"

"My *years*?" he interrupted. "You make me sound as much of a doddering ancient as your Veredian gardener."

"She was hardly doddering. My point is that you are probably three times Tristan's age."

"As are you."

"As am I."

Her calm acknowledgment left him with nothing to push against. That was Oneira, he was fast learning. She was as insubstantial as a dream and as perversely persistent. You poked at her, tried to contain her, and she wafted away, then returned to haunt you, over and over again. "You were saying?" he finally asked in resignation.

"Oh, you'll let me finish now?" she asked archly, though a smile curved her lips. "I harbor no illusions about who Tristan is and isn't. But he *is* pretty and I *have* been lonely, even before I retired and exiled myself. I've begun to realize that—why am I telling you this?"

"I asked," he answered simply. "In a manner of speaking," he added, realizing his motivations hadn't been at all pure.

"My enemy," she mused, "with whom I've spent a pleasant afternoon of intimate conversation."

"The world made us enemies, not we, ourselves."

She cast him a glance of silvery interest. "Do you think, under other circumstances, we could have been friends?"

"I think we are on our way to being friends now, even given current circumstances."

She laughed, then saw he was serious, and shook her head, pulling a strand of crimson hair out of her eyes. "Tristan is uncomplicated," she said firmly, as if convincing herself. "I've never had good luck with sex, but he's . . . practiced at it. He's attractive, available, interested—" She didn't pause as he snorted. "And he doesn't know to be afraid of me."

Ah, and there it was. And here he was. "I am not afraid of you."

She stopped, and not only because they'd reached the final landing above the beach, the pink-pebbled shore framing her like a lighter shade of her startling coloring. Her eyes both wide with surprise and full of suspicion, she looked to be groping for a response.

"I'm not afraid of you, Oneira," he reiterated. "And I can say that knowing *exactly* who you are."

"You do not know me," she countered, though it came out breathless.

"I know you better than anyone in the world, I'll bet. I know what you're capable of. I know how that power isolates you. Just as you know me."

"I know only what's in your dossier, and a few observations, mostly while you were asleep."

"So, we'll correct that."

"What exactly are you suggesting, Stearanos?" she demanded, sounding angry, sparks in her gaze, long, vivid locks of crimson whipping about her in a breeze that wasn't entirely natural. She made his hair stand on end with wariness and made him want to kiss her in equal measure.

"You know what I'm suggesting," he answered with deliberate calm, counterbalancing her anger. "But let me make it clear.

Don't waste yourself on that pretty boy. He's not good enough for you. Consider my suit instead." There. He'd said it, and ripped himself open to her scornful refusal.

"*You.*" She infused the single word with a universe of improbability.

"Why not me?" He ticked off the points on his fingers, all the logical reasons he'd been listing in his head, practically since the moment he laid eyes on her. Possibly before that, when he only guessed at what his mysterious thief might be like. "We're of an age, of equivalent power, similar life experiences, shared interests. We find each other attractive and—"

"I never said I find you attractive," she interrupted, and he grinned, pleased that she hadn't argued any of the other points and that she was clearly—by the sudden flush on her strong cheekbones—dancing the line of truth.

"You didn't have to say so," he teased, enjoying stoking her outrage. "For myself, I'd tell you that I find you incredibly beautiful and profoundly sexually compelling, except that you've heard so much of that drivel dripping from Tristan's lips I suspect you've become inured to it."

She opened her mouth and closed it. Then shook her head. "I have no words."

"That's fine. I do. Why not give me a chance? Why not give *us* a chance?"

"Oh, I don't know, because you could kill me?"

"If you were afraid of that, you'd never have tweaked my nose in my own library."

She firmed her lips over an objection, implicitly acknowledging the truth of that, studying him thoughtfully. "There's a reason sorcerers don't consort with one another."

"Yes, but you're retired with no intention of returning to your former career. Isn't that true?"

"Absolutely," she answered with firm conviction, but then fixed him with her penetrating gaze. "Are you planning to invade the Southern Lands?"

He gave that one due consideration, then replied with a question. "Is that something you really want an answer to?" Holding up a hand, he stopped her reply. "If you're no longer involved in the wars of the world of men, then these are things you don't want to know. That you'd be better off *not* knowing, for plausible deniability."

She let out a long, slow breath. "I think that *is* an answer. Still, your point is well-taken. Were the queen to discover that I knew of invasion plans and did nothing, Her Majesty would be most displeased. To the point of accusing me of betraying the crown."

"Could she do anything to you?" he asked, curious for himself, also. "Obviously the geas had to be removed when you paid off your contract."

Oneira nodded absently, thinking about the ramifications. "Even without that absolute control, she could make things difficult for me. I want to be left alone and not have to kill anyone ever again, not battle an army come to punish me for being a traitor. There are so many more of them than us, after all."

He nodded in grave agreement. Unless they were willing to murder thousands or millions of innocents, sorcerers could always be overwhelmed with the numbers of mundane bodies the monarchs could throw at them. "Our relationship would be a secret then."

"Our relationship," she echoed in turn, rolling her eyes.

"If you agree to have one," he replied agreeably.

"Such a tepid word."

"Would you prefer 'affair'?"

She eyed him. "That feels like putting the cart ahead of the horse. As for secrecy, yes to the necessity of that, though Tristan knows about you."

"He doesn't know who either of us truly is," Stearanos countered, excitement rising as she seemed to be truly considering the possibility.

"That's not the only reason this is a bad idea. We could accidentally incinerate each other in an argument over what to have for breakfast."

"We'd never argue over that," he pointed out relentlessly. "We like the same food."

She planted her fists on her hips. "We're arguing now."

"No, you're arguing—over something considerably more consequential than what to have for breakfast, I might add—and I'm making my case." He grinned at her consternation. "And wearing you down, aren't I?"

She gave him a look of pure frustration. "This is a ridiculous proposal. We don't even know if we're compatible."

"You didn't know if you were compatible with yon Tristan when he deposited himself on your doorstep."

"Yes, but I can make Tristan leave."

"Whereas you can't control me," he acknowledged with a nod. "Likewise, Dreamthief. But isn't there an appeal to that? There is for me."

Pursing her lips in sardonic disbelief, she raised her brows. "It drove you crazy that I could waltz past your wards and into your library, that I could put everyone in that overstuffed castle of yours to sleep—including you—and that you couldn't do a thing to stop me."

"True," he immediately agreed, enjoying her surprise that he didn't argue the point. "Which is why you have nothing to fear from me. We'd meet as equals."

She gazed at him, lips parting for words that didn't come. Encouraged, he continued.

"You drive me crazy, Oneira. You fascinate me. I am interested and aroused. I want more." He'd closed the distance between them as he spoke, ending up close enough to her to feel the warmth of her skin, to catch the scent of herbs from her hair. She had to tip her head back slightly to hold his gaze, refusing to give any ground.

"You're bored is what you are," she observed without rancor.

"I was. Not anymore. You're the most interesting thing to happen to me in a very long time."

"I'm not happening to you."

"We're happening to each other. Give it a try, Oneira. You have only your loneliness to lose. Let me show you how it can be."

Her gaze dropped to his lips, her resolve wavering. "What do you suggest?"

"A kiss."

For some reason that amused her, her silvery eyes alight with laughter as they lifted to his. "It never rains but it pours," she murmured, then continued before he could remark on that. "You intend to wake the sleeping beauty with true love's kiss?"

"I never said anything about love, true or otherwise," he countered. "And if anyone in this equation is the sleeping beauty, it's me. All due to *your* spellcasting, I might add."

"You're hardly the picture of sweet and virginal innocence."

"And not beautiful, I know."

"All right."

"All right, what?"

"Kiss me," she prompted, a glint of challenge in her gaze. "Convince me that you're better than my pretty poet."

He growled under his breath at the invidious comparison—no pressure, or anything—but he'd done it to himself. Moving slowly, he slipped a hand to the back of her neck, surprisingly slender, her skin satin, her hair a silky veil cascading over his arm that tempted him to take more, to thread his fingers through it, perhaps wind the length around his fists. But he leashed his increasingly urgent passion, easing in, aware of her tense wariness. She wasn't afraid of him, not as an enemy anyway, but she was a cautious soul, not one who made herself vulnerable easily, perhaps ever.

Softly, with all the gentleness in him—which wasn't much, as he was a hard man who'd lived a life of ruthlessness—he lowered his lips to hers.

23

Such hard-looking lips shouldn't be so soft, so utterly magical.

A low, animal sound escaped her at the exquisite sensation. The Stormbreaker's magic seeped into her via the hand at the back of her neck and his mouth, the only places they touched, just those two points of contact almost too much to bear, breaking barriers she'd erected within herself. Where Tristan's kisses had been skilled, cleverly stirring desire, Stearanos kissed her like a key fitting into a lock, unleashing something in her she hadn't known lived inside those internal walls.

The key turned.

The lock gave.

And something in the world shifted.

Like and unlike, his magic lashed the inside of her skin, ruthlessly controlled and constrained by the equations he used to explain his powers to himself. She imagined him quantifying her, exploring her mouth with a restrained fervor that felt half as if he engaged her in battle and half as if he starved for the taste of her. She met him with her own challenge, her own hunger. Her own yearning to yield to this extraordinary passion between them.

With a groan, he wrenched himself away and she caught at him before he could carelessly back off the landing. It wasn't far to the beach, but rocks lay at the base of the cliff, sharp and treacherous. Dangerous shoals they navigated. Aware of it also, Stearanos stared at her, his eyes wild. Then he laughed, tossing his head back and releasing the belly-deep sound that seemed to come from an entirely different man than the taciturn sorcerer who'd turned up to shatter her wards.

"That was extraordinary," he informed her, turning his hands to grip hers. He'd scrambled her thoughts so thoroughly, she'd forgotten she was holding on to him. "Do you feel this?" he asked in wonder, studying the shimmer of their combined magic. "Of course you do," he answered for her—and good thing, too, as her thoughts were still scattered to the four winds—and lifted those piercing eyes to hers, then narrowed his. "I've never experienced anything like that," he said in a low, intense voice.

Neither had she, but she wasn't about to tell him as much. Tristan would be far, far safer to dally with. Engaging with Stearanos on an intimate basis would be playing with fire—literally and figuratively—with as devastating results as if they dueled. And here she stood, her lips tingling from his kiss, battered within as if from a storm, holding the hands of a sorcerer who might as well be a wild beast, the way his hunger reached for her even now. Yes, he had it tightly leashed, but what about when he lost control?

Or when she did.

"Tell me I've made my case." Stearanos stopped short of making it sound like a demand, but not by much. He was a man accustomed to getting exactly what he wanted, exactly when and how he wanted it. At the moment, he wanted her, but what then? What happened when he grew bored—again—and tired of her? Could her already war-weary and tattered heart heal from that? "Give me something, Oneira," he coaxed, gaze searching her face.

"I thought I already did," she replied, marveling at how calm and poised she sounded, given how thoroughly he'd rattled her.

He smiled, a brief twist of those remarkably stirring lips, a flash of humor there and gone again, leaving only the intensity behind. She pulled against his grip on her hands and he instantly released her, concern clouding his expression. *Give me something.* She couldn't give him what he was asking for . . . Could she? No. Not without risking more than she could contemplate losing.

"Besides," she added, "even if I wanted to give you more, it's not possible right now as I'm having my menses."

Stearanos made a soft growling sound, closing the distance between them. "Is that supposed to deter me? I'm not afraid of a little blood."

Of course that didn't work with him. She'd have to try giving him what he'd come for. Reaching into the pocket of her gown, she extracted the novel and extended it to him. "Here is the one book and I'll pay you for the other."

Barely giving the book a glance, he shook his head. "Return it when you're done reading it."

"Stearanos, I—"

"Will return it when you're done, as you promised to do," he finished for her. "When you're done, come and return it to my library. Put everyone else to sleep if you must—though I'll tell everyone to stay out of the library at night and they'll heed my wishes—but leave me awake, please. So we can at least talk."

"At least?" Her pulse, still leaping unreasonably from that staggering kiss, stuttered at his suggestive tone.

"Conversation. I can give you recommendations for your next read," he said, still in that sultry tone. "Discover what you . . . like."

"I really don't think that's a good idea." And now her voice quavered. *Would you prefer 'affair'?*

"It's an excellent idea and you know it."

No, she only knew it was a tempting one. "Let me pay you for the rose cultivation book then."

"It's priceless. Literally. There are no other copies in existence." He managed to look pleased about it.

"I need that book, Stearanos, or the roses won't survive."

"Then keep it. My gift to you. I must concede that you are correct—you have the greater need. I only hope that you'll keep me apprised of how the roses are doing."

"Perhaps you could come see them," she offered impulsively, regretting it when his stern visage cracked into that wolfish grin.

"Thank you," he replied gravely. "But I won't impose. Not until you've decided what to do about me."

The man seemed to be able to read her thoughts, aggravating and infuriating. "Maybe I've already decided." Though she hadn't, had she?

"When you're certain instead of a maybe, you can inform me of your decision. Madame." He bowed, crisp and military, nothing like Tristan's elaborate ones. "I await your visit." Again with the wolfish smile. "We can take turns, exchanging visits."

"Is this another of your traps?" she asked with renewed suspicion. "The sort you dress up as invitations."

A light of surprise gleamed in his sere face. "You do know something about me. No trap, Dreamthief. I would never deprive you of your hard-won freedom, even if I could."

"You couldn't," she retorted.

"I know," he returned, sounding more pleased than rueful. "You're like your animals. Powerful, magical, you stay only where you choose. I'm asking you to choose me."

"If I do visit, I'll likely just return the book while you're sleeping," she cautioned him, ignoring the flutter of pleasure at those words.

"Your prerogative, obviously," he allowed, "as I have yet to discover a way to counter your enchantment, but I reserve the right to keep chipping at the problem of warding your magic—and to name you a coward if you do elect to avoid me."

Ugh. She hated that he knew how to get to her, but he did.

Giving him a narrow glare as she pocketed the novel again, she said, "I am not afraid of you, Stormbreaker."

He eased closer, overwhelming her with his powerful presence, tempting her to touch and take. "Aren't you?" he taunted. "I think you are afraid of me, a little bit, though not in the way you meant just now. Neither of us is practiced at being vulnerable."

Her throat tight, heart feeling overlarge in her chest, she denied it with a crisp shake of her head, not trusting her voice or words. With a sigh of regret, he stepped back. "Of the two of us, you are the one who boldly takes what she wants—your freedom from debt, my books, the roses. I didn't think *you* would be the one to be too afraid to take anything else you want."

"You are assuming that I want *you*," she retorted, stung.

"I don't have to assume. I know. That kiss went two ways, sorceress, and you cannot pretend to me that you didn't feel what I did. The question is whether you're willing to come to me and ask for it, thief. No more stealing from me."

"Or else?" she challenged recklessly.

His gaze glittered with answering challenge. "You forget you asked me to remake your wards. They're mine to manipulate now."

"I can replace them with my own," she fired back, regretting that lapse.

He shrugged. "Any ward you can make, I can break. In that arena, I have the advantage. I won't exploit it lightly, but I will use it if I have to. Treat me like your enemy and I will be one."

Her breath caught. "You wouldn't *dare*."

"Wouldn't I?" he asked almost idly. "You know my reputation, Oneira. You decide how far you want to push me."

"You know my reputation, too. In a duel between us, I would win," she spat.

"Are you sure?" He leaned in, lips grazing the shell of her ear as he whispered in it. "I don't think you are—which makes me an irresistible challenge."

"It doesn't," she snapped, jerking her head away, willing her traitorously aroused body to simmer down. She'd been far too long without sex. That was her problem. "Besides, I won't steal from you again, so this exchange of threats is moot."

He shrugged, unperturbed. "Then I look forward to your visit." He turned to face the sea, then looked back at her, smiling warmly as if they hadn't just had an extraordinary exchange. "This has been fun. A pleasant afternoon of intimate conversation with my alluring enemy."

She groaned, and cast her eyes to the sky. "Leave already, Your Eminence. However it is that you plan to go. Not via the Dream, I assume."

"No." He shuddered, and she didn't think that was all a pretense. "I'll leave that to you." He waved a hand and a small ship appeared, rocking on the waves just offshore. Squinting against the light on the water, Oneira cursed herself under her breath for not having known it was there, an aggravation exacerbated by Stearanos's knowing smile.

"Not as fast as traveling by Dream, but quicker than an ordinary ship with a bit of judicious tinkering with distance, and not nearly as treacherous." He had the audacity to wink at her. "Stealthy, too. No one in all the world can detect my travels in this ship, so your secret is safe with me. Call me and I will come to you. Otherwise, I'll await your visit."

"You will wait a long time," she informed him with all the dignity she could muster.

"Yes, Dreamthief," he replied with the solemnity of a vow. "I will. I'll wait forever for you, if need be. I am a patient man, something about me you'll find most rewarding."

With that stirring promise, he turned and walked across the

beach, then across the dancing waves, not altering his stride in the least, nor giving any evidence, even to her sorcerous senses, that he'd used magic to do it. Handy trick, making himself appear to have divine skills. He stepped into the little craft, standing there clearly visible with no sails to obscure him. Lifting a hand in farewell, he and the boat simply faded from sight, until he was gone, as if he'd never been.

Oneira trudged back up the long and winding flight of steps, the afternoon sun against the cliff face as hot as midsummer, the trek wearying as it hadn't been since her early days living there, her thoughts whirling and gnawing over the problem Stearanos presented.

Would you prefer 'affair'?

She could not afford to have an affair with the overpowering sorcerer. Her lifelong enemy, she reminded herself, and for good reason, no matter what he said about the world deciding it instead of them. The world knew what happened when magic-workers of their respective abilities clashed. Entering into any sort of relationship with Stearanos, let alone an intensely sexual one as all evidence indicated it would be, would be a world apart from dallying with someone like Tristan.

Yes, she could control Tristan, as Stearanos had astutely and uncomfortably observed. She could banish Tristan with a small mental nudge in his dreams. More important, she could handle Tristan. She liked the young poet, found him charming and amusing, for all the same reasons Stearanos found Tristan wanting.

If she admitted Stearanos within the silent white walls of her interior self, he would not be expelled again so easily—and not only because he would fight her with his considerable tenaciousness. She didn't trust herself to be able to excise him if it became necessary.

And that was a serious problem.

By the time she reached her garden at the top of the steps, seeing it anew as Stearanos would have observed it on his arrival, she'd made up her mind. Her answer was no. There could be no other answer. She would find a way to return the novel without encountering him again, in all his disturbing presence.

She snorted in disgust at the arrogant sorcerer, the sheer audacity of him baldly proposing she come to him for sex. Saying he knew she wanted it. As if she found him so overwhelmingly seductive that she'd throw caution to the winds. That thought gave her pause. Sorcerers—particularly those poised to be pitted against each other in some war—were known to employ such tactics. What better way to undermine her enmity and determination to defeat him than to pretend to woo her?

Except that she'd told him she was done with war and she thought he'd believed her. He'd even offered to keep their putative friendship a secret. She refused to call it a relationship *or* an affair. He'd understood, as he'd intuited so many other things, how important that secrecy would be to her. Not that it mattered, as there would be nothing *to* keep secret.

They'd never have any contact again. That was for the best.

Never mind that the prospect cast a shadow of sorrow over her. Compared to everything else that grieved her and weighed on her heart and conscience, losing a lover she had never had meant less than nothing. She must keep that truth firmly in mind.

"Is he gone?" Tristan asked hopefully when she found him in her own library, small and sparse compared to the Stormbreaker's. The poet sprawled attractively, harmlessly, in her favorite reading chair, several more books scattered on the floor. "I hope you don't mind," he added, waving a languid hand at the books. "You were gone so long, I grew bored. I missed you," he added, his full lips in a pout, extending that hand. "Lovely Lira."

Annoyed that Tristan now seemed far too boyish and soft

after the stern and stirring Stearanos, Oneira made herself take the offered hand and smiled at him. "I don't mind," she said, although it did kind of bother her, especially the book upended pages down, so it sprawled open, spine in the air. You'd think a poet and scholar would have more respect.

"We're out of wine," Tristan said, giving her a hopeful smile. "I looked, but didn't find a wine cellar in this place. But if we want more at dinner, then . . ." He trailed off expectantly.

Oneira glanced at the lowering light. "We only just finished lunch."

"Oh." His face fell. "Were you not planning on eating again? I suppose you've been away from court for so long that you've grown away from the custom of a late supper."

"Why do you assume I've ever been to court?" She withdrew her hand, not enjoying Tristan's touch as she had before. Curse Stearanos for ruining this, too. She couldn't imagine bedding the poet now—and not because Stearanos had asked her not to. *Don't waste yourself on that pretty boy. He's not good enough for you. Consider my suit instead.*

She shook the sorcerer's rough urging out of her head. No, with Tristan she was now too acutely conscious of the power imbalance between them, and the fundamental dishonesty of taking him to her bed under false pretenses. Picking up the abused book, she saw that one of the pages had creased, and set it to one side. She'd repair that later, when she could use magic to do so.

"Is that an incorrect assumption?" Tristan asked with a concerned frown, sitting upright. "I didn't mean to offend, my lady. You clearly have immense wealth and access to magical conveniences. It would be strange if you had never attended our glorious queen."

Glorious, indeed, Oneira thought wryly, but didn't say aloud. No sense being unkind to the lad—now she was thinking like

Stearanos—and upsetting his worldview. He was young, painfully so, and didn't know better. "I'm not offended," she told him lightly, adding a smile that came straight from court etiquette. "I have been to court, as you correctly guessed, but not for some time."

"I knew I'd remember if I'd ever laid eyes on you before," Tristan said with earnest sincerity. "What can I do to please my lady? I've taken terrible advantage of your hospitality and must find a way to repay you. I could sing for you, if you like?"

A private performance by a poet worthy of the queen's court was a generous offer in every part of the world—and yet Oneira wanted only to be alone with her thoughts. And she felt abruptly weary, no doubt from the initial battle to hold her wards against Stearanos, then keeping up her guard in case he violated his guest vow. She hadn't thought he would, but caution was, as ever, her watch word, and she'd maintained a low-level readiness, just in case, the Dream at the edge of her fingertips, ruthlessly under control.

"I've some studies to pursue," she told Tristan. And a book to copy over, so she could return it to its rightful owner. "I think I shall have to leave you to your own devices this evening."

His face fell into disappointed lines, rather gratifyingly. "*All* evening? Then . . ."

"All evening," she affirmed. "Help yourself to any food you like. I'm afraid there is no more wine." Perhaps that lack would help to dislodge him and send him on his way. "I'll see you off in the morning." Yes, that felt right. Stearanos and his invidious offers had nothing to do with it. She didn't really want Tristan. If she did, she'd have taken him to bed the night before, or allowed that morning to progress further. More's the pity, as her body seethed with frustrated desire.

"See me off?" Tristan repeated, truly upset now. "I *have* offended you, my lady."

"Not at all." She offered him a reassuring smile, resisting the urge to pat him on the head. "I am a recluse accustomed to her own company. It's simply time for you to go."

He nodded, dropping his gaze, his entire demeanor downcast. "I understand. I won't impose on you any longer."

"Make a list of any supplies you need," she offered, "and I'll see what I can fulfill. I won't send you away empty-handed."

"But you *will* send me away," he replied, seeming truly distraught. "Is there anything I can say or do to change your mind?"

"No," she answered, not unkindly. "It's simply time."

❧

Despite her weariness, Oneira barely slept that night—and not for thinking of how she could have slaked her body's needs with the obliging Tristan. No, as she lay amid her nest of pillows, her animals sleeping soundly around her, Oneira gazed up at the starry sky turning in its slow wheel, and thought about Stearanos Stormbreaker.

She'd spent the remainder of the afternoon and all evening sequestered in her dome, copying over the book on rose cultivation until her eyes blurred, wishing viciously that she knew a spell for replicating books. There were no such spells that anyone knew of, contributing to the rarity and value of the things. Back in her academy days, the librarians had often railed against that lack, urging the students to adopt the goal as a personal project. That sort of effort would never be helpful for wars or acquisition of the sorts of things wealthy clients would hire them to do, however, so no one ever took up that particular torch.

Now she felt the librarians' pain. What she should do, she reflected repeatedly, was abandon trying to cultivate the Veredian roses, full stop. That would be the wise decision. She could uproot the roses, return them to the ancient gardener—where they arguably belonged—and return the books to Stearanos, forever severing any connection to him.

By doing that, she could backtrack to where she started, unwinding the coil of this treacherous path where one thing had led on to another. If only she could so easily unlearn what she now knew. If only she could erase the imprint of his mouth against her still-tingling lips, undo their conversations, unsee him, unknow him. Rid herself of any sense that he lived in the world.

As restful as eliminating all memory of him would be, she also knew she wouldn't do it even if she could. Those moments she'd shared with Stearanos shone with a radiance that she couldn't bear to give up. Never had she felt as vibrantly alive as in his presence, whether verbally sparring with him or companionably chopping vegetables.

It made no sense, but there it was. She would never see him again, but she would treasure those memories. And she would keep her roses, devoting herself to nurturing them in lieu of growing any sort of connection between Stearanos and her. That was in line with her original objectives, and she liked that vision of herself: living alone and silently, puttering in her garden, growing roses and eating simply, while Stearanos seduced women and fought wars, far from her silent white walls.

That was another aspect of Stearanos and his life that she should very much bear in mind. She didn't care whether his king would be attacking the Southern Lands, beyond a gut-deep loathing of what the war would bring the world. And that was clearly the plan. His careful nonanswer confirmed it. Still, Oneira had no loyalty to the queen, no interest in thrones or governments. If she'd learned nothing else from all her years of service, she'd grown to understand that all rapacious rulers were the same. They all pleased only themselves, took as much for their own self-aggrandizement as they liked, slaked their own desires at the expense of everyone else.

The people who truly suffered from the wars of the nobility were those who gained nothing from them. And those people she could do nothing to protect. She'd learned that, too.

But Stearanos . . . Once he plunged himself into fighting his king's war, he'd be covered in metaphorical blood, freshly spilled. He'd reek of death and the agonies of the dying—all the things she'd fled. She would not be able to be around him. That much was clear. Even if she could get past everything else, she did not take the danger of being seen as betraying the queen lightly. Part of the terms of her retirement had been a vow not to act against the queen in any way.

No, Oneira would continue on the path she'd forged for herself, clearing her own trail through a wilderness of conflicts and competing priorities. She would live alone and quietly, until she was ready to lay herself upon her bier and be done with this life. Or enter the Dream forever.

Same and same.

And yet, though she absolutely believed in the correctness of her resolve, as the boundaries of consciousness blurred with sleep, the longing Stearanos had stirred in her returned full force. She'd thought that part of her, the desire to touch and be touched in turn, had long since died, along with so many other, softer aspects of her humanity. But it seemed she'd only been slumbering and now found herself tossed in a tumult of erotic awakening.

In time, those needs would dull again, and die a peaceful, final death.

In the morning, she went down to send Tristan on his merry way. Before the day had lengthened, she would have regained the peace and silence of her solitude, if nothing else. She hadn't felt loneliness as something painful until Tristan arrived. Once he was gone, she'd return to that place where longings did not plague her. She would make sure of it.

"I must throw myself on your merciful understanding," Tristan said by way of greeting, looking harried, sullen, and beseeching all at once. "I'm afraid Galahad has pulled up lame."

Oneira held herself still, beyond irritated by this development, and also suspicious. Quite convenient, when Tristan so clearly didn't want to leave. But she accompanied him to the stable, only half listening to the poet's tale of going to Galahad first thing, ready to groom him and saddle him for the day, only to find him favoring the hoof on the side that had been injured. Tristan had tried walking Galahad to work out potential stiffness—knowing very well he'd overstayed his welcome, for which he apologized profusely—but he was greatly concerned that attempting to go any distance today, even with Tristan leading Galahad, would only injure the horse further.

Oneira quelled her doubts and annoyance as she examined Galahad for herself. After all, the gelding didn't deserve her ire. He turned his head, snuffling at her, and she gave him a bit of apple she'd tucked in her pocket for him as a farewell gift. She ran her hands over his flank, using passive magic to sense what went beneath the skin. The scratches were healing nicely, but the ligaments in his haunch had become inflamed, hot and tight beneath her touch. He barely put weight on that leg, just resting the hoof on its point, and when she encouraged him to walk in a circle, he hopped rather than use it.

Letting out a long-aggrieved sigh—the only emotion she

would allow herself to show—she turned to Tristan and managed a smile.

"You're right," she said. "Galahad cannot travel today. Probably not for several days. I'll look up a poultice to brew, something to relieve this inflammation." She did not point out that Tristan should have been exercising Galahad more over the last couple of days, as that should have occurred to her, too. She'd been too long out of practice in dealing with horses and poor Galahad had suffered for it. As Tristan expounded on his relief and gratitude, she soothed the gelding, feeding him another bit of apple. "We'll get you fixed up, you'll see," she whispered to the horse.

He nickered and bobbed his head, as if in agreement, or perhaps in a bid for more apple. As Oneira turned to go back to the house to find a recipe for an appropriate liniment, she spotted Adsila, perched on a beam overhead. The kestrel cocked her head, the ring of gold around the obsidian glinting, as if in warning. Frowning to herself, Oneira wondered at it, walking back to the house and listening to Tristan's assurances that he'd be a helpful and invisible guest.

Oneira didn't visit. Not that night, not the next. Stearanos told himself he wasn't surprised, but had more trouble convincing himself that he wasn't disappointed.

The cagey sorceress wouldn't capitulate easily. That much had been certain from the beginning, even when she was only an anonymous thief. Still, he'd half believed he'd convinced her to at least engage in a friendship with him. They'd had that much, an unexpected gift, and he knew in his bones that she'd recognized that, too.

And then, the passion between them . . . How could she fail to recognize *that*?

Perhaps she had and ran scared of it, frightened of how that overwhelming desire could immolate the people they'd been. If she didn't have the vision to see that they'd emerge from that fire as new people, people they wanted to become, then she deserved her loneliness.

That's what he told himself. Over and over.

Better that than acknowledging the bitter and far more likely truth, that she was happily indulging in her uncomplicated and youthful poet. Eager to please her and no doubt endowed with the stamina to do so, Tristan had probably erased any thought of Stearanos from Oneira's mind. Stearanos could understand that, even wish her well, be generous in his heart and mind for her. He wasn't at all bitter about it. That's what he told himself. Over and over.

He threw himself into the work, researching the plans for

228 · Jennifer K. Lambert

conquest, constructing the maps, composing the strategy for conquering the Southern Lands as a musician would approach a symphony. Math and music shared a great deal in common, both metaphors working for him to frame his magical thinking.

In this way, every line of attack became its own instrument. The bass rhythm of the foot soldiers set the beat that would propel each battle, carrying the momentum of the war. The navy and the cavalry set the harmonies, weaving in and out, lighter and darker tones, sometimes methodically surging, other times shooting through, fast as lightning. The melody grew from those, the magic-workers with their solos, the fantastic creatures of earth, sea, and sky, singing a song of irresistible might.

Through it all, he added the counterpoint of supply lines, underscoring every other melodic component. Food, water, shelter, healers. Here and here and here, a consistent pulse allowing the symphony to grow and thrive.

Aware of the overall structure, Stearanos designed the opus of the war. The opening salvos to set the tone, perhaps with an overture of threats, along with posturing disguised as diplomatic forays. A flurry of intensifying attacks to drive toward a crescendo, diving into the downbeats of extended siege. Then the final build to the true climax, all of the instruments coming together, adding their parts to become a force greater than the simple sum, a building wave to wash away everything in its path, a grand finale of ultimate victory!

Then the denouement, the falling action into resolution, some callbacks to the original overtures, pained and pointed reminders of the peace they'd once enjoyed and could once again establish. A new regime, a golden era, looking forward to a bright future. Peace and prosperity.

He almost convinced himself those final resonant chords of peace would be the end. But not quite.

Sitting back in his chair, Stearanos became aware that the sun had set while he worked, the library shrouded in shadows. With a wave of his hand, he lit all the lamps at once and surveyed what he'd wrought. It was surely his masterwork. A brilliant blend of the magical and the mundane. Without Oneira, the southern queen couldn't hope to stand against them. Her remaining magic-workers, her armies and defenses would topple one by one, until she found herself kneeling before His Majesty, yielding everything to her new overlord.

In his satisfaction, in his sheer pleasure at his own genius, Stearanos could almost forget the true and bloody cost this war would exact. Easy to focus on the bass rhythm of marching feet and forget the individual minds that rode with them, each with their own hopes and dreams, their wishes for fruitful, rewarding lives that had nothing to do with conquest of lands they'd never enjoy for themselves.

Oneira had made him think too much about war and its cost— and their role in it. Perhaps she was correct that any continued conversation between them could only lead to grief and sorrow. Already Stearanos felt a kind of weary despair that threatened to erode his resolve. Or perhaps that was the erosion of his promise not to bother her, not to venture again past her wards unless she invited him. He'd been a fool to leave the decision in her hands. Even as he'd said the words, he'd known he handed her too much power.

But then, she'd possessed all the power from the beginning, the Dreamthief running stealthy circles around him. When he'd punched through her wards, he'd felt a rush of vindicated triumph, which had faded the moment he'd laid eyes on her and known her for what she was: not merely a thief, but the one capable of stealing his heart for all time.

No, he wasn't surprised that she'd never come back to his

library. Oh, she'd find a way to return that novel. Knowing her, she'd return both books, just to be extra certain that he'd have no leverage on her. Sorcerers were very careful about getting themselves into positions of breaking promises or incurring debt. Even when wreaking spells of terrible destruction, a magic-worker meticulously followed established rules of engagement. There was zero margin for anything but complete honesty between the sorcerer's will and the manifestation of magic. The sorcerer who breaks faith in the external world of consensual reality runs the risk of destabilizing their internal reality.

Even a sorcerer like Stearanos, who used quasi-objective reality like numbers, equations, and advanced mathematics to shape his magic, had to acknowledge to himself that it was all a construct. That's how he understood magic, but the numbers didn't actually and in truth govern the magic. The manipulation came from him. For a sorceress like Oneira, who dealt primarily in the realm of the Dream, where reality bent according to whim as much as to disciplined thought, she would be even more wary of blurring her own lines of truth and lie.

With a growl of restless frustration, he launched himself from his chair to pace across the room to stare at the note he'd left her, undisturbed on the shelf for days. It enraged him that she wouldn't take up his challenge, that she wouldn't allow them this chance. And he understood why, also. His respect and admiration for her grew as a result. Oneira drew clear boundaries and she'd walk away rather than risk violating them. No wonder she was the one to retire, to exile herself rather than tolerate another moment fighting the wars of men.

The wonder of it was that she'd lasted as long as she had. Whereas he . . . well, he'd been one to capitulate to what was asked of him. Just this moment, he'd drawn up an elaborate, stirringly brilliant strategy to win a war he didn't care about, and why? Because he could. Because he'd been told to and he'd always done what he was told.

He paced back to his desk and splayed his hands over the work. A work of genius. Stearanos tightened his fingers into claws, the paper bunching beneath the rictus of his despair and rage. He should tear it apart, throw it in the fire.

Let the mobs come for him. What did it matter? He had nothing to live for.

At that moment, just as he'd resolved to do it and give himself up to whatever punishment Uhtric would devise—though Stearanos could hardly be more in debt—his exhausted dispiritedness morphed into a deeper wave of sleepiness. Belatedly, he identified the reason, the source.

Oneira.

He knew the flavor of her magic, the irresistible siren call of her enchantment sending him to sleep, to dream. She was coming. And she was not leaving him awake.

Stearanos didn't bother fighting the spell. He'd tried and failed before. This was her strength, her sole kingdom where she ruled and he was but a powerless denizen. But, as the Dream roared up in all its drugging, sapping release, dragging him into its arms, sweet, soft, and promising surcease, he seized the quill and defiled the once-crisp lines of his plans with a single word. The one challenge that pierced the high walls of Oneira's determination to shut him out.

Coward.

❧

Oneira stepped out of the Dream and into the Stormbreaker's library—not at all surprised to see Stearanos there, slumped over his work again. Sound asleep, as she'd intended. Good. He might have the power to smash through her wards, but he couldn't resist her ability to put him safely out of commission.

What she didn't expect was the stab of acute longing at the sight of even the back of his head, his unbound braids spilling over to puddle on the desk. She'd spent the last several days convincing herself that his visit, that *he*, had been something less than her memories suggested. That her imagination had conjured him from wistfulness and yearning. She wasn't able to pretend that it had all been a dream, as she understood dreams far too well to delude herself to that extent, but she had been able to decide that the kiss couldn't have been that potent. That the conversation hadn't been so stimulating. That his interest in her must be far more transient and far less intriguing than it had felt at the time.

That the temptation was nothing she couldn't withstand.

How wrong she'd been, on every point. Even fast asleep, Stearanos was even more potent, more vivid and tantalizing than her most lurid fantasies had served up.

Not that the revelation changed her mind. She'd made a decision and she was sticking to it. No more of this ridiculous vacillating.

Moving with brisk determination, she made herself go to his shelves, to replace the novel and the book on rose cultivation in their precise spots. But, when she went to put the novel away, though the exact space had been left empty for it, she found a folded note sitting there slantwise, so she'd have to at least move it in order to replace the book. With a sigh, she extracted the paper with her barest fingertips, seriously considering consigning it to ash with a small burst of flame, leaving it for Stearanos to find on his plush and pristine rug.

Except he didn't deserve that. He hadn't done anything wrong or aggressive by issuing his seductive invitation. She couldn't even blame him for breaking her wards and forcing a confrontation, as that was understandable, even expected.

Checking to be sure he still slept soundly, she unfolded the note and read.

> *My dearest Dreamthief,*
>
> *As you're reading this note, I assume you took the coward's way out and I'm sleeping, unable to enjoy your company and conversation. So, I must make do with this.*
>
> *Did you like the novel? I read it some time ago and don't recall the details—and, of course, was unable to reread—but I remember being vaguely dissatisfied with the ending. Thoughts? If I could hear them, I'd offer a recommendation for your next read. As it is, I must guess. I suggest* When the Sea Shall Give Up Her Dead. *You'll find it on the bookshelf on epic love affairs. It would please me for you to <u>borrow</u> it—I must be specific that I won't consider this a theft—and would delight me even more if you would trust me enough to keep me awake so we can talk about it. What harm, Dreamthief? What risk?*
>
> *Wake me up now. I promise only conversation, if that's all you want of me.*
>
> *Your Em*

Oneira growled to herself in annoyance, glaring over at the sleeping Stearanos, master manipulator and tempter, dangerous even when completely under her power. Pocketing the note, with no intention of either replying or waking him up to be even more distracting—nor of borrowing any more books—she went to replace the rare book on rose cultivation. This time she wasn't at all surprised to see something in its spot. Another folded note, on top of a long, thin box. Unable to resist her curiosity, though she knew he was using that weakness against her, she pulled out both. She read the note first, this one much shorter.

> *You better have made a copy. If you let those roses die or return them to the ancient gardener, I will haunt you the rest of your days. Meanwhile, until yours bloom, this one reminded me of you and your extraordinary hair. You, minus the thorns, that is. (Which is hardly you at all, come to think of it.)*

"You can try to haunt me," she informed the sleeping sorcerer, though she couldn't help smiling. How well he'd guessed how she'd handled the problem, and the options she'd considered. Pocketing that note, too, she opened the box, and released another sigh. This one not of exasperation and weariness, but from some place deep inside that hadn't yet withered away from enduring too much of the horrors of the world.

It was a rose. Not a Veredian one, of course, but unlike any rose she'd ever seen. Mostly a golden ivory, its petals were shot through with pale pink streaks from the base that coalesced to gather into full, bright crimson at the tips, as if it had been dipped in fresh blood that had wicked its way up to concentrate there. And yet, while the echo of blood should have bothered her, in this context it didn't. Perhaps because it seemed to be about life, not death. The scent, spicy and sweet at once, intoxicated her with its loveliness. The entire rose seemed only about beauty, nothing harsh or hurtful to it. Examining it closely, she saw that Stearanos had indeed clipped off all the thorns, leaving them scattered in the bottom of the silk-lined box.

"Ha ha, very funny," she muttered at him, bemused and amused. He wouldn't clip her own thorns so easily. Though she'd intended to step back into the Dream immediately after she returned the book to its rightful place, she succumbed to the very minor temptation of drawing closer to Stearanos, dropping the clipped thorns into a pile on his documents. In doing so, she caught the hurried scrawl, the message he'd left, naming her a coward, scowling at it.

As if a childish taunt would erode her resolve. She'd seen enough of war to know that the brave died far more often than anyone else. Bravery was an overrated quality that best served the nobles and generals who stayed well back from the front lines. Exercising justifiable caution was something else entirely.

Averting her gaze from the additional temptation to peek at his plans for conquest, she turned away and opened a door into the Dream. Then hesitated.

What harm? What risk?

She'd restored the balance between them. They'd become something of friends.

She was weary of Tristan's inane company.

A small bit of conversation couldn't hurt, could it?

What harm? What risk?

Feeling as if she stepped off her own cliff with the drop to a raging sea below, Oneira took a breath, and allowed Stearanos to wake.

Stearanos swam up from the deep sleep, from indigo dreams of calming rest, his mind clearing as the enchantment released him. One thing he had to give Oneira—her spell gave true sleep, replenishing and delicious. Likely she could make it otherwise, pitching her victims into nightmares and soul-terrors, ripping their unconscious apart so they awoke exhausted and harried. Even though she hadn't exempted him from her enchantment, at least she'd been kind about it.

Then, as he became fully aware, he sensed her presence, instinctively bracing to shield himself from attack. He opened his eyes. Slowly, he lifted his head, seeing the pile of clipped thorns atop his scrawled challenge to her. He smiled, having predicted she would do that, thus greeting her frown with his pleased expression.

"You ruined your document," she informed him crisply from the other side of his desk. "A waste of high-quality paper."

"Absolutely worth the expense," he replied, taking her in. She could be a dream herself, impossibly lovely and magical, a creature from fantasy. Remaining poised there, she looked as if she might disappear at any moment, a faint numinous glow surrounding her, blurring the edges.

It was the Dream, he realized. She stood on the threshold of it, ready to step back and disappear. If he focused his sorcerous senses on it, he could make out the faintly iridescent outline of a portal and swirls of movement within it. The more he looked, the more colors he saw beyond that doorway, the echoes of creatures so fantastically alluring that he longed to chase after them. He didn't realize he'd half risen to do so until Oneira spoke, interrupting his rapt fascination.

"It's not wise to look too closely at the Dream while awake," she warned him. "It's not meant for our waking selves. To observe the Dream from a conscious state invites dreams into your waking reality, and there lies madness."

With effort, he focused on her instead, on her clear, silver gaze, that hair spilling around her in crimson glory, the exact shade of the petal tips of the rose she held. "Then how do you move about in it and exert conscious control over the Dream?"

Her lips quirked in a secretive smile. "Sorcery."

"Why leave the door open then, if it's so dangerous for me?" he asked.

"I . . ." She actually looked somewhat abashed.

"Wanted an easy escape route?"

"There is rarely anything easy about escaping," she retorted, almost primly, her eyes glittering with some emotion he couldn't quantify.

"Then come in and close the door behind you," he invited. "Tell me how you liked the novel you borrowed and returned."

She narrowed those eyes, still hesitating on the threshold of a dream. "The shelf is behind you. How are you so sure I returned it?"

"First of all, it's you. You would not have come here until you could return it, and you're not one to delay. Also, it's part of my talents as a posotomancer. My sorcery allows me to quantify most anything. I know where everything in my house is and isn't."

"Thus the obsessiveness."

"I prefer to think of it as attention to detail."

"Hmm."

238 · *Jennifer K. Lambert*

Her gaze rested on him, pensive, weighing her options. Stearanos had an odd sensation of unreality, as if he might be sleeping still and dreaming this conversation, that she might evaporate at any moment and become something else. He rubbed his eyes and focused on her again.

She let out a huff of impatience. "It's having the Dream open. You're awake, but it's getting to you. I should go."

"Stay," he countered immediately. "Please? I have wine."

After an eternity of hesitation, she stepped fully into the room, the Dream closing behind her with a snap he felt all through his magical senses. A faint odor lingered in the air, the sort both familiar and rarely named, like petrichor or oud. A shimmer of magic glistened like ice crystals forming from the humidity in the air on a brutally cold day in the northern wastes. Oneira waved her hand at the miasma impatiently, looking like someone clearing obnoxious smoke from their face, only her efforts worked, vanishing the residue as if it had never been.

"Apologies," she said. "I should not have left the doorway to the Dream that wide open for so long. I didn't intend to."

"You also didn't intend to stay, but I'm glad you did." He rose and went to the wine, tipping the bottle to show her it was unopened, the seal around the cork intact.

She smiled wryly, gaze lifting to his. "I would not have lingered if I thought you meant to poison me."

"As if I could."

"As if you could," she acknowledged.

He used magic to remove the cork, sinking the correct numbers into it to assess its circumference and decrease it enough for the air pressure he increased inside to ease it out.

Oneira raised her brows. "A handy trick."

Pouring a glass, he handed it to her. "Useful for impressing the ladies."

"Do you often entertain ladies you're intent on impressing?"

"You're the first," he admitted, clinking his glass against hers. "An admission that doubles as a toast."

Her eyes on his, she sipped, making a low sound of pleasure that reminded him of how she'd hummed when they kissed, the desire he'd ruthlessly leashed hitting him hard in the groin.

"So, which is it," she asked, slowly spinning the stem of the goblet between her index finger and thumb, "do you not entertain ladies, or do you not care about impressing them?"

"I haven't had a lover in years, but when I did, I never brought them here. And no, I didn't care about impressing them. As you succinctly noted, for our sort, finding a lover who isn't terrified of us is a challenge. Impressing them would be not only redundant but would pale in comparison."

"Our sort," she echoed.

"Yes. We are of a kind, you and I. Will you sit?"

She cast her gaze about the room. "Your rusty entertaining habits make themselves known. All of your chairs are singles."

In consternation, he noticed she was right. Poor planning. "You sit in the armchair," he pointed to his reading chair by the fire, "and I'll drag my desk chair over."

"No need." That same luminescence shimmered, the unnamed scent unfurling in the room, and a doorway outlined itself in the air. Fascinated, he observed as the reality of his library dissolved within the rectangle, and the Dream uncoiled in all its unnatural landscape.

"Don't look directly," Oneira reminded him, and he quickly averted his gaze, aware of the fuzzy sense of being not quite awake.

He felt the portal close right as Oneira told him it was safe to look. There sat a new chair beside his, like and unlike, as if reflected in an imperfect mirror.

"Handy trick," he said with a smile.

"Useful for impressing the gentlemen."

"Ah, Oneira, I am already beyond impressed." He did not add that he obviously knew which other gentleman she'd been entertaining, nor did he ask if she'd bedded the puppyish poet, much as the question burned on his tongue. To distract himself, he went to examine the chair she'd conjured. "It looks just like mine."

"Nearly," she replied, scrutinizing it with professional objectivity.

"Nearly" was the operative word, as it seemed very much like his chair, but subtly altered. The color of the oxblood leather didn't quite match. Nor was it, he determined on closer examination, upholstered in actual leather. Instead the material had a satiny give that wasn't unpleasant, but also felt oddly unreal. The studs all lay in the same pattern as his chair, but bore varying sigils instead of the matching embossed stars in the brass of his, and they served no actual purpose, the upholstery seamless, enveloping the chair like a coat of glossy paint. Most extraordinary, the clawed feet of the wooden legs extended actual talons in a gradation of ochre to ivory, looking for all the world as if they belonged to a living animal.

"Do you mind the oddness?" Oneira asked curiously, observing his intent examination.

"I'm fascinated," he admitted. "Is everything you pull from the Dream like this?"

"Only if I don't take the time to refine it. Objects in the Dream are like . . . well, think of how things seem in your dreams. They are familiar, and very nearly like what you know in the real world, but also ever so slightly different. If I pluck something from the Dream and do nothing else to it, I'll usually get a close approximation of what I want, but it will never be confused with something from the real world."

"Usually?" he queried, increasingly fascinated.

She grimaced. "Something like a chair of this sort is fairly easy to find, because people furnish their dreams with common items. The more specialized or uncommon an object, the longer it can take to locate in the Dream and the more work I have to do to alter it to blend with the waking world."

"And how do you that, the altering?"

Her lips quirked in a half smile and she gestured to the wine bottle. "Sorcery, yes?"

He nodded, considering. "Can I sit in it?"

"Yes, but you should take your own—" She huffed out a breath as he sat in the one she'd made from the Dream, running his hands over the arms with interest. "Fine." She sat in his usual chair, perching on the edge and holding her wineglass in both hands, the rose in its box on her lap.

"The things I saw in your house didn't have this odd—all right, I'll say it—dreamy feel," he noted.

"Dreamlike is probably more apt."

"Dreamy," he returned, snuggling into the chair. "Like sitting in a cloud. Can I keep it?"

She ignored that. "You didn't see my entire house. Only the kitchen and the outside."

"True, but you have that blissfully ignorant mundane lad staying with you, so it can't be too odd or he'd wonder."

"Ah." She saluted him with her wineglass. "You, as a posotomancer, have greater sensitivity for noticing such things, as you, in particular have that gift for detail." She nodded to herself as he acknowledged that truth. "But, that's part of the skill of being an oneiromancer, the shaping. Very few things that come directly from the Dream are useable. For example, food is no more nutritious than it is in a dream."

"That's why you grow and make your own food."

"That's not the only reason."

"I know."

"Do you?" She looked intrigued and he blessed her native curiosity.

"Yes. I only grow beautiful useless things." He gestured to the rose in her lap. "But you've inspired me to try my hand at vegetables."

Glancing down, she picked up the rose as if she'd forgotten about it, twirling the stem between her thumb and forefinger as she had with the wineglass. "You grew this yourself then?"

He raised his brows. "You're surprised? You knew I love gardens and know plants, and that I have a particular interest in roses."

"That doesn't mean you do the work yourself," she replied, meeting his gaze evenly without a hint of chagrin.

"With my own hands." He held them up, showing them to her, front and back, as if that demonstrated anything.

"I wondered why you had dirt under your nails," she commented.

He suppressed a surge of excited satisfaction. She'd examined him closely while he slept, to know that.

"Why do you do it?" she asked, silver gaze intent, and he realized it wasn't a challenge, but genuine interest. Thinking about her own motivations, perhaps.

Studying his hands, still turning them back and forth, he saw how like his father's hands they were, something he hadn't noticed until that moment. A working man's hands, unpretty, callused, hardened, the knuckles bigger than they used to be. None of the metaphorical blood on them showed, only the scars of manual labor. Symbolic of something, though he didn't know what.

"It's different, isn't it?" he mused. "All those years we spent learning to control those childhood accidents." He glanced up at her, assuming she'd had similar experiences to his, and she nodded minimally, old pain in her eyes. "Then studying magic, improving and amplifying our ability to manipulate these unseen, untouchable forces." He waved his hands, at a loss for the appropriate words.

"Inhabiting unreality," she filled in.

"Yes." He breathed the affirmation. "You understand."

Her lips quirked. "Perhaps more than most. It doesn't get more unreal than the Dream, but then, I don't really know how posotomancy works."

Interesting, to have the opportunity to explain his craft to someone who was both new to his precise skill set, but knowledgeable enough to understand the explanation. The academies kept the various specializations sequestered from one another, encouraging secrecy and isolation. "You said you pull from the Dream and then use your sorcery to shape it. It's similar for me in that I reach into the underlying reality of an object by assessing it, I find its dimensions and then alter those to make them be what I want."

Her expression rapt, she considered. "So very interesting. The underlying magic is, of course, operating in the same way, but you use quantification to alter objects to suit your purpose. I do the same, only for me it's not at all mathematical. More intuitive."

"Just our modality for manipulating reality differs," he agreed. "Which makes sense, since we all have some ability to work magic in all the traditional disciplines, just particular strengths in certain arenas."

"Or weaknesses." She grimaced. "I've never had much ability with numbers and my rune work is rudimentary."

"I noticed." He nearly laughed in the face of her indignation. "Oh, your wards are good enough to keep out the mundane world and probably most magic-workers. Just not a wardbreaker of my caliber."

She wrinkled her nose at him, looking suddenly young and impudent with it. "When one is an oneiromancer, wards and other boundaries of the world are irrelevant. As you learned first-hand, Lord of Wards," she reminded him archly, even playfully.

"That's true until someone breaches *your* wards," he persisted, eliciting a huff of annoyance from her. "I can strengthen your wards for you," he offered, as if that weren't a huge breach of etiquette and protocol.

She stilled. "You can't do that."

"In point of fact, I can. You had me fix what I broke."

She waved that off. "That's entirely different. What you're proposing smacks of collaboration, of *alliance*." She dropped her voice on the final word, as if fearing they'd be overheard.

"Is it really an alliance if you're retired?" He refused to drop his voice. His wards were the best in all the world. No one would overhear them.

Oneira was shaking her head slowly back and forth. "You know that's forbidden. *This* is why they keep us apart, why they sequester us by specialization at academy. Why the most powerful among us are tutored privately. It starts chummily enough, then we start chatting about our work, confiding our methods, then we begin to think we're friends, that we can be allies."

"We *are* friends."

"We do not command our own loyalties," she retorted, annoying him by refusing to acknowledge his words.

"Because they stack the deck against us when we're too young to know better and unable to escape them," he countered. "They bind us to their blood geas, trap us in debt and isolate us, pit us against one another. Isn't sharing information a way for us to assert control over our own lives?"

"I already did," she answered with a smile of satisfaction, though her gaze went shadowed.

"Yes, you did. I'd love to hear how you pulled it off."

All hint of a smile fled her countenance. "I should go."

"Please don't. You haven't finished your wine. We can speak of something else."

With a mutinous press of her lips, she took a sip of wine and looked at him. The silence stretched out and she moved in the chair restlessly. "What else do you want to talk about?"

So many things, but he firmly shifted his mind off all of them. "How did you like the novel?" he asked again. "Do you agree with my thoughts on the ending?"

She barely moved, her head nodding a breath of acknowledgment. "Ah, of course you know I picked up that note."

"And replaced the book, yes. Thank you. Both books, I perceive. I hope you copied the other?" Otherwise he'd find a way to make her take it.

"I did." She cocked her head. "How did you know?"

"It was the logical assumption, unless you had Tristan do it. I imagine he has a fair hand at transcribing."

"And let him see that incredibly valuable rare book?" Her brows climbed in astonished remonstration. "I would not be so foolish."

No, but she was foolish enough to keep the glorified minstrel about. "Then he hasn't moved on yet."

"I told him to be on his way," Oneira replied, her brows falling into a knot of irritation, "but his horse pulled up lame."

"How convenient."

"You and your paranoia. I examined the horse myself and have been treating him. He's honestly injured."

Stearanos only nodded neutrally. He had no doubt the horse was honestly injured—and had gotten that way through dishonest means. Still, he wouldn't push Oneira into defending the duplicitous lad. "So . . ." He was unable to restrain the question, no matter how jealous he'd sound. "How is he in bed?"

"The horse? I wouldn't know. Rather unwieldy, I'd think."

"The poet."

"None of your business."

"That means you don't know."

She glared daggers at him. "Incorrect. That means I'm not discussing it with you."

"Why not?" He leaned his elbows on his knees. "I'd love to know what you like, what you don't like, what you fantasize about."

Her expression went very still, color gracing her high, strong cheekbones, lips pressed firmly together. "I'm not discussing any such thing with you."

"Why not?" he repeated, sitting back in the chair and casually sipping his wine. "It's better to have this conversation before we have sex, so I know how to make it good for you."

"Because we are not having sex!" she burst out, setting her glass down on the side table too vigorously, so that it splashed. Without breaking stride, she flicked a finger to vanish the spill. Sending it into the Dream? he wondered.

"That doesn't mean we can't discuss it," he replied easily.

"For me it does."

"You never told your previous lovers what you liked beforehand?"

"You say 'previous' like you are my lover, which you are not, Stormbreaker," she bit out, her color even higher.

"I infer that means you did not. Could be the problem," he murmured sympathetically. "Difficult to obtain ideal results that way."

"Problem?" she inquired icily, her tone a contrast to her heated cheeks.

"You said you hadn't had good luck with sex," he reminded her. "Perhaps it was less ill luck than a woeful lack of preparation."

"You are teasing me mercilessly," she accused.

"Something I enjoy," he allowed. "Worried that you can't best me in this sort of duel?"

That got her. "I can't be coerced, Stormbreaker, no matter how highly you think of yourself."

"I know," he reminded her.

"I really should go." This time, she stood and dusted her hands on her skirt, a pristine white that shimmered like new-fallen snow.

"Don't go yet," he coaxed, rising also. "There's more wine. And we didn't finish discussing the novel you read."

She fixed him with a pointed glare. "I didn't care for how it ended."

"I guessed you wouldn't." Neither of them were talking about the novel anymore.

"Yes, well. It's easy enough to begin. The challenge is in the execution and culmination."

"Are we talking about sex again?" He'd tried for a teasing jest—and regretted his attempt immediately.

Oneira was one of those who grew cold with anger, her face paling and tightening. "You are no fool, Stearanos, so don't play the role. It sits ill on you. We cannot continue this thing we've begun. It must stop now."

A hiss of unheard magic allowed the tendrils of the Dream into the room, that sense of the edges of things blurring, the scent with no name—though he didn't see the portal light yet. He still had a chance. "Don't let this be the end," he said, nearly begging. "You promised that I could come see the roses."

The onrushing Dream backed off somewhat. "I never *promised*," she hissed.

"You said so, and for people like us, our words bind us."

She visibly seethed, unable to deny the truth of it. "They won't bloom until midwinter," she said stiffly.

"I'll come then. Or before, to see the progress of the bushes themselves. Just drop me a note. You know where to find me." He rethought that. What if he'd embarked on the conquest and wasn't here?

She read it in him. "Via the Dream, I can find you anywhere, Stormbreaker. Something you should remember, lest it be your downfall."

"You don't frighten me, Oneira," he said softly.

"Then you're a fool," she replied with ice in her tone. The portal to the Dream opened wide, with no warning from her, a flexing of her power.

"Oneira." He had to fight not to look in the open doorway. Unobscured by her body, the landscape beyond swirled in unnatural shapes, scents, sounds, and colors, enthralling, disturbing, and alluring.

She stepped in to block his view of the Dream, giving him a look both exasperated and ever so slightly apologetic. "What?" she asked, putting a world of weariness into the single word.

He picked up the rose where she'd discarded it, replacing it in its box, closing the lid, and handing it to her wordlessly. "It would be grievous indeed to refuse a gift already accepted."

Putting out a hand, she took it, then gave him a long, considering look. "Goodbye, Stormbreaker."

"I wish you wouldn't call me that," he said on impulse.

She cocked her head, predictably curious. "Why not?"

"It's not accurate, not a name I chose. Call me Em, instead. For just between us."

"There is no just between us," she replied on a sigh.

"Until next time, Oneira." He bowed and, by the time he straightened, she'd disappeared, vanishing like a dream upon awakening.

❧ 27 ❧

Oneira stepped out of the Dream and into the room under her crystal dome, pressed a hand to her stomach, and fell to her knees. None of her animals were about, the night sky still thick as it curved against the transparent sphere. Stretching out her senses, she verified that Tristan slept soundly, sadly alone in his bed, dreaming inconsequential fragments of things.

"Curse Stearanos," she muttered to herself. All of her problems had begun when she'd succumbed to the temptation to visit his library. She'd been so much better off when she'd kept to her white walls and silences.

One opening had led to another. Trading notes leading to her thinking flirtatious thoughts, opening her wards to Tristan and thinking about bedding him, Stearanos arriving on her doorstep and then asking her what she liked in bed! She pressed her hands to her still-hot cheeks. A woman her age shouldn't feel this way. She'd been the one to make the joke about true love's kiss, but Stearanos had awakened something in her she'd long thought dead, something that Tristan, for all his skilled seductions, had failed to arouse.

She hadn't even touched Stearanos this time and her body pulsed with desire, her mind swirling with erotic thoughts. He'd been so compelling, with his thoughtful questions, his sharp face alive with intelligence, those long fingers inviting fantasies of how they might feel on her. And the memory of their singular kiss making her think of nothing else but asking for another.

Almost not believing she could feel so aroused from nothing

but a conversation, she slipped a hand beneath her skirts, her skin sparking to her own touch. Her sex throbbed with need and she cupped herself, her tissues swollen and slick as they had never been any time she could recall. Pressing her fingers into that sweet ache, she shocked herself by immediately climaxing, the orgasm wrenching her with sharp, convulsing pleasure, so she ended up face down, curled around her hand, out of breath.

With Stearanos filling her mind. *Sorcerer.*

She huffed out a laugh, and kept laughing. That release, too, feeling as necessary a purging as the other. Flopping onto her back, oddly at peace now, she watched the slow turning of the wheel of stars until she fell asleep.

And when she dreamed, they were all her own.

The next day brought a messenger.

Oneira knelt in the garden, diligently weeding the peas, occasionally pausing in the task to stake up a stray vine. They were flowering, the blossoms colorful and sweet smelling. Lounging in the shade nearby, Tristan recited an epic poem for her that she hadn't heard before. She did enjoy listening to his tales. With his fluid voice mingling with the distant surf and the humming of bees, the sun warm on her back, and fertile earth beneath her, she was relaxed, even happy. The arousing conversation with Stearanos felt like a pleasant daydream, immediate in the keen pleasure of that shimmering, lively desire, distant enough to be simply a remembered pleasure. She could indulge in her memories of him in the loveliest way.

Then her wards pinged.

For a moment—brief, but far longer than she liked—she actually hoped it was Stearanos. Foolish of her, as Stearanos didn't politely knock. Stearanos didn't do polite anything. No, that wasn't fair. Once they'd established their truce, he'd been excruciatingly correct with her. With the exception of some startlingly frank conversation.

Oneira kicked herself for the palpable disappointment she experienced. She should be *relieved* it wasn't him. But if this wasn't him, then . . .

Her wards pinged again, more insistently. Focusing her senses, she arrowed her attention to the familiar point on the road to the world of men, from whence Tristan had come and should have returned already. Why had she even kept the road? She should fill it with forest. Nothing good came of the wretched thing.

That opinion was only confirmed by what she saw: a young man in the queen's livery.

Internally she groaned, once again cursing Stearanos. This had to be all his fault. She didn't know exactly how, but she had no doubt it was. She'd love to ignore the messenger. Or, better yet, fry him on the spot with a judicious bit of lightning from the Dream, though that would violate her resolve not to cause any more deaths and, besides, the poor man *was* only the messenger. She could summon a nightmare to chase him away, however, with no lasting damage done.

She discarded that impulse immediately. If she didn't receive the message, the queen would only send more and more. It had never mattered to the queen that Oneira turned her messengers away, unanswered. Zarja simply continued to hurl missives at her like squirrels barraging interlopers with nuts. Better to find out what Her Majesty wanted, send a polite, but firm refusal, and go back to her quiet life.

Waving Tristan to silence, she stood. "There's a messenger at the road," she explained, brushing the dirt off her hands.

Tristan bounced to his feet with enviable agility and swept her a florid bow. "I can go for you, my lady."

"I need to go down and release the wards," she reminded him.

"You let me through the wards from the house." His brow furrowed. "Though I suppose you never have shown me the mechanism."

And never will. She gave him a pleasant smile, tempted to pat him on the cheek, but she'd established a no-physical-contact rule between them and intended to keep it. Not that she was tempted by him any longer, but she wearied of fending off his advances. "I don't intend to let a messenger *inside* the wards. He can pass along the message and be on his way again." She wasn't letting anyone else, anyone human, inside her wards. Look what had happened with the two exceptions.

"But, my lady, what if he is required to wait for a reply?"

"Then he can wait for a reply."

"On the road?" Tristan sounded almost plaintive.

"I assume he is equipped to pass the night outdoors, if necessary," she replied caustically. "If not, he can journey back to the nearest village."

"A day's ride away!"

"Then back to wherever he came from this morning," she replied implacably, attempting not to lose her patience. Oneira wasn't accustomed to being questioned and Tristan had grown far too familiar with her. Past time for him to move on. Fortunately, Galahad had nearly healed enough for the journey. "Why do you care, Tristan?"

"It would just be nice to have some new company," he answered, a hair away from sullen.

"I'm sorry my company is so tedious."

"I didn't mean—"

She waved him off as the wards pinged again, insistently. "I can always send my reply to Her Majesty with you. Then you can be back at her court and in all the stimulating company you like."

"This is the queen's messenger?" he squeaked in equal parts alarm and excited glee. "My lady is a confidante of Her Majesty?"

Oneira regretted the slip. This was one of the many reasons that prevaricating, even lying by omission, landed one in a tangled web. "Not a confidante," she corrected. "But I have, on certain occasions, performed services for the crown. Now, wait for me here." She stopped short of telling him to be a good boy, and sighed at herself for ever contemplating bedding him. She blamed Stearanos for that, too, whether it made any sense or not.

"But I should go along to protect you," Tristan protested weakly.

"I have my animals." She walked away, Adsila winging in to light on her shoulder, Bunny bounding up from the sea steps, dripping wet and shaking himself dry. Moriah melted in from the shadows, black fur hot from whatever spot the cat had found to sunbathe in. Their presence would keep Tristan away. He tried to pretend the animals didn't frighten him, but it was clear there was no love lost between any of them. Her animals tolerated him and left him mostly alone, which was all she required of them.

Oneira unlocked the gates, passed through, and locked them behind her. The path wound down the hillside to the road. Not far. Stearanos was at least partially right in mocking her ward-building ability; she hadn't been able to construct them at as great a distance from the house as she'd have liked, and he'd reconstructed them along the same boundaries.

She was not, however, taking him up on his offer to strengthen her wards either. She snorted at the audacity of the suggestion, not for the first time. Oh yes, have your nemesis "improve" your defenses. What a brilliant idea.

Her wards pinged yet again, and she strolled into view around the bend, the messenger officiously tapping a gilded cane against the invisible wall. He spotted her, his eyes going wide, possibly at the sight of her animal companions, though his gaze remained fixed on her. "Your Eminence, Sorceress Oneira," he gasped, going to one knee and bowing his head.

This was why she'd made Tristan stay behind. "You have a message for me?" she inquired coolly, refusing to give any sort of welcome.

"Yes, Your Eminence. I could not pass the wards."

"Nor will you. Her Majesty promised to leave me undisturbed." Fat lot of good *that* promise had been, as happened with most promises the mundane made.

"Begging your pardon, Your Eminence"—the man's throat squinched nervously around the words—"but Her Majesty advised me to ask Your Eminence to recall the terms of the agreement between Her Majesty and Your Eminence and that—"

"Yes, yes, yes," she interrupted impatiently. This was one of the many reasons she'd hated court. The endless repetition of titles made every conversation excruciatingly long. Technically she'd shed that title when she retired, but she didn't bother saying so to the messenger. He'd never comply with calling her anything less.

"I'm aware of all the agreements I've made," she added with asperity. In those agreements were the only two reasons for the queen to have violated Oneira's solitude. "You may leave the missive and depart."

"With deepest apologies, Your Eminence, I'm to see that you receive the missive, then await a reply."

Score one for Tristan. "Set it there and draw back twenty paces," she advised the messenger. Not that the thoroughly mundane gent could do anything to her, but it pleased her to be difficult. It salved her irritation—and exacerbated her concern over just what the queen wanted. It couldn't possibly have to do with incipient conquest from the north, spearheaded by Oneira's archnemesis, could it? Oh no, who could think it?

With a show of reluctance, the messenger laid the ornate scroll on the ground before her wards, then led his horse back the required twenty paces before turning to watch. Oneira dissolved a small patch of the wards, took hold of the scroll, and brought it through, holding it up in demonstration as she mentally knitted the hole together again. "I'll be back with a reply. You may wait or return later."

"I'll wait, Your Eminence," the man replied, somewhat glumly.

Tempted to ask Bunny to remain at the road to glare at the hapless messenger through the transparent wards, Oneira acknowledged that she was being petty. It burned that the queen had dared to breach her privacy, and Oneira was taking out her frustration on everyone but the deserving target. She trudged up the path, all of her animal friends with her, and focused her ire on the one person whose fault this undeniably was: Stearanos.

❦

Oneira took the missive to her private study, the one she'd prevented Tristan from noticing by spinning an illusion out of the Dream. That was far easier for her than warding it against him. There she could relax and perform magic without being concerned that he'd see more than was good for him.

She spent some time checking the scroll for hidden traps or compulsions, more out of a reluctance to read the contents than any real concern. Paranoia belonged to Stearanos, and besides, Zarja wanted something. Her Majesty wouldn't do anything to anger Oneira, now that she couldn't force her obedience. Unable to procrastinate any longer, Oneira unrolled the scroll.

Adsila, still on her shoulder, peered at the ornate script also. Oneira scanned the document, then read it a second time more carefully. The third read gave her nothing more and she sat with her head in her hands for a very long time.

Stearanos should've had little time to stew over Oneira. Not her obstinate refusal to acknowledge the connection between them, not her precipitous departure that evening of her visit, and not the fact that she hadn't visited him again.

She'd said she could find him anywhere, but she hadn't done so. He hadn't been surprised that she didn't show while he was at His Majesty's court, meeting with the war council, though her frank and wry intelligence would've been a welcome breath of fresh air in the stultifying atmosphere of posturing and power wrangling. Much as he longed to be in her company again, for her to visit him under Uhtric's nose wouldn't be wise. And Stearanos had been busy from waking to sleeping, so he shouldn't have had time to think about her.

Which made no difference at all.

Even as Crown Prince Mirza paced the council room—the king had yet to put in an appearance, apparently sincere in his resolve to completely hand over the campaign to his son—uttering grandiose ponderings on how best to celebrate the victory of the war they'd not yet begun, Stearanos imagined Oneira in her gardens. The spring blooms would be giving way to the more robust blossoms of full summer. Although, he supposed, on her cliff over the sea it would remain cooler most of the year. She wouldn't get the weight of summer heat as he did at his castle. Even being on the coast, his place was too low and too sheltered for all but the most vigorous ocean breezes.

258 · *Jennifer K. Lambert*

She'd be working in her garden, perhaps reading books in the shade, surrounded by her animal companions. Hopefully she'd gotten rid of that puppy, Tristan, by now and—

"Don't you agree, Your Eminence?"

Stearanos jerked himself out of his musings to find Crown Prince Mirza looking down his imperious nose with impatient expectation. Though Stearanos hadn't been paying attention closely enough to know exactly what the prince was asking, he could be fairly certain that, whatever it was, he did *not* agree. All the other men around the council table watched him expectantly, most with expressions of doubt and trepidation. *Aha—no one agrees.*

Stearanos made a show of gravely considering—always advisable for stroking the prince's ego, regardless—and quickly reviewed the conversation in his head. Right, yes, they'd been discussing where Mirza would receive the queen's surrender. Stearanos should have been able to take pleasure in the universally lavish praise for his plan. Everyone had declared his strategy nothing short of genius. Yet, he only chafed at every well-meant compliment. He knew his strategy was brilliant. He only wished he could shake the feeling that he should have thrown the thing into the fire.

But the deed was done and no taking it back. The only way forward was through, so no foot-dragging.

"According to my strategic plan, Your Highness," Stearanos said, "the last battle will ideally take place on this plain." He rose from his chair to indicate the location on the map. "Regardless of the actual location, we can only tie up these final conflicts after the citadel has fallen. We need to be certain that they cannot resupply from these locations." He tapped them in turn. "Or they'll be able to outlast any siege we—"

"Yes, yes, we've been over that," the prince interrupted. "I don't need to revisit the tedious details. Follow your strategic plan. I don't care. I simply want to have the victory celebration at the citadel, so all the populace there can see me with their former queen kneeling at my feet while their nobles pledge fealty to me. Perhaps we could add a victory parade! March our soldiers through their streets, perhaps with their chained queen on display. Naked, and weeping." Mirza paused, enjoying the imagined spectacle with a decidedly unsavory expression on his narrow face. "Serves her right for daring to take a man's role in the world."

Stearanos couldn't help thinking of Oneira—as usual, but especially then—and how she would deal with the loathsome Mirza. Turn his nightmares against him, no doubt.

"Your Highness," General Khanpasha put in, nodding to Stearanos, "it's a stirring vision, and a well-deserved celebration of your sweeping victory, but if His Eminence's strategy succeeds, we'll have destroyed the city long before the final battle."

"Then we must leave it intact," the prince insisted. "Alter the plan, Stearanos. I insist. I'm certain your genius is up to the task."

Stearanos slowly sat again. He couldn't tell the prince no, but this couldn't possibly work. "Your Highness, I am gratified by your faith in me, but the citadel is the center of the queen's power. All of her mages and sorcerers are located within it, with sorcerers dedicated to protecting these key positions . . ." He started to rise again and the prince waved him down irritably.

"I'm aware of the key positions, Stormbreaker," he bit out.

"I apologize, Your Highness," Stearanos replied, willing himself to find a way through this. "With those sorcerers safe within the citadel, we can't hope to win any of those key positions. We have to take the citadel before then."

"The entire point, *Your Eminence*"—Mirza ground out the title, as if highly doubtful Stearanos had earned it—"of this conquest is that Sorceress Oneira has retired and vanished, likely never to be found again. Probably dead."

Stearanos fought to school his expression, to give nothing away, much as he wanted to say something like *not so dead or vanished as you might think.*

"The Southern Lands are undefended," Mirza continued. "Otherwise we wouldn't be doing this at all."

Admiral Bartolomej cleared his throat. "Your Highness, while the absence of the sorceress Oneira makes this conquest possible, Queen Zarja still commands a considerable stable of sorcerers, mages, and other magic-workers. His Eminence is correct in his strategy—in fact, I'd call this the keystone of his strategy. Unless those sorcerers are neutralized, we cannot hope to deliver the victory Your Highness so richly deserves."

"The Stormbreaker is better than any of them. He can ward our forces from their attacks. Use storms to break them," Mirza added with a laugh.

"Your Highness," Stearanos said, trying to govern his temper, and setting his teeth against the misconception. Few people understood the origin of his nickname, but most knew he was no weather mage. "I am but one man. I cannot be everywhere at once and my power isn't unlimited. And, while I can ward our forces against direct magical attacks, I can't ward against indirect ones, such as the very earth being turned against our armies."

The crown prince visibly fumed, looking around the table for support and, judging by his reddening face, finding none. "I don't care," he snapped out finally. "The victory celebration will be at the citadel, with a parade of our forces, and Queen Zarja in chains. Figure out a way to make that happen or I shall assume that you are not the best my father has to offer as he's promised me."

The prince strode out, slamming the door behind him, leaving the tableful of generals, tacticians, sorcerers, and Stearanos in silence. "Did Mirza just threaten to tell Daddy on us?" Admiral Bartolomej inquired of no one in particular.

They all, except Stearanos and the admiral, looked about nervously. Stearanos had warded the room against sound and Admiral Bartolomej had worked with him long enough that they trusted each other utterly.

"Admiral Bartolomej," Stearanos asked after scrubbing a hand over his face, "is there any way to assail that beach with the citadel intact?"

"With Sorcerer Gürsel watching over us and sinking my ships with his hydromancy?" Admiral Bartolomej shook his head. "I ran up against him before, you know, and I've read the war records. No navy has succeeded against him."

Exactly as Stearanos knew, but it had been worth posing the question.

"Neither can my foot soldiers make any progress on land while Sorcerer Tlaloc is able to open up chasms under their feet. As you noted, Eminence, he can swallow entire armies between one moment and the next," General Khanpasha added soberly. "We might as well drown them all at sea on the way there as attempt that." He sighed and looked to Stearanos. "Is it at all possible you could take out these sorcerers personally, without us attacking the citadel?"

"Duels?" Stearanos replied. "I could defeat any of them in a duel, but they'd never agree to such a confrontation. They have no incentive to face me, particularly knowing they have no hope of defeating me. In addition, Queen Zarja has no reason to receive any diplomatic overtures, especially ones suggesting sorcerous duels they'd have to know they can't win."

"Not duels," General Khanpasha corrected. "Stealth. Assassination. Could you do that?"

"No," Stearanos answered definitively. "First of all, Zarja would have passive defenses in place to respond to any kind of attack, and those alarms wouldn't be subtle or quiet, so stealth isn't feasible. Second, I have no way to travel there except physically, nor to enter the citadel without a major working to break the citadel wards, which, again, would not be stealthy."

"There's a rumor that the sorceress Oneira could do that," one of the younger tacticians volunteered. "The tales say she could penetrate any ward, put an entire castle to sleep, and pick off anyone she chose, leaving them dead for the others to find when they awoke."

"Or kill them with their own nightmares, even awake!" put in another with gruesome enthusiasm.

"Oneira is an oneiromancer," Stearanos said with a touch of irritation. "I am not. I cannot do what she does."

"Then maybe we need an oneiromancer," the first tactician replied defiantly.

The circle around the table burst into laughter, gratifying for Stearanos's slightly bruised ego.

"Young man," Admiral Bartolomej said with plenty of condescension, "all the world has sought an oneiromancer of Oneira's abilities. There are none. She was one of a kind, a formidable foe." With a wry smile, he glanced at Stearanos. "I can't believe I'm saying this, but I actually kind of miss her."

"We *all* kind of miss her," General Khanpasha said in his gravelly voice. "At least," he added, "in theory. Had she not retired, we wouldn't be facing this ill-advised conquest. Despite His Eminence's excellent strategic plan, even with it unaltered, we'll suffer tremendous losses. Our victory is by no means guaranteed and, if we do win, we'll be faced with defending two huge territories, separated by an ocean, with our forces decimated. Any ambitious ruler out there will be tempted to nibble at our edges and we'll be spread too thin to stop them."

He gave Stearanos a long and weary look. "The previous détente saved us from this. No one was willing to pit you two against each other. I hope none of you will report me for a traitor, but is there any way to find Oneira and convince her to return to her queen's aid? His Majesty will retract his declaration of war, in that case."

"But will Mirza?" someone quipped.

"Daddy will handle his restless prince," General Khanpasha replied without looking at the wit, his gaze focused on Stearanos. "Uhtric wants an easy victory, not a protracted and losing enterprise. Not even for his son will he risk what he has now. Your Eminence?" he prompted.

"Khanpasha," Stearanos answered wearily, "you are well aware that sorcerers at our level don't socialize. Even should we wish to, it's inadvisable."

The general, experienced and savvy, returned his gaze steadily. "I wouldn't ask this under any other circumstances."

Stearanos weighed how to answer this. General Khanpasha's idea was an excellent solution. With Oneira in place, this war would evaporate and they could go back to their homes and the business of living rather than generating more death and destruction. Up until a few weeks before, he could have honestly answered that even if he could and did find her, he had no way to convince her of anything.

Now he wondered. Did he have any influence with her? Their relationship, if you could call it that, felt so new and tenuous that he was wary of putting it to the test.

Oneira would refuse to participate in anything that brought death, that was certain, but what if he could promise her it wouldn't come to that? That all she need do was return to the queen's court for a little while, to act as a deterrent, and then the war would go away. She would want to save the people from what promised to be a horrifically destructive war. General Khanpasha wasn't wrong about the aftermath. Both kingdoms would face endless attacks in the coming years if they went ahead with this war, and Mirza wouldn't be able to defend the Southern Lands. The destruction and violence wouldn't end with this conquest, but would grind on—likely reaching even her isolated corner of the realm.

She could be convinced, possibly. But would she forgive him for asking? She'd have to reenter a world she hated, one she'd won free of at great cost. Oneira had found peace in her white walls, with her gardens and her animals—a peace he envied—and his asking this of her would shatter what she'd built for herself.

Either way, if she refused or if she agreed, he'd lose whatever fragile trust he'd gained with her. And they would perforce be enemies again, and therefore unable to become friends, or more. Even though she'd held back so far, she'd been thinking about his offer, he knew. Asking her to do this would put paid to that forever.

But wouldn't it be worth it, to save all those lives? It would be utterly selfish of him to prioritize his own happiness, theoretical happiness at that, over hundreds of thousands, perhaps millions of lives. Then again, how could he possibly ask this of her, the one thing he knew she'd resolved never again to do?

"Your Eminence?" General Khanpasha prodded again. "Could you find her?"

"She doesn't want to be found," Stearanos hedged, not a lie, but skirting the truth uncomfortably. "It's nearly impossible to find a sorcerer who doesn't want to be found."

"Nearly, but not entirely?" Admiral Bartolomej pounced on the sliver of opportunity. "Can you make the attempt?"

"As soon as possible," General Khanpasha put in. "All that we ask is that you try, Stearanos. And you know we wouldn't ask if the situation were any less dire. If His Majesty didn't hold me in debt, I'd refuse to participate."

"As would I," Bartolomej agreed on a sigh. "But none of us are free to act."

"Only Sorceress Oneira is," Khanpasha mused. "Our longtime enemy is now our only potential savior. An irony I'm sure she would savor. You could put it to her that way, Stearanos. We only ask that you try."

Blowing out a long breath and kissing his chance for happiness goodbye, Stearanos nodded his assent, unable to make himself speak the words. At least he'd never really counted on being happy anyway.

"Can't you tell me *anything* at all? Not even a teensy tidbit?" Tristan wheedled, at his most charming and with a winning smile. They were sharing tea in the garden, enjoying the late afternoon light and her most recent attempt at baking cookies. Tristan had pronounced them edible, but would be improved if she used sugar instead of honey. She liked them fine, especially dipped in the herbal tea concoction she'd assembled to complement the anise and rosemary flavor of the cookies. "Lovely Lira," he continued in a lyrical tone, "just a whiff of what the queen said would be more excitement than I've had in my entire life."

"It's really nothing exciting," Oneira told him, yet again.

"Then you can divulge the not exciting," he replied with a laugh. "Oh, please, please. I've never known anyone important enough to receive a message from Her Majesty. I need to know, for my poems, how a queen speaks to a reclusive noble. You must be so valuable to the queen to receive a royal messenger, one who awaits your reply. He's still waiting, isn't he?"

"Of course," she answered absently, still pondering the most polite way to tell the queen no without getting herself into trouble. She shouldn't have to be on the horns of this particular dilemma. Curse Stearanos and his clever war.

"Poor fellow," Tristan murmured sympathetically, then flushed when Oneira raised a brow. "I have reason to know how inhospitable that stretch of road is."

"It's not storming. I sent him food and drink. Royal messengers are accustomed to the travails of the road. He's fine."

"He's a *royal* messenger, not a traveling tinker," Tristan argued, then held up a hand at her sharp look. "All right, all right, spare me your glowers, beautiful lady. I didn't mean to displease you. If you won't tell me what the queen's letter says, will you at least tell me what your reply shall be?"

"Wouldn't my reply reveal the content of Her Majesty's missive?" Oneira asked, laughing at his persistence.

"Not if you're cagey about it," he replied, wagging a finger at her. "Though you have perceived my strategy, clever lady. I hoped to sneak around your obdurate silence." He sighed dramatically. "I shall have to go to my grave never knowing."

Oneira shook her head, his antics helping to lighten her mood. Now that they'd taken sex off the table, and the poet had entirely—well, mostly—stopped trying to seduce her, she enjoyed his company far more. He was entertaining and merry, knowing thousands of tales and songs, always good for a jest.

"All right, fine," she said, deciding it couldn't hurt to divulge the thrust of the missive without giving any context. "She invited me to attend her at court at the citadel and—"

Tristan's gasp interrupted her, every line of him alive with excited delight. "You're going to *court*, at the *citadel*, to attend the *queen*? Oh, Lady Lira, please say I can go with you. I'll be your faithful servant in every way, just please take me with you." He'd fallen to his knees, lifting the hem of her gown and kissing it fervently. "I knew there was a reason that storm dropped me on your doorstep," he continued reverently. "All I've wanted all this time is an opportunity to return to Her Majesty's court. Please say yes."

He was so artlessly enthusiastic, so truly sweet that Oneira almost felt bad to be the one to dash his hopes. "Tristan," she said gently, laying a hand on his soft hair, much as she would with Bunny or Moriah, "I'm refusing the summons."

Tristan lifted his pale-skinned face to gape at her, a portrait of horrified disbelief. "But . . . But you *can't* refuse the queen," he stammered. "She's . . . the *queen*," he said, emphasizing the word as if Oneira had somehow failed to understand. "Her Majesty must be obeyed, in every way," he added in a slightly odd tone that caught Oneira's attention. Tristan's gaze had unfocused and he shivered visibly, his attention seeming far away. She quickly assessed him for magic, but found nothing more than she ever had. He was thoroughly mundane.

"I'm not a fool, Tristan," she said sharply, snapping him out of his rapt state. To her relief, his eyes met hers again, his usual sparkle in them. "Don't be concerned for my sake," she told him reassuringly, attempting to soften her sharp edges. "I am able to refuse the queen's invitation. I have dispensation." Her Majesty would be thoroughly displeased, but Oneira could live with that. What she couldn't live with was returning to the citadel to assist with a war, especially knowing Stearanos would be on the other side of it.

"Couldn't we go for just a little while?" Tristan pleaded wistfully, still on his knees. "A day or two, and then return home."

It made her uncomfortable that he was kneeling like a supplicant and that he'd referred to her house as home. Stearanos was right in that much—she'd let Tristan stay far too long and become much too attached to her. She prodded him to get up and sit in his chair again.

"I'm not going at all," she told Tristan. "I left for a reason. Her Majesty knows this. She just hoped . . ." What? "That I'd recovered from what sent me here to begin with." There, that was the truth. "But I haven't."

Tristan blanched, uneasy, subtly edging away from her. "Plague?" he whispered.

"No." She nearly laughed and had to drag it back. If only what plagued her was curable. "It's more complicated than that. Suffice to say that the reasons that brought me here remain the same and so I will be writing a reply to Her Majesty regretfully declining on the grounds that I must stay where I am." And fervently hope the queen accepted it without too much fuss. Oneira didn't look forward to a fight—especially as she still wouldn't kill any soldiers who arrived to forcibly escort her to the citadel—but she wouldn't go back. She'd die first, which could be easily arranged.

"You should face your fears, Lira," Tristan said decisively. "That's how you overcome them."

"I am not afraid," she replied softly, irritated enough that menace leaked into her mien and he withered ever so slightly. Poor guy. Stearanos had that much correct—the young poet was no match for her, with her internal darkness and independent nature. There was a reason she'd spent most of her life alone. She wasn't a woman who could have lovers. "Truly, Tristan. I'm not angry with you, but let it go."

"Then what are—" he bravely forged on before she cut him off.

"I am resolved," she finished for him. "And I will not be persuaded otherwise."

"Nothing I can say would alleviate your concerns?" he asked miserably. "I'd stay by your side the entire time."

She refrained from telling him that particular promise was more of a threat than an enticement—though the image he evoked did serve to remind her of how it would be at court, all of those people packed into the citadel, thronging the narrow, winding streets, weaseling their way into the palace proper, spending and seeking favors. A headache formed between her brows, a bright star that threatened to grow and burn all her thoughts away. No, she could not go back there. Not for any reason, not for anyone.

"I'm sorry," she said, although she wasn't. A polite white lie that barely registered. She put her hand over Tristan's, eliciting a woebegone smile from him. "This is not something I'm able to do."

"I understand." He turned his hand to squeeze hers, then let it go. "I was just really excited to have a chance to get back to court. To see the *queen*," he added with longing, before dragging his attention back. "The likes of me don't receive many opportunities."

"I'll tell you what," she said, making a bid to solve two problems at once. "I will give you my reply to Her Majesty, with the stipulation that I trust only you to put it into her hands. You can travel with the messenger to the citadel and that will give you entrée to the court. I'll even add a personal note of reference and recommendation."

She owed Tristan that much for putting up with her moods, for changing her mind on him, for leaving him alone so often. Not that a personal recommendation from the dread sorceress would hold much water with the queen, but Tristan wouldn't know that. And it *would* get him into court. With his charming ways, he'd no doubt soon find other sponsors, other older women eager enough to have a young and virile lover in their beds.

"Oh, my lady!" Tristan gushed, looking as if he might fall to his knees again, stopped by her warning look. Instead he took up her hand once more and pressed a series of kisses to it. "How can I ever thank you?" His handsome face fell. "How can I ever leave you, though?"

Smoothly, she extracted her hand from his enthusiastic grip. "It is I who am thanking you," she replied, focusing on that and ignoring the last question. "You've provided a lonely woman company, despite my gloomy moods."

"You are never moody," he declared gallantly, then gave her a long, serious look. "I'm only sorry that you never admitted me to your bed. You know how much I desire you, Lady Lira. Perhaps if we'd become lovers, then . . ."

"But now our time is done," she interrupted, stopping any further discussion there. While she regretted not purging this stifled desire from her mind and body—all the fault of Stearanos—she congratulated herself for resisting Tristan's further advances. No doubt many women could enjoy no-strings bed games in that scenario, but she'd learned she firmly wasn't one of them. She wasn't casual about that sort of thing. Unfortunately, at the other end of the spectrum lay Stearanos and his knee-watering offer, which was the farthest thing from casual she could imagine. And also something she could never do, for entirely different reasons.

Tristan was watching her in miserable expectation, clearly unsure what to say, unwilling to jeopardize the gift she'd offered.

"I'll go write the missive," she told him, "and you can take your leave."

"Take my . . . you mean, leave this afternoon?"

"It's for the best. Galahad is ready and no sense delaying good-byes." All true. Plus she was eager to have her silence again.

❧

As is the way of these things, in the wake of Tristan's departure, Oneira found her much-craved silence ever so much more, well, *silent* than she recalled.

She, Bunny, Moriah, and Adsila saw Tristan through the wards at the road. The animals had never quite taken to the young poet—and vice versa—but they attended the leave-taking for reasons of their own. The queen's messenger was not at all pleased to have gained Tristan as a traveling companion, nor that the unwelcome companion carried Oneira's reply. She had laid a light enchantment on the messenger to prevent him from revealing Oneira's true identity. Tristan would discover the truth once he arrived at court—if not before, in some other way—but that couldn't be helped.

Once they were gone, the wards duly sealed behind them, Oneira tried to settle into her previous schedule again. Without success. She felt as if she tried to wedge her feet into a pair of favorite old shoes from years ago, finding she no longer fit into the life she'd led before Tristan's arrival.

Before Stearanos, truly, if she was being honest with herself.

She tried to think back to who she'd been when she first came to the cliff, building her house—*Did you make these steps? Spectacular work*—extracting a measure of peace from the smoking remains and blood-drenched despair that had driven her into exile. Where that nothingness of being entirely alone had been restful once, now the emptiness of the house weighed on her, the silence within the walls too heavy. She worked in the garden, tended her roses, played in the sea with Bunny, who also kept her company on a long hike into the mountains while Adsila traced circles in the sky above them.

She was there, high in the hills, when she felt the knock against her wards, startling her into alertness. Her house was becoming as trafficked as the citadel.

The process feeling far too familiar, she focused her senses to determine who'd violated the sanctity of her retirement this time. It was too soon for a reply from the queen, and it had been too long for Tristan and the royal messenger to have turned back, even for an emergency. Besides which, she'd made it clear that they should never return, either of them, an edict that Tristan had received with piteous sorrow and the royal messenger with easy relief.

The visitor wasn't on the road to the world of men, however, and she had to correct her initial assumption, scanning for the correct direction . . .

The sea steps.

Stearanos.

She stilled, hating that her heart pounded with heightened excitement. What was *he* doing here, especially when he'd said he'd await an invitation? She had very specifically and carefully *not* stolen from him again. It seemed he was being polite, however, nothing more than that light knock on her wards, standing back, knee-deep in the surf, until she answered. He sensed her attention, lifting his head to meet her mental gaze and giving her a sardonic salute along with a slight twist of his thin lips, an expression too severe to be called a smile.

How aggravating that he'd caught her away from home. She didn't care to make him wait, lest he take it into his head to break her wards again and then taunt her with his ability to do so. Neither was she going to admit him through the wards into her home without being present. Deciding it was the best option, and though the Dream was thin and tenuous at that time of day, she told Bunny to meet her at home, and stepped into the Dream, for the short series of steps to greet Stearanos.

The waves surged around his boots, Oneira's whimsical pink-pebble beach stretching to the cliff on the other side of her wards. The view wavered ever so slightly with the invisible wall between, an indication of her less-than-expert warding, which he had faithfully replicated when he reconstructed them. Of course, only a purist like himself would care. Still, Stearanos took pride in his ability to set wards that were truly undetectable to all but magical senses—until the un-wary mundane stumbled into them—and he planned to grab on to every bit of superiority he possessed over Oneira.

Perhaps she was correct that they'd always compete to some extent, but he didn't mind that. It would keep things interesting. *If* she ever forgave him for what he was about to ask of her. It seemed she hadn't yet detected his presence, despite that he stood so close to the wards they shimmered against his face, as palpable as standing near a fire in a cold room. He could teach her to fix that, too. Ah well, no sense delaying any longer. Time to beard the dragon in her den and face her ire. Or disappointment in him, which would be infinitely worse.

Tapping against her wards with his magic, he politely knocked this time and awaited her notice. Almost immediately, she *looked* at him, from somewhere above. Meeting her insubstantial gaze, he gave a little salute. With a bit of surprise, he realized she wasn't gazing at him from inside her wards, but from somewhere outside of them. Where was she? It irritated him irrationally not to know.

She vanished, and for a moment he wondered if she'd ignore

him, and what he'd do in that case. He'd promised not to punch through her wards again, but even without that, he could make himself obnoxious and annoying enough that ignoring him would become a trial to her very quickly. Again, not really in line with his purpose.

Discovering she wasn't inside her wards changed things, however. Could he find her in that case? Several spells for locating a known person came to mind, though she doubtless wouldn't like that either.

To his relief, the point became moot. The Dream tickled the edges of his mind with unsettling unreality, more familiar to him now, and then she stepped onto the shore. She stood there, a couple of arms' lengths away, startlingly vivid and lovely. Glaring at him with a frown knitting her high brow. "What do you want?" she demanded ungraciously.

"Hello, Oneira," he said, unable to resist needling her, just a little. "It's lovely to see you, too."

"Except it's not lovely to see you," she countered. "You promised you wouldn't return without an invitation."

"And here I am, standing in the sea that belongs to all, awaiting that invitation."

Her frown deepened to an outright scowl. "I should extend my wards to deeper water."

"You really should," he agreed. "I could assist with that, and teach you a few other tricks to make them better all around."

"I don't want to learn any of your tricks, Stearanos, magical or otherwise." She pressed her lips down, as if withholding any further incautious words, and he grinned at her revealing slip of the tongue.

"So you have been thinking about my potential tricks," he said, observing how her light blush deepened. "I've thought of little else," he confided.

"Clearly you don't have enough to do," she informed him crisply.

"In truth, I have far too much to do to be thinking of you as much as I have been, but it turns out I'm weak where you're concerned."

She laughed, a dry, disbelieving huff. "Why are you here?"

"I need to talk to you."

Raising a brow, she conveyed her doubt and disdain. "*Talk.*"

"Only talk," he promised, then figured he'd better leave the option open for more. "Unless you decide otherwise. But yes, my primary objective is a conversation."

"About what?"

He mirrored her raised brow. "It's sensitive. Not with your wards between us."

"I really don't think it's a good idea to let you in." She glanced off to the side, an inscrutable expression on her face. "For more reasons than you likely suppose."

"Then you come out. We can talk somewhere besides knee-deep in saltwater if you'll tell me where to meet you. The road?"

"Not the road," she replied with perplexing immediacy, her gaze shooting silver back to his. "Not anywhere," she corrected. "It would be unwise of me to leave the protection of my wards."

"Up until a moment ago, you were outside of them," he pointed out.

"How do you know that?" She sounded more curious than defensive now.

He tapped his temple. "I know wards. When you *looked* to see who knocked, I sensed that you *looked* from outside your wards, rather than from within. Where were you?"

"Walking in the mountains," she replied absently, her mind clearly still fixed on the question of him perceiving that she'd been outside her wards. "Could other sorcerers do that—sense when I'm outside my wards?"

"Maybe a handful in all the world," he answered honestly, "and they'd have to know you like I do."

"You don't *know* me, Stearanos," she corrected stiffly.

"More than most," he offered with a smile. Adsila flew into sight from over the edge of the cliff and arrowed downward. To the surprise of both humans, the kestrel shot to Stearanos's shoulder. He was so pleased, he squelched the wince of pain as Adsila's talons pierced the thin shirt he'd worn. He'd chosen it because a woman once commented that it suited him, and because it would demonstrate that he came unarmored and unarmed. Well, as much as a sorcerer ever could be. "Look, even Adsila approves."

She fixed the tiny raptor with an irritated glare. "Traitor."

Adsila chirped and rubbed her beak against Stearanos's cheek. "Let me in, Oneira. I won't harm you."

She sniffed. "As if you could."

"Exactly."

Gazing at him a moment longer, she relented. "Oh, very well, but don't make me regret this. And you leave the moment I tell you to."

"All you have to do is ask." The wards shifted, opening a passage the width of his shoulders, and he stepped through, wading the short distance to her. She held her ground, as always, inclining her head in a formal greeting. "Do I get a kiss hello?" he asked, unable to resist teasing her.

"So much for 'only talk,'" she retorted.

"I feel I should point out that this *is* only talking and I did ask politely."

"Nothing is ever *only* with you, sorcerer," she grumbled, but he caught the hint of amusement in her tone.

"I could say the same of you."

They stood there a moment, face-to-face. Not close enough to kiss, but not far from it. She studied him, thoughts obscure behind those clear silver eyes. "Well, come up to the house then. Are you hungry?"

"For food made by your fair hands? Always."

"Someone has been practicing his extravagant courtier's flattery."

He fell into step beside her, bemused by how right it felt. All this time of thinking about her and missing her should have been an indicator, and yet he hadn't quite expected that this, just walking beside her, would settle the restless unhappiness that had been plaguing him. "Not flattery, because I mean it honestly, but I have been at court of late, and that obsequious language has likely filtered into my head. Think of my mind as ink stained and needing a good wash to restore it. Intelligent conversation with you will have it handled within an hour."

She slid him a sideways look. "Should you be telling me that?"

Tempted as he was to riff on his metaphor, he figured he might as well not dance around it, as he'd have to admit to it before long, regardless. "No, but what I need to discuss with you all falls under the umbrella of confidential information I shouldn't be sharing, so there we are."

She stopped, one foot on the next step, looking upward and not at him. "I cannot advise you in a war against the queen. I gave my oath to Her Majesty."

"Nor would I ask that of you," he replied solemnly.

"Then what do you ask?"

"You want to discuss it here, halfway up the stairs?"

Glancing at him with a ghost of a smile, she said, "Apropos, as we seem to be caught between worlds in several ways."

He answered her smile with a wry and rueful one. "Painfully true."

"But no." She resumed climbing. "I offered to feed you and we might as well be comfortable while you tell me whatever thing has darkened your gaze so."

Following after, Adsila still riding on his shoulder, Stearanos wondered at the woman's ability to see into him so easily.

31

Oneira didn't care for how much she liked having Stearanos there. As before, he rolled up his sleeves—this time a lovely silk suitable for court, a deep color that flattered him—and helped her to prepare the simple meal. Because of the darkness in his aura, she set the little table out in the garden, thinking the sunshine and vibrant life might help dispel whatever grave topic he brought to destroy her peace.

For destroy her peace he would. She knew it as surely as if she'd drawn cards to read the future, not something she did anyway, as it wasn't her strength and people never made good decisions from that knowledge.

The two of them worked in companionable silence, then carried the salad and bread out to the garden, along with a pitcher of iced herbal tea. Stearanos had raised a brow at her more liberal use of magic—such as icing the tea—and she simply said that Tristan had gone on his way. Not when or why. Stearanos looked pleased but said nothing in response. Wise man.

Adsila observed from a nearby branch, Bunny and Moriah, lying on the grass in the shade and sun, respectively, all at ease around Stearanos as they'd never been around Tristan. Ironic, as Stearanos was the dangerous one and Tristan utterly harmless.

"Excellent salad," Stearanos told her. "I love the flavor these orange flowers add."

"Nasturtiums."

"We don't have those."

"I can give you some seedlings."

"I'd like that. Some other time, as I'm not at home to tend my garden at the moment."

Oneira figured that was as good an entrée as any. "So you mentioned, when you said you've been at court. Plotting your war, I imagine."

He sat back, the gravity that had enshrouded him upon arrival and that had briefly lifted falling again like a black cloak about his shoulders. "It's not *my* war—I'd like to be very clear on that— but yes."

She considered telling him of the queen's summons and her own refusal. Decided to wait.

Stearanos, stern to the point of forbidding, watched her warily, as if uncertain of her in a way he'd never before revealed, even when they'd been on the point of dueling. The sunlight played on the silver strands in his dark braids, left to hang over his shoulders, and he laced his fingers together on the table where he'd pushed aside his empty plate. "I won't dance around it. As you already know, my king is planning a war against the Southern Lands."

"That does not mean you should tell me anything about it." In truth, she didn't want to know. Even this much made her feel vaguely ill, panic fluttering at the edges of her vision at the memory of what she'd done.

"I don't want to, but I feel I should. Without getting into specifics of the strategy, which I firmly believe will succeed—"

"Since you crafted it."

He met her gaze steadily, seriously. "Since I crafted it, yes, with every intention of resounding victory."

"Do you expect congratulations?"

"Quite the reverse. I want to stop it."

That took her aback. Not at all what she'd expected. "I feel I should point out that the simplest way to stop something is not to start it. Though I know that's easier said than done."

"True, but it's exactly what I have in mind: to stop it before it begins."

Her unease curled into dread. "I'm not going to like this, am I?"

He lowered his eyes, shaking his head in one sharp movement. "No, but I'm asking anyway. Because I need you to help me."

She laughed, a sharp peal of near hysteria before she dragged it back, realizing he was deadly serious. "Not possible."

"I believe it is. You said you'd hear me out. Then, if you still want to, you can say no, and I'll accept that as your final answer."

Knotting her fingers in her lap, sliding slickly together with a cold sweat that had nothing to do with the midday warmth, she nodded reluctantly. *All you have to do is say no. They can't make you do anything.*

"Those of us on the king's war council discussed—"

The king's war council? "Discussed me?" she cut in sharply. "You told them where I am?" She tensed in alarm, Bunny raising his head with a growl, hackles rising.

"Easy," Stearanos said, to both of them, expression stern, but voice gentle. "No, I told them nothing. Only that I would try to find you, since they begged me to."

"I won't be bought by your king or your war council," she fired at him. "You should know better than that."

"I do know better, which is why I'm not asking for that. Would you relax and hear me out?" Impatience edged into his tone.

She sat back—though she was anything but relaxed—lifting a hand in resignation, waving him to go on.

"Without the king's knowledge, the council has calculated to the best of our ability what will result from my brilliant strategy." His voice was bitterly sardonic, flattening as he went on, tallying for her, relentlessly and methodically, the cost of this war that had nothing to do with her.

She closed her eyes as the numbers washed over her. He kept details to a minimum and, as much as possible, she divorced the strategic part of her own mind, honed by decades of war, from trying to predict the order of conflict, the potential locations of the various battles. Some of them, though, were easy to guess. The predicted casualty numbers staggered her, as he intended them to. What truly gutted her, as Stearanos warned her it would, though he remained stoic in his recitation of the numbers, was the future he painted for both realms, overextended, supplies attenuated, weakened to the point of being a dying carcass for the vultures of the world.

He eventually concluded his soul-crushing summation, blessedly ending the onslaught of horror. Only when the silence stretched out did she reluctantly open her eyes, finding him regarding her steadily, expectantly.

"I don't know what you expect I can do to stop any of this," she said. "It's your war, not mine."

"I know," he replied. "I'm not expecting, but asking: will you come out of retirement?"

"*No.*" The denial erupted out of her unbidden.

"Just to provide the brakes that you always have."

"Absolutely not."

"Not to fight. Only long enough for His Majesty to hear that you have returned to the queen's court. They won't dare attempt this war with the threat of you on the other side. Don't you see how simple and elegant a solution this is? You can stop this before it begins. Only you, Oneira."

She did see. She saw and she hated that he was likely right. But she . . . could not do this. "I can't," she said, a broken creak of a refusal. "Don't ask this of me."

He met her eyes gravely. "I *am* asking. *We* are asking, all of us indebted to Uhtric—and you know what that means, his holding our contracts, our debt, and what it will mean for us should the king discover our actions. I wouldn't ask it if I could think of any other way. Please, Oneira."

"You didn't have to craft such a brilliant strategy, Stearanos!" she hurled at him, suddenly and incandescently furious, startling Bunny anew with her outburst. Moriah only gazed at her calmly, having listened all along. "I am not responsible for correcting a situation *you* created."

"I know you're not." Instead of meeting her anger with his, he yielded, turning up his palms. "And yet, I cannot unmake what I've made."

"Again, *your* problem," she hissed, her fury transcending heat and chilling to ice.

"My *fault*," he corrected. "But the problems this war will create will belong to all of us. They will reach even this pristine place."

"Then I'll find another."

"And continue to run, Oneira?" he asked softly. "You cannot run all your life from who you are, from the road that's brought you to the here and now."

That brought her up short. "Is that what you think I'm doing— running? You couldn't be more wrong. Running from the truth is what *you* are doing, Stearanos. You, blithely going along, doing as you're told, burying your head and pretending you're just an employee, but this war couldn't happen without you."

"Do you think I don't know that?" he fired back, in a temper at last. "I don't have the luxury of being able to retire, Oneira! My debt is crushing. I have no idea how you paid yours, but I cannot escape the geas that binds me. Even if I sold everything I own, I'd still owe three times that amount. I don't have your freedom to putter in the garden and divorce myself from the woes of the world."

Thrusting herself to her feet, fingertips tingling with the desire to open the Dream and throw something truly hideous at Stearanos, Oneira struggled to master her seething rage, all the more intense for having chilled. She knew this place in herself, where her skull plates felt as if they folded in tightly, where she became the warped and amoral creature capable of anything to free itself.

"My *freedom*," she sneered. "Do you have any idea what price I paid to escape the wars of men? No, you don't. But I paid it and not so I could *putter* in my garden, but so I could . . . could—" The words stuck in her throat, her breath caught painfully in her chest.

With detached shock, she realized she was perilously close to tears. Yet again. In all these years, she hadn't wept. Not since that day when the academy took her away, and she sobbed in the arms of her mother, who had handed her over, that look of mingled terror and revulsion on her face. Oneira hadn't known to identify those emotions then, but she'd known very well that she'd been a bad girl. So bad that they didn't want her anymore. Didn't love her.

Worst of all, they'd been right. Anyone could argue that she'd been a child, that her family had acted unfairly, out of fear and ignorance. But, in the end, Oneira had proven them correct in their foulest assumptions: they'd birthed a monster, a being capable of unthinkable and unthinking destruction. One not only able to commit the vilest of crimes, but willing to. She'd grown into an anathema, and she had only herself to blame.

"Could what, Oneira?" Stearanos asked softly, with more compassion than she could bear.

Yanked back from her thoughts, spiraling down into the dark pit of despair, she stared at him wildly, having nearly forgotten he was there. *Why* was he there? To ask her to do the impossible, appealing to the conscience she utterly lacked. Well, she'd show him.

"So that I wouldn't become what *you* are," she spat, aiming to wound and noting her success as he flinched and paled, as surely as if she had flung a night terror at him. "You can find your way out."

She turned her back on him, and fled.

32

Stearanos sat there by himself for a long while, only Oneira's animals keeping him quiet company. The garden was so lovely and peaceful, so full of riotous color, soft sounds of nature and sweet redolence, that he hated he'd been the one to bring the horrors of war and the brutality of the outside world into it. But those creeping wounds from violence would find their own way in to permanently destroy not only this pocket of paradise, but everything good and lovely in all the world.

For the sake of the world, he couldn't leave Oneira to her well-earned peace.

Thus, eventually, he went to find her. He wouldn't leave things between them so unresolved, not with her so upset. She'd exhibited wilder behavior than he'd ever expected to witness from the preternaturally calm sorceress. Passion boiled beneath that ice she'd layered over her heart to keep from feeling all she felt. He should have known, because he was the same.

He found her in a large room at the center of the house, the white walls devoid of decoration. All that kept it from being entirely empty—besides her—was a rectangular block shaped like an altar that seemed to merge seamlessly with the floor. Fresh flowers from the garden adorned it, draping over the pristine surface with verdant and colorful glory.

Oneira sat on the floor with her back braced against it, knees drawn up and arms wrapped around them, head bent and turned so one cheek rested against her knees, her hair a brilliant, crimson cloak falling all around her, calling out notes from the flowers surrounding her. A sunbeam sifted in from a skylight overhead, illuminating the tableau with warmth that only highlighted her crumpled posture. Stearanos briefly wished to be a painter with the skill to capture it all. *Oneira in Despair*, he'd call it.

"I thought I told you to leave," she said tonelessly, without raising her head or otherwise acknowledging his presence.

"You issued a statement of fact," he corrected. "I can, indeed, find my way out. You did not tell me to leave."

She lifted her head then, silver eyes fulminous. "You really want to quibble semantics?"

"When it lets me stay a bit longer to talk this through, yes."

"Stearanos," she sighed his name wearily, "go a—"

"Don't," he interrupted. "Please. Let me stay a little longer."

"I don't see the point," she replied, but didn't tell him to go.

"About what I'm asking," he began, "you would only—"

"You know what war is, Stearanos?" she asked, her gaze as keen as Moriah's. "It's all dick-swinging. All men wanting to be the herd bull."

He couldn't really argue that. "What about your queen?"

"She's not mine," she answered immediately. "Besides, she's the same, lacking an actual dick or not. Just glorified monkeys, the lot of them, flinging poo and trying to hog all the bananas."

He choked on his laugh, though she remained bitterly serious. "Where does that put us—which animal metaphor are we?"

"We're monkeys, too, ones with more power than a monkey should ever have. And do we use it to make sure there are bananas for everyone? No."

"Maybe we still could."

She smiled, briefly, slightly, wistfully. "That would be something."

Heartened, he stepped closer, running light fingers over the precise edge of the altar. No, not an altar at all, he realized. "Is this a bier?" he asked, almost to himself.

She gazed up at him, a vulnerability in her expression he hadn't anticipated. "Dramatic, isn't it?" she asked, though it wasn't really a question. Uncoiling gracefully to her feet, she rearranged a spray of what he'd call baby's breath. "This was one of the first things I installed when I built this house. The centerpiece, as it were."

"You came here to die," he realized with a frisson of cold horror, the possibility that she'd have passed from the world without him ever having met her like an arrow to the gut.

She slid him a sideways look, tucking a long lock of hair behind her ear, shrugging one shoulder. "In a vague way, yes. I was . . . in a state, I suppose the court ladies would say. I was too numb to decide anything, but I made this bier, yes, and the hall to hold it. See how the skylight lets the light fall just so? I had this image of laying myself upon it, and decaying gracefully in the white-walled silence of this space." She shrugged again, huffing a nonlaugh. "As I said, dramatic. But I find I like putting the flowers on it every day, a kind of ritual acknowledgment of why I came here and how I may eventually still go."

"How would you do it?" he asked, both to ascertain how close she'd come and to match it with his ideas of how he might make his own escape.

"I'm not entirely sure. At first I was so exhausted, so . . . empty, that I thought I could simply lie down and drift away. If that didn't work, I thought I'd simply step into the Dream and not return."

His scalp prickled at the idea of being lost in the Dream for all eternity. "Don't you take your body into the Dream?"

"I can do it both ways," she answered thoughtfully. "To travel, yes, I can go physically, but I can also go with only my mind and leave my body behind."

"To lie on this bier, amid the flowers, highlighted by sun and moonlight."

She actually laughed, not heartily or musically, but not the dry huff of the bitter nonlaugh. "Vainglorious of me, I know, but . . . I have no one to mourn me. It's up to me to create my own memorial."

"Your animals would miss you."

"At first, perhaps, but they had independent lives before they came to me and they'll go on without me."

"*I* would mourn you, Oneira," he confessed quietly, partly a plea, the intensity of the moment vibrating through him.

She turned to face him. "Stearanos," she said with gentle gravity, "you also have had an independent life before me and you will go on without me. We barely know each other."

"I feel as if I've known you forever." He faced her also, feeling inadequate to convince her of any of the things he needed her to understand. "What if I don't want to go on without you?"

"Now who's being dramatic? There's only room for one on my bier," she answered lightly, deliberately misunderstanding him. "Get your own."

Following impulse, his own aching desire, he slipped a hand under her hair to the silken back of her neck, and kissed that tempting mouth. He caught her by surprise, her soft lips open and unresisting. He'd thought it to be a quick kiss, a demonstration of all he seemed inadequate to put into words, but she caught her breath, that quick hitching of instant desire, and kissed him back, fervently, with surprisingly honest and ardent passion. With a groan of utter raw need, he gathered her close against him, her slim body yielding, as soft as he was hard, winding his hands through her hair and pressing her to him. She opened her mouth, a heated gasp that entangled them further.

A fine tremor ran through her, and she placed flat palms against his chest. Though he braced for it, told himself he'd accept her refusal with grace, she didn't push him away. Instead she dug her fingers into his chest, the thin shirt providing no barrier, so even her short nails scored him as deeply as Adsila's small talons. He shuddered, wanting those deft and clever fingers over him everywhere. And yet . . .

"We shouldn't," he breathed, breaking the kiss, then belied his resolve by immediately diving in to sip once more of her sweetness, and again, and again.

"I'm tired of talking about death, of thinking about it. About war and famine and destruction," she replied, evading his lips long enough to catch his gaze and hold it, her eyes a darker gray, serious and intent, her mouth deeper red from his rough kisses. She dragged those sharp, nimble fingers down his chest, those hands that grew roses and kneaded bread dough, tensile, drawing life from him and giving it back with shuddering passion. He wanted her like he'd never wanted another woman, with bone-rending desperation. As if she could make him whole again, draw out the rot and the bitter cynicism and make him, too, into something life-giving and good.

She opened his shirt and replaced her caressing fingers with her mouth, hot and sweetly wet, kitten teeth nipping his nipple so that he convulsed and vised his hands on her. "Wait," he managed to say, "we haven't talked about—"

"Enough of your talking, Em," she murmured against his skin, biting into his pectoral harder so that he nearly yipped with startled pain—a sensation that transmuted immediately into frenzied arousal, as if she'd wrought an alchemical reaction in him, his edges and control fraying, blurring. As if he'd been pulled into the Dream, where rules and boundaries no longer applied. He found himself bunching her white gown in his fists, pulling it up her long, slender thighs, over her gorgeously rounded hips. She was naked beneath and he groaned at his inability to do anything but savage her.

"Turn around," he whispered, and she complied, bracing her hands on the bier. Drawing the gown up, he savored the sight of her nakedness, the fawn-colored skin a paler gold beneath, her bottom generously full, her waist narrowing above the sweet flare of her hips, spine a long, elegant arch. And she trembled under his hands as he traced those curves, her breath coming raggedly, skin twitching like a fly-stung horse as he touched the hollows and rounds of her. He pulled the gown over her head and tossed it aside, beyond tempted to kick her ankles apart and plunge into her. But he leashed his feral desire, gathering her hair to the side so he could enjoy an unobstructed view. She remained pliant beneath his hands, whimpering in encouragement now and then.

He pressed his throbbing groin against her perfect ass, laying himself over her and reaching beneath to gather her full, weighty breasts in his hands, her taut nipples poking hard into his palms. She hummed in desire and he kissed the side of her neck.

"Where is your bed?" he asked, throaty, nearly a demand.

"No. Here." She turned in his arms, facing him in all her glory.

He lost himself in her stunningly sensual loveliness, her nipples bloodred as her lips, the crimson triangle at her crotch incredibly seductive. Then the sense of her words penetrated. "Here?" he echoed, as if he hadn't heard her correctly. "On your bier?"

She laughed, throaty and musical, full of feminine mystique and power. "Yes. Perhaps there *is* room for more than one, if we align correctly." Placing her hands behind her, she hopped up onto the hard surface, laying back so her crimson hair spilled over the sides and the sun from above gilded her flawless skin. Blossoms fell to the floor and the scent of crushed leaves spiraled through the air. She spread her legs, and held her arms out to him. "A bit of a wrangle, but I'm sure you can manage."

He wanted nothing more than to take her up on the offer, and yet . . .

Narrowing her eyes in implicit command, Oneira wiggled her fingers, along with the rest of her, just in case he'd somehow failed to notice the blatant invitation. "Why do you hesitate? This is what you want."

"But is it what *you* want?" he ventured, kicking himself, but also wary. He wanted her for more than a moment, here and gone.

"Obviously," she answered in a considerably cooled tone, edging toward displeased sorceress.

Perversely, that aroused him even more. And yet. "Oneira . . ." He said her name like a prayer, like an oath. "Why are we doing this?"

She dropped her outstretched arms and rolled her eyes to the skylight above, heaving out an exasperated groan. "I should have gone with Tristan. He wouldn't have asked questions."

Edging a hip onto the bier, he sat beside her, not so resolved that he resisted trailing fingers along the hollow beneath her rib cage and over the smooth round of her belly. She softened under the caress, but continued to watch him with suspicion. "You never bedded Tristan, then?"

"Not that it matters," she replied testily.

"Not that it matters," he agreed, though privately he thought it meant something that she hadn't. Tracing the lines and curves of her, he found a pattern of freckles beneath her left breast that reminded him of one of the constellations in the northern skies. He raised his gaze to hers, finding she watched him curiously, less irritated and impatient. "You know I want you," he said slowly, "more than I've ever wanted anyone else, but this feels less like wanting and more like avoiding."

Her face set into lines of strain, shadows darkening the eyes she quickly shifted away from him as she stared stonily into some middle distance only she could see. "You say that as if you've discovered something surprising. I should think it would be obvious to you. Avoidance is all any of this is." She waved a hand in a grand gesture that managed to be bitterly ironic. "I've made a palace of avoiding, of hiding. Even of running, as you accused me."

"It wasn't an accusation," he replied, knowing he finally touched on the heart of the pain that plagued her like a disease that continued to claw at her, a parasite so deeply embedded that it flourished within her, feeding and growing ever fatter, while she wasted away from nourishing it.

She stabbed him with her silver gaze. "Careful, sorcerer. You dance the edge of a lie." Pushing herself up, she scooted off the other side of the bier, scattering flowers in her wake, a few stuck to her bottom where it flared like the sweet curve of the belly of a lute.

"Between friends," he said, "pointing out each other's self-destructive behavior is a loving insight, not an accusation."

Snagging her gown from the floor, she pulled it on, releasing that cutting laugh of hers that held so much sorrow and anger. "Are we friends, then?"

"Aren't we?" He gathered the remains of his shirt, mentally declared it a total loss, though sacrificed to a good cause.

"I'll give you a new shirt," she said, looking chagrined.

"Only if it's made by your hands," he returned with a smile. "Not from the Dream."

"That would take forever. I have nothing to make it with."

"You have the wool you spun."

She looked confused.

"On the mantel over the fireplace in the other room, there's a skein of wool. It looks soft."

Her brow cleared. "That?" She laughed a little, ruefully and with bemusement. "It's Bunny's fur, and a bit of Moriah's. When he first came to me, he was a ragged mess and I had to clean up his coat. Then Moriah wanted the same attention, and I had a big pile of fur that . . . Well, it was simply a diversion, a way to deal with the excess."

"It's powerfully magic." He'd sensed that easily. Whatever she'd spun into the fur, the care and attention, the love, she'd transformed the yarn into something potent and unique. "A shirt woven of that by your hands would be special indeed. That way I could carry something of the peace and silence of your white walls with me."

She was watching him with a curious expression, taken aback in some way he hadn't intended.

"Not to presume," he added, "but if you were so inclined, that would be my wish."

"You're a strange man, Em," she finally said, as if she'd discovered the answer to a complicated equation.

He grinned. "You've just now figured that out?"

Firming her lips, she shook her head. "I can't give you what you want."

"Not even to save the world?"

"Not even for that. I'm too selfish."

"That is not how I'd describe you."

"You don't know the height, breadth, and depth of my selfishness."

This was at the dark heart of her, the thing she'd done that ultimately sent her fleeing from the world. "Will you tell me about it?" he asked.

She stilled, sorrow freezing her face. "You'll be horrified. You'll never see me the same way again."

"I've done terrible things, too."

"Not like this."

"I want to hear it anyway."

"To pass judgment, to decide on my sentence and whether I should attempt to atone by helping to stop your war?"

"No, Oneira." He took her hand, cold and slick as ice in his. "Because I'm your friend and I'm willing to listen."

O neira didn't quite credit his stated motiva-
tion, but she'd also never had a friend, so she
wouldn't know. Certainly no one had ever offered to listen to
what pained her. At the same time, Stearanos truly didn't know
the extent of what she'd done in her desperation to escape the
trap she'd found herself in, the damage she'd done as a result.
She didn't think she could bear to see the look in his eyes when
he knew the truth.

But telling him—showing him in vivid detail what she was—
would also serve to send him away forever, which is what she
needed to happen. She only wished he'd taken her up on the offer
of sex first. Who knew that the ruthless sorcerer with his rapacious ways and frank invitations would be the one to hold back,
to cling to niceties?

He stood there before her, the hard planes of his chest bare
to her gaze and still showing the marks of her teeth and nails,
his lean face almost ascetic, silver-limned braids snaking over his
broad shoulders, asking about her troubled history instead of
plowing her as most mindless men would have. She wanted to
put her hands on him again, but it seemed she was fated to never
have a man inside her as long as she lived. Fitting.

"I won't make it through the recitation, but if you trust me, I
can show you," she said.

"I trust you," he replied with a quirk of his stern mouth.

"Then you're a fool."

"A fair accusation."

"A loving insight," she corrected wryly, "regarding your arguably self-destructive behavior. Come with me." She led the way to her dome, wondering to herself why she was doing this. Perhaps Stearanos wondered, too, as he followed only after a long moment of hesitation.

"Where are we going?" he finally asked as they climbed the spiraling staircase to the tower. Then, before she could answer, he added, "To my eternal doom, I suppose. This is when I'll be immolated by Dream fire and catapulted from the cliffs."

"If I immolated you in Dream fire," she replied, nearly laughing despite the queasiness of her gut, "I wouldn't have to pitch you from the cliffs as there'd be nothing left of you."

"How do you know?" he countered. "There might be a few bone shards and ash."

"All right," she agreed, "any ash residue I would sweep off the cliffs, but I'd retain the bone shards for witchcraft."

"Do you know witchcraft?"

"No," she admitted readily, "but I'm well educated and thus know that the bones of powerful sorcerers are much in demand." She banished the final ward and politely gestured Stearanos into the domed room.

He stepped in and whistled, low and long, turning in a slow circle with hands on hips, surveying the expanse of sea, forest, mountains, and sky, all brought startlingly close by the fine and flawless crystal. "This is incredible, Oneira," he breathed, and she flushed at the sincere praise, surprisingly pleased and terribly flustered by it. "You made it from the Dream?" he asked, glancing at her.

"Yes. If it can be dreamt, I can make it—with the suitable caveats and explanations attached to that statement, of course."

"I wish you could teach me." He actually sounded wistful. Enough so that she briefly considered what it would take to ground him in a few principles of oneiromancy. Before she could reply, he spoke again, his head tipped all the way back as he scanned the sky. "I feel as if I'm flying above the world."

"The crystal does that, makes it all feel much closer."

Sliding her a look, he raised a brow. "Should I mention how flimsily you warded the access?"

She waved that consideration aside. "Enough to dissuade a curious young poet from invading my privacy. I wasn't trying to keep out someone like you."

He grinned at her, that wolfish baring of teeth that shattered the granite sternness of his hard-lined face, a smile that shouldn't be remotely charming—with none of Tristan's artless sweetness—and yet affected her so much more profoundly. "I'm flattered to be welcomed into the heart of your home, if not into your own heart. Why here?" he asked, sparing her the need to reply to that outrageous remark.

"Lie back and be comfortable. This is the easiest way for me to show you."

Looking bemused and incongruous, the big man lowered himself to the cushion-strewn floor, picking up a pillow and giving it a long look. "These are a bit . . . uncanny."

"From dreams," she explained. "Bits and snatches of people's dreams that I left in them. I think they're pretty."

With a noncommittal whuff of breath, he bunched up a few of the uncanny pillows to prop up his head and, kicking his feet around, squirmed himself into a relatively comfortable position. Folding his arms, he stared at her expectantly—and like a man who suspected he might soon be the butt of a joke.

Oneira accessed the Dream, opening a small portal that allowed it to infuse the crystal of the dome with its darkness, but confined there through her will. Though dreams weren't restricted to the night, they flourished there best, and the absence of light is the fabric of the Dream, like rich soil from which plants grow. The Dream swirled over and around them now, a deep and fantastical fog. Stearanos made a sound, a grunt of wary surprise.

"It's only a representation of the Dream," she reassured him. "A projection of my mind to this substrate. It can't pull you in or disorder your perceptions."

"Ah," he breathed. "Is this how you see the Dream? It's different from how I perceived it, those glimpses through the doorway you opened in my library."

"The Dream is as different for everyone as our own dreams differ from one another, but yes—this is how the Dream appears to me."

"A truly wondrous ability."

"I'm going to show you something not at all wondrous. Something nightmarish, in truth, from my own memories."

He paused. "Will you come lie with me?"

"Why?"

Huffing a laugh, his voice came warm from the darkness. "Sometimes things are less terrible when shared."

"Nothing will make this less terrible." But she picked her way through the pillows toward his silhouette where he sat up, reaching for her, a deeper shadow within the swirling shadows, and allowed him to draw her against his side, taking shelter in his stalwart strength, even though it was pure illusion and nothing could shield her from the truth.

Not allowing herself to procrastinate any longer, Oneira called up her personal nightmare, allowing it to play out larger than life. The client coming to her from a distant land, offering a fortune to eradicate an enemy so thoroughly they could not return from it. How she'd agreed, seeing her way to freedom at last.

She'd gone to Govirinda, on leave from Queen Zarja and drunk with the prospect of the fortune she would earn. With visions in her mind of dumping a bag of coin at the queen's feet, Oneira had unleashed a storm upon the island paradise, devastation straight from the Dream in all its apocalyptic phantasmagoria.

Never had she had carte blanche to do anything at all. Usually clients wanted to take possession of a place, not destroy it. Heady with the power of opening the Dream and funneling the darkest elements into the waking world, Oneira slipped the leash on her control.

Feeling ill, much as she longed to look away, Oneira made herself watch. *You did this thing,* she reminded herself remorselessly. *You can at least bear witness.*

Stearanos didn't move, didn't make a sound, as all around them the epic storm boiled. Centuries-old trees spun like twigs and drove through solid rock. The air blackened as the winds of fury tore up topsoil, barely obscuring the screaming shapes of people and animals alike. The sea hurled itself over the land, sweeping away what little remained until there was nothing left of the island but bare rock. Not even a scrap of a rosebush.

"The disaster that befell Govirinda," Stearanos whispered in awe. "That wasn't a cataclysmic typhoon or earthquake. That was *you.*"

"A one-person disaster," she whispered, knowing she didn't deserve to be held in the circle of his arm, and yet unable to refuse herself the simple human contact. On the sphere above, she played the afterimages of the barren landscape, over and over again. Making herself look at what she'd done. "So you see—I am not a redeemer, only a destroyer."

"You can change that," he told her, his arm drawing her closer against his side, still gazing up at the horribly sterile devastation she'd wreaked.

"You don't understand," she said, stirring restlessly, ready to move away, but he held her with gentle firmness. "I didn't mean to unleash that extent. I opened the Dream and lost control of what it did. In the moment, I failed to . . . Stearanos, I'm a monster. I didn't care who and what died, only that I got free. You know the story of the wolf that chews off its own paw to escape the hunter's trap? Well I chewed up everything and everyone else, escaping intact."

"Not entirely intact," he whispered in the dark. "You shredded your heart in the process."

Shredded your heart. That hit home hard enough to make her gasp at the sudden transformation of the chronic ache of despair into an acute pain.

"And now you work with your hands, growing things. The roses," he realized, "they lived on that island."

"Yes. I don't know why the gardener trusted me with them."

"Maybe she's a sage, to know that's what your heart needed to heal."

"Though I don't deserve to heal."

"We all deserve to heal, to become better people, Oneira. The trick is doing it."

She didn't know. She couldn't think about it. "Moriah gave me advice along those lines once, that even the sages do not know how the heart heals."

"Moriah's advice is a bit obscure."

"I haven't found hers terribly useful thus far."

"When did she say it to you—was there context?"

Thinking back, she blushed to recall it, cringing at the vulnerability, though Stearanos already knew the worst of her. She laughed softly in her embarrassment. "After I manipulated your dreams, inserting the image of that bunny."

"So, it was you who put that image in my dreams—the fanged rabbit chewing up a book." He let out a sigh of disgust. "I knew it had to be you."

"I thought you would figure it out immediately. It was so impulsive and foolish, revealing the nature of my magic to you. I didn't understand what was wrong with me to take such an idiotic risk that would allow you to identify me. I still don't."

He turned onto his side, keeping his arm around her, adjusting her hair with his other hand, then smoothing it down the long line of her body, petting her. This sort of cuddling was totally new for her—and was something she couldn't have imagined with Tristan. Certainly they wouldn't have shared these difficult secrets. "Maybe," Stearanos said quietly, "you took that risk because you *wanted* me to know you."

"Why would I have wanted that?" she asked, breathless, yearning, aching with grief, regret, and—bizarrely, given the moment—desire intermingled.

"Because I'm the only person who can understand the terrible power of what you did, the desperation that drove you to do it, and still offer forgiveness."

Tears welled up in her eyes for the second time that day and she felt like that child she'd remembered being, wanting to sob in her mother's arms. Only this time, the arms weren't thrusting her away; they were holding her close, with something that felt like love. "How can you forgive?" she gasped, words broken through the choking sorrow. "I can't forgive myself."

"I forgive," he answered, kissing her tears away. "It can be easier to forgive others what we cannot forgive ourselves. You committed a great wrong, but so have I."

She believed that, given his reputation and the tales told of him. "I suppose neither of us has led a blameless life, but have you done anything this terrible?"

"Is there a measure of such things?" he asked, sounding bleak. "Some of what I've done weighs on me more than others and I can't always say why it's those and not the others. It's not always the most deaths or the worst devastation. Certain faces, moments—those haunt me, give me nightmares."

"I saw some of them," she said, hesitating to confess it but feeling she should tell him. "When I first looked for you in the Dream, I caught a glimpse of your dreams—I didn't mean to pry, but I can't quite help seeing. Most people never know that I have."

"Unless you tell them."

"Unless I tell them," she agreed, "which I've never done before."

"Why tell me now?"

"It feels important, because of . . . this."

"This?" He stroked his hand over her bottom and down to her thigh, lifting her leg so it draped over his hip, snugging them together, her gown riding up.

"Perhaps," she answered breathlessly, tipping her head back to see his face.

"Can you banish my nightmares?" he asked abruptly, a tinge of hope in his voice. "I've heard of oneiromancers who—"

She laid a finger over his lips, stopping the flow of words. He kissed her fingertip, drawing it gently into his mouth in a way both physically stirring and somehow sweetly intimate. Her heart, always a stone lump in her chest, fractured a little, riddled with longing for more and more and more.

"I can't do that for you," she told him with regret, "though another kind of oneiromancer, one trained in mental healing, could. Think of me as a devastating flood when you're asking for a bit of rain. I'm just not able to work with that kind of precision."

He curled his stern lip in disdain. "You're the only one I'd trust inside my head. I'll pass."

"That's a disturbing level of contradiction, that you'd trust me when you know what I'm capable of doing."

"But will never do again, as you've demonstrated by living this life. You've done your best to atone, to take steps to create instead of destroy."

She shouldn't accept the comfort he offered. She didn't deserve any of it, and yet she couldn't make herself push him away. This rough and powerful sorcerer did understand, astonishingly enough. Still, she had to laugh, the sound bitterly cutting. "Growing a few roses—that we don't know yet will survive and that were fine where they were—hardly makes a dent in the sheer scale of what I destroyed."

"It's not a mathematical equation, Oneira," he replied softly. "All we can do is try." His lips, trailing down her wet cheeks, found her mouth, kissing her with salt-tinged sweetness. This time, as his hands traveled over her, the desire lost that keen, desperate edge of before, instead swelling like throbbing music, the softer strains of grief waxing into something greater, deeper, more profound. She caressed his bare chest, not digging her fingers into him like claws of need this time, but savoring his skin with cautious fingertips, then tasting him with lips and tongue as he murmured her name and pulled away enough to draw her gown over her head.

Naked against him, she devoured his skin, that lean, hard body with its myriad scars covering the entirety of him. With lips and hands, with her own skin, she consumed him with a hunger less avid than languid, as if she absorbed him through her pores, a healing balm that penetrated to her darkest, agonized depths. His caresses were a benediction, his kisses a psalm of reverence and joy. She hadn't expected to find this sort of peace, this swelling joy, in another person. She'd only experienced the like in the clean, thin air of the peaks or the surging of the sea against the sand or in the rustling leaves of the forest, the dense buzzing of honeybees on heavy-headed blossoms, the thick silence of white snow piling up against her walls. They were of a piece, all of it, she realized. And this, too, was life.

As Stearanos murmured words of sensual affection, touching her as if needing to explore every hollow and crevice, as he moved against and then inside her, she found the shredded tatters of her heart drawing together, not healing, not whole, not yet, but no longer shedding blood, no longer waving in a storm wind and eroding into less and less and less. In its place, there seemed to be a growing and filling, a sense of more than there had been in a very long time.

She cried out her completion against him, shuddering and dissolving along with him, he chanting her name over and over so that it sounded like a low song, the sort a wolf might howl, or a whale or loon call, one end blending into the beginning of an infinite loop.

Oneironeironeironeiro.

They lay intertwined, shrouded in shifting darkness, their edges blurring into the other, magic blending into new shades. She was unwilling to move or speak, not wanting to shatter the fragile bubble of peace. Not quite an illusion, but a delusion, perhaps. Nothing that could last.

"Oneira," Stearanos murmured, "look at your dream."

She opened bleary eyes, muzzy with tears and the dregs of overwhelming desire, and turned her head to look. No longer filled with the barren landscape of Govirinda, the dome billowed and furled with roses, the iridescent indigo of Veredian rose petals made a shifting sea of loveliness, a paean to color. Oddly, of hope. Of blooming in the full dark of midwinter.

"This, too, is part of you," Stearanos murmured, one hard thigh sliding between hers, his big hand flat against the small of her back. He kissed her, drawing her gaze away from the spectacle. "This is you, Oneira."

She considered that with some wonder. It had been so long since she'd thought of herself as anything but a destroyer, a generator of nightmares and death and destruction. And here she was, a woman sticky with being made love to, perhaps having made love in return, being held as if she were something precious rather than vile. "The roses were only entrusted to me," she answered, even knowing it wasn't a direct answer, even though Stearanos hadn't asked a question. "I didn't create them."

She banished the Dream from the dome, letting go of her illusions, revealing the colorful sunset sky. They'd been in there for hours.

"There are all kinds of creation," he said, kissing her forehead. "Many ways for us to atone, to change the direction of things."

She, of course, knew what he was asking now. And that he looked to make his own atonement, to change his own direction, though he wouldn't be able to free himself of his debt onus. Letting out a sigh, she buried her face against his skin, inhaling his scent, wishing she had the magic to prolong this moment for all eternity. But no magic in the world could accomplish such a feat. So much power between them, and yet so little ability to make their lives what they wanted and needed them to be.

But she could do this one thing. For him, for the world, a tiny bit of sacrifice. "I'll go," she said, her lips inscribing the decision against his skin like a vow. "I won't kill. I won't engage in battle magics, but I'll go to the queen's court and let the news be known, so your king will rethink this war."

He took a deep and ragged breath, gathering her close, again pressing a kiss to her forehead. "Thank you," he breathed. "I know what it will cost you."

She shook her head slightly. "It costs me only my pride and a bit of aggravation. Retiring, going into exile . . . I can see now that I was only indulging myself, walling out the world instead of taking action to mend what I broke."

"I think that crawling away to lick your wounds and finding a measure of peace, a steady foundation from which to build again, doesn't count as self-indulgence."

"Is that what I've done? That might be a generous interpretation." But she smiled as she said it. She might not deserve this care, this understanding and forgiveness he offered so easily, but she was beyond grateful for it, drinking it up and filling the parched cracks in the profoundly shattered aspects of her humanity.

Perhaps, over time, repairing them.

They slept together in the crystal dome, waking under the slow wheel of glittering stars to make love again, and again, seemingly insatiable for one another. Time stood still, a feat impossible to accomplish by any magic, but apparently easily effected by new lovers. Oneira felt as if she'd been transplanted to a different world, one where just the two of them existed, where there was only sweetness and warmth, beauty and affection. The past fell away and only the now mattered.

More, it seemed possible for her to exist in that world, one friendlier to her way of being, where she could find a way to continue living, perhaps even flourish, given enough time nourished by Stearanos.

Inevitably, however, dawn arrived, proving that time hadn't stopped, only slowed. They lay entwined naked together, their intimacy so seamless that his skin felt like her own. In the growing light, she traced the fine white scars on his shoulder, and he made a hum of pleasure like a cat purring.

"How did you get these scars?" she asked.

"You don't know the story?" He raised his head, levering onto his bent elbow to gaze down at her, his braids tumbling to glide against her with the fine silkiness of tiny snakes.

She searched her memory, then shook her head. "Nothing springs to mind."

"It was a long time ago, one of my early battles—and biggest mistakes." He grimaced ruefully, tracing the sensitive skin along her collarbone. "Uhtric had won the final battle, which I foolishly believed ensured our victory. He entered the city to take the palace, and I had him and his invasion force warded from attack—I was at least that smart—but I failed to account for the presence of the ruler's personal sorcerer."

Oneira winced in sympathy. "A desperation defense."

He nodded. "She was a transformation mage. Not tremendously powerful, but she loved her king and gave the last of her life energy in that final attempt to save him. She transformed my umbrella ward into glass—and threw it at me."

"Ouch," she breathed, barely able to imagine it, not sure what an adequate response would be.

"Yes. I very nearly bled out. If a healer mage hadn't been right with me, I likely would have."

Oneira believed it, having seen for herself how the scars covered every fingertip of his skin, like a stained-glass window leaded in white. "I didn't know wards could be transformed that way."

"They can't, if the wardmaker constructs them properly. I've since learned better. I could teach you."

"Hmm." Tempting, but she had other questions. "And why do they call you 'Stormbreaker'?"

He snorted. "You want to hear of all my humiliations, don't you?"

"At least the only two there are," she returned drily.

"At least three," he corrected, "having been bested by an oneiromancer in my own home."

"Shall I apologize?" she inquired archly. "You shouldn't have assembled such a tempting library if you didn't want to lure visitors to it."

"My favorite method," he replied warmly. "Bait the trap with something irresistible to the prey one desires."

"And you believe you've captured me?" She'd tried to sound

taunting, but a giggle escaped her as he wrapped her in an inescapable embrace, nuzzling the join of her neck and shoulder.

"All evidence indicates as much," he pointed out, laying his body over her, neatly pinning her in place.

"Stormbreaker," she prompted, and he exhaled, lifting his gaze to the pinking sky.

"It's a misnomer," he replied, meeting her gaze again. "A weather mage provoked me into a duel. He threw all sorts of storms at me, as you might expect from that type, and I warded against them, biding my time until he exhausted his magic."

"Seems like a reasonable approach, if there aren't others you need to protect, and if your magic in sustaining the wards can outlast theirs hurling lightning at you. Takes patience, though."

He grinned at her, a wolfish cast to it. "I'm a patient man, I told you."

Yes, and as he'd demonstrated repeatedly over the course of the night, so much so that she flushed at the memory.

"I love that you blush for me," he said in a gravelly voice, brushing his lips over her warm cheeks.

She would not be diverted. "So, 'Stormbreaker' because you broke his storms?"

"I may be patience, but you are persistence," he commented on the breath of a laugh. "No, my wards broke—just as he'd nearly run out of magic and had only rain left, but a lot of it. I was soaked in seconds."

"So, it should be Stormbroken?" she asked, keeping a straight face with effort.

"But for a poetic rescue, yes. Probably the bard felt sorry for me because, in the very next moment, I slipped in the quite copious mud and slid ass over teakettle down a considerable hill."

She tried not to laugh, but the hilarity broke out of her and she emitted a gargling snort.

Stearanos glared at her. "She laughs at me," he commented dourly.

"It's just that . . ." She gasped, lost control, and laughed entirely. "The image of you . . . so dignified . . . sliding down that mud slope . . ." She couldn't get out any more, laughing helplessly.

Stearanos waited her out, his sternly set lips twitching, until he finally smiled, then laughed, too, shaking his head. "It's good to hear you laugh," he confessed. "A real laugh."

Reaching up, she ran her fingers over his lips. "It's good to see you smile a real smile."

He kissed her fingertips. "You've given me a reason to smile, Oneira." Pressing kisses down her arm, then up her throat to her lips, he kissed her lavishly and lingeringly. Then he broke the kiss and delivered a stern look. "But you owe me a story now."

"Any story?" she inquired, languid and saturated in the pleasure he brought her. "Or a particular one?"

"Tell me about paying off your debt. Not what led to it," he said, soothing her as she tensed. "I'd love to hear the good part. What did it feel like?"

She hadn't thought about how that had felt in so long, overwhelmed as she'd been by the horror of how she'd gotten to that point. Stearanos sounded so wistful, his eyes full of a longing she remembered all too well, that she found she wanted to share that feeling with him. "It was . . ." She paused, searching for the right metaphor.

"I didn't expect to feel much of anything," she explained, trying again. Pushing up, she rolled him onto his back, taking her turn to survey the bounty of male beauty spread before her. He gazed up at her, eyes dark, braids spilling black-and-silver over the colorful pillows. "I was so numb, so emotionally eviscerated after . . . well, you know. But I wanted it done with. I'd already committed the crime; I wanted my prize, however ill-gotten.

"I took that chest of gold and carried it into Zarja's court. I don't know how I looked, but there was this astonished silence. You know how court is never completely silent?" She continued when he nodded in understanding. "I'd never heard it like that—as if everyone held their breath at once. And Queen Zarja, she just watched me come toward her, this look of terror on her face. I nearly felt bad for her, but . . ." She breathed a laugh, tracing the lines of his scars. "I dumped out that chest of coin at her feet—dramatic, I know—and it was as if I released the weight of all those years. It all dropped away and for the first time in my life, I owed no one anything at all."

Stearanos listened, lips slightly parted, no tension in them, wonder in his gaze. "I can't quite imagine," he said in a hushed tone.

"It wasn't at all what I'd fantasized, all those years. You know, as you do." She touched those lips with reverence.

He nodded. "Yes, I know."

"We joke, don't we? About those who hold our contracts controlling us with leashes, but that's exactly how it felt. Even before the geas was gone. As if I'd been tethered and was suddenly free, like I could float away, weightless."

"Or disappear," he suggested quietly, "to live alone in the quiet."

"Exactly."

"I'm glad you reappeared, Oneira."

Moved, she bent to kiss him. "So am I," she whispered against those lips she loved so well. He slipped a hand under her hair, feathering a caress at the nape of her neck, drawing her into a deeper kiss, quickly heating.

Conversation done for the time being, they didn't speak again except in incoherent sighs and murmurs, as the sun rose, painting the crystal dome a blazing gold.

314 • *Jennifer K. Lambert*

Oneira could have stayed there with him, in that bubble of intimacy, forever. Like all things, however, their idyll came to an end.

They finally arose and took on the small tasks of bathing and dressing, easing into the greater demands the day would bring. She made a shirt for him from the Dream, resisting the urge to color it with dream images, instead making it a somber gray.

She came into the kitchen with it to find Stearanos grilling pancakes, liberally sharing them with both Bunny and Moriah, who sat on their haunches snatching the tidbits he tossed them out of midair, as if they were house pets instead of immortal magical creatures. He made a syrup of honey, drizzling it over fresh berries he'd gathered while she was bathing, and they ate in the garden, talking of nothing important—flowers, the weather, books.

At last, their plates empty but for sticky residue, he stood. "I'll wash up and then I'm afraid I must go."

"No, you cooked. I'll wash." She stood, too. "I'll walk you down."

"Do me a favor?" he asked. "Wait up here. I have this image in my mind of you standing on the cliff's edge and watching me go."

She cocked her head. "When I first visited your library, I never imagined you would be a romantic."

Sweeping her up in his arms, he kissed her thoroughly, leaving her breathless, body aching with desire, heart sweetly raw. "It's your fault," he informed her seriously. "You have bewitched me, sorceress, body and soul, and I'm in love with you."

She froze and he laughed, bestowing a kiss on her nose and releasing her.

"You don't have to say the words, Oneira. It's enough—more than enough—all you've given me. Once we've stopped this war, I'll be back to visit, as often as you'll allow. And you can come to my home. I'd love to show you my garden. After this is over, we'll have all the time in the world."

"For the first time, having a long life sounds like something I actually want," she admitted.

He smiled, briefly, a thin slice of wonderment. "I know what you mean. In the meanwhile, if you need to make contact, it will be up to you. You can find me, you said, anytime, anywhere."

"Yes, though it may not be safe for me to come to you physically, even via the Dream."

"Then talk to me in my dreams."

"Stearanos, I don't think . . ."

"Please. I'm asking." His lips quirked teasingly. "I need to hear from you. Or you can leave a note."

"That led to trouble before," she reminded him, aware she was holding on to him, fingers curled into his shirt, her body unwilling to let him go no matter how she told herself she must.

"That led to this." He kissed her again, as if demonstrating, deeply, passionately, filling his hands with her hair, seeming to be savoring her for the time of privation to come. "I regret nothing," he said against her lips, then showered her face with kisses. "Between us, that is," he added, finally lifting his head, gaze roving over her face with sober reflection. "You're right—I should never have let this war planning go so far. I didn't have to construct such a devastating strategy."

"I suspect it's not in you to do less than your very best," she replied on a sigh. "Part of your compulsive nature, no doubt."

He mock growled, hands tightening on her. "I'd take offense if I didn't know you were the same way."

"It's true," she admitted. "Maybe they know that about us and reinforce it during our educations, ensuring that—even if we hate our clients and their wars—we can't do less than our utmost for them."

"Something for you to consider in how you executed your assignment with Govirinda," he said, his expression grave and compassionate.

She nodded, unconvinced, and also unwilling to evoke the ghosts of that darkness when she still had him in her arms, in the sunlit morning, her belly sweetly full. "If I need to, I'll contact you via your dreams," she said, returning to a safer topic.

"Will it be all dream symbolism or will I know it's you?"

She hesitated, considering that. "You would know that it's not a normal dream. It would feel especially vivid and memorable, and you would sense my magic, as you did before. But since you're not an oneiromancer, other than that, I don't know."

He frowned. "I'm a sorcerer; I can learn oneiromancy."

Spreading her hands in disbelief, she gestured widely. "Now? As you're leaving. You propose to learn an entire branch of sorcery that's wholly new to you and for which you have no natural inclination."

"It's not *wholly* new. I learned the principles at academy."

"Theory only," she said, not a question.

"Well, yes. The instructor wasn't a specialist and claimed it would be dangerous to—"

"It *is* dangerous, Em," she interrupted. "People can get lost in the Dream, even talented oneiromancers before they hone their skills."

His scowl deepened, his considerable power mantling about him in his displeasure, reminding her that the sorcerer who'd been her nemesis was still contained within the man who'd become her lover. Stearanos would never not be dangerous. "I'm no naïve student, Dreamthief. I'm an experienced sorcerer with skill in wielding magic that rivals—if not exceeds—your own."

Narrowing her eyes, her pride very much intact, she replied, "I could defeat you, under the right circumstances."

"We'll never find out," he retorted. "To return to your question: yes, now. When else? Teach me some fundamentals of practical oneiromancy. Enough for me to have some control over the

Dream, to be able to speak with you and know I'm doing so, and in return, I'll teach you a few wardmaking tricks."

"I already know wardmaking and—"

"After a fashion," he interrupted with a sly grin, and she huffed at him. "Oneira darling, be reasonable. We each have skills the other lacks. It's foolish not to help each other. After all we've shared. After all we will share." His voice dropped to a deep purr and he stroked a finger along her arm, bared by her sleeveless gown.

He did have a point. "Fine," she muttered ungraciously. "You show me yours first."

Eyes sparkling with pleased mischief, he gently chucked her on the chin. "I have all along."

It turned out that Stearanos had more to teach Oneira about wardmaking than either of them would have predicted. He was surprised, in truth, that her wards had been as solid as they were, given her methods. She approached the endeavor in a decidedly dreamlike way—no surprise there, he supposed—going about it with more intuition than internal logic.

"More math, less creativity," he chided her. "You're not shaping something from the Dream. Stick to the waking world and what *already* exists."

She slid him a glittering, silvery glare. "I am, demonstrably, working only with the waking world. No portals to the Dream anywhere. Even *you* should be able to sense that."

"Play nice, Dreamthief." He had to suppress a smile at her ire. All passion and prickly pride, his lover. "I know you can't have been taught wardmaking the way you're doing it. I'm simply saying that you've drifted over time, as you grew into your greatest power, adapting those other skills and applying them to this. But indulge me and try it my way."

With a last glare, muttering something under her breath, she did as he asked, applying herself with diligent intellect and patient focus—and smiling broadly when she succeeded in mimicking his technique. "I can see your point," she admitted grudgingly.

"You're welcome," he replied. "I know I'm an excellent teacher."

"Ha ha. And thank you."

"Now, teach me how to open the Dream."

She let out a long breath, a vertical line between her fiery brows. "Em, there are really good reasons they didn't teach you how to do this."

"Reneging on the deal?"

"No. I just—" She stopped herself with a headshake. "Be careful. And do exactly as I say."

Despite his confidence in his own abilities, Stearanos found himself struggling to follow her very simple instructions. The Dream was there, just beyond the edge of his perception, like one of those dreams immediately forgotten upon awakening, forever out of reach. He reached for it, though with his hands metaphorically tied behind his back, and it slid away from him, again and again.

"I feel like I'm trying to open a door with my teeth," he grumbled after the nth failed attempt.

"In a way, you are," Oneira observed, "in that you're trying to use a totally different faculty. Besides which, you are very much a person rooted in the rational world. The Dream is irrational. You have the magical ability to complete the task, but the logical aspect of your mind is resisting the nonreality that is the Dream."

He eyed her. "Are you saying I deep down don't *want* to access the Dream?"

Tipping her head, she acknowledged that. "You pointed out that I tend to approach every magical problem intuitively, which makes sense. The Dream is a construct of our unconscious and subconscious selves. We're not meant to enter it awake. Your subconscious knows that and may be guarding you."

"I can control my subconscious," he asserted, annoyed when she smiled at that, clearly amused. "What?"

"I suppose you think you can force yourself to relax, too," she retorted.

"As a matter of fact . . ." He trailed off, catching on too late.

"All right, I see your point. But how do I stop myself from *intuitively* stopping myself?"

"Clever, but this isn't a riddle to solve. In other words," she continued before he could reply to that, "I don't think you can."

"I can." He'd never failed at anything magical before and he wasn't about to declare defeat already. "Show me one more time."

"Fine, but this is the last try. You're beginning to tire and it's an even worse idea to attempt this at less than your sharpest."

"I'm not tired," he protested, hearing the burr of irritation in his voice and having to acknowledge to himself that she might be right. He was no longer a young man, to stay awake all night making love to a woman and then attempt difficult sorcery. "One more try, and that's it," he agreed, more calmly, offering a rueful smile to acknowledge her point.

"I know it's not in you to give up on a challenge," she replied, gray eyes soft with an affection she wouldn't put into words. Not yet. "All right, clear your mind of all other thoughts. Allow the conscious mind to relax."

He sat cross-legged on the grass, the sunshine warm and golden, birdsong and surf in the background, Oneira before him, strikingly beautiful with her crimson hair unbound and cascading about her, expression serious and intent. Dream magic coalesced in that unnamed scent and he followed the soothing, entrancing sound of her voice as she talked him into a meditative state. Concentrating, extending his sorcery with precision, he reached mentally for the slice of Dream she held stable for him.

And this time, connected.

The Dream shimmered and billowed into his mind, making him feel as if he indeed were dreaming. He made a thought into a blade and sliced with care, opening a very small portal—Oneira had been insistent on that—just enough to allow him to peer in.

The landscape that greeted him reminded him of home in

some way, and then he recognized a sense of those bleak steppes that had been his home for the first nine years of his life, before his impoverished family sold him to the Minot Academy for Extraordinary Children. The off-kilter hut, leaning away from the prevailing northern winds, stood in the middle—though with additions he didn't remember. Curious, he stepped toward it and found himself inside suddenly, without knowing how he'd gotten there. And it was all wrong inside, with a black lake taking up the floor, floating with crimson rose petals.

No, that was blood. As he bent close to examine them, about to dip in his fingers to test his perceptions, a shadow even blacker sharked beneath the surface, then lunged upward.

And froze.

Oneira stood there, hand extended to hold back the monster, giving Stearanos a ferocious glare. "Let go," she told him.

"What?" He wasn't sure what she meant. Confused, he cast about him and the walls faded, becoming a blizzard so dense he couldn't see her anymore. The snowflakes became glass, slicing him everywhere, and he howled in pain and shame.

"Em." Oneira emerged from the whiteout. "Wake up. It's only the Dream. Close the portal. Wake up."

Wake up?

Wake up!

With a shock of realization, he remembered himself and returned to his waking body with a hard thud of pain. His skull throbbed and he opened his eyes to glaring daylight—and a furious Oneira glaring silver daggers at him.

"What did I tell you not to do?" she hissed.

"Enter the Dream," he answered with chagrin, knowing now what had happened. "I apologize. I didn't realize that I had. Thank you for pulling me out."

She heaved out a sigh and nodded. "It wasn't unexpected. But now you understand why you must never attempt this without me to assist you."

Nodding soberly, he tapped his temple in a salute of acknowledgment. He did understand, with visceral immediacy and more than a little terror, exactly what she'd been explaining. No longer academic, the prospect of being lost in that shifting landscape with nothing to tether him and allow him to escape . . . He physically shuddered.

Oneira observed it, lips flattening in sympathy. "It's unsettling, I know. But I'm relieved to see you afraid. I wasn't sure you could be."

"I'm well acquainted with fear, Dreamthief," he replied drily.

"Yes," she said, her voice hushed, and she gazed back at him, silent in the shared understanding. "I wouldn't have liked to lose you in the Dream," she finally said.

He accepted that admission, which amounted to a declaration of love from anyone less contained. "I don't want to leave," he told her.

"And yet, you must. So must I, if your plan is to work."

Standing, he offered her a hand up. "It will work, and then we can continue what we've started. At least I'll know you in my dreams when you come to me," he added pointedly.

"I probably won't," she cautioned him.

"I hope you will." He kissed her, gently, almost chaste, since he'd already stayed long enough to excite suspicion back at King's City. "I'll dream of you anyway."

❦

Oneira gazed up at Stearanos, still trembling inside from the close call, warm from even that light caress of a kiss. Completely unsure what to say to him.

"Be careful at the queen's court," he continued in a more serious vein, gripping her arms a bit too tightly. Then, seeming to realize it, he released his hold and slid his hands softly up and down, soothing her, or possibly himself. "I know you don't need my advice, as you've ably survived without me all these years, but . . ."

"It's nice to know that someone cares," she said. "And I will be careful."

"Hopefully it won't be long. You can make your presence known. His Majesty will stand down. Then you can come home to your peace and quiet."

"Yes." She started to say more, then stopped, feeling as if she might be somehow jinxing their prospects. "That would be good," she finished, aware of how uncertain she sounded.

"Thank you for doing this." He frowned, searching her face for what troubled her.

"I'm not doing it for you." She managed a smile for him, though it felt sad on her face. "It's the right thing to do. Goodbye, Em."

"Farewell," he corrected, stepping back and taking her hand to kiss it, "thief of my heart."

As he'd asked, she stood on the cliff's edge, watching him descend the winding steps to the pink-pebble beach, Adsila on her shoulder, and Moriah and Bunny on either side. Once he sailed into the fold of reality he used to travel, she stood there a moment longer, enjoying the sea breeze blowing her hair back from her face, the warmth of the sun, the sound of the sea, the afterglow of a truly miraculous night.

Perhaps it was the dregs of the nightmare he'd almost succumbed to, the leave-taking, or the ending of a glorious interval, but a dank feeling of depression settled over her, despite her valiant efforts to keep her thoughts elsewhere. She busied herself with cleaning the dishes and restoring the kitchen to order, then checked her garden a final time, particularly the Veredian roses. They'd begun to leaf out, looking less like sticks and more like actual rosebushes, though still unbeautiful, and she fretted over how they'd do in her absence.

But there wasn't anything she could do about that. Hopefully— that word again, that seemed to promise disaster rather than hope—she'd be gone only a few days, a week or two at most. She couldn't use magic to see that the roses were watered, so she'd have to hope for rain. Oneira had never been much in the habit of hoping for things, so it sat ill with her.

Otherwise, she used magic to ensure the rest of the garden would flourish, and closed down the house to the extent she needed to. Bunny and Moriah would remain behind, so they would need to come and go as always. Adsila clung to her shoulder with the apparent intent of coming along to the citadel. Finally, she strengthened her wards, using the techniques that Stearanos had taught her. His system really was better. She'd have to tell him so, the next time she saw him.

If there was a next time.

She wished the feeling of foreboding would lift, but it never did.

At last, satisfied that she'd done all she could, with Adsila on her shoulder, Oneira stepped into the Dream, to return to the world of men and their wars.

"Have you heard the news?" General Khanpasha asked Stearanos quietly, laying a finger alongside his nose briefly before dropping it again. "Word is that the sorceress Oneira has returned to the citadel to aid the Queen of the Southern Lands in her time of need."

Admiral Bartolomej, accompanying the general, gave Stearanos a long look. "I don't know how you pulled it off, Your Eminence," he said, also sotto voce, "but well done. Well done, indeed."

They stood outside the council chamber, having been summoned by Crown Prince Mirza to attend an emergency meeting. It had been days since Stearanos left Oneira, and the image of her standing on the cliff above as he sailed away was still burned into his mind. He fancied he smelled her on his skin, recalled the ghost sensations of her touch, the sardonic lilt to her voice, the clear insight of her gray eyes.

A thousand times a day he thought of her, wondering what she was doing at that exact moment. Every night he willed himself to sleep with an eagerness bordering on desperation, hoping she'd visit his dreams. Every morning he awoke with vestiges of wild dreamscapes that Oneira strolled through, Adsila on her shoulder—and sometimes it seemed she paused in her journey to glance over at him—but nothing that seemed deliberate or real.

He abided by his promise not to attempt to open the Dream himself.

Now, at last, their gambit had delivered. So why did he feel so unnerved? General Khanpasha and Admiral Bartolomej both radiated relief, stopping short of vociferous congratulations only out of discretion. They both clearly believed that Stearanos had successfully stopped the war. So why couldn't he believe it?

You just need to hear the words, he consoled himself. *Then it will be real and you'll know what you asked of her was worth it.*

The council chamber doors flew wide, opened by the crown prince's personal guard. His Highness waited at the head of the table, fingers steepled against it as he leaned toward them, the polished blackwood surface reflecting Mirza's face, which already loomed large due to his pose. Stearanos misliked the manic gleam in the prince's eyes and hoped that foreboding, too, was only a product of nerves.

"Be seated, gentlemen," the crown prince declared in a tone of command. "Not you," he said to the aides and lesser commanders who'd collected in the hall to file in behind the three of them. "You lot can wait. Close the doors." The crown prince waited impatiently for the guards to shut the heavy double doors, then shot Stearanos an imperious look. "Ward for silence, Your Eminence."

Suppressing his annoyance at the crown prince's condescension, Stearanos did as he was told, nodding at Prince Mirza to continue.

"I have two pieces of news—one distressing, the other the best possible," the prince informed them, attempting a serious expression, one disrupted by his sizzling excitement. He flexed on his steepled fingers, as if doing miniature push-ups on them. "The first is that the sorceress Oneira has returned to the citadel!"

General Khanpasha assumed an expression of sincere dismay. "This is distressing news, indeed, Your Highness. Clearly we will be unable to go forward with this conquest. A pity, as the strategy crafted by His Eminence is—"

"Is utterly brilliant, yes," the crown prince crowed. "So brilliant that even with the infamous Oneira on their side, we cannot fail. This is the best possible piece of news, not the distressing one."

"Your Highness?" General Khanpasha posed the title as a question, his gravelly voice faint with a dawning horror Stearanos shared.

Suddenly the pieces fell into place, his persistent, vague dread crystallized. They'd played this entirely wrong.

"Think of it!" the Crown Prince ordered, straightening and waving his hands in a wildly expansive gesture. "I will go down in history as the monarch to have defeated the Southern Lands, even with the mightiest of sorcerers in all the world on their side. You, Stearanos, will enjoy similar fame. Anything less than this would have been a pale victory, everyone knowing we only succeeded because your nemesis stepped aside. Now they will know our might and all will cringe before us. Gentlemen, this is a banner day for us."

"Your Highness," Stearanos began, not at all sure what he would say next. All he could think of were Oneira's bitter words. *It's all dick-swinging. All men wanting to be the herd bull.* If ever there was a herd-bull wannabe, it was the crown prince, forever fighting to escape the immense shadow cast by his father. "There are good reasons I have never been pitted against the sorceress Oneira." *Because I love her.* He shook that thought away. "I don't know that I can defeat her."

"Nonsense, Your Eminence," Mirza said with a winning and practiced smile. "*I* know you can do it. Everyone in this room knows, don't we, gentlemen?"

The other men agreed with a semblance of enthusiasm, the dread in their haunted gazes mirroring his own.

"My father didn't have faith in you, Stearanos," the prince continued, "not the way I do. I believe in you as he failed to do. In the end, he lacked the courage of his convictions. Age will do that, make cowardly dotards of those once-stalwart rulers, reducing heroes to frightened fools. But never fear! I am the leader you've needed. I am not afraid! In time, we shall rule all the known world. And to think it began here." He actually teared up a bit, gazing out the window. "I have been chosen for a great destiny and I shall not falter."

General Khanpasha and Admiral Bartolomej slid Stearanos discreetly pleading looks of utter panic.

"Your Highness," he ventured. "What says His Majesty of these developments? I designed my strategy based on the assumption that the sorceress Oneira would not be a factor in the equation. Perhaps we should revisit—"

The prince glowered, his mood darkening instantly. "I believe in *you*, Sorcerer Stearanos. Do you fail to return me the favor?"

Stearanos could not think of any possible way to answer that question with any level of honesty. Fortunately, the prince spared him, drawing himself up with self-importance and assuming a mask of grief. And here came the distressing news. Stearanos braced himself, reasonably certain of what it would be.

"Unfortunately," Crown Prince Mirza said, looking from one face to the next, "I must share with you, my trusted advisors, the truly distressing news that my father recently experienced a seizure. Only his personal physicians, myself, and now you, are aware of this terrible event." Mirza cast down his gaze, his shoulders sagging. "His Majesty has entered into a state of unconsciousness from which the physicians say he will never recover. His mind is gone and his body will soon follow."

The murmurs around the table were sincere in their aghast sorrow. Stearanos grimly reflected that under no other circumstances would this assembly have experienced such authentic anguish over the incipient fall of a tyrant who'd made all their lives a misery. To think that Stearanos had once looked forward to this day with a sense of optimism. Of course, once upon a time, Mirza had been a charming and enthusiastic boy, not the hubris-filled young man who now stood before them, so pumped up with his own vision of himself that his pretense at grief frayed at the edges after only moments. Very likely he'd conspired to murder his father, and none of them could do the least thing about it.

The old king had been right in his foresight and wrong in his solution. There seemed to be a great deal of that going around.

"Enough of this sadness," Mirza abruptly declared. "Father wouldn't want us to grieve."

Absolutely untrue, as His Majesty would expect the entire kingdom to mourn for at least a year. He'd probably left precise instructions to that effect. Not to mention that the man wasn't even dead yet. Stearanos had never imagined he'd feel sorry for Uhtric, but he *could* imagine what manner of dire magic Mirza had employed to fell the king with a debilitating stroke that not even the best physicians in the entire realm could mitigate. Trapped within an unresponsive body would be a nightmare of epic proportions.

"Stearanos," Mirza said, "you will rework your strategy to account for the influence of Sorceress Oneira and present it to the council tomorrow."

Stearanos didn't bother to argue that it wasn't enough time. No amount of time would allow him to develop a way to counter Oneira's unique skills. He only hoped that she would find a way to nullify Mirza's conquest without destroying them utterly—and shattering her barely mended heart in the process. What *would* she do? For all that he'd confidently declared his knowledge of her, he found he had no idea. If only she would come to him in dreams, then he could pass along this devastating news.

Their plan had failed. Not only that, but he'd dragged her into the middle of a war where they might yet be pitched against each other.

"I want the sorceress in chains, too," Mirza added with a light laugh, all pretense of grief fled. "They'll make a nice set piece, that pair of women who dared to defy the natural order. It will be a pleasure to teach them their proper place in the world. Don't you agree, Your Eminence? Perhaps I'll gift you with the sorceress after you break her, to keep as a pet."

"I'll begin reworking my strategy, Your Highness," Stearanos said with perfect honesty, as a plan had already occurred to him. There was one way to ensure this war would fizzle before it began, one person without whom it could not happen.

Stearanos had to find a way to tell Oneira to kill him. The sooner, the better.

❧ 37 ❧

Oneira stepped out of the Dream and into the grand throne room at the citadel. Might as well make an impressive entrance. It would help create the appearance of a free agent granting Her Majesty a boon, rather than the refugee returning to the scene of her shame with her ears down and tail between her legs.

The queen was holding court—Oneira had peeked ahead of time, to ensure the effectiveness of her grand entrance—and Zarja sat upon her throne in all the radiant glory the riches of multiple kingdoms could provide. Funny how Oneira's time away had changed her perceptions. The queen looked more like an ordinary woman dressed up in jewels and finery than anything more potent than that. The queen's court, too, looked smaller than ever, packed to the gills with richly dressed people, and stinking like old fish.

All of them gaped at her like those stranded fish. Gaping most outrageously of all was Yelena. Oneira gave the other sorceress a jaundiced eye, not at all surprised to see that the woman had jumped at the opportunity to take Oneira's vacated place at the queen's side, but somewhat surprised that Yelena had clearly beaten the quite stiff competition for the plum position. Not everyone hated the job like Oneira did. And now Yelena, recovering from her shock, but not her long-established enmity, glared at Oneira like a teenager suddenly realizing their crush's long-lost love had returned and would take them away.

To extend the analogy, Queen Zarja was gazing at Oneira

with the incredulous hope and starry-eyed happiness of that long-lost love. Then Oneira saw who stood at the queen's other side and her heartbeat faltered.

Tristan.

The young poet regarded her with a woeful look of puppy-ish regret, essaying a smile full of both wistful charm and tentative apology. Oneira realized she'd said his name aloud. She also realized, far too late, that Yelena's expression of outrage had morphed into one of vicious delight. Far, far too late, Oneira remembered Yelena's skill with psychic magic. No wonder Tristan had seemed so merrily uncomplicated. Yelena had made him that way, the perfect tool of sabotage.

The other sorceress had struck a blow that Oneira had yet to fully register.

Tristan bowed, deep and with courtly elegance. "My name is Leskai Orynych, Sorceress Oneira. I beg your forgiveness for my pretense with you about my identity on the grounds that you did the same with me."

Oneira tore her gaze from the young man she'd so underestimated, Stearanos's scathing words about the pretty poet's convenient arrival on her doorstep ringing in her ears, and focused entirely on the queen. "Your Majesty," Oneira said, mustering a polite tone and inclining her head. She need not bow, not any longer, nor would she.

"Sorceress Oneira," the queen breathed, life and hope flooding her face with color. "Dare I believe you're here because you've changed your mind about aiding me in the war?"

No, Oneira longed to say. *No, I want nothing to do with you and your wars.* But she trapped the words behind smiling teeth. "I do not wish to see this realm overrun with war," she replied honestly. "So, I am here."

Yelena, face rigid, bent to whisper in the queen's ear.

"A moment, Eminence Oneira," the queen bade.

Tristan trotted down the steps to bow again to Oneira. "I hope you're not frightfully angry with me," he said with a merry smile, as if it were all a joke. "The queen is a stern mistress. If it helps you to forgive me, she punished me dreadfully." A haunted expression crossed his features, fleetingly hinting at the man he'd once been, vanishing again into blithe nothingness. "I only did her bidding."

"To convince me to accept her summons." Of course that had been his goal. And she'd fallen for the gambit, after a fashion. Except that Stearanos had been the one to convince her. But surely *he* had been sincere in his reasons.

"I tried." Tristan—no, Leskai—shrugged, back to his cheerful persona. "And apparently I didn't fail, for here you are!" He leaned in closer, whispering. "If you could find it in your heart to mention to Her Majesty that it was my persuasion that brought you here, I'd be ever so grateful."

"Is your horse truly named Galahad?" she asked inanely, not at all sure why that occurred to her first.

He grimaced, rolling his eyes dramatically. "No. He was named Lucky. Isn't that a boring name? Galahad is ever so much better."

"And the injuries?" she asked, thinking poor Lucky hadn't been.

Leskai attempted a repentant moue that came off more sulky than anything. "Self-inflicted, I admit. Sorceress Yelena gave me a tool to mimic the attack. But all in the best of causes, serving Her Majesty!"

"And Lucky pulling up lame so conveniently? You did that. Harmed a horse and not yourself that time."

A look of stubborn anger crossed Leskai's face, hinting at that true self she hadn't before perceived in him. "In service to the queen," he insisted. "For a powerful sorceress, Oneira, you focus on decidedly odd things. Living alone and not using magic. Eating like a peasant. He's only a horse. It hardly matters what happens to a horse in the grand scheme."

Oneira had no words, and Leskai wasn't a whole human being anyway, so she clenched her teeth over them.

"How's your friend, Em?" Leskai asked with glittering curiosity. "He's a sorcerer, I'm sure. What's his real name? You can tell me. I'll keep your secrets. Promise."

She opened her mouth to tell Leskai where he could shove his promises, but the queen waved Yelena away just then, and beckoned Oneira closer. Then, surprising Oneira tremendously, the queen rose and stepped down, holding out her hands to greet Oneira on level ground, as if they were equals.

"Whatever I possess or may command, Your Eminence," the queen spoke fervently, "is yours for the asking. I am so appreciative that you chose to aid me in my hour of need."

Oneira raised a brow, keeping her expression otherwise impassive lest she reveal her true feelings. "So much so that you sent Leskai to seduce me into seeing things your way, Your Majesty?"

The queen had the grace to assume a chagrined mien, giving a far more convincing performance than Leskai had, whether she felt that way or not. Oneira was betting on not. "I was desperate, Oneira," the queen said in a lowered voice, squeezing her hands and looking earnestly into her eyes.

All around them, courtiers gazed upon them with naked envy—including Leskai and Yelena—and Oneira was excruciatingly aware of the multiple honors the queen bestowed upon her in this moment. Yes, it was all an attempt to further manipulate her and, yes, Oneira would trade any honor to be back inside her white walls at that very moment.

"Not for myself, but for my people. And Leskai is a harmless sweetmeat," the queen added with a wicked smile. "I thought you would at least enjoy him in your lonely exile. I intended no malice, only . . . an enticement, to remind you of the pleasures of court. You have always been like a sister to me. So few women understand what it's like to wield the power we do, the pressure and the responsibility."

The queen would never understand how very different the two of them were, alike only on the surface. Leskai looked on anxiously, clearly concerned that he was the topic of their conversation. They all played their games, caught up in the dance of wealth and power.

Oneira didn't believe for a moment that Zarja had acted on her people's behalf rather than her own, but no one deserved what the threatening war would bring.

The queen went on, encouraged by Oneira's silence, as people in power tended to be, thinking that they commanded the other person's attention along with everything else. They would make plans, she said. The queen would share intelligence from her spies, which wasn't complete, but was adequate to predict the coming invasion. They could wait until King Uhtric's forces landed on their shores and perhaps Oneira could send them all to sleep to be slaughtered. Or would Oneira prefer to dispense with the invaders before they ever left their shores? In which case they'd have to move quickly.

Sickened by the thought, the foul odor of roasting meat clouded her brain with old memories. Then Oneira realized the odor was more likely the citadel kitchens preparing the evening meal; no less revolting for that, though. Oneira demurred, saying she'd review the intelligence first. *Let the stalling tactics begin.*

The queen was fine with that, saying with sincere happiness,

"Simply having you here is likely deterrent enough. I'll see to it that their spies 'discover' that information immediately. They'll likely elect not to risk their ill-advised conquest and then we can choose how we'll deal with them."

Oneira only hoped that plan would work as Stearanos had seemed so confident that it would. She couldn't seem to banish the persistent sense of dread that insisted this wouldn't be so easy. She'd changed the balance of power by retiring, shifting the lines of what was possible. The exact parameters of the realignment remained obscure, but she sensed it, just as she intuitively understood the flow of the Dream, its waxing and waning, the endemic elements contributed by dreamers and the foreign intrusions that changed the warp and weft.

The queen had assured Oneira that her rooms had been held intact for her return—another demonstration of Her Majesty's high regard for the sorceress, to keep empty such a generous space in the crowded citadel, and an additional irritant that the queen had been so certain of Oneira's eventual return, which Oneira had proven correct after all. It rankled that, despite all her certainty and resolve, she'd ended up back in the same place. Stepping into her rooms seemed like pulling on an old skin, one she'd shed and left behind and now no longer fit. Nothing about her rooms had changed. She'd walked away and left so much behind, intact, and they'd been maintained in a pristine state, which only pointed up the ways in which she had and hadn't changed.

Drifting about the space, she felt like a ghost inhabiting another person's life. And she couldn't help thinking of Stearanos. The queen had dangled a harmless sweetmeat of a young poet before her, a gift and a temptation, but it had been her enemy, the flinty and forbidding Stearanos, who had proved to be the one to penetrate her defenses, to pry her from the silence of her white walls.

She still didn't know what to think of that.

❧

Oneira endured the passage of days, hating every moment of being trapped in the citadel, the endless meetings planning their defense against conquest, attitudes ranging from despair to glee, everyone looking to her with calculating expectation. News continued to roll in from the queen's spy network, though none of it was actually new information. If Oneira's return to the queen's court had created an impact, the effects had not yet rippled outward. Some of the generals and advisors hinted around asking Oneira to spy via the Dream, but no one dared ask outright and Oneira didn't offer.

That was one positive change from before. She was a free agent now, present of her own will, and not subject to any kind of pressure. She had slipped her leash and they were careful of her.

Except for Leskai, who cheerfully continued to play on what he clearly considered to be an intimate friendship, willfully or blissfully ignorant of how his betrayal affected her. He seemed to think mutually hiding their identities from one another canceled out any trespasses, and he traded on his supposed influence with Oneira, spending that dubious coin to maneuver his way through the court. Finding it easier, Oneira mostly ignored him. She didn't need his meaningless apologies or effusive praise, bemused that he still referred to them as friends.

She didn't contact Stearanos, much as she longed to. Instead, she kept to herself, with only Adsila for company, coming to the realization that loneliness cut the deepest when one was surrounded by people.

Then the day came that brought actual news: the devastating information that not only had Oneira's return to court not snuffed out the conquest before it began, but that King Uhtric had been declared dead and the Crown Prince Mirza had taken the throne, along with adopting a renewed fervor to begin his reign by adding the Southern Lands to his empire. Their navy had amassed, due to set sail within days.

The court in a turmoil of panic, talks resumed about how to best deploy Oneira as a weapon. Feeling like nothing more than a magic sword to be wielded as others saw fit, wrestling with the harsh reality that her worst nightmare had come true, Oneira absented herself from those council meetings, another form of exile, leaving the world of men and wars for the nominal silence of her rooms at the citadel.

That night, for the first time since they'd parted, she walked the Dream to Stearanos.

She'd thought she might have to wait for him to be asleep, knowing him to be embroiled in his own court where he'd no doubt be forced to keep courtiers' hours. But she found him, already dreaming, reaching him more easily than ever, as if the path between them had shortened, like a trail worn with use, the gates to his mind invitingly open.

He dreamed badly, too, full of the chaos of war and the stink of the dead and dying. Black and bloodred rivers ran through a smoking landscape, shrieks of agony in the air, that peculiar scent of disrupted human flesh and shattered hopes thick in his dreaming. Oneira couldn't relieve him of those nightmares, no more than she could excise them from her own dreams, but she could create a place for him to exit them for a while. Grudgingly, she admitted to herself that she could not have accomplished this if Stearanos hadn't insisted on learning those rudimentary techniques of oneiromancy.

Working methodically, in an effort both well within her expertise and also entirely new to her, she constructed a Dream version of a garden, a blend of her own and the one belonging to the ancient gardener. She filled it with Veredian roses, as she imagined them to look in full bloom, and set a table with honeyed tea and cookies. Casting a critical glance over her creation, she thought it looked perhaps too romantic. Certainly too much so for the conversation they needed to have.

And yet, she wouldn't change it. She'd created it with loving intention and that manifested in the Dream.

Opening the garden gate, she extended a path to Stearanos, where he raged on a hillside over the endless sea of battle, naked and impotently flinging fireballs that immediately fizzled and became venomous serpents that turned on him, slithering up his legs, burying their fangs in his flesh. The path to her garden arced to him like a rainbow, radiating light and peace. Oneira sent Adsila to fly along it, just in case Stearanos doubted who invaded his dreams.

But he'd already leapt onto the bridge, running down the path and bursting into her garden, Adsila winging behind him. He raced to embrace her, stumbling when he passed through her and into a rosebush she quickly denuded of thorns. The dream roses couldn't harm him, but he could feel pain and she'd spare him that as much as possible.

Stearanos recovered his balance and turned to her, holding out his arms in hope and bewilderment. "Oneira? It's really you."

"Yes, it's me," she answered, a giddy smile stretching lips that hadn't moved out of their stoic set in far too long, absurd joy bubbling up in her.

"I dreamed of you so often," he confessed, moving closer, "but I somehow knew it was only my own mind and never truly you. And yet, I still can't touch you." He passed a hand through her arm, disappointment creasing his brow.

"This is only a dream," she reminded him. "I control it, but neither of us is physically present. Only Adsila is."

"Since you control this dream," Stearanos said, gesturing to his nudity, "could I have some clothes? It seems I'm always naked in my nightmares of war."

"A dream metaphor for vulnerability," she commented, clothing him in his typical style, resisting the urge to dress him in something according to her whimsy. This wasn't a meeting for mischief. "Very common. Would you sit?"

He eyed the tea and cookies. "Can I?"

"The dream is as real as any you have on your own. Just as you eat and drink in dreams, or experience any sensation, it will be the same here."

"Except for you," he said with a half smile that looked more sad than anything. "I've dreamed of making love to you, Oneira, and that felt real."

"But it wasn't." Her own sorrow rose up to meet his. "I am both more and less real than the Oneira in your dreams."

"Thief of my heart," he said softly, then sat at the table and ate a cookie. "Tastes like dust."

She sat also. "I could make you experience a flavor, but that would be far more invasive than even this. I'm not comfortable manipulating the dreams of other people, as I think I've told you."

He regarded her somberly. "So this is an excursion."

"Yes." She looked around at the lovely garden. "I've never done anything like this before, but I wanted this time with you to be . . . memorable, I suppose."

"That sounds terribly final," he said, going still.

"We're at an impasse." She spread her hands. "With the old king gone, your prince is now wearing the crown and is determined on conquest."

Stearanos nodded, full of grim regret. "We have tried to talk sense into him, but . . ." He scrubbed his hands over his face, his skin aging into deeper lines, his dreaming self reflecting the weariness of his spirit. "My gambit failed. I failed you, Oneira. Hearing that you'd returned to Queen Zarja's court only inflamed the prince. He is indeed determined. He is, perhaps, not entirely sane, seeming to believe that all the world exists only to serve him. I'm not sure he grasps that other people have lives and thoughts independent of him."

"I'm sorry, Em."

He smiled, a flicker, mostly sorrowful. "No, I'm sorry. I pulled you from the peace of your white walls for nothing."

"Not for nothing." As she said the words, she realized the truth of them. "For a dream," she said, smiling at the wordplay. "We both made decisions for the right reasons, with the best of intentions."

He dropped his hands but still looked harshly tired, his smile rueful. "There are sayings about good intentions leading to bad places."

"Those are about intentions without commitment," she replied, very seriously. "About capricious choices and surface appearance, not engaging wholeheartedly in a plan to make a positive change."

"What are you planning, Oneira?" he asked, eyes narrowing in suspicion. "Even in your dream self, I can see that you are up to something—and that I won't like it."

"This *is* the real me, so you see truly. Tell me . . ." She hesitated. "You've tried everything to stop this war from your end."

"Except for one," he said abruptly, leaning forward.

A flurry of hope whirled through her. He'd thought of something she hadn't.

"You can trap me here in the Dream, can't you?" he asked.

She regarded him with genuine horror. "I would not do that. Not to you." She wanted to say not to anyone, but that was perhaps not true. "Never to you."

"You have to," he replied with urgency, flexing his hands as if he longed to take hold of her. His fierce face took on a light of determination, the radiance of the martyr set on self-sacrifice. She recognized it well. "I thought that *with* you, the war couldn't happen, but I was wrong. The truth is that *without me*, it cannot happen."

Stunned, she attempted to think of an argument against that. He had indeed thought of something she hadn't. Except it was the one thing she couldn't do. All this time she'd had a list in her mind of everything she'd resolved never to do again. Now it turned out that she would do any of those things, and the one that was complete anathema had never made it onto the list. Hadn't even been conceivable.

He was likely right. Without Stearanos, Crown Prince Mirza had no hope of succeeding in his conquest.

Stearanos saw her waver, nodding emphatically. "You see the truth of it. Trap me here in this garden you've created. You can come and visit me. We can at least talk. It wouldn't be so bad. It's peaceful here, and so lovely. Are those truly Veredian roses in bloom—is that how they look?"

"That's how I imagine they look," she answered, feeling a desperate grief shredding her from within, a violent storm eroding the cliffs of her resolve. "I've never seen one bloom."

"They're so beautiful," he said wistfully. "Even if I can never see them in life, you've given them to me here. It's a gift beyond price. Keep me here. Let me never wake up."

"Stearanos, listen to me: you can't dwell in the Dream. No one can. The human mind isn't meant to dream forever. You'll go insane. And your body won't survive being untenanted."

He shrugged, giving the appearance of nonchalance she knew wasn't real. "So I'll eventually pass into death. It's no more than I deserve, Oneira. You, of all people, would understand that."

"I do understand." And she did. But she loved him too much to sacrifice him, no matter how great the cause. "I brought you here so we could say goodbye."

"Goodbye? Then you won't visit me here. That's all right. I understand."

"I'm not consigning you to the Dream. No, don't argue. My mind is made up. I only wanted . . ." She let out a sigh. "You were right about Tristan. Only that's not his true name. The queen sent him to seduce me back to her side."

No vindicated pleasure from Stearanos. Instead he winced. "I'm so sorry. I know you were fond of him."

"As one might be of a foundling puppy," she replied, then had to be honest, even now, even in the Dream. Particularly in the Dream. "The betrayal hurt, however, and I had to know—you and me, Stearanos, was it real?"

"As real as any dream can be," he answered with gravity. "If you're asking if I was only in this to manipulate you, remember that you came to me first. I didn't expect you either, Oneira, but I wouldn't change anything." He grimaced. "Except that I'd make it so my plan worked."

"If your prince disappeared." She posed the question carefully. "If he vanished, would another step into his place to wage this war?"

"You can't do that," Stearanos said, reaching for her futilely. "You vowed never to murder again."

"I perceive that the answer to my question is no," she said evenly. She'd known as much. The queen's spies had spoken truly: the old king had no other designated heirs. Instead multiple candidates would jostle for the throne. The kingdom would be thrown into chaos, likely fragmenting with the infighting. There would be war and death—inevitable with the world they lived in—but Stearanos could perhaps stop some of it.

"Don't do this, Oneira," Stearanos begged, his face a rictus of grief and fear. "Not for me."

"I can't consign you to the Dream, Em," she said softly, resolute in at least this. "Perhaps that solution makes the most sense, but my heart won't allow it. I love you too much."

He stared at her, thunderstruck, joy and revulsion warring with each other. "I've longed to hear those words from you, but not like this. Please don't sacrifice yourself to save me. I'm not worth it."

She smiled ruefully, amazed at how full her heart could feel, even in the face of this ending. "I'm doing this to hopefully save a bit more than that. I created this problem, with my selfishness and weakness. Now I'll solve it my way. I'm just sorry that your hands will be full, dealing with the chaos that will ensue. At least I can ensure that you will be able to choose of your own free will who to aid. I know you'll choose wisely."

"What are you talking about, Oneira? Don't do this. I'm begging you not to do this. Sit and talk with me. Surely there's another way."

She shook her head and stood. "I've thought and thought—and I know you have, too. This is the only way, and even this isn't perfect. You'll have your work cut out for you." She smiled at him, letting the warmth, the love she felt, shine through, imbuing his dreams so he'd remember, just as she'd made this place for them with love. "I know you're up to it. I've done what I can. I've arranged for the queen to pay your debts. That's my price for stopping the war before it comes to her shores."

He was shaking his head, fighting the dream to reach her. "No. I don't want that. It's not worth losing you."

"You lose me regardless," she told him as gently as she could, aware of tears coursing down her cheeks. "I can't survive causing another death. I can only choose which murder will be my last and then deal myself the consequences for doing what I'd vowed not to."

"Oneira, you can't—"

"I can and I must," she interrupted firmly, then tried on a smile. "At least I've answered Moriah's riddle. I've learned how the heart heals. Take care of my roses, Em." She released her hold on the dream and let it begin to unravel.

"Oneira!" Stearanos shouted as the dream dissolved. His voice echoed through the Dream, a forever shout of love and longing that would weave itself into the very fabric of the Dream.

A fitting epitaph, she supposed. And far more than she deserved or expected.

 38

Oneira stepped out of the Dream and into the vast palace of the King of the Northern Lands. She'd used power with profligate abandon, putting everyone to sleep within a league—including and especially Stearanos, who now slept dreamlessly.

She could give him that much, a deep slumber, out of reach of the nightmares that plagued him. She owed him that, given the chaos he'd assuredly wake to. Gazing down at his sleeping face, Oneira allowed herself one last look at him, this severe man who shouldn't be so beautiful to her. He'd been the easiest point of travel, so she'd used him for this penultimate journey through the Dream, stepping into his grand rooms in the imperial palace. It wasn't because she wanted to see Stearanos in the flesh a final time, to take in his scent to carry with her into eternal sleep, she told herself. Oneira had always been very good at lying to herself.

Stearanos had been thrashing in his sleep, legs tangled in the blanket that barely covered the lower half of his body. His chest bare in the guttering light of the fire, he lay twisted, one arm outflung, his mouth still open on that last dreaming shout, braids caught around his neck. Unable to resist, Oneira straightened him, letting her fingertips glide along his skin, marred by those thousands of scars, savoring the feel of him, and the magic beneath. Lifting his arm, she tucked him under the blanket, feeling oddly tender.

Arranging his braids on the pillow, Oneira bent and placed a soft, lingering kiss on his lips, beyond tempted to allow him to wake. "I love you, Stearanos," she whispered. "Against all reason and sense, it seems I do. Too late, but there it is." She kissed him once more, wondering if he'd wake to taste her on his lips. "Sweet dreams. My hope for you, though I cannot deliver."

Feeling the weight of all she couldn't do, wishing more than anything that she could crawl into the circle of his arms and stay there forever, letting the world go on with its vicious spinning without them, she acknowledged the dream for what it was—irrational and insubstantial—and left him there, peacefully sleeping.

She moved through the winding corridors, dimly lit with torches for guards and servants to perform their nocturnal duties, passing them occasionally in sleep where they'd lain down. Over time—and via horrific mistakes—Oneira had learned to make her victims sleepy first, so they'd succumb gradually, rather than falling face-first into whatever was in front of them.

It was quiet, but not silent, snores and occasional guttural cries of dreamers ringing out, barely louder than the crackle of low-level torches. The Dream billowed around her, burgeoning with dreamers, ready to pour into the waking world.

She found the prince through his dreams, easy enough to locate even amid other dreams of glory and bloodlust. To her surprise, Mirza was in the king's bedchamber, not his own. He slept draped over the bed, holding his father's empty, barely living body, the distinctive miasma of decaying meat filling the air. Several attendants, possibly a physician, slumbered in chairs around the room, or curled on the floor.

Going to the other side of the bed, Oneira laid a hand on the old king's brow, his skin cool, crisply thin as dried onion skin. He'd been sent into the Dream. Somehow his traitorous son had found an oneiromancer capable and willing to commit that crime, depriving the man of ever moving on, trapped forever on this side of death. From what Oneira knew of the king, he hardly deserved her sympathy or pity, but neither did she. Because she could, and it seemed right, she did what the other oneiromancer had not or could not: she severed the final tie to the decomposing body, allowing the spirit of the man to fully enter the Dream, or perhaps even find the realm of death as his old form became fully a corpse. He'd been declared dead and now truly dead he would be. All things must complete the cycle of life and death. That was inescapable.

Then she turned to Mirza. Until that moment, Oneira had been planning a straightforward murder. She'd killed so many people, in so many ways. It should have been a simple dispatching.

And yet, somehow, in the stuttering steps toward healing her heart, she'd gained the ability to feel again. She hadn't killed anything in all this time, and now she'd kill this sleeping man, hardly more than a boy.

Strangely, he reminded her of Leskai, whom she should despise, but couldn't.

She couldn't hate this self-absorbed princeling either, no matter how horrible. Leaning over the bed, she touched a fingertip to the prince's temple, finding him in the Dream, where he frolicked through battles, crowned with glory, chased by seeping regret. He turned, a man lost in a surreal landscape, surprised to see her there, wondering at the vividness of her walking into his mind. As she severed his connection to his body, he held up a hand, calling to her.

She didn't listen to whatever it was he said.

❧

From there it was simple to go home.

She did not return to see Stearanos again. Instead, she stepped fully into the Dream, withdrawing the sleep enchantment behind her like a curtain, allowing them all to wake in their own time. All but the prince, who would sleep forever.

She stepped out of the dream and into her garden, lit by early morning sunshine, the flowers seeming to shiver as they opened their petals to the light and warmth. Bunny and Moriah sat there patiently, waiting, as if anticipating her arrival, and Adsila flew out of the Dream behind her.

Realizing she was weeping, silently and copiously, Oneira embraced them in turn, then went to see her roses, Adsila on her shoulder, Bunny and Moriah on either side of her, her hands buried in their fur. The four of them gazed on the rosebushes, which had survived her neglect, but were far from lush. She would never see them bloom now. She could only hope that they'd survive without her to tend them, because she couldn't allow herself to live any longer.

So many things she regretted, none that she could change. Not now. Not any longer.

Making her way laboriously inside, feeling as old as her true age, as if her body had finally given up on trying, she wrote one last note, giving it to Bunny and Moriah, in case they decided to stay.

With the sun rising golden, as ever oblivious to the chaos and death below, Oneira gathered her favorite blossoms and decorated the bier for the final time. As she laid herself upon it, she gazed up through the unending tears at the light spilling from above, just as she'd envisioned from the beginning.

It was a more difficult farewell than she'd imagined when she first arrived. But then, she'd gained companions, become a different person, fallen in love. She didn't want to say goodbye to it all, but she could only take this one last step. She owed it to all the world.

Closing her eyes, remembering Govirinda as it had been, green and blossoming with life, Oneira stepped into the Dream and let go.

EPILOGUE

Long months later, in the short days of mid-winter, Stearanos finally escaped the clawing demands of a fractured kingdom, at last making his way to the pink-pebbled shoreline of Oneira's home. The beach had frosted over in the dark of the year, with its long nights and fractious seas.

Oneira's wards were down, as he'd expected. She'd done as she promised in that last, brutally vivid dream, and taken Mirza out of the world forever, leaving only his unblemished body behind. She'd vanished, also, though Stearanos knew where she'd gone. He'd been half-afraid that her home would have crumbled in her absence, falling like her wards without her magic to power them, but she'd wrought well, building to last, and the white walls of her house stood like the memorial she'd wanted, shining pure against the gray and turbulent skies.

Snow and ice coated the winding steps up the cliff, and he used magic to clear and dry them as he went. No sense risking a fall and he rather thought Oneira would appreciate the housekeeping effort. Huge pawprints had melted into the snow and frozen there, giving evidence that her animals lived there still. Indeed, before Stearanos was more than halfway up, Bunny came racing down to greet him with slobbering enthusiasm.

They climbed together, Stearanos clearing the path Bunny and Moriah had made through the deepening snow that piled against the walls in gentle, pristine slopes. Knowing what he'd find within, Stearanos delayed a bit longer, detouring to the rose

NEVER THE ROSES · 351

bed Oneira had dug and tended with her own hands. There, stark against the backdrop of winter white, the Veredian roses bloomed, midnight purple, gloriously fragrant—and exactly as Oneira had imagined for them in her dream.

Using no magic, he plucked a single blossom, pricking a finger in the process, a drop of bright red blood falling against the snow. Carrying the Veredian rose inside, he went to where he knew Oneira would be.

She lay on her bier, as cold and white as stone, the flowers beneath her withered and dried, her crimson hair spilling to the floor. Grief stabbed him through the heart, even though he'd grieved for her all this time. Coming close, he touched the still skin of her face. From a distance, she could seem to be sleeping, but no. She was gone.

Moriah rose from her curl beside the bier, nosing his hand. "She found her question and answer," the black cat said in her low purring voice, surprising him that she spoke and then not. "Not everyone gets to choose the manner of their absolution."

"True," he granted, his voice choked with tears. He laid the rose on her breast, a final living blossom in tribute to her. "I wish she'd waited to see the roses bloom, however."

"It was never about the roses," Moriah said.

"I know."

Bunny trotted up to him, something long carefully draped from his fangs. Stearanos took it, bemused by the color and texture until he realized what it was. A bit of yarn pierced a folded note attached to it. His eyes nearly too blurred with tears to read, he opened it, blinking furiously to focus.

> *My Dearest Em,*
> *I knew you'd come and I'm glad you did, if only to receive*
> *this last note and gift, unlovely though the latter may be. I blame*

Bunny, but a promise made is a promise kept—though weaving you a shirt turned out to be beyond my skills and the amount of available yarn. Instead you now own what I believe to be the only scáthcú scarf in existence. Wear it in good health.

The house is yours if you want it. If not, please take the roses to your garden and tend them in my memory. You always did have the prior and greater claim to them.

Thank you for healing my heart, for being both the question and answer.

Live well for me. Look for me in your dreams. I can only hope they'll be sweet.

With infinite love,
Your Thief

Stearanos wiped the tears away and folded the note. "You won't slip away from me so easily," he informed her silent figure. "You've stolen my heart and I can't live without it."

With Bunny and Moriah observing, Stearanos laid himself beside Oneira on the bier, gathering her close, and laying his face on the pillow of her glorious hair, still a vivid crimson. Clearing his mind, he summoned all of his magic, and prepared to open a door with his teeth.

If anyone could survive the Dream, it was Oneira.

If anyone could find her, it was Stearanos.

ACKNOWLEDGMENTS

First and foremost, many thanks to all of my friends who—when I kept referring to this story as "the book I'm not supposed to be writing"—finally chorused, "Jeffe, clearly this IS the book you're supposed to be writing." You all were right and your support means everything. A partial, but not comprehensive list: Grace Draven, Jennifer Estep, Darynda Jones, Mary Robinette Kowal, Susan Lee, Megan Mulry, Kelly Robson, Jim Sorenson, Carien Ubink, Maria Vale, and Charlie Whittock. If you were part of the chorus and I've forgotten to list you, many apologies. I heard you at the time and your voice helped.

Along those lines, immense gratitude to my agent, Sarah Younger, whose faith in me never wavers. When she asked if I'd made progress on either of the projects I was supposed to be working on, I had to tell her no. "Actually I'm writing something I'm not supposed to be writing. It's weird but it fell on me from out of the sky and insisted on being written," I said. And she immediately replied for me to send it to her when I finished. Even when I told her I thought she wouldn't like it, she insisted. She read it in record time and emailed: "Jeffe, you've created your own fairy tale and it's magic." I'll remember those words all my life.

Practically, thanks go to Sarah Goslee, Libby Stigaard Ilson, Mary Anne Mohanraj, Elaine Robson, Marin Untiedt, and Stephanie Zalewski for critical input on spinning yarn and weaving.

I am so grateful to the amazing team at Tor. I often talk about how a great reason to go with traditional publishing is that experience of having a fantastic, smart, and enthusiastic group of people supporting the book along with you and I have that in abundance with these people.

+ To my editor, Ali Fisher—so many thanks for the way you love this story, including crying in an Uber over the ending. From that first call where you waxed enthusiastic for half an hour over everything you liked in this story to your insightful, thoughtful, and compassionate edits, every moment of working with you has been a joy.

+ To my assistant editor, Dianna Vega, who valiantly took up the torch while Ali went on parental leave, your enthusiasm, humor, and eye for detail are amazing. So grateful for you!

+ Many thanks to Nicole Hall, copy editor extraordinaire, for the perfect kind of edits. Detailed copyediting without pedantry is a real gift. Doing so with grace and humor is even better. You rock.

+ Appreciation to Emily Mlynek, director of marketing at Tor, for thoroughly and patiently answering my impatient questions. Thank you for indulging me.

+ Cheers to Bramble publisher, Monique Patterson, who I've known for—decades? Whoa!—through various publishing houses and conferences. It's so great to finally work together. The words you said to me at ApollyCon 2024 meant so much. Something else I will always treasure.

+ To Devi Pillai, president at Tor—thank you for your personal touch and behind-the-scenes enthusiasm. You're doing great work at Tor and everyone is noticing. Looking forward to seeing what you do next!

+ Gratitude to the rest of the Tor team: publicists, Libby Collins and Jocelyn Bright; Rachel Taylor in marketing; jacket designer, Lesley Worrell; managing editor, Rafal Gibek; production editor, Ryan T. Jenkins; and production manager,

Jacqueline Huber-Rodriguez. A special shout-out to Caro Perny, publicist at Tor, who treated me like part of the family long before I ever signed. And who sends me books!

This book started as a conversation with works by two other writers, something I've never done in such a profound way. But, like the elements of the Dream, they invaded my story brain and entangled to birth Oneira's tale. Writing something like this can feel like a struggle, to balance the sense of homage with theft. My friend and crit partner, Jim Sorenson, suggested thinking of this as a conversation, which helped immensely in framing this effort.

The works that collided in my mind at a difficult time in my life—think Eddie Norton telling Helena Bonham Carter in Chuck Palahniuk's *Fight Club* that she'd met him at a very strange time in his life, as skyscrapers imploded into flames around them, collapsing to the ground—are led by Patricia A. McKillip's *The Forgotten Beasts of Eld*. Readers of that distinguished work will no doubt immediately grok those elements here. I fully honor them and humbly hope that my end of the conversation is worthy of their immense influence.

ABOUT THE AUTHOR

Jennifer K. Lambert lives in Santa Fe, New Mexico, with her husband of over thirty years, his chocolate-lab assistance dog, two Maine Coon cats who assist no one, and plentiful free-range lizards. She also writes as the multi-award-winning and bestselling author of sixty-six published titles, Jeffe Kennedy, primarily in epic fantasy romance, and is a past president of the Science Fiction & Fantasy Writers Association (SFWA). She is represented by Sarah Younger of Nancy Yost Literary Agency.